A GOVERNESS OF WISE YEARS

The Governess Bureau, Book 6

Emily E K Murdoch

© Copyright 2022 by Emily E K Murdoch
Text by Emily E K Murdoch

Dragonblade Publishing, Inc. is an imprint of Kathryn Le Veque Novels, Inc.
P.O. Box 7968
La Verne CA 91750
ceo@dragonbladepublishing.com

Produced in the United States of America

First Edition February 2022
Trade Paperback Edition

Reproduction of any kind except where it pertains to short quotes in relation to advertising or promotion is strictly prohibited.

All Rights Reserved.

The characters and events portrayed in this book are fictitious. Any similarity to real persons, living or dead, is purely coincidental and not intended by the author.

ARE YOU SIGNED UP FOR DRAGONBLADE'S BLOG?

You'll get the latest news and information on exclusive giveaways, exclusive excerpts, coming releases, sales, free books, cover reveals and more.

Check out our complete list of authors, too!

No spam, no junk. That's a promise!

Sign Up Here

www.dragonbladepublishing.com

Dearest Reader;

Thank you for your support of a small press. At Dragonblade Publishing, we strive to bring you the highest quality Historical Romance from some of the best authors in the business. Without your support, there is no 'us', so we sincerely hope you adore these stories and find some new favorite authors along the way.

Happy Reading!

CEO, Dragonblade Publishing

Additional Dragonblade books by Author Emily E K Murdoch

The Governess Bureau Series
A Governess of Great Talents (Book 1)
A Governess of Discretion (Book 2)
A Governess of Many Languages (Book 3)
A Governess of Prodigious Skill (Book 4)
A Governess of Unusual Experience (Book 5)
A Governess of Wise Years (Book 6)

Never The Bride Series
Always the Bridesmaid (Book 1)
Always the Chaperone (Book 2)
Always the Courtesan (Book 3)
Always the Best Friend (Book 4)
Always the Wallflower (Book 5)
Always the Bluestocking (Book 6)
Always the Rival (Book 7)
Always the Matchmaker (Book 8)
Always the Widow (Book 9)
Always the Rebel (Book 10)
Always the Mistress (Book 11)
Always the Second Choice (Book 12)

The Lyon's Den Connected World
Always the Lyon Tamer

Pirates of Britannia Series
Always the High Seas

De Wolfe Pack: The Series
Whirlwind with a Wolfe

Welcome to the Governess Bureau

You are most welcome, sir or madam.

When the nobility and gentility of England are at their wits end, they send a discrete note to Miss Vivienne Clarke's Governess Bureau. Only accepting the very best clients, their governesses are coveted by minor royalty, with every governess following three rules:

1. *You must have an impeccable record.*
2. *You must bring a special skill to the table.*
3. *You must never fall in love…*

CHAPTER ONE

December 15, 1815

WITH EVERY WORD Vivienne Clarke read, it grew worse. How was that possible? Why was this newspaper article so absolutely damning?

> *But of course, the proud Miss Clarke—who rarely, if ever, actually delivered the duties of a governess herself—has been too proud. Whilst others have attempted to inform her of the dreadful practices of her precious governesses, the proprietress of the Governess Bureau has turned a blind eye to their seduction of the dukes and lords they purport to serve.*

Vivienne blinked. Surely the editor would not have printed such a letter. But no matter how much she blinked, rustled the thin paper of *The Observer*, or looked away from the offending lines and then back again, the words remained the same.

Despite herself, she continued reading.

> *Just when it seemed possible that Miss Clarke could scrape back some respectability—landing the prestigious placement of a governess with the Quintrells of Quintrell Hall, a relation of the Astor family—Miss Clarke proved once again that her*

judgment itself is in question.

The offending governess not only wed the gentleman of the house, a Mr. Thomas Astor, Esq., but it has been revealed by our correspondent that they had been married for several years.

Vivienne snorted. *Well, really.* If they were going to attempt to discredit her, the very least they could do was be accurate.

It was a Mr. *Timothy* Astor, Esq. that Miss Herriot had married, and they had not been wed several years. Just one.

A twist of her stomach told her that her petty attempts to justify it all would convince no one. The fact remained that the Governess Bureau was supposed to deliver governesses, not wives, to the aristocracy and nobility of England and Ireland.

The scandals...

Her gaze was dragged inexorably back to the page.

It is certain in this correspondent's mind, at the very least, that the Governess Bureau will be forced to close. Which family would be brazen enough to put their gentlemen at risk?

Really. Vivienne threw the newspaper back onto her desk and glared at it so fiercely, it was rather a surprise it did not burst into flames.

Gentlemen at risk. Vivienne was no expert, but she was certain the gentlemen in question bore at least half the blame for all the scandals and marriages. Why, it could not be her girls' fault entirely.

Guilt tugged at her heart as she thought back over the last few years. Well, Miss Meredith Hubert did not help herself with the Duke of Rochdale. That was probably her fault. She had been disappointed to hear Miss Anne Gilbert had become the Countess of Clarcton—there were some funny rumors she had decided not to credit, despite the rapidity of their spread.

Vivienne rubbed her left temple, which was starting to ache. It was scandalous; there was no way around it. The Governess Bureau was supposed to provide ladies of skill and talent in the schoolroom, not the bedroom!

The very thought made her cheeks flush, and she pushed it aside. She was surely far beyond such nonsense. In her fifteen years of owning and managing the Governess Bureau, *she* had never been tempted away by a client.

Her gaze caught something on her desk. A different newspaper, this one opened at the "Letters to the Editors" page. A heavy sigh escaped her as she saw the words "Governess Bureau". Knowing she would regret this, Vivienne pulled it toward her.

Dear Sir,

I am horrified to see the emerging scandal of the so-called Governess Bureau featured in so many of London's reputable newspapers—and my wife advises me that she sees it mentioned daily in the scandal sheets.

How can this be permitted in England, in this modern age? How can one trust a lady coming into one's house if they seem hell-bent on securing the affections of any gentleman who will have her?

I have resolved, sir, to avoid governesses entirely. Who can tell whether they once belonged to such a nefarious institution? No, my children will go to school. We shall just have to hope the notorious Miss Clerke does not take it into her head to enter the profession herself.

I remain your faithful servant, etc...

Vivienne scrunched the page into a ball and dropped it into the wastepaper basket.

Well, really! As though they were not perfectly aware she was Clarke, not Clerke!

It was easier, perhaps, to focus on the indignity of having her name spelled wrong in print than the horrible words they used to describe her and her precious Bureau.

Notorious, nefarious, scandalous...

Heat blossomed across her cheeks at the mere thought of those words. It was so unfair; how could they consider her to blame for such things?

She had three rules, and they were easy to follow. She'd added the third, of course, after Evangeline...but that was years ago. *Thanks to that marriage at the beginning of the Bureau's history,* Vivienne thought darkly, *she had been sure never to permit that mistake again.*

Every governess knew it was forbidden to fall in love. It had worked perfectly for years. And then it hadn't. Why, if she had only managed to stop—

"Miss Clarke?"

Vivienne blinked and assumed the stoic, rather cold expression she utilized whenever at the Bureau. No one should feel too comfortable around her; it was an approach that had always served her well.

"Yes?" she said stiffly to the young lady who had so rudely opened her office door without knocking.

Miss Wroth inclined her head. "I thought I'd let you know in person, I'm giving my notice."

Pain—and just a hint of panic—rushed through Vivienne's heart. "I beg your pardon?"

"My—notice," said Miss Wroth slowly, as though the owner of the Governess Bureau was hard of hearing. "I am leaving the Bureau."

Vivienne knew she should respond immediately with some sort of cutting remark, but none came to mind. It was most distressing. "Why?"

Was that embarrassment on the governess's face? "Well...well, I've waited above a month for a placement, Miss Clarke, as you well know, and...there hasn't been one. I've got to earn a living, Miss Clarke, and the longer I stay here, the more people will think I'm...well. A *Bureau* governess."

She had known the reason, deep inside, but still. It was painful to hear it spoken aloud.

Vivienne attempted to rally. *She would prevail. The Governess Bureau was not over.* "Take heart, Miss Wroth. I am sure something will come up soon. A nice earl or perhaps a duke."

The look Miss Wroth affixed her brooked no fools. "Really? You are sure. How sure?"

For a horrendous moment, Vivienne opened her mouth, but no words came out. It had never happened before; she was renowned, she knew, for her quickness of speech. Why, she had even overheard her governesses describe her as "frightening", which had given her a little joy and just a little more sadness.

But to lead a business, as a lady, one needed a little fear. It left one isolated, to be sure, but it was worth it. *It had been worth it.*

Still scrabbling for something to say, Vivienne realized there was nothing but the truth, painful as it may be. "Do not worry, Miss Wroth. I will ensure you are given a good reference. I am certain you will find a new position swiftly."

The tinge on Miss Wroth's cheeks grew. "I...ahem. Actually, Miss Clarke, if it is all the same to you...I would rather not have a reference from the Bureau. Good day."

She was gone, the door snapped shut before Vivienne could respond.

Until that moment, she had been able to ignore most of the bad press. People would always criticize a woman's endeavors if less than perfect. She was accustomed to it and did not expect adoration from the public, merely from her governesses and the Bureau's clients.

She did not expect perfection from them, either. Some governesses and clients were not good matches. It could take two, or at the very most, three governesses to satisfy a duke or countess.

But now it rather seemed as though fifteen years—her entire life's work—was over.

A dull ache settled in her chest at the thought. *Over.* The hours, the sweat, the tears, the determination to prove to the world she could do it. The frustration at being overlooked as a woman, the sacrifices she had made...

All worthless.

Vivienne found her hands clenched into fists in her lap. She tried to relax them, focusing on each joint in her fingers.

Fifteen years. Months and months of her life, she would never get back. The Governess Bureau had been her life's work, her evidence of a life well-lived. And it was gone.

Vivienne swallowed, her throat dry. *And it was worse than that, wasn't it?*

Her way of life. Her income. Her reputation.

All three were in tatters. Without the Governess Bureau, Vivienne had nowhere to go, no roof over her head, no way to protect herself.

Swallowing, throat like sandpaper, her gaze dropped not to the newspapers but to the pile of letters which she had put off opening. There could be nothing good in there.

Vivienne picked up her letter opener. How bad could it truly be?

Miss Clarke,

I am writing to complain about Miss Dewey, the governess you placed with me last month.

Though my little Oliver tells me she is remarkably clever, for a woman, I have noticed a rather troubling trend of my brother visiting us for Sunday lunch.

As per your advice, I had invited Miss Dewey to join us for that meal once a week, to integrate her with the family at just the right level as befitting her status, but now my brother is determined to attend also.

What is the meaning of this? How dare you permit such things to occur?

I expect your apologies in the return post, along with your advice as to how to prevent my brother from turning up every Sunday at a quarter to one in the afternoon.

I remain,
Mrs. A. Thwaite

"Dear God in Heaven," Vivienne said aloud to the empty room as the letter fell to her desk. "Am I to support such arrogance?"

Why was it her fault that her governess was liked by the woman's child? I If Mrs. Thwaite's brother wanted to attend Sunday lunch, so be it. He could wish to do so for a number of reasons!

Vivienne hesitated. *A number of reasons.* After some thought and some scratchings on a scrap piece of paper, she had three potential options noted down:

> *Item one. Mrs. Thwaite's brother is taking a wholesome interest in his nephew. Likely?*
> *Item two. Mrs. Thwaite's brother has an inferior cook and prefers his sister's cook. More than likely, as a bachelor.*
> *Item three. Mrs. Thwaite's brother is in love with Miss Dewey.*

Vivienne glared at the piece of paper. *Drat.* Even she was starting to fall into that trap.

She couldn't allow this type of thinking to continue—within herself or with Mrs. Thwaite. It took Vivienne just ten minutes to write the following reply.

> *Dear Mrs. Thwaite,*
>
> *Thank you for your letter. I am delighted to hear that you and your son are pleased with Miss Dewey, one of our pre-eminent governesses.*
>
> *It sounds to me that your brother has a fine brotherly affection for you and for your boy. I would encourage him to spend more time with your son, naturally, but do not believe there is anything amiss in his weekly visits.*
>
> *I am your faithful servant,*
> *Miss V. Clarke*

Vivienne tried to look at what she had written from the rather irate perspective of Mrs. Thwaite. Would she take offense? Was it possible to read more into it than she had intended?

Her left temple was throbbing now. Vivienne sighed, put her

note aside, and reached for the next letter. As her gaze moved down it, her heart sank.

Miss Clarke,

I have not received a reply from my note of last week, and Oliver is starting to get concerned that his governess is going to "run away with Uncle John." I have therefore taken the liberty of removing your governess and have no further need of her or your services.

Mrs. A. Thwaite

Vivienne sighed, reached out for her note of reply to the irate Mrs. Thwaite, and dropped it into the wastepaper basket. It was starting to get rather full.

This was starting to become a disaster, partly her fault, of course, for not bothering to open up the post when she should have done.

Miss Dewey... Vivienne had to concentrate to bring the face of the woman to mind, there had been so many governesses at the Bureau. Her face appeared in her mind. She was not the sort of woman to be fishing for a husband; it was outrageous to suggest so!

A curl of uncertainty halted her, however. She had thought the exact same for Miss Helena Patrick and look how that had ended.

Vivienne sighed and rubbed her head. She had been so certain, so confident in herself when she had sent out those governesses to their positions. Each time, it had ended...not precisely in a scandal, but only thanks to the discretion of the gentleman in question.

It always reached the press eventually.

The pile of letters still waiting to be opened sat menacingly. Vivienne knew it would be page after page of clients relinquishing their governesses, ruining her, one letter at a time.

How could she give assurances to any of them when love

seemed to occur whether anyone planned for it or not?

Hot prickles were starting to irritate her eyes, and it took Vivienne a few moments to realize what it meant. She was about to cry. She couldn't remember the last time she had cried. Blinking back the hot tears violently, Vivienne cleared her throat in the silent room.

"I am not defeated," she said to herself, as though that would help matters. "I am not going to be beaten. The Governess Bureau will survive."

How, she was not entirely sure. She had worked far too hard to just give up now.

There was a way. Just because she could see no way to salvage the Bureau's reputation, that did not mean it could not be done. Besides, it was not as though she could have foreseen this sort of nightmare. This had happened out of the blue.

There had been one idea. It had floated through her mind a few weeks ago, and she had been foolish enough to consider it. Vivienne flushed and pushed it away.

No. She would not lower herself. It would be the very last resort, going to him.

After taking a deep breath, Vivienne knew she had to face the worst. She needed to look through the ledger and see how many clients the Governess Bureau had left. That meant reading all that looming post.

It took almost an hour, but by the time the clock over her mantelpiece was striking half-past, she had done it. Vivienne felt as though she had aged ten years.

There was no need for people to be so cruel, was there?

Still, it was done. Vivienne's exhausted eyes meandered down the ledger, which kept track of all the clients and governess she had sent them. Lists of people, rows of payment...and over and over again, they were crossed out.

Vivienne swallowed. Every row on this page. So many clients had heard the rumors—*the entirely false rumors!*—about the Astor marriage and had returned their governesses.

All that money, all that potential income. All that damage to her reputation.

It did not seem possible that the Bureau would survive.

It was not merely the money, Vivienne knew. It was her connections. Their ability to recommend her to other families. She had even started to receive requests from ladies who were once children of the Governess Bureau years ago.

Vivienne took a deep breath. But not all was lost. Something would look up, something would brighten things. It was not as though she had no clients...

As her eyes scanned the pages looking for a row not crossed out, her heart started to beat faster. None on this page. None here. The third page offered no clients either.

Panic started to rise, no matter how many times Vivienne tried to shove it down, turning page after page without finding a single customer. Was that it, then? Was the Governess Bureau essentially closed? *There!*

The last row on the last page. Heart now pattering painfully, Vivienne looked along the row to see who it was. Her stomach contracted as she saw his name. *Of course, it would be him.* It was not as though her year had been a disaster. There was always room for more agony.

Edwin, Viscount Bysshe.

Vivienne closed the book, then opened it again. The name remained the same.

How could she be so unfortunate? Why was someone from her past—*him*, of all people—on her books at all?

That was the trouble with running a successful business, she supposed. Sometimes specters from one's past decided to revive themselves...

As much as she hated to even consider the thought, now she needed him. She needed Edwin—Viscount Bysshe—not because he was a client, but because he was her only client.

Vivienne glared at the name written down in her ledger as though that would make the man himself, wherever he was, feel her ire. It was unfair. Of all the gentlemen her hopes could rest on, it had to be him.

Was it possible to salvage the reputation of the Governess Bureau with just one client? She had started with just one client. No one had expected her to do well—a woman, a governess, without a husband or father to champion her.

A slow smile crept over her face. *Yet she had succeeded.* The Governess Bureau had, for a time, been the most splendid, most well-respected place to source governesses in the country. Dukes, lords, earls, all had flocked to her.

And they would again.

Precisely how she would restore her reputation with a Bureau governess for Edwin, she was not yet sure. It would depend on the governess and the monthly reports she would send back. The question was, who to send?

Rising from her desk, Vivienne smoothed down her gown and ensured to hold her head up high. She would not permit her governesses to see how downtrodden she had become, thanks to the scandalous reporting in the papers.

She was Miss Vivienne Clarke. She had built an empire, and nothing would end it.

Smiling grimly, she stepped purposefully to the door. Who to send? Her determination flickered and then died as she opened the door to her waiting room to see…

One person.

In months past, this place was bustling, packed with governesses with excellent reputations, all desperate to be considered worthy by her—by the Bureau—for a position.

The noise would have crept under the door to her office, and she had been irritated then. She missed the noise now. Her governesses had abandoned her. They had not wished to be tarred with the Bureau's brush, so they had left. Uncomfortable silence filled the place as Vivienne looked around the large room, seats empty.

All save one.

The only woman still in the room rose to her feet, and Vivienne saw with a jolt that it was Miss Rachel Herriot.

Or at least, Miss Rachel Herriot, as was.

"I thought you left my employ," Vivienne said stiffly, "to do something foolish."

Rachel smiled. "I got married."

"Yes, that."

The governess laughed—or at least, the woman who had once been a governess. Vivienne could see now that she bore all the trappings of a recently married woman: the plush fur collar around her pelisse; the velvet reticule, heavy with coin; diamond earbobs peeking out from a resplendent bonnet. The dazzling smile of a woman well pleased.

"I thought you may be stern," said the newly minted Mrs. Astor with a laugh. "And you have a right to be, I suppose. The Governess Bureau rules are perfectly clear, and I did break one of them."

Vivienne sniffed rather than reply. She saw no reason to give Miss Herriot—Mrs. Astor—the satisfaction of hearing the pain in her voice.

Mrs. Astor took a few steps closer. "Miss Clarke, were you not ever in love?"

Edwin's face forced itself into Vivienne's mind before she had the wherewithal to prevent it. That laugh he gave only for her, the feeling of his fingers entwined in hers—

"No," said Vivienne stiffly. "Never."

Pushing the Viscount Bysshe from her mind was a challenge, but she managed it. Vivienne was not about to permit him to overtake her thoughts again, not after he had monopolized them so selfishly all those years ago.

She had promised, when it had all collapsed, that she would never see him again. She certainly would not speak his name as a response to such an impertinent question.

"I am for France," said Mrs. Astor breezily, appearing not to require an answer to her inquiry. "I thought I would stop by the

Bureau before I left. After our encounter at Almack's, I must admit that...well..."

Vivienne could not help but be intrigued. There was a worried look on the woman's face, one she had not seen before. Spies did not usually have time to be concerned.

"I read the papers this morning and yesterday's," Mrs. Astor said in a conspiratorial whisper, "and I thought...well. I am worried about you, Miss Clarke."

It was perhaps the most embarrassing thing anyone could say to her. Worried about her? Worried—*about her?*

As she neared forty years old, Vivienne had prided herself in her self-sufficiency. She needed no one—certainly no man—to care for her. She had the Bureau. Built it single-handedly.

No one had worried about her. Some had feared her. Many had respected her. A few, she knew, wondered if they, too, could throw off Society's expectations and start their own businesses.

But worry about her?

"You do not have to worry," Vivienne said stiffly. "I—"

"Are you sure?" interrupted the persistent Mrs. Astor. "Because the things I hear—your reputation quite ruined, governesses being returned to you left, right, and center—"

"I actually have a rather impressive client on our books right at this moment," said Vivienne, tasting the bitterness of the lie on her tongue.

Well, what else could she say? Rachel Herriot—Astor now—had been the height of discretion, of course, all Bureau governesses were, and it wasn't that she did not trust her—but Vivienne had no desire for anyone to know just how desperate things had become.

One client. *Him*, of all people.

Vivienne took a deep breath. "I am sure the winds are about to change, and I will be fighting off both clients and governesses with a stick," she said as impressively as she could manage. "In fact, I was about to ask you whether you wished to reconsider your journey to France. There is no shame, I think, in a governess being...being wed."

It was a desperate plea, and Vivienne could see in Mrs. Astor's eyes that she knew it. *A married governess? What nonsense!*

The woman smiled a little too knowingly for Vivienne's tastes. "I may not have all my memories back, Miss Clarke, but I do recollect that you are a good person. Very good to me, even when you had no requirement to be so. I am sure you will discover a way out of...of whatever situation the Bureau has found itself in. Good day, Miss Clarke."

Vivienne inclined her head automatically as her tongue scrabbled to find words to induce her to stay—but Mrs. Astor had gone.

Sighing heavily, she dropped onto a chair in her now empty waiting room.

She was left with no choice—no choice but one. It was something she could not have countenanced a year ago, not believed possible, but it appeared all other options were gone.

Now she had to face it, to save the reputation of the Governess Bureau, there was only one person who she would be able to call on, to rely on.

Herself.

Many years though it had been since she had taken up the schoolbooks, she had been a governess. She would have to return to it, perform the duties herself. Close up the Bureau in London, and have post sent on to her to...

Vivienne swallowed and closed her eyes as though that would make it easier to even think the name. His name.

Edwin, Viscount Bysshe.

Fate was cruel indeed. But she was not a woman who would permit circumstances such as these to overwhelm her. She would better herself, she would rescue the Bureau from the mire in which it had fallen, and she would return to London, triumphant.

Vivienne opened her eyes. And no matter what happened, no matter the circumstances, she would never permit herself to be tempted to return to the past and...and *entangle* herself again.

That part of her was dead. The Vivienne Clarke he had known was gone.

Whatever was once between her and Edwin, it was over, never to be repeated.

CHAPTER TWO

December 19, 1815

Edwin knew that look. He had seen it countless times and knew there was absolutely nothing he could do to prevent Laura from speaking her mind.

It was not going to be pretty, but then the twelve-year-old had never been taught to hold her tongue. That would all be changing.

"I do not wish to be here," said Laura petulantly, pushing a strand of hair from her face, eyes fixed upon him. "I don't see why I have to be, and I refuse to behave."

She said the last few words as though she were an empress laying down the law.

Edwin sighed. His temper was notoriously short at the best of times, his tongue usually uncensored, and those around him likely to suffer because of it.

He had promised himself, when Laura had first arrived, that she would never hear a cross word from him. When had he first broken that promise? *What sort of father was he?*

"You will behave if I tell you to," he snapped, unable to prevent himself, despite his best intentions. "Laura!"

"You cannot tell me what to do," said the girl, lounging flat and most unladylike on the sofa in the drawing room, one cushion behind her head and another on her stomach. "You don't get to dictate all the rules around here!"

Edwin glared, and she glared back. *It was so infuriating*, he thought darkly. There was a special hell reserved for fathers of outspoken daughters.

And only twelve years old! Still a child. How she would be when approaching adulthood, he dreaded to think. His stomach clenched. Best he didn't think about it.

"I said, you cannot tell me what to—"

"I absolutely can, and I absolutely will," said Edwin firmly, hoping his tone sounded resolute and paternal instead of irritable with frayed nerves. He walked from the fireplace where he had been stoking the flames to the window. Frost still clung to the edges of the glass. "And I won't put up with that sort of cheek, Laura Bysshe, so heed me well."

Perhaps he should not have glanced over his shoulder with those final words. Laura should certainly not be sticking out her tongue. A slight tinge colored her cheeks as she was caught in the act, but there was a familiar defiance in her glare.

Edwin turned back to the window and sighed. *Dear God*. If anyone had told him being a father was this difficult...

Well, that was neither here nor there. One could not return to the past and undo one's decisions. *No matter how much one may wish to.*

The trees in the garden shivered as the howling winter gale clutched at the bare branches. From this side of the house, where the drawing room was, the parkland was most visible. Dry, cold winter had given way today to a storm.

Not an auspicious beginning for the arrival of...he would not think of her.

Edwin's jaw tightened. Some Christmas this was turning out to be. Laura was as bad-tempered as she had ever been—perhaps the worst he could remember—and he was no better. That was the trouble when you put the two of them in a house together. Without the buffer of Henrietta, they were far too likely to lock horns.

Not that his wife had been much help when she had lived. A throbbing pain jolted along Edwin's jaw, and he relaxed it. He would not think of her. He would not punish himself like that. He had suffered more than enough when she was alive.

Something tinkled. Edwin turned to see Laura now poking at the Christmas decorations the servants had put up in some hope of bringing festive cheer to the place.

Unlikely. Edwin turned away from the girl. Celebrating Christmas had never been something he had been particularly interested in. Laura had been amused by the wrappings for a few years, but then it was just want, want, want.

Nothing was ever enough. Had he not given her everything?

"I'm not going to behave when she gets here, you know," came the plaintive voice behind him. "No matter what you say."

Edwin sighed and lowered his head, resting it on the window pane. He should have expected this. It was normal, wasn't it, for a child to resist the intrusion of a governess?

They should have found one for her years ago, he thought wretchedly. Twelve years. Wasn't it too late to start teaching her some manners? But Henrietta had been adamant the girl needed no instruction, and it had all been too painful, too complicated for Edwin to think about.

And then his wife had died, and here he was.

"You will be respectful to your governess," Edwin said without turning around. "You will, Laura, or have me to answer to."

The words were wrong, he knew it as soon as the words were out of his mouth, but there was no taking them back.

Edwin cleared his throat, but no other thoughts came to mind to soften what had already gone before them. *Damn and blast it, why were girls so complicated? Didn't girls want governesses?* To share their secrets and that sort of thing? Her mother gone, he had expected Laura to leap at the chance to have another woman in the place.

Apparently, he could not have been more wrong.

It had been no surprise to Henrietta that he'd had no sisters. Just brothers—two elder brothers. Edwin had shrugged when Laura had first arrived. A daughter. That was fine. He knew women. Some of them he even liked.

But nothing had prepared him for the continuous onslaught of raising a daughter.

"No matter your personal feelings, Laura," Edwin said with a heavy sigh, watching a willow tree thrash about outside, "you must welcome and impress this new governess. Yes, impress," he added, not seeing but hearing the snort of derision. "I want you on your best behavior if you can remember what that looks like. Her failures will not be your own."

Her. He had not said her name, had not yet managed to do it. Not that he was a coward. No coward would have requested her to come, would he?

After all these years, it was hard to believe she would be here. Here, in his home. After such disappointment fifteen years ago, he would finally put Miss Vivienne Clarke in her place.

There was a heavy sigh behind him. "But I don't want a governess in the first place."

Edwin turned away from the window and saw Laura lying face-up on the carpet by the fire, gazing at the ceiling. He hid a smile. It was one of Laura's more wild habits. When everything became too much, she just lay down and stared at the ceiling.

He could hardly blame her. The ceilings at Byhalden Lodge really were spectacular. Gods and goddesses, cherubs, fruit and waterfalls, all in dazzling colors with gold leaf in the—

"I don't need a governess!"

"It's not about what you think you need," Edwin said stiffly. "It's what I think."

Laura sighed dramatically. "I never get what I want."

Raising a hand to his head, knowing a headache was imminent, Edwin said, "Enough."

There it was: the tension around his temples, the growing frustrations of his daughter increasing the pressure in his mind. He couldn't remember being this difficult as a son. Perhaps that was a difference between sons and daughters. Perhaps it was the difference in generations.

Did everyone have such a hard time, constantly having to balance politeness with firmness? It was a small miracle he didn't shout at his daughter on a daily basis.

Whatever the reason, Laura was a handful. Was it perhaps just his bad fortune to have a daughter this rebellious?

"And I don't see why I am the one who has to be on their best behavior," said Laura from the floor. "Isn't it the governess who has to impress me, not the other way around?"

Edwin snorted. "I very much doubt we will be impressed, Laura."

Not after all he had heard about the Governess Bureau she created. Scandalous, that's what he heard. That each and every one of the governesses Vivienne—Miss Clarke—managed to find were one step away from the whorehouse. Harlots, every one of them.

How else could you explain how many marriages had come out of it? Why, in the last year alone, there had been at least two—and those were the ones he had heard about. How many had she been able to stifle, to keep from the press?

A strange sort of pleasure trickled through his lungs. He had known it all those years ago when they had—well. He had told her the Bureau would fail, didn't he? Had told her there was no point trying, that the attempt would be impossible.

And he had been right, hadn't he?

Despite that, Edwin found there was more sadness than happiness in his heart. Miss Vivienne Clarke. What a woman. She had been impressive then and was surely only more beautiful with—

No. He must not think that. She had broken his heart, as well as dazzled him. Edwin cleared his throat to dislodge thoughts of her.

He would not permit her to entice him again.

There was a sniff from the carpet. "I heard the servants saying this Governess Bureau of yours—"

"It's not mine!" snapped Edwin. *The very idea...*

"Whatever," came the uninterested response from the girl lying near the fire. "That it wasn't very good. They were wondering why you bothered to find someone from there."

There appeared to be a permanent scowl on Edwin's face whenever he was around Laura. Something that he needed to address. *The sheer cheek, the servants criticizing his decisions—and within earshot of Laura, too!*

Not that he could blame them for their assessment. The Governess Bureau had indeed lost its reputation these last few years—the last six months especially. Once the province of governesses for minor royalty, he was not aware of anyone who had bothered to seek a governess from it in some time.

That was the trouble with gossip. It got everywhere.

"Never you mind," Edwin said shortly.

"Never you mind," imitated Laura, followed by a snort of laughter.

Rather than speak his mind—which would have been rude to a gentleman, insupportable to a woman, and unforgivable to a child—Edwin chose to turn back to the window. The storm was growing. He would have to ask his butler, Harris, to go around and light the lamps early at this rate.

It was moments like this, moments of weakness when he wished that his wife was still here. The desire left as fleetingly as it had come.

Edwin knew he should never have married. That's what happened when one married for money. One was guaranteed none of the pleasantries that matrimony for love offered.

It was wrong of him, he knew, to be relieved that she was gone. Perhaps if Henrietta had been in any way amiable; if she had attempted to love him, had been pleasant to him at any time, or had wished him well for a single moment, he would regret her loss.

But she was gone. The illness had been quick, and she had not suffered.

Now he was left with the girl with no real idea what to do with her.

"You could always write to this Bureau and send her back."

"No," said Edwin absent-mindedly without looking around. "No, I won't do that."

He wouldn't give her the satisfaction—Laura or Miss Clarke.

Either Vivienne—Miss Clarke—would arrive and fix everything, and he could finally settle into a life with his child, or...she would fail.

Edwin smiled bitterly. Either way, eventually, he would emerge as the victor.

The instant the thought occurred to him, he felt the pathetic nature of it all. Here he was, a viscount, conspiring against a woman who rejected him over a decade ago. If a friend had mentioned this to him, he would have laughed, then counseled the man to look to the future and ignore whatever woman this was in his past.

If only it was that easy.

Besides, it was not as though he had much else to occupy him. The entire York neighborhood had descended to London—something he had told Laura quite categorically they would not be until she was older—and viscounts had little to entertain or distract.

Edwin sighed, his warm breath misting up the cold glass. *Was this what middle age was?* Bitterly concocting plans to humble women who offended him years ago? Wasn't he better than this?

The memory of that mortifying conversation when it all fell apart resurfaced in his mind. The pain of that moment, the agony of realizing that she was walking away, seemingly without thought or heart...

Edwin's resolve hardened. He would prove to her that this Governess Bureau of hers was a foolish idea. He would be the one proven right after all these years.

He heard the scuffing of the carpet and turned to see Laura reaching for the door.

"You will stay here," he said stiffly. "Sit down—like a lady, if you can manage it."

Laura sighed as she dropped her hand, then dropped into an armchair. "Really, Edwin. This governess of yours isn't even here!"

A sting shot through Edwin's heart. "Call me Father," he said stiffly. "I think that is her carriage now."

There was no one else expected at the lodge today, and that carriage appeared to have traveled quite some distance. It came along the drive right before the drawing room, then swept around the house toward the front door.

"Fine. *Edwin.*"

Edwin did not rise to the bait. His concentration was far more focused on the woman who was now surely descending from her carriage onto the drive. *His drive. To his front door.*

She had never been to the lodge. There had never been any cause for her to come. What was she thinking, now, as she looked up at his manor house? Would she be impressed? Did he want her to be?

The rush of emotions and confusion unsettled him. *He was the master here*, Edwin told himself sternly. He was the one in charge, and no one, not his daughter, not the woman he had once hoped to marry, not anyone, was going to get the better of him.

A voice. Footsteps in the corridor. His stomach lurching, Edwin wondered hastily whether he should be seated when Vivienne came into the room. Would he then rise, or would he treat her as the servant she was and merely incline his head?

As shivers rustled up his spine, it was in that moment he knew he was not ready to see her again. *This had been a mistake.* Even after all this time, after the suffering of her loss, after his marriage, and the arrival of Laura, she still had a hold on him.

Would he recognize her? Did she even remember him?

He was playing with fire, flames from the past which would burn him.

But it was too late now. Whatever he had hoped, whatever resolve he had intended, he could no longer ignore the footsteps getting closer and closer. What should he say when—

"You look strange, Edwin," Laura observed with that clarity only a child possessed.

Edwin cleared his throat. No matter what he attempted, Laura would always call him "Edwin." He would never allow her to see how much it hurt him. *Not yet.* That conversation, complicated as it was, could not be held today.

This was not the time.

The voices were growing louder. In a sudden spurt of speed and panic, Edwin left the window and rushed toward the sofa. He fell onto it in a messy heap, his legs attempting to both fold and not fold themselves to look natural.

How did one sit? How was it possible he had forgotten something as simple as this?

There was a distinct look of bad temper on Laura's face, but it could not be helped. *Any governess worth her salt*, Edwin thought wildly, *would be accustomed to a frosty welcome from children.* No one likes to be told what to do.

They were right outside the door. With each second seeming to elongate as Edwin attempted to adjust his cravat to a more impressive knot, he could not ignore his lurching heart.

It hurt, but it was nothing like as painful as the original betrayal all those years ago. Whatever happened in the next few minutes, no matter how charming she was, how beautiful, he would not permit himself to be taken in.

He had fallen for that trick before. That path was well-trod, and it did not go well.

"Why do you hate me?" hissed Laura just as the door handle started to turn.

"I am certainly tired of you!" snapped Edwin, pushed beyond all endurance.

It was a mistake. He had not meant to say it, the words harsh and cruel even in his mind. But they had slipped out, the tension of the moment removing his restraint.

It was a sentence he bitterly regretted. "Laura, I didn't mean—"

"Miss Vivienne Clarke, my lord," said Harris smoothly, opening the door and ushering in a mature woman with blonde, almost silvery hair.

Edwin both attempted to stand and stay seated at the same time. The result was a rather awkward writhe on the sofa, and he was not surprised to see his butler's eyebrows raised.

Laura snorted.

Edwin could not chastise her. Not with the vision of beauty standing inexplicably before him, as though she had stepped through time.

In a way, he could hardly believe she was actually here. *Miss Vivienne Clarke.* When her letter had arrived, he had assumed she was jesting or that she would change her mind and decide to send another governess in her place.

But there she was. The same elegant expression, the same shrewd eyes, the same mouth—*best he not think of that*, Edwin thought hurriedly.

The same and yet different. The same eyes, yet they were accompanied with a few lines which had not been there before. There was more silver in her hair than he had first spotted, and yet she was still the woman he had...

Edwin swallowed. *She came, but why?* He had wanted to see her, had known this was just a foolish excuse to take another look at the woman who had ended his hopes for happiness. But why was she here? Had she wanted to see him—had she missed him?

Dear God, it was frightening how little she had changed. Edwin shifted slightly in his seat as she curtseyed to him and then to Laura for good measure.

This was supposed to be a good idea, a brilliant idea. It had felt almost humorous when it had first come to him. He had written off his letter to that Bureau of hers the same moment.

It did not seem so clever now.

Harris had gone, though Edwin had not noticed him departing, and that left just himself, Laura, and Vivienne. Miss Clarke. Was he supposed to say something? Was there an appropriate way to do this?

How did one address a woman who came to your house as a servant when she could have done so as your wife?

"So this is her, is it?"

"Laura Bysshe!" Edwin said, scandalized. He knew he needed to say something else. Chastisement to his child, an explanation, perhaps even a welcome to Miss Clarke.

Nothing came to mind.

A brittle smile appeared on Vivienne's face, and Edwin most unfortunately melted in his seat. Heaven's above, but she was beautiful. Fifteen years had come and gone, and she was perhaps more beautiful than before.

There was a certain elegance and grace that only came to a woman with maturity. It was why some of the mamas at Almack's looked far more likely to find a match than their childish daughters.

Edwin swallowed. *It was not supposed to be like this.* He was the master here, but he was hardly master of himself. It was tricky, that was the problem—looking, and at the same time, not looking.

The brittle smile on Vivienne's face widened. "Had a good look?"

Edwin coughed. *Blast.* "Nothing much to look at."

"Not that anyone would tell," Vivienne quipped swiftly, "by the look on your face."

Heat seared Edwin's cheeks, and he looked away. Their first conversation in fifteen years, and he was already the loser. How did she do it? How did she utterly command a room?

A woman of no real birth, scant wealth, and great education. Such a woman could rule the world.

Laura was staring curiously. "You look hot, Edwin."

"Father," corrected Edwin, more out of habit than anything else. "And I have no idea what you are talking about."

"As usual," said Vivienne calmly. "You must be Miss Laura Bysshe, young lady. Your father hasn't done the decent thing and introduced us, so I suppose we will have to shift for ourselves."

He was at sea. Edwin knew he should have expected this. Vivienne had always been the swifter of tongue, even all those years ago. Being bested in a conversation, however, was not a pleasant experience and one he usually avoided at all costs.

How was he to extricate himself from such a disaster?

"I am Laura," his daughter was saying haughtily. "And I don't need a governess."

Was that a wry smile on Vivienne's face? Edwin could barely tell. He was attempting as best he could not to look at her.

That was the trouble with Vivienne Clarke. He had reveled in her wit as a younger man, as a third son of a minor viscount, he had no issue with her lack of fortune nor her common surname.

It had been Vivienne who had captivated him. Who had dazzled him. He had been entirely taken in. He had had nothing to offer her then, and it had not been enough.

The bitterness had seeped into his heart once more, and he forced himself to remember who he was now. A viscount; a wealthy one, at that. A gentleman respected in his home, usually, in his neighborhood, and in London.

He did not need to relive the days which could have been.

"The best the Bureau could offer," he said aloud, interrupting Vivienne's conversation with Laura. "I suppose I should have expected nothing less."

He allowed a sneer to appear momentarily on his lips before smiling politely.

Vivienne did not miss a thing. "Yes, I am here. You requested the best from the Bureau, and here I am."

Her gaze met his own, and it was enough to transport him in time. Food had no taste, wine had no buzz, and there had been nothing anyone could do—save a death in the family—to bring him back to himself.

And here he was, nearer forty than twenty, and slipping back into that state once more.

Damn. He had made a mistake. Miss Vivienne Clarke should never have been invited to Byhalden Lodge, but he was hardly going to admit that to Laura, let alone the woman who had broken his heart fifteen years ago.

There was nothing to do but continue and hope her resolve weakened before his did. If she cared at all. The way Vivienne was looking at him now, it was as though they were indifferent acquaintances.

Which Edwin supposed, in a way, they were.

Before he could say anything else, Vivienne's gaze had left him and moved to Laura. "Now then, Miss Bysshe, why don't you show me your schoolroom."

"Better to have a tour of the house first," cut in Edwin. *Anything to undermine her, to show her he held no feelings or emotions that would mark him as the weaker of the two.*

Laura looked between them. "Do you two know each other?"

It was rudeness beyond what Edwin would normally accept, but in this moment, he had nothing to say but, "No."

The word was echoed by Vivienne. It was all very well for him to say they had never met. This was his home, his child, he was the master. It would be degrading for him to admit to an acquaintance to a servant. But for her to deny him? To pretend the affection they had shared had never existed? *How dare she!*

Edwin swallowed. "I do not know Miss Clarke at all."

"I completely agree," Vivienne said coldly. "You do not. Now, Miss Bysshe, the schoolroom. On the west side of the house, I think your butler mentioned?"

Their conversation faded as the door shut behind them.

Edwin dropped his head into his hands. He had never expected a miracle, but that had been a disaster on a scale even he had not expected.

CHAPTER THREE

December 25, 1815

THE LAST HAIRPIN scraped along her scalp and made Vivienne wince. It was impossible to do without a looking glass, and perhaps she should not have attempted it.

Looking around the small bedchamber she had been assigned by the wary yet welcoming housekeeper, Vivienne sighed. It was quite a come down from her luxurious apartment over the Governess Bureau in London.

There, her drawing room had overlooked St. Paul's Cathedral. The bells which had rung out each hour and for Evensong on a Sunday had been the perfect accompaniment to her books and a small glass of red wine.

Many an evening had been spent there after a long day of negotiations at the Bureau, Vivienne alone in the blessing of silence, enjoying naught but the book, the wine, and the bells.

Not so here. Vivienne's nose scrunched up as her gaze took in the small wooden bed pushed up against one wall, the small window with a cracked window pane, the threadbare curtain, the small chest of drawers—the complete absence of a desk.

She would have been offended on the behalf of any Bureau

governess to see such living quarters. To suffer them herself would be an entirely new experience.

Vivienne took a deep breath. But that was neither here nor there—as was the fact that she would be spending Christmas, most unusually, in the company of others.

Alone, that was how she preferred her Christmases. The delights of Mrs. Cooper, her cook, tasted in the gentle silence of the wintery afternoon. A treasured box of truffles, chosen weeks before from Fortnum & Mason. A new pair of gloves, or a bonnet perhaps. Some small trifle that Vivienne could justify purchasing. And that was enough.

Never one to crave the company of others, there had been years in the past during which governesses of the Bureau had been between assignments and living in the guest quarters she kept above the Bureau.

Vivienne smiled, despite herself. On the rare occasion of that coinciding with the December Adventtide, it had been pleasant to share a quiet luncheon with them—but by late afternoon, she would, as was her habit, creep back to her own rooms and enjoy the solitude.

Not so here. Vivienne could well remember the hustle and bustle of a great house during Christmas. More stewing and baking than the kitchens knew what to do with, all noise and excitement—particularly with children in the house.

All she wanted was to be left to her own devices—but not at Byhalden Lodge.

Vivienne had received no direct instructions, though it had been nigh on a decade since she had last been a governess herself, forced to sit with the family through a grueling hours-long Christmas dinner.

A hairpin slipped out of her hair to the floor. Vivienne leaned down to pick it up. That was one of the problems with age. It took with it not just the fresh bloom of youth but also the thickness of one's hair. Every year, it appeared to be thinner.

If only there had been a looking glass in the room, she thought irritably as she looked around. It was thoughtless, indeed, for no one to consider that she may wish to review her appearance before descending downstairs.

Not that she had anyone to impress, of course.

Vivienne forced herself to think about anything but the man who had assiduously avoided her—most successfully—since she had arrived at the lodge. She had not thought it possible, but then, it had been many years since she had lived in a house this large. All those corridors, hidden passageways, rooms that ladies were expected never to enter.

He had probably been hiding out in the smoking room or the gun room, Vivienne thought with a vicious smile.

Why, in a way, he reminded her of...who was it? The master at her last position. Really, it was ridiculous she could not remember his name, but then it had been many years ago.

Now she came to think of it, Vivienne thought, her smile fading, she could not recall the name of the child she had cared for either. Strange that one could spend almost every waking hour with a person for two years and then not remember them.

She would be grown now, of course. She had been—what, almost fourteen?—when Vivienne had left her. She had cried, Vivienne remembered now. Both of them had.

So she—Josephine!—Josephine could be married. Perhaps with children of her own.

Vivienne shivered. Her Bureau may be down—for the moment—but it would rise again.

There was a knock at the door.

"Come."

She really must remember that she was the servant here, Vivienne scolded herself silently as the door opened and a rather surprised housekeeper opened the door.

"Mrs. Jenner," Vivienne said as warmly as she could muster.

The housekeeper looked astonished at the rapidly changing temperature of the governess's voice but appeared to ignore it. "My master thought you may appreciate this and wonders how he managed to forget it in the first place."

There were rosy-pink dots on her cheeks, a distracted look in her eyes, and a looking glass perfectly sized for propping up against a chest of drawers in her hands.

Vivienne pursed her lips. *Well, it was all very obvious what had happened.* Edwin—*the viscount,* had purposefully neglected to include a looking glass in her bedchamber, and now he was making a point about how vain she was. *The cheek!*

"Thank you," Vivienne said coldly. Did she know, the housekeeper? Did anyone know of her and Edwin—of their history together? "And thank your master, too, I suppose."

The last two words slipped out before she could stop them. Mrs. Jenner's eyebrows shot up as she placed the looking glass gingerly on the bed.

"Yes. Right. Well," she said uneasily. "I'll be going then."

The door closed with a snap, and Vivienne closed her eyes with a sigh. Really, managing the politics here was going to be difficult, if not impossible.

Why did the dratted man have to make such a point of sending her a mirror? Did he think she in need of improving her toilette? Did he think her ugly now?

Vivienne opened her eyes and slowly brought a hand to her face. Her fingers traced the lines around her eyes and mouth.

She was changed, she knew that. She did not need a looking glass to feel the changes in her body over the years. She was not the young lady who had mooned about a certain young gentleman all those years ago, and she was not ashamed—most of the time—of the woman she had become.

But still. No one wanted reminded of the decades which had passed, surely?

Her small traveling clock chimed once from the chest of drawers. Vivienne glanced at it. One o'clock. She rose and moved to the door, ignoring the looking glass entirely. She was not here to impress anyone, certainly not the master of the house. If there was something incorrect about her dress, he could tell her to her face.

Edwin. The gentleman's face soared into her mind as Vivienne closed her bedchamber door, but she pushed it away. She would not allow her mind to be consumed by him.

She had struggled enough when…when it was all over. She was well-practiced at this, had not needed to even attempt it for many a year. Just because she was here now, living in his house, teaching his daughter…

Vivienne swallowed as she reached the top of the stairs. *Poise and calm. That was what she needed.*

If he had been anyone else, she could not help but think as she started to descend the staircase, she would have considered purchasing a small gift in London to bring with her. Nothing too impressive or expensive, of course. She had no wish to appear a sycophant—a token of her goodwill.

But she had done no such thing. Besides, it was supposed to be him, the master, who gave presents! It had been mortifying that morning at breakfast.

In that instant, she was transported back to that morning. The smell of the tea brewing in the large stoneware pot in the center of the long, servants' table. The clattering and noise of the kitchen maids as they continued cooking away, sweating over sauces in preparation for Christmas luncheon.

She had sat beside Mrs. Jenner and opposite the butler, as was due her station. Vivienne had noticed only a small kerfuffle as the master's valet entered and found his position taken, but she had said nothing, and it was all resolved.

Vivienne had smiled at the time. *The politics of servants.* Well, it was important, rank and position, no matter where you were in the social scale. Clinging on to what you had was almost a British pastime.

But it had become awkward when the butler had started handing out small parcels. Nothing particularly impressive; each had been wrapped in brown paper with string, little name tags written in a script Vivienne almost recognized.

There was universal joy at this sight.

"Been waiting all year for this!" one footman had exclaimed.

"You bet," said a maid, a cup of tea in one hand and a small parcel in the other. "I promised me Mam I wouldn't open it until tomorrow when I was with her. What a temptation!"

And Vivienne had smiled indulgently. It was easy, in a way, to smile at these countryside servants who probably had never seen London: the markets, the apothecaries, the haberdasheries, the modistes.

The smile had cracked and then disappeared as Harris, the butler, sat down and started hastily buttering his toast.

"Got to get back upstairs as soon as possible," he said impressively to the table at large. "His lordship depends on me."

Vivienne looked at her plate. *No small parcel for her.*

What could it contain that she could not procure? She forced her face to remain calm. A few sweets, perhaps? A handkerchief for the ladies, some snuff for the men. Nothing she could not buy herself. She did not want a gift from Edwin, Viscount Bysshe, anyway.

Still, it had not gone unnoticed.

"My dear Miss Clarke, you are without a gift!" Mrs. Jenner's voice carried the entire table—it seemed to Vivienne—turning to her.

Vivienne smiled icily. "I am sure his lordship was not expecting me to arrive so quickly, and so did not make provision for such a trifle."

She had thought her words carefully, but they did not explain the looks of irritation from the other servants. Her words had also not proven to be the balm of conciliation she had hoped for her own heart.

It grieved her, and Vivienne could not have explained why to be so left out. Of course, that man would want to separate her from the others. It was a slight, and she knew it.

Vivienne reached the bottom of the staircase without realizing it, her reminisces of that morning absorbing her attention so utterly that she attempted to continue going down a non-existent step.

The jolt to her stomach made it swoop up most unpleasantly, and Vivienne tried to distract herself by looking around the hall.

It was rather impressive, though she would never admit as much to Edwin. *Him.*

Byhalden Lodge, despite its name, was no lodge house but a rather impressive manor. Built in the Stuart style, all beautiful-patterned bricks, the interior was quite modern. Very elegant, Vivienne noticed, a frown appearing on her brow. What a shame. She had rather hoped she would not like Edwin's home.

She had always wished to see it when—

But no. Returning to what had once been—or could have been—was too painful. She had promised herself she would not.

Straightening up, Vivienne looked around the hall and realized she was faced with a rather awkward conundrum. All her luncheons since she had arrived had been taken with the servants. That had been made clear to her by Harris, and Mrs. Jenner had informed her that she would be dining with the family on Sundays.

Vivienne had approved of the arrangements. Just enough civility to demonstrate that she was respected, but just enough distance from Edwin to prevent any more awkwardness than had already taken place.

But this was Christmas…

It had been customary, when she had been a governess, that at Christmas and Easter, the governess dined with the family. Or was that just the habit of that particular family? It was too long ago now, and Vivienne could hardly remember.

What did she teach her governesses? Thinking as quickly as she could manage, Vivienne tried to recollect what advice she gave her governesses for just such a dilemma but could not think of a single thing.

Had she really permitted her governesses to go out into the world with such a murky rule? It was most unlike her. Why had she not considered it before?

A discomforting sort of lurch impinged on her stomach. Had she been out of the field too long? Had she spent too long in her office, in the streets of London, in her silent and comforting drawing room? Had she forgotten, in effect, how to be a governess?

Vivienne stood, irresolute, between the dining room door and the door that led to one of the servants' corridors. Which way should she go?

It was the perennial debate for governesses, of course. Partly servant, but far too elevated to be considered a servant; not family; not a guest. A strange sort of status.

That was the trouble, Vivienne thought darkly, *of coming here.* In London, she was the owner and proprietress of the Governess Bureau. That had respectability. She knew where she stood with almost everyone in Society. But here?

Vivienne bit her lip. It was a most discomforting sensation, feeling out of place. No clear direction. No way to know where to belong.

And in this situation, a most definite need to decide. Should she enter the dining room and risk the wrath of the family for being overfamiliar? Or hedge her bets and go toward the servants' hall and risk offending the family as they waited for her?

Years of being the most powerful woman in the room, of her governesses respecting her, of potential governesses to the Bureau fearing her...

It was all gone. To be brought down to this level...

Vivienne swallowed. *For now,* she reminded herself. It was deeply unpleasant for now, but this time would pass. She was going to rescue the Governess Bureau's reputation, she was sure. By next Christmas—perhaps even by Michaelmas—she would be back in London in her rightful place, the head of the most respected governess business in the country.

"What are you doing?"

Vivienne turned hastily to see Laura, all dressed up in her

Christmas finery. There was a scarlet ribbon in her hair and a look of peevishness on her face.

A smile crept across Vivienne's face. *Laura Bysshe.*

Vivienne was sure she should be grateful there was but one child to care for. Some households, she knew from examining her ledgers, requested a governess for five, six, or even seven children. A challenge indeed, but not one any Bureau governess balked at.

Despite this, Vivienne had been relieved to hear Edwin had only one child. She could not entirely explain why; perhaps it was the hope that he had been unhappy in his marriage, a thought which had once crossed her mind, but she had ignored just as swiftly.

She was not that sort of woman. At least, she did not think she was.

The trouble was, of course, that since her arrival at Byhalden Lodge, she'd had little time with Miss Laura. Lessons had not yet begun, at her father's insistence, and were to commence in the New Year. That left Vivienne with little to do other than explore the lodge, a rather awkward endeavor, and Laura with nothing to do but avoid Vivienne, which she had performed admirably.

But no longer, it seemed. Vivienne swallowed. This was the time to build a rapport with the child, as she so often instructed her governesses. It was only now that she was starting to realize just how much easier that was to say in a room in London, as opposed to standing before the child one was supposed to befriend.

"Good afternoon, Miss Laura," Vivienne chose as an opening statement.

The last thing a governess should do was admit weakness, but Vivienne knew she was at the disadvantage. This was Laura's home, her father; her life being upended with the arrival of a governess. She was an Honorable, whereas Vivienne was a mere clean and respectable Miss.

And there was something about her, something Vivienne had

not quite put her finger on yet. That she was a rebellious child could be in no doubt. Had she not herself heard the child call her father "Edwin"?

There was something going on here, something Vivienne did not yet know. And that worried her. Knowing things was what she did.

"I said, what are you doing?" repeated Laura, her eyes narrowing.

Vivienne's smile did not waver. "Oh, just looking around at—at the paintings."

She raised a hand at the paintings that lined the hall. It had been the perfect opening for an engaging child to exuberantly tell the governess all about them, but it appeared Laura had little interest in performing.

"Why?" she said. "They are boring."

Vivienne glanced at the paintings. She really should have paid more attention to them before using them as an excuse for why she was here. Laura was right; most of them were very dull. Hunting scenes, a few landscapes of what was presumably the local neighborhood, and a raft of what appeared to be family portraits.

"Come now," said Vivienne in an attempt to deepen the conversation. She had to get Laura on her side somehow. "Are you not interested in your ancestors? These people lived in these very rooms, walked these very halls, share your blood. They do not interest you?"

For some reason, it was entirely the wrong thing to say. A look of deep hurt crossed her face, her eyes downcast, and her hands came together and pinched her thumbs.

"What are they to me?" came the sullen reply.

It was such an unusual response, Vivienne was for a moment utterly at sea. *What were they to her?* She had always met with children who were fascinated with their ancestry, particularly those for whom a title formed part of the family tree.

But Laura was clearly quite distressed. *Sugar*, thought

Vivienne hastily, habit completely removing all chance of a curse word. *How had she managed to get into this tangle?*

"Well, you will step in their footsteps," she tried, hoping to salvage the conversation. "Their victories and achievements are yours. You bear their name. They are your family."

She had been, as far as Vivienne could see, nothing but politeness and encouragement. Trying to get Miss Laura on her side was the important thing with an only child. They had no one else to cling to, so it was easy to engage their friendship—particularly one without a mother.

Yet if anything, Laura looked even more upset. Though her eyes sparkled with unshed tears, she managed to look up and meet Vivienne's eye. "You don't know much about me," said the girl. "Do you?"

Before Vivienne could reply, a door opened, and Edwin entered the hall. Her heart twisted, then attempted—and failed—to beat normally. Its flutter caused her lungs to tighten, everything within her to freeze.

If only he wasn't so handsome. She may have aged, but Edwin Bysshe looked as though he had just skipped the last ten years and decided not to engage with them at all. He looked closer to five and twenty than five and thirty.

Vivienne's heart hardened. *That meant nothing.* Perhaps he had learned nothing in those years, either, unlike her. Her years had been spent gaining wisdom and understanding, and his? Marrying, siring a daughter, and nothing else.

She would wear her gray hairs as medals for the battles she had fought.

"What are you two doing out here?" Edwin snapped, utterly misreading the temperature of the room. "Go into the dining room. Did you not hear the gong?"

Without waiting for a response, he strode past them into the dining room.

It was a small relief, Vivienne had to admit, to leave her rather tepid conversation with Laura—and to have it established, once and for all, where she should be dining.

Still, it was not the most pleasant of interactions. His respect for her was clearly lacking, and Laura was more than old enough to pick up on that. The last thing she needed was for Laura to start speaking to her in such a disgraceful manner.

The dining room was silent when Vivienne entered. Edwin was seated at the head of the table, Laura waiting for a footman to pull out her chair. Vivienne hesitated, then moved to the seat beside Laura, further away from Edwin than if she had sat the other side of him.

The last thing she needed was to lose her head and sit close to him.

Polite conversation, that was what she needed. Though the silence was comforting, in a way, Vivienne knew it was her responsibility to guide the family into pleasant, Christmastide conversation. How difficult could it be?

Very, as Vivienne swiftly discovered. It appeared Edwin was absolutely impossible. No matter what topic she attempted to introduce as the first course was brought in, he had nothing to say about it—nothing at all! It was as though he had brought her here to insult her!

Vivienne swallowed. Her first three attempts—the weather, the local neighborhood, and what they had received for Christmas—had been utterly ignored. Even Laura was refusing to meet her eyes.

What was wrong with these two? Fathers and daughters were, Vivienne knew, not always the closest of family members, but these two had no one else but each other. Yet they did not even appear to wish to meet each other's gazes.

More to distract herself than anything else, Vivienne picked up one of the many forks beside her plate. There was an emblem on it she could not quite make out.

"Do not play with the cutlery," came Edwin's curt words. "You are not a child."

Vivienne bristled. *She certainly was not!* "I was merely looking at the crest."

Edwin snorted. "You don't know it by now?"

It was a cruel thing to say, and a cruel reminder of how they had looked at it together years ago, when Edwin had been but a third brother. The temptation to snap back, to remind him of his impertinence with a little impertinence of her own, was growing within her—but a clatter of a soup spoon against a bowl brought Vivienne back to earth.

She could not speak her mind with Laura here. *The things she wished to say...*

Vivienne smiled coldly. "Fine."

Placing the fork down, she looked around. The dining room was decorated with the same elegance of manner. Surely not Edwin's own style. From memory, he had very little. His wife's, then?

"Can't you make pleasant, polite conversation?" muttered Edwin.

"Can't you?" she snapped back.

Her words echoed into the silence, and Vivienne forced herself to take a deep breath. *She was better than this.* She was refined, a lady. Title or no title, she had taught the women who had taught the next generation of gentry and nobility how to behave.

She would behave.

"I had thought," she said stiffly, "of starting lessons with Miss Laura on January the first. A new year. A new beginning."

"Nonsense," came the immediate critique from her master. "Laura will start her lessons on the second."

Laura was staring intrigued at Vivienne, who attempted to ignore the child's gaze. She was being made to look a fool before her pupil, a great challenge. One she would overcome.

"I thought I would spend some time," said Vivienne slowly, "understanding what Miss Laura already knows, and then—"

"Don't you have a curriculum?" Edwin asked his soup spoon, refusing to look at her. "Something standardized, something you would expect every girl of Laura's age to know?"

It was becoming more and more difficult to keep her temper,

but Vivienne was determined to. She would not be the one to lose it.

"I find it better, in general," she said as calmly as she could manage, "to curate everything to the child."

Edwin sniffed as the soup bowls were removed and the second course brought out, but he said nothing. In a way, this was even more irritating. Why could he not be civil? Was it so difficult?

Vivienne knew she should hold her tongue, but the words slipped out. "You're just out of date and old fashioned."

"I am not—"

"What is going on?" Laura interrupted, her roast chicken and vegetables utterly ignored. "What are you arguing about?"

The tension in the room grew. Vivienne berated herself silently, for she was supposed to be the model of decorum. She should control herself.

Neither she nor Edwin said anything.

A mischievous smile crept over Laura's face. "If you cannot agree, perhaps I should not have lessons at all."

"Your mother wanted you to be well educated and have all the opportunities a girl of your birth deserved," snapped Edwin, finally looking at his daughter, "and so do I."

Though Vivienne was not aware of anything particularly scandalous or cruel in his words, Laura colored and looked down at her food.

It was sufficient to raise Vivienne's curiosity. The mother, the woman Edwin had married. She had purposefully not investigated, other than the name. Henrietta Chester. The surname had not meant anything to her, and she had been surprised to see the notice of death almost a year ago.

Not that she had been looking for it.

"Just eat," said Edwin stiffly. "Both of you."

Vivienne obeyed. It was rather galling to be so subservient, but there appeared to be nothing to be gained by speaking. This was going to be a rather challenging assignment.

Chapter Four

December 27, 1815

SNOW FELL SOFTLY past the mullioned windows as Edwin paced the length of his study.

What was becoming of him? Pacing like an old man in a novel? He tried to stop at the window to watch the dusty flakes drift past, falling onto the lawn below, covering it with a sugary soft of fluff.

It was no good. Only by moving could he force his mind to consider his options.

A fire crackled in the grate, a welcome warmth in the cold chill of the house. At least the snow had arrived after Christmas Day. Harris had said himself—it would have been a challenging festive period if the supplies from York had not made it through.

What was Christmas without plum pudding?

An image flashed through Edwin's mind, the taste of the plum pudding, the scrape of his spoon against his bowl...and the look of a woman staring across the table, her disregard for him showing absolutely no hint of respect.

Edwin swallowed. He had been stiff yet polite, and she still delighted in irritating him! All that nonsense about how she was going to teach Laura, he was her father. Shouldn't he have a say in his child's schooling?

But no, Miss Clarke was the expert. Miss Clarke could brook no opposition.

Even Laura had noticed the nonsense they managed to get themselves entangled in. *Dear God, that she should spot it.*

The snow was falling heavier now. Edwin threw himself bad tempered into his chair by the desk. Within moments, he had risen again. More pacing, then he returned to his chair.

This was ridiculous. He was no lily-livered fool of one and twenty. He had grown up a great deal since that time, hadn't he? Married, with a child?

Edwin swallowed. He should be better than this, so why wasn't he? What sort of hold did Vivienne—did Miss Clarke have over him that he simply could not break?

Even from this vantage point, he could watch the snow drifting down heavier now. The lawn would be almost covered, the soft green verges coated in a blanket of white. Pristine.

Why was it so difficult to restore one's life like that? Why couldn't one's choices be made clean and new again? *If only he could go back and...what, change things?*

"Utter nonsense," Edwin said aloud in the silence of his study.

What would he change? He had been the one to ask her to marry him. She had been the one to say no. One could not force a difference of opinion upon someone else, no matter how much one wished to. No matter how much one tried.

Forcing himself to harden his heart, Edwin clenched his jaw for good measure as though that would prevent him from saying the things that would surely make a fool out of him.

He should not be the one with regrets. He should not be the one wondering what could have been. What had he done? Offered Vivienne everything; everything he was, everything he had, everything he could be. And what had she done?

Rejected him. Refused to listen, forced him from her life, refused to see him again.

His life had become nothing but pain and misery and loneliness for a time, and it was her fault. He had not rejected her—the very idea! No, it was Miss Vivienne Clarke who decided she was too good for the son of a viscount.

A tight throbbing pain appeared just under his right ear, and Edwin forced himself to relax his jaw. He could not go back. The idea of groveling before her again, tears in his eyes, begging her to reconsider her decision... No. He would not force himself through that pain.

And it was only right, wasn't it, that now he had the upper hand for their first time in their acquaintance, now he was the one who could say yay or nay, that he made her life as difficult as possible?

Edwin felt the righteousness of it. She had been cruel to him, spiteful when he had nothing but his pride—and now he could do the same to her.

Even thinking it made Edwin's stomach twist painfully. He was not a cruel man...was he? Never before had he been tempted to force another person down when they were already down on their luck.

Yes, he had wished to see her once when he had been married, and Laura had joined them. Just for a moment, he wanted Vivienne to see a glimpse of the life she could have had.

The feeling had faded over time. Now he was faced with the opportunity to make everything difficult, and Edwin both embraced and loathed the part of him that wanted that.

Edwin rose to his feet with a heavy sigh and resumed the trudge up and down past the windows, which were growing dark now.

It had all seemed so simple. Invite a governess from the damned Bureau to his house, prove she was not worth her salt, and send her back. A small punishment for the woman who had altered the course of his life irrevocably.

Instead, it was not some simpering girl, eager to impress a viscount who had arrived, but Miss Vivienne Clarke herself.

Edwin swallowed. It was mightily unfair that his heart skipped a beat whenever he thought of her name. She was not enduring reminders of deep emotion every time she looked at him—he would bet on it. If he had known he would experience the same patterings of affection as he had all those years ago...

Impossible. Edwin cleared his throat as though that would clear up the matter. It was nothing but the echoes of an affection long dead, surely.

And now he was paying her!

"Stuff and nonsense," muttered Edwin, reaching the globe in the corner and pushing it around, watching the countries of the world appear, then disappear out of sight. "Nonsense."

After all that had happened, after her refusal of him for money, for that was what it was, even if she said it was for other things—to think that she was in his household now and being paid by him to be here! *Him, paying her!*

It was ridiculous. True, Edwin was under no illusion that if wages were not available, Vivienne would not have come.

Unless...unless things were truly as desperate as they said. As the newspapers alluded. As all the gossip cried with vicious laughter. Unless the Governess Bureau was truly in trouble.

The very words were bitter on his tongue, and Edwin vowed to restrict himself from saying them as much as possible. *Governess Bureau.* The reason he—

No. He would not even permit his mind to go there.

The fact was that Vivienne would not have come here, debasing herself as a governess, even further as his governess, unless things were desperate. *It was true, then.* The Bureau, that dratted institution, was falling apart. He was, perhaps, the only one who could save it.

Edwin sighed and fell into his armchair by the fire. He'd had it moved up here years ago, against Henrietta's wishes. It left an odd number in the drawing room, but was most comfortable here when his work, little as it was, tired him.

"Order a new one!" she had screeched at the time. "Why take

that one?"

"Because," Edwin had said calmly, "I like this one."

The soft fabric was worn smooth at the edges. Edwin stroked it now, the softness and familiarity of the chair calming him. *Had he made the right decision all those years ago?*

The intrusive thought was gone as quickly as it came, but Edwin could not ignore it. *Decisions, decisions.* They were always easier to make from an armchair, *with the gift of hindsight*, he thought wryly.

Had he made the right decision when she had asked him to—but he would not think of that. The wind howled outside his window, and Edwin glanced at the panes. Night had fallen. It fell so early now, in the depths of winter.

No, better to concentrate on the decisions before him now, on the things he could seek to change at this moment.

Edwin's jaw tightened unconsciously. Had he made the right decision in writing to that damned Bureau? Was he making the right one now by keeping her here? Would it be better, easier on him, if she were to leave? Even if that would mean she had won.

No, he could not do it. Edwin crossed his legs, moving his feet closer to the warmth of the fire. No matter how many times he would wonder—and perhaps he would look back on this and believe he had made a mistake—he would continue. He had decided on this course, and a little concern would not shake him from it.

Miss Clarke would remain and be the governess of Laura. Either she would succumb to the realization that her precious Bureau was finished, over—or he would order her away, sending her away in disgrace. It would all lead to very much the same thing.

The door behind him opened, then closed quietly. Edwin did not look around. It could only be one person; Mrs. Jenner was in York, visiting a sister, and Harris had requested some time to put the Christmas silver to bed.

There was only one person he had ordered here, and there

was no mistaking that scent.

By Jove, he had to forget that scent. Edwin tried to forget the numerous times he had smelled it before as they sat together on a sofa, laughing away as a card party continued without them, or pressed up against each other in a carriage, hidden away in a box at the opera, or entwined together as they stole kisses, heated and desperate and fearful of discovery...

Edwin cleared his throat. He was supposed to be ignoring those memories. Those wonderful images were both sweet and painful and must be forgotten.

He had to stay the course. What sort of man would he be, changing his mind?

"You asked for me?" said a cold voice.

It was the icy temperature of her tones that allowed Edwin to cool his own ardor. She was still standing behind him, had not the decency to move across the room and stand before him—but perhaps that was a mercy.

He did not need Vivienne Clarke before him to see every line, every inch of her. To know precisely what she looked like happy, sad, irate, confused, joyful.

To know she was glaring at him right this moment.

He had expected time to soften the memories; to gently ease him from obsessive love, or whatever it was he had found himself in all those years ago, into kind remembrance, and then disinterest. And yet...

Yet if he was honest with himself, and Edwin was certain he would never speak these words aloud, but if anything, those feelings had done naught but increase. Multiply.

Miss Vivienne Clarke. What a hold she had over him.

"You need to leave."

Edwin had not intended to say the words. They had been crying out in his mind for so long—ever since her carriage had first pulled up outside Byhalden Lodge—that it was a wonder, really, that it had taken this long for them to spill out. But spill out they had.

There was a gasp, then silence. Silence that elongated and remained quite still, until Edwin could bear it no more. He rose and turned around.

There she was. *Vivienne.* In the glowing snowy light of the study, she seemed alit in silver, her hair glowing, her skin radiant, a knowing smile upon her delectable lips.

Edwin's stomach lurched, then something a little lower moved, too. *Damn.* How was it possible that each time he saw her, she was more beautiful, more powerful, more dominant in their connection?

He was the gentleman, he was the viscount, this was his house! Yet there she stood, utterly in control of the situation. *Damn and blast.* He should never have got into this mess.

He should never have brought her here in the first place. Too many memories, too much pain. Too much regret, all seeping into his soul. It was too late.

Vivienne arched an eyebrow. "I must leave?"

Edwin nodded. "Y-You must leave."

Damn his pathetic tongue!

The eyebrow raised further. "Unable to handle me?"

"No," said Edwin swiftly, but as he had nothing else to say, it all felt a bit foolish.

Yes, he wanted to say. *I cannot handle the reality of you, a living, breathing woman. The remembrance of you was painful enough.*

"Well, I cannot see any other reason why you would not want me here," came the crisp reply, Vivienne's eyes not leaving him. "Does Miss Laura's education not matter to you?"

It was his own fault. Perhaps he should not have ordered her to his study before he had entirely worked out what he was going to say, as though there was a perfect set of words that could make her disappear.

Edwin could feel the tension running down his wrists into his fingers, the temptation to clench them just inches away. But he would not. He would not give her the satisfaction.

It was not as though she could understand. Few could. He

had promised himself, promised Henrietta, that he would never speak ill of Laura to anyone if he could help it.

In the main, he had kept that promise. Few would hear criticism of her from his lips, no matter the inducement. He was not about to critique his daughter now, not to Vivienne, anyway. She would not understand. Few people would. That was why few people knew.

A slow smile crept over Vivienne's face, and for a heady moment, it was as though the last fifteen years or so had fallen away, as though they had returned to the happy days they had once enjoyed. Halcyon days, days they had believed would continue onward, forever.

They had ended, of course. Ended too soon.

But they had been open and honest with each other; their hearts had been shared freely, when whispered nothings held truth, when everything he had wanted in life was in her.

The feeling was so visceral that Edwin shivered. They had been everything to each other, once, and now look at them. Barely able to have a civil conversation with each other. Hardly able to stand in the same room and not lash out in anger and pain and regret.

Edwin rubbed his temple. *This was getting ridiculous.* He could not be overwhelmed by the presence of a mere governess, even if it was Vivienne! The last thing he needed was to lose control. Lose control, step over to her, pull her into his arms, tell her he regretted it all and wanted to—

Edwin's gaze caught hers and saw to his alarm that she seemed to guess what he was thinking. *Hell's bells, that was the last thing he needed.* He had to get a grip of himself, had to restrain himself from revealing just what he was thinking all the time.

He cleared his throat. The sooner this conversation ended, the sooner she would leave.

"When I sent to the bureau…I didn't expect you. I thought—well, that someone else would be sent. You know. A governess."

Edwin tried to repeat the words in his mind the moment they

were out of his mouth. Did he sound the fool? Was it possible that she could hear the pleading tone underneath his voice, the desperate need to be understood?

The last thing he needed was to be exposed, for his emotions to betray him.

Yet it was not he who appeared exposed. Now Edwin concentrated, he saw what was surely impossible—two pink dots appearing in the cheeks of Vivienne Clarke.

Was she...surely the woman was not embarrassed?

"I am well aware you were not initially expecting me," she said in that haughty manner he knew so well. "But when it came to it, I...There was no one else I could send."

Edwin frowned. "No one else you could send—no other governess wished to lower themselves to care for the child of a viscount? My title not enough for your precious Bureau?"

He had not intended his ire to seep into his words, but they were said now—and they did not have the response he had expected.

The two pink dots on Vivienne's cheeks deepened in color. "No, it was not that."

Silence fell between them, a silence which felt heavier, somehow, as the snow settled along the mullioned windows.

"Well?" said Edwin a little more aggressively than he had expected. "Why then?"

Only then did Vivienne's eyes become downcast, her gaze leaving him and moving to the carpeted floor. "Because...because there was no one else I could send. There was no one else."

Edwin took a step forward. "Do you mean to tell me...you are the last governess of your Bureau?"

The idea was fantastic—surely impossible—yet in the silence, Vivienne nodded.

A strange sort of elation rushed through Edwin's body. *It was true then.* The problems at the Governess Bureau were not merely speculation or gossip or mean-spirited hopes. The Governess Bureau was going to end.

"I had heard there were problems," he said aloud, attempting not to sound triumphant, "but then you can never tell just how much is true in those London papers."

Vivienne nodded but said nothing. Her eyes were still downcast, and there was a strange sense of defeat that could not be expressed in words, but her whole body was shouting.

The elation only continued, making Edwin feel giddy. It was a strange feeling: the sense of a glorious achievement, a relief that what had once pained you was over—yet he had done nothing to achieve it.

The Governess Bureau was gone. Dead, in all but name. The paltry excuse Vivienne had used not to marry him was over.

Even as these thoughts rushed through his mind, Edwin was not so absorbed to ignore the expression on Vivienne's face. There was pain there, and it cut into his own soul—until he hardened his heart.

No, he must not feel sorry for her. This Bureau was the reason she was not his wife. He would not permit himself to feel regret that it was over.

"You should not have chosen it over me," Edwin said quietly.

That got her attention. Vivienne's bright eyes rose and pierced him, the pink in her cheeks gone and an icy expression once more on her face.

"I made the right choice," Vivienne said, flaring up. "You are so miserable, Edwin! You think I would have preferred a life here, in the freezing north, where we could be miserable together?"

Her words cut deeper than she could ever know. Edwin stared at the woman who, but for one different decision all those years ago, would have been the dearest, most beloved person in his life. In the world.

Yet she had done the unthinkable and chosen a business over a gentleman offering his hand, his affections, his name, everything he was. The Bureau had been barely even formed then, and still, it had a greater claim on her heart. Her own independence had been more important than their affections for each other.

Vivienne was still glaring, and Edwin forced himself to ignore the pitiful, fanciful thoughts of what had mattered more with the beauty of hindsight.

He was the fool here. That he could have had affections for such a woman—a bold, determined, selfish woman! A woman who only did what she wanted, who had no thought for others!

Edwin swallowed. No matter how much he attempted to revile her, he could not. Best that he remove her from his sight, the whole reason he had summoned her here.

The Bureau was gone, failed, finished. If only he had known that all those years ago. Would he have waited? It was a rather confusing thought, one he would have to revisit when he did not have an irate Vivienne Clarke standing before him.

After all, he had married Henrietta so swiftly precisely because he could not imagine a situation in which Vivienne would be free, free from the Bureau's grip and willing to love again.

Dear God, his marriage had been a mistake. Not that he would ever admit it to Vivienne, at any rate.

She was still standing there, glaring, and though he remained completely silent, she misunderstood his silence.

"I will restore the Governess Bureau to its former glory," she said stiffly. "No matter what the newspapers say, there is good within it. I will return it to splendor and prestige, its reputation and mine will be salvaged. Even if it takes until Laura is wed."

It was a length of time Edwin could never have considered. Vivienne here, until Laura was wed? But that—that could be years! It would be years, at least six or seven.

Vivienne Clarke, living in his home, sleeping along the corridor, dining with him once a week...for years?

No, absolutely not. Edwin's mind was overwhelmed, intense emotions he could not name spinning his head, making it impossible to think properly. One thought remained.

"No—no, you need to leave now," he repeated. She had to leave. He could not put up with her presence any longer, it was agony. *He did not deserve such torment.* "That is an order."

But Vivienne did not move. She did not look particularly impressed. "I think you will find that I will stay, and I will do an excellent job. I am the governess you never knew you needed, my lord."

The last two words were spoken with such anger that Edwin took a step backward. It was not his custom to be dictated to in his own home—to be dictated to at all!

Who did this woman think he was?

"You do not get to decide whether you work here or not," he said irritably. "When I say you must leave—"

"And on what grounds, precisely, are you dismissing me?"

Edwin opened his mouth, spluttered a few syllables that made absolutely no sense, and made the decision to close his mouth.

Damn and blast it, why was he utterly incapable of speaking coherently when he needed to! This had never happened with Henrietta—did not happen with anyone.

Vivienne's smile had returned. "I thought so. If your wife were here—"

"Well, she is not," snapped Edwin. He had to put a stop to this conversation, had to cut it short before he made even more of a fool of himself. "I am a widower, Miss Clarke, and a viscount, and my word here in my house is law!"

There were a few heartbeats of silence, and then—

"I will stay and restore the reputation of the Governess Bureau," Vivienne said calmly. She looked utterly unperturbed by Edwin's growing frustration, which of course, only increased his irritation. "That is the *only* reason I am here," she added with a knowing look. "Then I will be gone. You can be assured there will be no repeat of the…the entanglement we almost got into fifteen years ago."

It was difficult not to be insulted by her insinuation, Edwin thought. Did she really think that her prolonged presence would cause a—a relapse? That he would suddenly get on bended knee and profess his undying love?

Not for a second time, that was for sure.

Yet there was a strange sort of regret in his heart. Was it really so impossible that she would wish to once again receive his attentions? Was he that changed?

Without speaking, Edwin stepped over to the windows. Snow was probably still falling, but he could not tell. The utter darkness outside meant the glass was now more a mirror.

He examined himself quickly. His reflection showed a man who looked young for his age, or at least he thought so. The same chestnut hair as she had first met, the same square jaw.

"My lord?"

Edwin turned hastily, desperately hoping that she had not guessed his purpose.

"I will not be pushed out," Vivienne said quietly. "I will not return to London until I have restored the reputation of my Bureau."

Edwin smiled. "Or, I suppose, until its closure is absolute?"

He saw the answer in her eyes.

"Well then," Edwin said cheerfully. "We are agreed. Until your precious Governess Bureau is restored to its shining reputation—or it has completely failed and can no longer be resurrected—you will stay. But mark my words, Miss Clarke, I will be doing everything in my power to demonstrate to the world that you and your Bureau are finished. Finished, over and done with. Forever."

CHAPTER FIVE

January 2, 1816

THE SCRAPE OF the chalk on the blackboard was enough to set Vivienne on edge.

Not that it would take much today. The first day of lessons with Miss Laura Bysshe. It was an auspicious day. That's what she was attempting to tell herself—had been trying to tell herself for days.

It had been years since she had taught, years since she had picked up chalk and tried to remember not to wipe her hands on her gown. Years since she had faced a pupil who did not wish to learn.

Vivienne glanced back at Laura. She was seated quietly in the small chair and desk that had been procured by the butler.

She turned quickly back to the blackboard, her heart thundering. *She was not afraid*, Vivienne told herself silently as she continued to write the date in the top right-hand corner. She was not afraid.

Teaching did not frighten her. The idea of trying to convince Laura to be polite and to learn did not frighten her. The thought that she may be returned to London in disgrace by the gentleman who had once loved her did not frighten her.

The chalk snapped.

Vivienne jumped, startled at the sudden sound. There was a muffled giggle behind her which she chose to ignore.

The chalk felt strange under her fingertips as she knelt down to pick up the broken piece from the floor. Soft and yet grainy. Did they make chalk differently these days? Was it her memory that was failing her or was everything different?

Her heart was pattering most uncomfortably now, but she could not let Laura see that. The last thing she needed was for her charge to see just how unsettled she was.

Vivienne swallowed as she placed the two pieces of broken chalk on her desk. How long had it been since she had done this? Eons. Epochs. She could barely remember it.

But she was Vivienne Clarke, she reminded herself silently as her fingers reached out for a fresh—and hopefully less delicate—piece of chalk. The Governess Bureau was her creation, her child. She had brought it from nothing to riches, from obscurity to respectability.

And she would return it there.

Vivienne turned back to the blackboard. It currently said *January the sec*

Raising her hand, she continued writing the date. She would never justify her Bureau if she could not perform the duties of a governess herself. The hypocrisy would not be lost, even on her. Even if she wanted it to be. *If only she had stayed in touch with Evangeline.*

The thought seared through her most painfully, so suddenly that Vivienne almost dropped the chalk but managed to hold onto it.

Evangeline. Goodness, it had been forever since she had thought of her. Her friend who had begun the Bureau with her. The friend who had been happier to go out and work as a governess, start to build their reputation.

The governess who had betrayed her, fallen in love with her

master, and married him.

Vivienne's fingers became as white as the chalk she clutched so tightly. A betrayal she had never forgiven, a friend she had lost, and a woman whose insight and expertise would have been very valuable right now.

Perhaps she had made a mistake. Perhaps she had been too harsh on her friend. She, if anyone, knew the pangs of disappointed love. If only she could have persuaded Evangeline to stay resolute, not to marry that man, whatever his name was.

It was Evangeline's betrayal that had caused the third rule of the Governess Bureau to be created.

You must never fall in love...

How many governesses had followed in Evangeline's footsteps and betrayed her by breaking that third rule? Vivienne had lost count now. She would not punish herself by going back in the records to count them.

But now, with frost at the windows, a chill in the air, and a freezing cold schoolroom before her, Vivienne wondered just what she would give to have her original co-founder in the room there with her. Alongside her. Guiding her. Encouraging her.

It was all very well to be proud you had created something alone, but then you were left to celebrate it...alone. Survive in the hard times alone. Be alone.

Vivienne breathed out slowly and saw her breath blossom before her.

This was preposterous. She glanced at the grate on the other side of the room and saw, to her dissatisfaction, that it was empty.

Here they were, in the depths of midwinter, and the master of the house could not even see fit for a fire to be ordered for the schoolroom? Did he want his child to freeze to death? Did he want *her* to?

A wry smile crossed her mouth. *Well, perhaps*. His reception could certainly be described as icy, though she had expected nothing better. Had he not made it clear himself?

"But mark my words, Miss Clarke, I will be doing everything in my *power to demonstrate to the world that you and your Bureau are finished. Finished, over and done with. Forever."*

He wanted to chase her away. He wanted her to fail, to feel the failure, to glory in it. He wanted to watch her suffer, and she would not give him the satisfaction.

Cold? He was a viscount, a member of the nobility, Vivienne thought savagely. *He had no idea what it was to grow up cold.* To feel the chill in one's bones because your parents could not afford to feed the fire.

He underestimated her, as usual. Frighten her away? He knew her background, *or at least he had, once*, Vivienne reminded herself. It was possible he had forgotten, but she had not. A little cold was not going to frighten her away.

Vivienne turned to speak impressively as she opened the first lesson with her new pupil, but her words caught in her mouth.

Laura. She was shivering at her desk, her light shawl doing nothing to prevent the chill from descending into her bones. She did not even, from what Vivienne could see, have proper woolen socks on.

A sharp jab entered her heart. Was it Laura's fault that her father and her governess were at such odds? Should she be forced to suffer?

Vivienne swallowed. No one's heart could be stone when looking at a cold child. There was something deep within any person—*any person with a heart*—who would seek to care for such a child.

Laura should not be the one cold and feeling slighted, Vivienne thought bitterly. It should be her father.

And then the strangest thought rushed through her mind so quickly she was unable to halt it. *Laura could have been her child.*

Not precisely. Not exactly Laura, but perhaps a child like her. If she had married Edwin, if she had accepted his proposal and gone along with his demands of abandoning all her dreams for the Governess Bureau, then perhaps they would have had a child. A daughter.

A daughter like Laura.

Vivienne swallowed. She would not have the Bureau, true, but she would have a family. A husband, a child. A daughter to take after her. Then she would have been the one looking for a governess, trying to find someone to teach her.

It was a strange thought, one that reached into the depths of her heart, the parts which she had closed off many years ago and shone a light on them as brilliant as a wax candle. A life she could have lived. A life she declined, and now she faced the reality that perhaps the life she had chosen...

Vivienne cleared her throat. *No. She was not going to compare the two.*

"My goodness, it is cold in here, isn't it?" she remarked aloud. There had been far too much silence.

Laura nodded. "Edwin says he never wishes for me to be too comfortable."

Vivienne's mouth fell open. *Surely the man was not so barbaric!*

The girl nodded at the unspoken question. "He says that is how one becomes complacent."

It was impossible not to feel revulsion at the idea. *The man was mad!* He had not been this harsh when she had first known him, had he?

Perhaps she had not noticed. It had been champagne and trips to the opera, she remembered with a wry smile on her face. She had never seen him make these sorts of decisions, but perhaps she had been spending time with her eyes shut.

Her unconscious gaze had remained on Laura, but now she came to look at her, there was something remarkable about her that she had not yet noticed.

There was nothing of her father within her.

Vivienne blinked. The thought did not make sense. Of course, there would be something in Laura's face... or expressions... or carriage, that would mark her out as a Bysshe.

But the more Vivienne concentrated, the more she realized that there was little of Edwin in Laura at all.

Their eyes were different, his so dark, hers so light. Their cheekbones were different, the color of their hair opposing. Edwin was tall, whereas from what Vivienne knew of Laura's age, she was rather slight and petite. The only similarity, perhaps, was the haughty attitude.

Vivienne smiled at the thought, but her smile froze as a rather intrusive thought stopped her in her tracks. *What would a child of theirs have looked like? Hers and Edwin's?*

Her heart rocketed against the thought, rebelled against it, but it was not possible to ignore. *A child of theirs*.

It was a heady thought, throwing her mind into a miasma of rushed images, hasty thoughts, half-completed ideas. A child of theirs: her wit, her bravery, his directness and strength of mind. What such a child could have been.

Vivienne swallowed. *This was getting her nowhere*. She was certain the more time she spent with Miss Laura, the more of Edwin she would see in her. However, the answer could be simple, of course. It could be that Laura was the picture of her mother.

Jealousy tore through her heart before Vivienne could prevent it. The woman Edwin had married; the woman he had decided was better than her, more impressive than her—willing to give up everything, including her name, for him.

It was impossible not to wonder about her. Vivienne's questions about the mistress had been careful and delicate, but neither the butler nor the housekeeper seemed to wish to speak of her when she had lightly asked.

"Oh, she's gone now, bless her," Mrs. Jenner had said only yesterday as she distractedly attempted to calculate how many candles to order. "Best forgotten."

"I would not speak of the dead," had been Mr. Harris's response when Vivienne had delicately asked about her a few days before. "'Tisn't right."

This woman, the viscountess, had captured Edwin's heart in a way she had not.

Vivienne brushed the thought away. No, she would not permit herself to feel the sorrow. She was here as a governess, not as a prospective wife. *The very idea!*

She had made that perfectly clear to Edwin—to the viscount—and that was that.

"Miss Clarke?" Laura was staring, and only then did Vivienne realize she had probably been standing there for a few minutes without saying anything.

Vivienne smiled brittlely. "One moment."

The schoolroom had once been a bedchamber as far as Vivienne could tell. At the very least, there was a bellpull by where a bed could have been, and she pulled on it hard.

It took but a moment for a maid to open the door, a confused look on her face. "The green bedchamber is—oh, it's you."

Vivienne smiled as icily as she could manage. She had certainly had sufficient practice at the Bureau. The maid colored, curtseyed, and fell silent.

"Someone has neglected to light the fire here," said Vivienne coldly, her breath still blossoming out before her. "Rectify this mistake immediately."

"But the master—"

"—would not wish for Miss Laura to catch a cold," Vivienne cut across the plaintive remark of the maid. "Immediately, please."

It was not immediately, of course. These things never were, but within ten minutes, there was a small, growing blaze in the fireplace, and Vivienne could already feel the warmth.

Laura was no longer shivering, at any rate.

Vivienne returned to her desk, stood between it and her blackboard, and took a deep breath. *Right. Where was she?*

Ah yes. The first step of a lesson. Not the lesson itself, for the child would be taught something quite different. She would be taught to trust.

"Now, tell me, Laura," said Vivienne as brightly as she could manage. "This is a new part of the world for me, Yorkshire, and I know very few families here, save the Rochdales, of course. Who is in the neighborhood worth knowing?"

Laura snorted. "Very few. I find most of them dull."

It was a reasonable answer for a child, even Vivienne had to admit. It was rare that anyone attempted to entertain a child when there was hunting, shooting, and balls to be had.

"Fine," Vivienne said slowly. "But there must be some families of note your father knows well."

The question was rather simple, but Laura merely blinked as though she was attempting to be purposefully irritating. *Perhaps that was where she took after her father.*

"Miss Laura, who do you know in the neighborhood?"

Laura sighed. "Some families. Three or four, most of them dull. They are all in town for the Season. They go every year. We don't see anyone in the winter."

Vivienne nodded. It was perhaps the longest speech Laura had made in her presence, and it was a good one. Short, still, but succinct.

So for months of the year, the Bysshes were alone here in this part of Yorkshire. York was not too far away, otherwise, Mrs. Jenner would not go there to choose supplies, but far enough away for Edwin—for the viscount to keep his counsel.

Interesting. Why had he no interest in seeking company?

Vivienne smiled curtly. The room was starting to warm up; she could feel the tendrils of heat meandering across the room. Perhaps it would thaw their conversation.

"And what has your schooling been up until this point?"

Laura sighed, an insubordination Vivienne would never have accepted from one of her governesses. From a child, however, it was accepted—for now. "Hasn't Edwin told you?"

The continued rudeness had to be stopped, Vivienne decided. Calling her own father by his first name? *How did he allow that?*

"I must say, Miss Laura," Vivienne said stiffly, "I think it strange that you consider it appropriate to call his lordship that. Has not he asked you to call him Father or Papa or—"

"You…you don't know, do you?" Laura had spoken without malice, without glee, but with a certain amount of confusion.

Vivienne swallowed. If there was one guaranteed way to ensure that she felt off-kilter, it was to hint there was something important she should know that she quite evidently did not.

What had Edwin hidden from her? What was she supposed to know? How was she supposed to be a good governess if she…

Of course. Vivienne remembered the last words Edwin had said to her in his study. He had avoided her ever since that moment.

"But mark my words, Miss Clarke, I will be doing everything in my power to demonstrate to the world that you and your Bureau are finished. Finished, over and done with. Forever."

Vivienne breathed out slowly, trying not to let her confusion and disappointment show. *Of course.* Of course, Edwin had kept something vital from her. Of course, he had allowed her to start lessons without telling her something clearly crucial to her role.

It was a most dissatisfying feeling. When she had been at the Governess Bureau, her office had been like a kingdom. She had been its supreme ruler, and all had feared her.

The feeling of being utterly helpless was not one Vivienne was accustomed to, and she did not like it. She was the one supposed to be making other people feel nervous.

This was most irregular.

Laura was still staring, a smile creeping over her face. "You don't know, do you."

It was not a question but a statement. Vivienne opened her mouth to speak, but no words came out. *Was this what it was, then, to be utterly powerless?*

She closed her mouth, coughed, then said, "I am sorry, Miss Laura, what should I know?"

Vivienne attempted to speak stiffly, as though she was doing Laura a favor by permitting her to tell her something. It was a feeble attempt, and she could see immediately that it had not worked. Laura almost laughed, then stifled the merriment, while an amused expression remained on her face.

"I am sorry, Miss Clarke," said Laura, looking anything but. "But I thought that—well, I thought everyone would know."

Vivienne's patience was running thin. "Know what?"

Laura blinked. "Why, that I am adopted, of course."

Utter stillness entered Vivienne's body. The words echoed in her mind, her heart skipping a beat, her stomach frozen. It was such a surprise, there did not appear to be words within her to explain just what her mind was attempting to understand. Adopted. *Adopted!*

Laura was no blood relation of Edwin. That would explain the lack of likeness, to be sure, and the strange, cold distance between them.

"Are you not interested in your ancestors? These people lived in these very rooms, walked these very halls, share your blood. They do not interest you?"

Embarrassment shot through Vivienne like a bullet. *Dear God, had she really said those words? No wonder Laura had been offended!*

Not a whisper of any trouble with Edwin or his wife had ever reached London—but of course, she had tried to avoid any information about them. The last thing she needed was more information about how Edwin had immediately restarted his life without her.

Was it possible that everyone in London knew, and she was the only one who did not?

Laura appeared to confirm her suspicions. "How strange. I had thought Society would be full of that gossip when I was first brought here."

Vivienne took a deep breath. *She could not lose control of this schoolroom.* She was the governess here; it should be she who was settled and calm, and Laura who should feel permanently on the back foot.

If there was one thing Vivienne had learned—painfully, as it was—over the intervening years, it was that discomfort and pain and discord were no way to build a connection.

She would have to humble herself. Refuse to attempt to look impressive and clever. Speak from the heart, for once. At least it was to Edwin's child and not himself.

"I did not know," Vivienne said as calmly as she could. "No, I was not aware."

There was a strange mixture of pleasure and confusion on Laura's face. Did she wish to be mistaken for his birth daughter, or was she merely proud of having confused the governess?

Vivienne knew she would have to think about this later. Was this why Edwin was so short with Laura? Why he rarely praised her, engaged her in conversation, snapped at her so often? *Was this why she called him Edwin and not Father?*

She had never assumed that there would be any less affection between an adopted child and their parent than any other kind of child—though it was not as though Vivienne knew enough parents of any kind socially to make any sort of comparison.

And was not adoption fairly common? Children who could not be cared for, loving spouses who could not conceive... It solved a problem for everyone. Nature did not always deliver as people hoped.

"Yes, adopted," said Laura quietly. "At the age of around three, I have been told. At any event, I have few memories of my previous life and no real idea where I came from. That's why Edwin doesn't love me."

The ricochet of those words made Vivienne almost rock on her feet. She lowered herself carefully on the chair by her desk. *This was no time for standing.*

Her surprise must have shown on her face, for Laura continued, with all the gentle precociousness of a child who had spent a great deal of time thinking about it, "Please, Miss Clarke, do not worry yourself about it. I am accustomed to it by now."

Vivienne wanted to say something, but no words came to mind. What was she supposed to say to an adopted child who had so clearly decided her father did not love her?

Besides, it was not as though Edwin was giving her much

opportunity to refute the accusation. She had seen little, in the short weeks since she had been here, to suggest that Laura was anything but entirely correct.

He did not love her. What a terrible thing to think. What a terrible thing to see.

Vivienne swallowed. She had thought…nay, she had hoped to see Edwin in a better light than this, yet he disappointed her at every turn. Where was the man she had fallen in love with? Where was the gentleman who had whispered such sweet nothings into her ears when she had kissed him?

"How old are you, Laura?" Vivienne managed.

"Twelve years old," said Laura promptly. "Assuming that my birth parents told Edwin and Henrietta the truth. I never can tell. I am so small."

Vivienne thought privately that perhaps she was right. She was far smaller than she would have expected a girl of twelve to be—yet there were petite daughters. It did happen.

"Well," Vivienne said aloud, "twelve years old is a very interesting time for a girl. Not a child, becoming a woman…fathers and daughters can often find this time complicated."

The face Laura pulled could be best described as bored. "Do not try to pretend he cares for me, Miss Clarke. I told you, I am quite reconciled to it. I know he does not. I have a home, and for that, I am grateful."

Vivienne was unable to reply. Wise beyond her years, this child was, yet she clearly had to be. If Edwin's disdain and disregard for her had been this obvious ever since Laura had arrived at Byhalden Lodge, then no wonder Laura had little respect for him in his turn.

To adopt a child, then not to love it? What was wrong with Edwin? *It was as though*, Vivienne thought wryly, *the part of him that knew how to love had broken when she had refused his ridiculous proposal.*

How could she reassure Laura while at the same time be honest? There was little love there, at least from what she could see, and she knew what Edwin in love looked like.

A particularly wonderful carriage ride back to her apartments from a ball crept into her mind, but Vivienne pushed it aside. He had known what to say then. He clearly did not know now.

"Well," she said bracingly, "let us focus on history and geography for today, then tomorrow we can discuss math and the sciences."

It was a small miracle, to Vivienne's mind, that she managed to get through the day's lessons at all. Mercifully she had agreed with Edwin that Laura's lessons would only take place in the mornings for now, as the child became more accustomed to a regimented system.

By the time luncheon was called and Laura traipsed out of the schoolroom, having performed adequately for a child with no previous schooling, Vivienne was in a daze.

Adopted. Unloved. Uncared for. And seemingly aware that Laura knew all this and did not mind? No, Edwin Bysshe was not the man she had once loved.

It was so on her mind that, when Vivienne was descending herself to the servants' hall for her own luncheon, she almost did not notice passing Edwin in a corridor.

And then her mind caught up with her. "Edwin Bysshe!"

Edwin halted, confusion on his face. "Yes?"

"How could you?" Vivienne berated, with no introduction to her ire. "You have brought me here under false pretenses!"

Edwin looked coldly. "I have no idea what you're talking about. I told you the other day, I will ensure the Bureau will end, and in disgrace if I can manage it."

That was an entirely different problem, and Vivienne was determined to face only one at a time, troublesome man that he was. If only he wasn't so elegantly dressed today.

"You did not say that Laura—that your daughter was adopted!"

A flash of pain seared Edwin's face, one that Vivienne had not expected. It was gone in a moment as he regained control, but it did not make sense. *Why was he offended? What had she done, other than pointed out the lie by omission?*

"And what difference does that make?" he asked coldly.

Vivienne was caught off guard by this. *No difference,* was what she wanted to say. *No difference at all, save the difference you are marking out!*

But it was abundantly clear by the way he was looking at her that Laura had been quite incorrect; he loved her.

He loved her but hid that fact from his daughter. *Why?* Vivienne could not understand it. *Pride? Shame?* He always had been such a proud man.

"As I thought," Edwin said bitterly. "Look, this is nothing to do with you, Miss Clarke. This is not your problem. You are paid to do a job. I suggest you focus your attentions on—"

"But she is hurt by the lack of affection you show her," Vivienne said, desperately attempting to make him see. He did not deserve Laura, but that did not mean she would permit a child to go through her life under the mistaken belief that her adopted father did not love her. "You clearly care for her, yet you withhold—"

"Not your problem," repeated Edwin. "Be advised, Miss Clarke. Do not interfere with my relationship with my daughter."

He continued along the corridor, leaving Vivienne absolutely boiling with fury.

From where did this desire to self-sabotage come? Was it possible that her redemption of her Governess Bureau could be achieved with a father and daughter so unwilling to speak their minds?

Chapter Six

January 5, 1816

THE SPARKLING BIRDSONG from the tree overhead was the balm soothing Edwin's soul.

It had all started that morning. It had been weeks since he had gone out with his sketchbook. Edwin could barely remember when he had taken some time for himself, ignored the callings on a viscount's time, and escaped into the garden with his pencils.

It was only by accident that he was reminded of it. Searching through his desk that morning, he had accidently knocked two ledgers, which his butler had most inconveniently left, and amongst the papers which had slipped from the desk—there was his sketchbook.

Edwin picked it up.

Almost unthinkingly, he opened it up and allowed his fingers to brush against the textured paper. You could not buy anything like this quality in York. He had been forced to send to London for it when he had completed his old sketchbook.

Edwin had glanced at the window. Sunlight; wintery beams, cold but bright. Perfect weather for sketching.

After throwing on his greatcoat, a scarf, and his hat, Edwin strode across the hall and threw open the front door. The piercingly cold air hit him like a sledgehammer, but he breathed it in regardless.

There was something about the smell of winter that no other season had. Spring, summer, autumn, they were all about life: starting, growing, dying.

Winter was different. Not the absence of life, exactly, but the reminder that life needed to pause occasionally.

Edwin breathed in deeply as he strode along the gravel drive toward the garden. *Garden or parkland?*

The thought gave him reason to pause. There was little to do in the gardens at present, the statues wrapped in heavy white sheets to protect them from frost, green buds not yet appearing, bulbs nestled in the soil.

But that did not mean that he might run into someone. Anyone would be an intrusion when one was hoping to spend some time sketching, but if a certain two ladies were to appear…

Edwin breathed out heavily, watching his breath appear on the air before him.

Not the gardens today, then. If Vivienne—if Miss Clarke and Laura took a hearty walk in the cold, and the little he knew about governesses led him to believe that was precisely the sort of thing they would encourage, he would certainly see them. And they would ask questions.

Worse, and his fingers tightened around the sketchbook under his arm, ask to see what he was doing.

Decision made, Edwin's footsteps took him, instead, toward the parkland. It was nothing too impressive—a hundred acres of so of the finest woodland and moor that his ancestors managed to carve out.

Deer had rutted there in the autumn, the evidence of their antler sharpening along the trees. Edwin made a vague mental note to ask his steward whether any trees would need to be coppiced after such activities.

But he was not thinking as a viscount, not right now. The

title had never been expected, with two elder brothers before him. No, this afternoon was a chance to return to his earliest love. A wry smile crept over his face. *Whether Vivienne liked the idea or not.*

A large oak had fallen—what, about two generations ago? Edwin had sat on its sorry bough so often, and previous Bysshe generations before him, that it was smoothed into a seat.

Sitting down, Edwin pulled his scarf closer as the brightness of the sun dazzled him. It was disconcerting, being in such brightness with no warmth, but that was winter beauty.

Edwin placed his sketchbook on his lap and pulled out both fingerless gloves and a pencil from his pocket. It was one of his habits, one that always seemed to drive his valet mad. Almost every pocket, no matter the piece of clothing, had a pencil within it.

Mrs. Jenner had once told him, rather irritably, that if he could desist with the habit, then their laundrymaid would be much happier. Apparently, nothing ruined a load of washing as mangling a pencil.

Edwin gripped it purposefully and opened up his sketchbook to a fresh page. The sheer whiteness was slightly intimidating, but it did not remain virginal for long. His fingers moved quickly, his pencil drawing out the lines of the tree before him. Edwin's eyes darted up and down, between the real thing and the created thing starting to appear on his paper.

There was nothing like it. The coldness of the air, crispness of the light, the utter silence save the gentle wind in the leafless trees and the song of a bird above. Blackbird, maybe?

Time was immaterial. Time did not matter. Edwin's focus was the pencil, the paper, the light falling slowly, lazily through the branches of the tree before him. The darkness of winter, the cruelty—but also the beauty. The power. The majesty.

He should not have put off coming out here, doing what he loved. If only art could be a profession for a gentleman such as himself; if only he had been given the chance to…

Edwin smiled as he purposefully smudged a part of the bark on the paper. *If, if, if...no one won the "what if" game.*

Things could have been so different, he supposed. Everything could have been different. His whole life could have taken a different course.

He should be grateful, really, that he could still use art as a way of losing himself in something that harmed no one. Edwin knew many of his neighbors were waiting for him to remarry, or at the very least, take a mistress. It was not natural, one of them had told him only a few months ago before they traveled to London, for a gentleman to be so alone.

Edwin's breath poured into the air. The idea of bringing another woman into his life—it was already far more complicated than he had ever intended it to be. Laura...

No, his pencil and his sketchbook, that was the best way to calm him, to reduce the strain on his nerves, to give him all the sustenance for his soul that he required.

Henrietta had never understood it.

The pencil snapped in his hands. Edwin looked down, shocked at the sudden noise and violent motion under his fingertips. The pencil had broken clean across the middle, leaving him with a useless end and a stub of a pencil.

The bird flew off, taking its birdsong with it.

Edwin swallowed. He was no fool, for he knew he had broken the pencil at the mere thought of Henrietta.

He should never have married her. He should have known better. A foolish marriage, made in haste, Edwin was sure everyone thought she was with child. *What other reason*, he thought bitterly, *could a man have for rushing into a marriage?*

An image of Vivienne seared his mind.

To escape her, he thought dully. So convinced a marriage to another, any other, would rid him of those longings, would remove Vivienne Clarke from his heart, he had stumbled into the arms of the first woman who would have him.

Even Henrietta's father had advised against it. Edwin gripped the small stub of pencil carefully. That should have been enough to tell him that the whole dratted thing was a mistake. Still, he had persevered. He had persevered long after the small affection he had felt for her had faded, long after their attempts for a child had waned.

But that was the past. Edwin brushed his hair out of his eyes as though it was just as easy to brush aside the remembrance of a wife who was now gone.

He had come here to draw. That was what he should do.

Though the pencil was a little shorter than he was accustomed to, Edwin was a proficient enough artist for that to cease to be a problem after a few minutes. His eyes darted back and forth once more, the beauty of the world, the paper, the world, the paper...

Tension melted away from his shoulders without him noticing. The stress disappeared from his brow as it furrowed in concentration, seeking to represent the movement of the branches in a still medium. His fingers moved idly across the page, adding detail there, purposefully smudging to bring depth here.

It was as though his fingers knew precisely where to go; the drawing was there, just beneath the surface of the page, and all his pencil was doing was excavating. A hidden jewel.

And then the moment was over. Edwin blinked, swallowed, and looked down at the page. There was a perfect representation of the twisted, aged tree before him.

A slow smile crept over Edwin's face. There was something about the act of creation. Something nothing else could replace.

His left hand moved, fingers chilly, and turned the page. Another white, blank expanse, just waiting for him to create something. His fingers brushed across the whiteness, those which had smudged the previous drawing, leaving a gentle trail of lead.

Dear God, he had missed this. As the pencil started to work once more, tracing the lines of a different tree, Edwin wondered idly when he could justify coming out here again.

It was not as though he was very busy all the time. A viscount was no duke. There were no great calls on his time.

But there always appeared to be something to do. Nothing complicated enough to delegate, nothing important enough to feel impressive. Wage slips and order notes, invoices and letters from his accountant, lawyer updates on tenancy agreements, queries about land, about selling pigs, about when he would next be in London—

Footsteps.

The pencil scraped across the page, causing an unsightly line across the detailed stump he had been attempting. Edwin looked up, tension returning to his shoulders, eyes darting, looking for the instigator of the sound.

They were footsteps. Though Edwin could not see who, it was someone approaching. He did not want to be disturbed, but the only solution was to depart.

Pencil and stub thrust into his pocket, Edwin closed the sketchbook and was about to rise to his feet when—

"Oh, I do apologize."

The voice sounded embarrassed, almost shy. It was a gentle voice, though one he would have recognized quicker if it had been cold, icy, aloof.

Vivienne Clarke.

She had come into view now, stepping from behind the very trees he had been sketching. Heat blossomed in Edwin's cheeks, no matter how he attempted to prevent it.

Of course, of all the people who would interrupt it, it would be Vivienne Clarke. As sharp, painful embarrassment seared his heart, Edwin snapped the sketchbook shut and wished he had brought a leather band or something to close it.

This was ridiculous. It was his land! All he was doing was sitting on his land with a sketchbook. There was nothing embarrassing about it, surely—though the rational part of his mind seemed unable to convince his stomach of that fact.

"Nothing to apologize for," Edwin said, hardly aware of what he was saying but certain he had to say something. "You have free reign of the garden and the parkland."

He could hear the foolishness of his words as he said them, but it appeared he could do little to stop himself. *What was wrong with him? Why was anger such an intrinsic emotion whenever he spoke with Vivienne?*

Besides, it was hardly a secret that he enjoyed drawing, painting, art of all kinds. It was no shameful pastime, one that was in general encouraged in the aristocracy. And he was rather good at it. Edwin found he was standing, chest puffed out, defiance in every pore.

So why did this feel like an intrusion? Why was he furious, for some reason, that she had disturbed him? Why did he feel as exposed? Thank goodness his sketchbook was closed. Edwin clutched it, grateful beyond words he had closed it before Vivienne was too close.

She was still approaching, however, and appeared mightily unhappy. "Must you snap at me? Does every word out of your mouth have to drip with disdain when we converse?"

Edwin opened his mouth to speak, harshness about to pour from his mouth, but in that moment, a cloud shifted, and sunlight poured through the branches of the trees behind her, lighting Vivienne up like an angel.

Edwin closed his mouth. It was as though no time had passed at all. As though Vivienne had stepped away when refusing his proposal of marriage but now stepped back.

The elegance of her face, the warmth of her mouth, the intelligence in her eyes...it was all there. Something deep stirred within him, Edwin knew, and he could do nothing but stand in awe of the picturesque beauty she offered. She was...she was everything. Unchanged.

His rather irritating baby face had been one he had loathed when young and was only starting to grow into it—but Vivienne? She had barely changed at all, each small change only serving to accentuate her beauty, not lessen it.

If only she looked changed, Edwin found himself wishing, mouth becoming dry. *If only she looked nothing like the woman he had fallen in love with.*

Edwin dropped his gaze, the brilliance of her beauty too bright for his eyes. "No, you are...you are right. There was no reason to speak to you like... I apologize."

It was a relief, in a way, to get those words out. He should have said them long ago, and now they were out, there was a rather strange sense of joy. *He had apologized to her. Now they were even.*

"Oh," came the surprised response.

Edwin wished to raise his eyes again, take another look at her, unrestrained as it would have to be in the presence of others.

He should not have. Vivienne appeared wrong-footed by his small admission of guilt, and the wintery sun was still flowing across her, turning her blonde hair golden, making her crisp cream pelisse a silvery flowing gown.

Edwin swallowed. *What could he say?* He had spent most of the time since she had arrived at Byhalden Lodge adeptly avoiding her as best he could. He had even concocted business in York—utterly fabricated—to avoid Sunday lunches with her and Laura. Two birds, one stone.

Not that it had helped. He had received irritated glares from his daughter when he had returned late on Sunday afternoon, the darkness of the hall unable to hide her ire.

And it was Vivienne. *Vivienne, of all women in the world, that it could be!*

No, he had to get a grip of himself. He was the gentleman here, it was his home—he was a viscount, for crying out loud! He would not permit a governess to overwhelm him.

With a great effort, Edwin sat slowly back onto the branch and opened up his sketchbook. It felt like an impossible task, and his fingers did fumble slightly as they retrieved his pencil from his pocket, but he managed it.

"Thank you, Miss Clarke," he said lazily, looking down at his sketchbook as though she held no further interest to him. "You may go about your business."

It was his great wish that she would simply go away. Disappear. He could not have been more clear, Edwin was sure, that he wished to be left alone.

It was a wonderful thought, but Edwin was not entirely sure it was true. Even with his focus on the paper before him, he could feel her gaze upon him. Fighting the instinct to look up and meet it, Edwin focused instead on moving the pencil slowly across the page.

He would not look up. No matter how much he wished to gaze into Vivienne's eyes, he would not look up. He would master himself.

"You're sketching."

"Obviously," said Edwin without thinking.

Thought was becoming difficult. Why was his mind clouded with such intrusive images of Vivienne? Even without looking, he was entirely captivated by her presence.

When next she spoke, Vivienne was much closer to him than he had expected. "You know, at the very least, we should attempt to be civil."

"I...I am not sure how we can be civil," said Edwin, honesty seeping out of his mouth before he could stop it. "So much...so much has happened. Water under the bridge, they say, but it has been a flood."

"What utter nonsense."

"And can you remember to be civil? Do you remember how?" The words had been bitten from his tongue before Edwin was conscious of speech.

The cold silence that met his words was enough to finally induce him to look up. Vivienne was standing just a few feet from him, shivering slightly in the cold but clearly ruffled by his words.

"I have—you cannot say..." Vivienne swallowed, Edwin watching her chest heave as she attempted to find the words. "I have spent the last decade or so maintaining a respectable reputation in London. I think I know how to behave. What can be said of you, a-a country squire with little manners—"

"You think so?" snorted Edwin, his fingers ceasing to move across the page as he glared, heart thumping. *Country squire indeed!* "Fine. We both know how to be civil, but clearly, we cannot be so with each other. Fine."

Silence fell between them, a sticky, uncomfortable silence that Edwin hated. *Damn and blast it, if only she had gone away when he had suggested it.* All this tension, it was her fault. She had drawn him into it, forced him down this path.

He wanted to go—but that would feel too much like defeat. No, he could not be the one to leave. He would not retreat. He would not give her the satisfaction of knowing, even in the smallest way, that she had managed to get under his skin.

Even if she had.

There was too much unsaid between them, that was the trouble. Too much had occurred. *Too many sweet nothings whispered, too many kisses stolen*, Edwin thought furiously, his hand turning the page of his sketchbook merely for something to do.

Was it possible for two adults to maturely converse after such goings on, even if the said kisses had been years and years ago?

He would defy anyone to discover a way to do it. He had no comprehension of how to be when he was around Vivienne. She brought out of him all the darkness, the bitterness—when once she had encouraged naught but joy and hope and...

Edwin swallowed. *Dear God, he was weak before her.* If she asked him to kiss her...if she asked anything of him, he was not sure whether he could say no. As he looked up, her own eyes full of emotion, whether it be passion or hatred, it stirred him in a way he was sure Vivienne would not expect.

He needed to escape her, but how could he if she was always here?

A robin soared low behind Vivienne, Edwin's eye following it as a welcome distraction. Without conscious thought, he absentmindedly started to sketch out the creature. Wings out stretched, each feather a delicate demonstration of the soaring flight he knew he could not capture...

A shadow fell over his sketchbook. "You were always...always so good at sketching. I am glad to see that you have kept up the habit."

A smile crept across Edwin's face, despite himself. "Drawing comes naturally to me. I do not consider it a talent, more an expression of who I am. Like breathing."

There was a knowing chuckle. "The only thing that ever came naturally to you."

In another's mouth, in another situation, the words would have been vicious, but for some reason, Vivienne's words did not sound so. They sounded—wistful?

Edwin could not tell, and he was not going to make the mistake of glancing up. If anything would distract him, it was that.

"I think everyone has something they are naturally good at," he said quietly, his pencil darting along a feather to create definition. "Most people do, even if they have not found it yet."

It was on the tip of his tongue—a place of great temptation—to ask her about the Bureau. *How had it fallen? How, after so many years, had its reputation been lost?*

But Edwin knew better to speak of such a thing to Vivienne. Managing to hold himself back, he reminded himself that he had to have some dignity. She may have stolen the majority of it fifteen years ago, but he had retained some, and he would not lower himself to purposefully hurt her. He was not that sort of man.

"You are much improved."

"Th-Thank you," Edwin said hesitantly. *Dear God, what was wrong with him?* Why did he find it so difficult to accept her kind words?

Were they, perhaps, the first kind words she had spoken to him since that fateful day in the park? That day when he had bared his soul to her, and she had found it wanting?

"You draw most things?"

Edwin nodded. Finally, they had found a topic they could

converse on with little emotion. "I prefer things of nature to man's creation. Trees, leaves, birds, that sort of thing. I drew you once. Do you still have it?"

The words slipped out before he could think, and once said, could not be retrieved. Edwin's shoulders tightened, tension slipping into them as easily as a bird slipped along a breeze.

He did look up now.

Vivienne's cheeks were pink. She was carefully examining the stitching on her gloves. "No."

The sadness and sense of betrayal that flowed into Edwin's heart surprised even him. *Of course, she didn't have it.*

He had never felt so stupid. For a moment, they had been conversing...well, not quite like old times, but civilly enough. It was not as they had been; there was too much frost, and not just in the air.

But they had been polite. Polite was an achievement, and they had managed it for—what, all of two minutes?

Civility had always felt impossible between them, and now Vivienne had proved why. *She had not kept the drawing.*

Edwin could not put into words why it hurt so much. Why the idea of her destroying or disposing of a thing he had poured so much effort into was so soul-destroying.

"Of course, you didn't keep it," he muttered, dropping his gaze back to his sketchbook.

"What should I have done with it?" Vivienne's voice was low, quiet, with none of the coldness he had expected. "Hung it on my wall, a drawing of myself from the gentleman I refused to marry? Put it in a drawer somewhere, take it out when I was alone and lonely?"

Despite himself, Edwin looked up. "You have been lonely, then?"

It was not precisely something to crow about. He had wanted her to be happy; at least, eventually, he had managed to feel such graciousness.

Was she unhappy? Edwin found his gaze raking over her

features, attempting to discern whether she had spent the intervening years joyful and productive or miserable and alone. There did not appear to be any midground in his heart.

But this was none of his business. Edwin had to force himself to look away, to remember that the happiness—or not—of his governess was none of his concern.

Vivienne Clarke was nothing to do with him. *She had made sure of that.*

"What should I have done with it?" came the gentle question.

Edwin swallowed. He had absolutely no idea, but he was hardly going to admit that. No matter the months and years which had gone by, Vivienne had power over him, even if she did not mean to.

She...she did something to him. His body and his heart responded to her, her mere proximity enough for him to start to wonder what could be.

And he could not allow it. He would not fall into that trap again.

"You...you have to go back to the house."

As he looked up, he saw Vivienne raise an eyebrow. "I thought I had free reign of the gardens and the parkland?"

Galling as it was to have his own words used against him, Edwin could not argue. "Do you not have something to do for Laura?"

Only then, for the first time in their conversation, did he meet her eyes with no thought as to what he would say next.

She was so intoxicating. It was a wonder other gentlemen had been able to prevent themselves from offering for her, all those years in London. Perhaps they had. Perhaps she had rejected them all. Perhaps she was a widow, hiding that by using her maiden name. Perhaps—

Vivienne sunk into a low, clearly sarcastic curtsey. "Whatever you wish, *my lord.*"

Try as he might, Edwin was unable to stop himself watching Vivienne walk back toward the house.

He should follow her. The instinct was there—to catch up with her, to tell her just how he wished they could speak with openness and honesty. How he wished the impossible could happen, and they could return to that moment, and he could convince her, once and for all, to become his.

Edwin swallowed. He looked down, pulled out the page, and screwed it up, placing the paper in his pocket.

He turned the page, looked down at the white, clean expanse, and sighed.

CHAPTER SEVEN

January 12, 1816

THE WARM BUTTERED toast melted in her mouth, and Vivienne let out an unconscious sigh of happiness as the chatter of the breakfast table echoed around the servants' hall.

She had not even noticed that she had missed this. The coming together of people without titles, without expectations, to laugh and talk and eat together. The food that one had not prepared oneself, the delight in overhearing the conversation of others…

Simple pleasures. Pleasures she had forgone, Vivienne could see now, when she had decided to withdraw from her governesses, determined to create distance between them.

The privilege of owning the Bureau, she had told herself then. How many warm conversations had she missed? How much joy and laughter?

"And then I told her," a maid was saying further down the table, to the accompaniment of chortles from another maid and two footmen, "that the damned thing couldn't scrub up clean. It was painted black!"

The end of the story generated much amusement. Vivienne

smiled to herself as she finished off her slice of toast. *The simple things.*

Yes, she had forgotten them. Never raising herself up so high as that of a duchess or a countess, naturally, but still...she had lost something of the class she had been born into.

Not a servile class, nor an uneducated class, her father had balked against such ideas.

But a *working* class. Where one was warmed by one's efforts during the day and a communal fire in the evening. Where teamwork and collaboration and connection meant that great things were achieved, things one could not have done alone.

Vivienne reached out for another piece of toast and decided to treat herself by spreading liberal amounts of marmalade on it. *Marmalade.* An indulgence she rarely permitted herself in London at the Governess Bureau. When one was one's own employer, every single shilling made a difference.

Apparently, the Viscount Bysshe did not agree. *Why, his servants ate better than some gentlemen in London,* Vivienne thought as she bit into the sweet, tangy marmalade and toast.

She was certainly not complaining.

"—your turn, I definitely believe it is your turn," a footman was saying with just a hint of frustration opposite her to another of his station. "We agreed, every other week, and I spent most of last week—"

"But so was I. I was doing it, too!" came the retort.

The butler sighed. "Don't tell me you both polished the silver with the expectation that neither of you will serve at table this week? If so, you are sorely mistaken, I can tell you..."

Vivienne was careful not to smile at this snippet of conversation. Maids did not mind their jests being overheard. *But men, no matter their station in life, demanded respect in a way a woman never could countenance,* she thought idly as she watched the debate continue. Men had to be right. A man could never be proven wrong; it was alien to him.

"*You...you have to go back to the house.*"

"I thought I had free reign of the gardens and the parkland?"

A case in point, Vivienne thought wryly as she reached for her teacup. A gentleman who simply could not be wrong.

No matter what she said, Edwin would always be the person wronged. The fact she was left, abandoned and alone, in the cold and unforgiving city of London, with the reputation of a woman who had potentially been soiled by a son of a viscount...

"Here, let me pour you another cup of tea, Miss Clarke."

Vivienne looked up to see a warm smile on the housekeeper's face, teapot in her hand.

A weak smile crept over Vivienne's face. "Why—why yes, thank you, Mrs. Jenner."

It was strange, she thought as she watched the steaming amber liquid fall from the spout into her cup. Loneliness was an emotion she had known well at the Bureau, but she had always assumed it was the only option.

Who could befriend the ice queen as she had accidentally heard herself referred as by a governess who had been refused the position in a minor French prince's family?

It was why she had avoided being a part of the servants' hall when she had arrived at Byhalden Lodge, but even Vivienne would admit, she had been wrong.

Why had she been so worried about eating with the other servants? She was alone in the main, which was how she liked it, but merely being around so much hustle and bustle poured life into her veins. It was as though she had been asleep for many years and only now was starting to wake up.

And the irony was, of course, though again Vivienne would not own it, that she was better treated here, even in passing, than the few times she dined with the family.

The family. Laura was pleasant enough, in her way, though she kept her father at arm's length in a way that was painful for Vivienne to watch. If only the two of them could understand each other. If only Edwin could share some, any, of his emotions with his daughter.

But that was the problem, wasn't it? Vivienne sipped her tea as her thoughts meandered to Edwin. He simply could not share his emotions. Speaking of his feelings had been difficult enough when he had been, according to him, passionately in love with her.

Her cheeks were hot. *It was the tea*, Vivienne told herself. *Anyone observing her would surely assume it was the tea.*

"Miss Clarke?"

"What?" Vivienne snapped.

The footman who had spoken to her shrunk down in his seat. "I...there is one piece of t-toast left, and I..."

His voice trailed way, his eyes downcast, and shame washed over Vivienne as she saw what an impact she had had on the boy.

Dear Lord, he was probably only one or two and twenty, she thought. About the age Edwin had been when he...

Well. There was no going back to that now. The boy was gone, and the man who had replaced him was certainly not a person she would have fallen in love with.

"Thank you," she said aloud, as graciously as she could manage. "Thank you. If no one else wants it, I would be grateful to have it."

The toast was cold, perfect for marmalade. Scraping on the thick orangey compote, Vivienne was reminded of just how delicate the balance was in a servants' hall.

Everyone attempting to look impressive, no one with any real money, and the little power that some had—the valet, the lady's maid—could be lost at any moment. There was no longer a lady's maid at Byhalden Lodge, Vivienne had discovered quickly. What was the point when the lady of the house had died?

"Thank you," she reiterated to the blushing footman. "I-I misspoke earlier."

He nodded without saying anything and then rose to leave the table.

A flush of regret seared her stomach, twisting uncomfortably as she swallowed her last mouthful. *Had she accidently condemned her governesses to either loneliness or hunger?*

Because it was rather wonderful being here. The ovens kept the place warm, and there was a sense of...well, camaraderie, Vivienne would probably call it. A sense that without them, each and every one of them, the house would naturally cease to be.

"Have a good day, Miss Clarke," said a maid as she rose from the table.

Vivienne smiled. "And you, Abigail."

That was it, of course. Distinctions had to be maintained. Though she ate with them, the governess had one of the few honorifics at the table. Mrs. Jenner. Mr. Harris. Miss Clarke. Everyone else went by first names for the women and surnames for the men.

The question was, would she have benefited from any additional distinction by not eating with them?

Only the distinction, Vivienne thought dryly, *of being too stuck up to sit with them.* Was that what had happened to her governesses, perhaps? Had they been ostracized not due to any decision of their own making but because she had advised them poorly?

"Now tell me, Miss Clarke," said Mrs. Jenner comfortably as she once again refilled her own teacup. "How are you finding your feet here at Byhalden Lodge?"

Vivienne smiled, the warmth of the room, the tea, and her conversationalist's questions bringing depth to her smile. What would her life have been with a confidant? A friend, a true friend she could have relied on? After Evangeline married that man, she had been alone. Now, it seemed, her life was going in a different direction.

Still, she was unpracticed at the art of light conversation. "Well enough, I thank you."

The housekeeper blinked, clearly waiting for more. When none seemed likely to be offered, she added, "And so your lessons continue well?"

Vivienne hesitated. *They certainly did not, but she was not going to be the person to say it.* "Well enough, as I said."

The awkward tension grew, spreading from her navel to her

chest, to her arms, making her fingertips tingle. *Small talk, light conversation; whatever one wanted to call it, she was certainly not adept at it.*

She had counseled her governesses to remain aloof. Now Vivienne was reaping the rewards of such advice.

"I like her," she said suddenly, aware she needed to say more. "Miss Laura, I mean."

Mrs. Jenner broke into a smile. "A difficult child, I think, but one that has grown a great deal. Why, I remember when she first arrived…"

The housekeeper fell into reminiscences that Vivienne did her best to follow. It appeared that she was much wanted, a little rascal, and when she had first arrived, she had been bathed three times before they could get all the dirt off her.

Vivienne smiled, nodded in the right places, and allowed her mind to wander.

Mrs. Jenner was a good woman; the whole household was. Even Laura, in her way, was an interesting child. But she had not really answered the housekeeper's question. How had she been doing since she had arrived into the Bysshe family?

Vivienne's stomach lurched painfully, and she swallowed down the bile that rose. *Not well.* The little news received from London had been more newspapers speaking ill of her Governess Bureau, more notes from clients saying they were outraged that their governesses might even have *spoken* to one of the ill-reputed marrying kind, and even a note from a previous governess who asked, very politely, if Miss Clarke could refrain from mentioning that she had ever been part of the Bureau.

None of the missives had put a smile on her face. Vivienne had hoped, after a few weeks, that the furor would have died down. Instead, it only seemed to be growing. *Where was Miss Vivienne Clarke, head of the Governess Bureau*, asked a more recent headline which had tied her lungs in knots. *Had she fled London? Had she taken the piles of gold*—Vivienne had had to laugh at that one—*to France?*

The speculation was rife, and Vivienne was certain if she even attempted to put the rumors to rest by revealing the truth—that there were no more governesses in the Bureau, that she had been forced to take on the care of a child herself, and that it was the daughter of a previous gentleman caller of hers...

Vivienne's jaw tightened. *No.* There was no way to explain that without the scandal heightening. The last thing she wanted was to bring Laura into this, and as for Edwin—

But no. She would not think of him.

A quick glance around the room told her that none had noticed her rising temperature, least of all Mrs. Jenner, who was absorbed in her story.

"—the mistress naturally very fond, but there was always a coldness, I think that is how I would describe it, between the master and Miss Laura. I often said to Mr. Harris, if only they could..."

Vivienne smiled weakly. It was all very well for the housekeeper to share some of the history and gossip of the family. *What would the woman do if she found out that shecould have been her mistress?*

It was a strange sensation, and not one Vivienne enjoyed. The idea of being a viscountess, a woman in charge of a household this size—it simply did not happen to women like her.

"—take your plate, Miss Clarke?"

Vivienne blinked. A maid stood before her, hand out. "I beg your pardon?"

The maid smiled and indicated her empty plate. "Can I be so bold as to offer to take your plate, Miss Clarke?"

"What?" Vivienne said, mind utterly elsewhere. Then the words slotted into place. "Oh, yes, of course, thank you! Here, let me help you."

The maid's eyebrows raised in a good-natured smile. "My word, I don't think I've seen you offer to help clean up before! Trying to think of excuses not to go to that schoolroom?"

There was murmured yet good-natured laughter around the

room, but Vivienne flushed, nonetheless. *Was she really so aloof, so snooty? Had she been considered above her station?*

"Oh, go on with you, Hannah," said Mrs. Jenner with a knowing smile. "I'd like to see you do your job, not expect other people to do it for you!"

There was greater laughter here at the maid's expense, who continued to chatter away to one of the kitchen maids, and the conversation moved on.

Heat still poured through Vivienne's veins, Had she been so concerned about what others would think of her that she had inadvertently done herself a disservice?

Although no one was looking at her anymore and the conversation had most definitely moved on, Vivienne found she could not stop feeling self-conscious. Heated embarrassment rushed around her, but there was a nagging concern at the back of the mind that, perhaps, she had deserved such a remark.

"Oh, come now, Hannah," a footman said, jerking his head over at Vivienne. "You can't expect the likes of those who can read to be the same as you and me!"

There were chuckles at Hannah's expense, but Vivienne felt the slight just as keenly.

The likes of those who can read.

What would they think, these servants who spent their lives caring for, cooking for, and cleaning up after "the family," if they knew that she had grown up in a way much like they did? Were they really so different from each other?

"Oh, ignore the whole pack of them," the housekeeper said kindly, placing a hand on Vivienne's arm and making her jump. "Sorry, I did not mean to startle you. They're just a den of nonsense, this lot, and I would advise you to ignore them all."

Her smile was comforting but did nothing to quell the concern in Vivienne's heart.

"Yes. Yes, right, thank you," Vivienne found herself saying as she rose from the table. "But I really must—the schoolroom, Miss Laura will be… I will see you later, Mrs. Jenner."

She had risen from the table before the housekeeper could reply. Vivienne stepped away from the gossiping, cheerful, warm servants' hall and into the cold corridor.

She shivered. It really was a sudden change, the comfort of the bustling servants' quarters to the freezing corridors. One day, the British aristocracy would bother to learn—or pay—for their corridors to be heated, and they would all be a lot happier for it.

Byhalden Lodge was not a particularly large manor house. Ten bedchambers in all, Mr. Harris had proudly informed her, but the north wing was essentially closed off and only used for visitors.

This meant that it took Vivienne but five minutes to make her way to the schoolroom for the official portion of the day to begin.

She was pleased, upon opening the door, to see her charge was already waiting for her. There had been a debate not too long ago as to whether Laura wished to continue on with lessons, despite the short progress they had yet made. Her father had made it perfectly clear that lessons would continue, but Vivienne had been unsure just how far Laura would go to prove her point.

Her pleasure declined, however, as Vivienne stepped into the room and saw Laura had her feet on her desk and was entirely absorbed in a novel.

"Please put that away, Miss Laura," Vivienne said smartly as she stepped toward the blackboard. "There will be plenty of time for reading this afternoon when lessons are over."

"Why should I put it away? It's more interesting than anything you teach me."

Vivienne's outrage was absolute. *The rudeness, the disrespect!*

But against her instincts, she did not immediately chastise the girl. It never did, she had always told her governesses, to let a child see that they had truly offended you. Hiding one's emptions, being that sea of calm, that is what a child needs.

Vivienne knew all this. It did not particularly help in this moment, the irritation flowing through her quickly after her embarrassment downstairs.

A smile, brittle but present, stretched across her mouth. "I think you might be surprised, Miss Laura, by what we will cover today. We are focusing on history, and—"

"It's just so dull," said Laura with a heavy sigh, feet still on the desk and novel still in her hands. "All those names and dates, and nothing meaningful, and nothing really changing. I just don't see why I should have to learn it. So I shan't."

The words were said with all the confidence of a woman who had been a matriarch for many years, and in any other situation, Vivienne would have applauded her.

But in this moment, her emotions were already raw. She was not here to have fun or even earn a wage. All the money she received from the butler each week went to maintain the Governess Bureau, a building she could scarce afford. If she was not able to improve things soon, her debtors would start calling. If they had not already.

"My word," she said aloud. "I know plenty of children who would be grateful to receive such an education—would bite my hand off to have such wonderful books of history."

Laura rolled her eyes in just the same way Edwin did. "Fine. Go and teach them."

Without another word, the girl disappeared behind her book.

Perhaps if Vivienne had come straight to this moment from the Governess Bureau, she would have reacted differently. But the last few weeks had taught her something that being in London, several distances removed from the children they cared for, had kept from her.

Nuance. These hard and fast rules she had laid down for her governesses in her training—always to do this thing, and never to do that thing…

They all seemed a little foolish now. Hesitation was the key thing here, Vivienne felt. Besides, her memories of being a governess all those years ago were of calm, gentle, suppliant, well-behaved children. This sort of resistance was certainly not something she had expected.

So how had her governesses dealt with a child this obstinate? How would they have mediated the path between determined education and defiant repose?

A thought flickered through her mind, which made Vivienne smile. *Why, they asked themselves what Miss Clarke would do, wouldn't they?*

It was an unhelpful thought, and one that made her feel strange. *Best not to think about it.* What she needed to do was find a way into Laura's confidence. Until she trusted her, no governess would make any headway.

Vivienne took a deep breath, leaned forward, pulled the novel out of the girl's hand, and sat on her desk. None of these movements were particularly elegant, but there were done with such determination, Laura stared in shock.

"But that's mine!"

"Mine now," said Vivienne crisply.

Laura's mouth fell open. "But—but you can't take it away from me!"

"I just did," said Vivienne quietly.

When was the last time she had engaged in a battle of wills? Vivienne could barely remember. Perhaps with that Scottish laird who had refused to pay his last quarterly bill. She had beaten him down into submission by sheer force of will, and she would certainly not lose to a child. She was determined.

After a full minute, Laura looked down. "Fine. You're just like him, happy to order me about. Who am I to argue with you?"

There was only one person that Laura could mean by "him," and Vivienne certainly did not appreciate being lumped into the same category as Edwin, Viscount Bysshe. The man was a Philistine!

Vivienne took a deep breath. There was only one way to combat this, and it was to do something she would never have countenanced back in London. Indeed, if a governess of hers had suggested it, she would have coldly pointed out all of the many reasons why it was a bad idea.

But she had no other. And that meant she was left with one option.

"Laura," Vivienne said, choosing to leave off the "Miss" this time, "do you know why I am here?"

Laura nodded, her scowl remaining. "To bore me to tears."

"I am here from the Governess Bureau to attend to your education."

There was another stiff nod from the girl, but Vivienne could see she had piqued her interest. Had anyone actually told Laura why she was here? Did anyone talk to Laura about anything?

"And has anyone told you that I own the Governess Bureau? That it is my business?"

For some reason, this perked Laura up. "I did not know women could own a business."

A rush of satisfaction poured through Vivienne, a necessary balm for her soul. "Indeed, not many do. But there are no laws against it. Not directly against it, I suppose I should—but I digress. Yes, women can own businesses, can own property, and I do both. Not many, but I am one of those few."

Laura was sitting up now, feet dropping to the floor. "I did not know that. Why did you not tell me?"

Vivienne shrugged. "It was not important when we were first introduced, but now I need to tell you a little more about myself. You see, my Governess Bureau…due entirely to unforeseen circumstances, it is failing. It will fail, I believe, unless things change by Easter."

The girl's eyes were wide. "But that—that's sad. That doesn't seem right, especially as you probably started it all yourself, didn't you? You've worked hard, and now it's being taken away from you?"

She would go far, Vivienne thought. "I have come here to try to save it."

Laura looked at her hands. "I suppose I am not helping, then."

"No," said Vivienne curtly, but not unkindly. Enough speaking to Laura as if she were a child. In a few years, she would be preparing to come out into Society. "But you are a clever girl. You could make this easier for me if you chose to."

It was a testament to Laura's intellect that she did not immediately rush to agree. "And how would I do that?"

Vivienne almost smiled. *Yes, she was clever.* She would not commit to helping the governess until she knew what it would require—and more likely, what she would get in return.

She may be going against everything she told her governesses, but she had no choice. Surely none of them found themselves in difficult positions?

"Well, it would certainly mean proving your father wrong if you were to become a dedicated pupil," Vivienne said slowly.

That got her attention. "Edwin?"

Vivienne nodded. "He is very certain I will fail, and I wish to prove him wrong."

This could all be a terrible idea, Vivienne told herself. It could be a mistake, the beginning of her downfall.

But Laura was perking up, her eyes shining. "You mean we can plot against him?"

"Not *plot*, exactly," Vivienne said hastily. "Just a way to demonstrate to your father that I am an excellent governess. Then I can restore the Governess Bureau, return to London, and leave you to it. And in the meantime, if I find lessons go well in the early morning, well…I might just find that by eleven o'clock, I am able to do this."

In a sweeping motion, Vivienne handed the novel back to Laura.

The girl looked at it carefully and spoke without meeting her governess's gaze. "I…I wish I knew more about where I came from."

There was such a genuine curiosity and sadness in her voice. Vivienne wished she could give a different answer. "I am sorry, Laura. I don't know anything about your history."

Sadness overswept the girl's face. "I thought...well. I thought maybe Edwin told you."

Vivienne shook her head as she said dryly, "There is a great deal he does not tell me."

She probably should not have spoken so to the child of the house, but these were extenuating circumstances, Vivienne told herself. Besides, Laura nodded in silent agreement.

"Laura," said Vivienne slowly, "are...are you lonely?"

"Of course," said Laura simply. "No siblings, my parents—my birth parents did not want me, and of my new parents, one is dead. I am alone."

In any other circumstance, Vivienne would have said nothing. But this was no ordinary circumstance. This was no time to hold back.

"I'm lonely too," she said simply.

Laura nodded sagely, as though this was the sort of conversation she had often. "Why didn't you marry?"

And in that instant, Vivienne was transported back to that moment when it all could have changed. When she had two options before her and chose—what she knew—was the right one. Even if she had moments of regret.

The park was bright, the sun up, the place bustling, and yet Edwin had managed to find a quiet corner. A corner where they could speak privately, and she had attempted to tell him all about the Governess Bureau.

"—second client!" Vivienne had said excitedly, expecting her beloved Edwin to be just as excited as she was.

But there was a distant look in his eye. "But this Bureau won't be your life forever."

Vivienne had frowned. "Why not?"

And suddenly, he was on bended knee and saying words Vivienne had heard before but never truly believed, and he wanted to marry her—when the Bureau was closed.

And that was when she dropped his hand. "What do you mean," she had said, voice caught in her throat, heart beating, lungs struggling, "when the Bureau was closed?"

"Well, you can't expect me to—the Bureau is just...you'll be my wife!"

Vivienne had frowned, felt the distance between them growing. "The Bureau is my life, Edwin, everything I've built for the last two years. It's still in its infancy. I need time to get it fully—you really would not wish me to be a part of it, as your wife?"

And Edwin had risen to his feet, all softness in his expression gone. "You wouldn't marry me until this Bureau of yours was larger?"

Sorrow drifted from the memory to Vivienne, where she sat in the schoolroom.

Laura cleared her throat, and Vivienne looked up to see the girl smiling with a determined look. "I'll help you. We'll show Edwin what a success the Governess Bureau is."

CHAPTER EIGHT

January 15, 1816

IN A HAZE of blurry vision and blinking, Edwin looked hazily at the bottle. The bottle in his hand. His hand?

The smoking room came vaguely into view, then started to go blurry at the edges again. It had been doing that all evening, with increasing frequency.

He blinked again. The bottle of port he had been holding slipped and thunked heavily onto the carpeted floor. It sounded strange, a different pitch than he had been expecting.

Leaning down and finding to his surprise that his head immediately began to swim with dizziness, Edwin halted for a moment before continuing to lean down. His scrabbling fingers took a little while to pick up the bottle, which made no sense. He knew how to pick things up. Picking things up was easy. So easy.

As he straightened up, Edwin lifted the bottle to his eye line and saw, to his complete surprise, that it was empty.

Empty? This port was a 1783 special! He had only a few bottles in the cellars, guarded carefully by Harris, and it was empty! *Someone had drunk it.*

The bleariness continuing to encroach the edges of his vision.

The blaggard. Whoever had drunk the whole thing must have been greedy—it was nigh on full when he had first come in here a few hours ago!

The room shifted again, and Edwin let go o the bottle, which fell uncomfortably into his lap, as he waited for the room to stop moving again. *No. No, wait a minute.*

Edwin's thinking was starting to shift into gear. He could almost hear the mechanical squeaking of his brain, which was rather disconcerting. But no matter how much he blinked, the smoking room refused to come into focus. *Damned irritating.*

It was only then that the pieces of the puzzle fell into place—with a thunk rather like the one made when the empty port bottle fell to the floor.

Edwin raised a hand to his head and found both hand and head were heavy. *He had done it. He* was the culprit. He was the one who had drunk all the port. *All?*

He blinked down at the bottle in his lap. *Oh, dear.* Now that was unlike him. He was drunk. When was the last time he had got drunk?

Oh, you know precisely when, whispered a cruel little voice in his ear. *After the funeral.* Everyone went home, and Laura went upstairs, and you heard her crying, but you couldn't bring yourself to open the door and comfort her—and so you came here. The smoking room. The refuge from women that you've clung to all this time.

Try as he might, Edwin was unable to push the voice from his mind. *How could he?* The voice was his own conscience. He had got drunk, fool that he was. He had let Laura down.

Something hot and wet and sticky was on his face. The hand that had held his temple moved to his cheeks. Edwin blinked again, and his cheeks became wetter. He was crying.

Edwin swallowed, tasting the bitterness of the port. What sort of a man was he, who disappeared into drink in the hope it would solve all his problems? Was he that sort of man?

An image appeared before him, though Edwin knew it was

only in his mind and an outworking of the full bottle of port rushing through his system. *Vivienne.*

So beautiful. So elegant. So witty, though that did not seem difficult at the moment.

Plink.

Edwin blinked and looked down. A tear was slowly falling down the curve of the bottle in his lap. He was still crying.

Vivienne Clarke. If she hadn't waltzed back into his life, Edwin told himself righteously, *then he wouldn't have got drunk.* The fact he had invited her was forgotten.

If it weren't for Vivienne. If she had not refused him. If she had not broken his heart. If she had not pushed him into the arms of another woman. If Laura hadn't...

Edwin swallowed. If Vivienne had not appeared once again in his life. If he weren't forced to dine with her once a week. If he hadn't seen her laughing with Laura in the garden, making him feel so alone, separate from them...

A hiccup rocked his body so utterly, the port bottle slipped to the floor again. This time he left it there. What was he going to do—put the wine back in?

He snorted, then clutched the arms of the chair as the room swirled most alarmingly.

Ah, this was why he had vowed never to get drunk again. A small remembrance of the hangover that he could be expected to enjoy slipped into his mind and Edwin cursed.

No one replied. He was alone. Alone in the dark in the smoking room, the furniture lit only by the flickering fire he had neglected to tend. It was starting to die out, the flames low.

Edwin sighed, his head woozy, his feet heavy. A small part of him—flattened by the port—was attempting to tell him this was foolish. Embarrassing. Shameful. It was difficult to hear over the hum of the alcohol, fizzing through his veins, slowing his thoughts.

But he could still tell he was being ridiculous. Finding solace in a bottle; hadn't he proved, years ago, that was impossible? A prickle of self-loathing seared at his heart. He had already made a fool of himself. He just had to hope that no one found him in this awful state.

Besides, he had made so many mistakes.

"So many," Edwin said aloud for the benefit of the bottle lying on the carpeted floor, with the accompaniment of a hiccup.

Well, there was no one here, was there? Why not talk to himself. He was the only one likely to listen to him.

"So many mistakes you've made, you old fool," Edwin said heavily. "You think you can solve them now? Go back in time and change the decisions that led you to this misery?"

"Edwin?" A voice in the darkness spoke nervously.

Another time, Edwin would have been startled, wished heartily he had managed to keep his mouth shut and been concerned what the unidentified person had heard him say. But the warmth of the port was still in his blood, inoculating him from any real concern.

Blinking into the darkness in the direction where the voice had come from, Edwin stared. Eventually, a figure came into focus, and then a face.

"Vivienne," he said quietly.

How long she had been standing there, he did not know. He could not recall the door opening, though that wasn't saying much. He looked for the bottle for nigh on a full minute before realizing the damned thing had fallen to the floor.

"Helped myself," said Edwin with a wide grin, picking up the bottle and waving it as though for explanation. "Vivienne. Damn it."

Vivienne took a step toward him, and Edwin saw even through the haze of his drunkenness that she looked tired. *How late was it?*

Vivienne, here, watching him. Seeing him drunk. *Well, she was both the last and best person to see it*, Edwin thought hazily. Best person and worst. First and last. Person.

"See," he hiccupped, still waving the empty bottle as though it explained everything. "You agree, of course?"

"Who...who are you talking to?" asked Vivienne quietly.

Edwin could not entirely make out the expression on her face, but it was not good. How dare she pity him—or loathe him? Perhaps it was both. Perhaps he was too drunk. He had no wish to answer—yet there was such sternness in her voice that brooked no argument.

Edwin dropped the bottle. It finally smashed with a wonderful tinkling noise.

"Talking to?" he said, not looking down to where the smashed glass lay. "Talking to? You, I suppose, you're the only one here, aren't you? Wait, is Laura here?"

The thought panicked him, frightening him as nothing else had.

Vivienne shook her head slowly. "No, it's...it's only me, Edwin."

Relief made Edwin sink back into his chair. "Yes, good. Just you. You, Vivienne."

The words tasted strange, almost longing, as though if he said them with enough emphasis, he could make it true. Make it so that only Vivienne loved him. Vivienne was enough, wasn't she?

"But my point is, you agree, don't you?" Edwin said, words pouring from his mouth before he could think about them. "You agree I am a fool?"

Vivienne sighed. "You're drunk enough. Really, Edwin, what were you thinking?"

There was something about governesses, Edwin thought hazily. Something about the way they spoke. The tone they used. Something about the way they could look at you and instantly remind you of all the mistakes you had ever made.

Each and every one your fault, no one else's.

Edwin swallowed. He felt...wonderful. All the aches and pains of the day were gone. All the confusion and pain of Laura was gone. All the uncertainty of Vivienne was gone.

Vivienne. She was still standing there, staring.

"What was I thinking?" he repeated, a lazy smile on his face. "Not thinking, Vivienne. Feeling. Feeling...feeling sad. All the sad things. All the things I've lost, the people I've disappointed, and why, Vivienne? Why am I such a disappointment?"

He had rather hoped she would disagree with him, but Vivienne just stared. The low firelight flickered across her golden hair, the faint lines around her eyes. The swell of her breasts.

Edwin cleared his throat. "You think I'm a fool, but I know it. Mistake after mistake, and not small ones, Vivienne, big ones. Huge ones! Mistakes I can never take back, mistakes I have to live with, day in, day out..."

His voice trickled away. He was speaking nonsense. He knew that, could feel it, but what was the point in attempting to censure himself? It was all Vivienne's fault anyway. If she had just accepted him...if she had believed in him, that he would support her, that this Bureau nonsense wasn't necessary—well then, wouldn't they be happy?

"—no matter what I do, I can't change the past," Edwin found himself saying. "Even if I wanted to, which sometimes I do, I think everyone does once in a—"

"I am going to ring the bell for your valet," said Vivienne firmly, stepping toward the bellpull by the fireplace.

"No, Vivienne, wait." Edwin spoke instinctively and was surprised to find, in this one occasion, she had obeyed him.

She was close. *Very close*, now Edwin came to think about it. Standing right beside his chair, unmoving. Why was that?

Only when he lowered his eyes did he realize his hand had reached out and grasped her own. Her fingers in his, interlocking, entwined together. The heat of her fingers, it was the warmth he had longed for all these years.

Vivienne pulled her hand from his, and the moment, whatever it was, was broken.

"I don't want him to see me like this," Edwin said, his gaze dropping as shame started to replace the comforting warm buzz in his veins. "I don't want anyone to see me like this...dear God, what have I done?"

"You should just be relieved I didn't step in all this glass," Vivienne whispered.

Edwin smiled lazily. "Of course, you didn't, Vivienne. You're nimble. I've always said that. Nimble like a fox."

Was it just him, or was there a strange look in her eyes? Had he complimented her? Had he wanted to? Edwin was not entirely sure. Nothing seemed certain anymore. Nothing made sense. Nothing was right.

He watched as Vivienne bit her lip, attempting not to watch the way her soft bottom lip curled under her white teeth.

It could not be more evident that she did not know what to do.

"You know," said Edwin, as though this would help, "I regret marrying Henrietta."

He had intended to speak in a light, helpful tone, but his revelation did not have that effect. Vivienne colored, dark splodges of red appearing on her cheeks. It was most peculiar. Edwin did not understand it at all.

"You...you should not say such things," said Vivienne, her breath for some reason caught in her throat. "Especially not to me."

Edwin stared, then nodded solemnly, for that seemed to be what was required. "Probably not, but I-I'm drunk."

Vivienne sighed and looked to the heavens as though that would help. She was lit most appealing by the fire from this vantage point—not that she needed additional adornment.

It was strange how a woman could captivate him utterly, body and soul. Had anyone ever had this power over him? Edwin could not think of anyone—but then, thinking was starting to become rather difficult.

"God, I've missed you, Vivienne," Edwin whispered.

The dark red splotches on Vivienne's cheeks grew darker. "You wouldn't be saying that if you weren't drunk."

Edwin sighed. "No. No, I wouldn't. But that wouldn't make it any less true."

"I-I should leave—"

"Don't leave me," said Edwin quickly, reaching out for her but finding that Vivienne had stepped just far enough away so he could not touch her. "Not again, please."

There was something in the way she hesitated, the way Vivienne had clearly intended to walk away but now halted, looking with her sharp eyes—eyes, Edwin now noticed, that were softer than they usually were.

"You…" Vivienne seemed to have something wrong with her voice, but the second time she attempted to speak was stronger. "You never seemed upset I left you the first time."

If Edwin's mind had been in any way coherent, he would have spotted the danger signs. Had they ever spoken on this topic before? Had either of them been truly vulnerable about their feelings, shared what pain it had caused them?

Knowing full well he was only speaking plainly because of the port in his body, Edwin waved his arm expressively. "Big mistake. Huge mistake. Enormous mistake. Gigantic—"

"It was a mistake not to miss me?" Vivienne was frowning.

Edwin was not certain. "A mistake not telling you. Dear God, Vivienne, you think after all we shared, all I promised, that I would not miss you? I missed you like the winter misses the sun. I felt your presence all over London, unable to escape it, yet never truly enjoying it because I was apart from you."

She was standing still, her eyes fixed upon him, eyes unblinking. There was a deep emotion there, but Edwin was conscious he was far too drunk to comprehend it. He would just have to hope it was a positive one.

"And then I did the most foolish thing in my life and married you," said Edwin heavily. "No, not you. Her. Henrietta."

The words were coming from somewhere deep within him that had never seen the light of day before, and Edwin was vaguely aware that he should stop at some point.

But when? The words wanted to keep pouring out, and he

wanted to let them. There seemed to be no better time than when he and Vivienne were alone.

"Henrietta," she repeated.

Edwin nodded. "Henrietta. Oh, I knew I did not love her, not like I loved you, but I could not have you, and I was lonely. And the dowry—she had a rather large dowry, Vivienne, I admit, and I was a third son with no guarantee of title or fortune so…"

The words poured from him like water, like a dam which had been released after years of pent-up tension. They trickled, stronger and stronger with each word that preceded it, and Edwin could not attempt to stop even if he had wanted to.

And he did not want to. He wanted her to hear them, wanted Vivienne to understand.

Did she understand? Could she see how much he had wished to speak these words to her all those years ago when they had been ripped apart? When they had ripped themselves apart, despite all the affection they had for each other?

Exhilaration rushed through him. This was an excellent idea—the best idea he had ever had. Tell Vivienne how he felt— why had he never thought of this before? It was a genius idea. He had never had a better one.

"And with every day that passes," he said, warming to his theme, "I wonder if—"

"I think," said Vivienne, "that is enough revelations from you. Come on."

She stepped toward him and held out her hand.

Edwin smiled. Of course, she wanted to be close to him, and he wanted to be close to her. She understood, didn't she? She understood everything. Everything would be better now, now that they had talked.

Well, now that he had talked.

"You know," said Edwin quietly, "I have not touched you in almost fifteen years."

There was a knowing smile on Vivienne's face. "You touched me five minutes ago."

Edwin blinked. What was she talking about? Five minutes ago—surely not. Surely he would have remembered if such a wonderful thing had—

His fingers enclosed hers. A rush of something heady and glorious soared through him. Heat he had never known, a connection he had desperately missed, a desperate feeling that if he could not experience this touch, this rush, every day then...life would simply not be worth living.

Edwin's heart fluttered in his chest, his lungs tightening to make it difficult to take deep breaths, yet he felt wonderful. Wonderful. As though for the last decade or so, he had been dead. Or asleep. Not living.

He lifted his gaze to hers. Did she feel it, too? Surely she felt it, too, the same rush, the same warmth, the same knowledge, deep within, that somehow they had come home.

There was nothing in Vivienne's face save embarrassment. Why?

Edwin hiccupped, then giggled. Then he knew. *Dear God, he was drunk!* So drunk, he had forgotten he was drunk! It was a disaster. A disaster!

And Vivienne—Vivienne was here! Edwin looked up at her, her hand still clasped in his. He was making a complete fool of himself in front of the woman who he...

Whom he certainly did not wish to be a fool before.

Still, Edwin thought hazily, still unsure whether he was thinking clearly or making no sense whatsoever, *it was time with her.* Time he craved, no matter what he told himself when she had arrived here.

It was jealousy, sheer jealousy—or was it envy, he could never tell—whenever he saw them together. Them. Vivienne and Laura.

It was the closeness he wanted. The intimacy, the closeness with each of them. Yet despite Vivienne only being here weeks, they had already created the bond he wished for.

Why had he been forbidding himself the connection with

Vivienne? Edwin could not remember, not now she stood before him, and he held her hand. Her hand. Her pretty hand.

Why not allow himself what he wanted?

"Up we go," said Vivienne bracingly as she pulled on his arm, forcing him to stand up. "You have got to go up to bed, Edwin."

Edwin giggled as he felt the floor shift under his feet. "Goodness, isn't that a bit forward, Miss Clarke?"

For some reason, Vivienne colored. "I didn't—you know precisely what I mean!"

The next thing he knew—and Edwin was not entirely sure how she had managed it, some sort of governess magic to which he was not privy—he was standing outside his bedchamber. His own bedchamber.

Vivienne was beside him, propping him up for some reason. Perhaps because the floor was spinning most disobligingly. Yes, that was it.

With some effort, she reached out while still holding him upright and opened the door before him. "There you go."

Edwin blinked. *That was not right.* "You are not coming in?"

Vivienne's face was so much closer than he was expecting. It was thrilling. It was precisely what he wanted. "That...that would not be appropriate."

Edwin sighed. "I suppose it probably was not an appropriate idea to invite you here in the first place, but here we are."

Finally noticing that the door was in fact open, Edwin stumbled forward, pulling Vivienne along with him. She gasped at the sudden movement, and Edwin dimly felt the inappropriateness of what he had just done—but it came from such a long way away.

She pulled away as he staggered toward the bed, sitting on it heavily and focusing with bleary eyes on his boots.

"Boots," said Edwin firmly.

For some reason, that did not remove them. It took a great deal of tugging until they were off.

"I-I should—I should really go, Edwin," said Vivienne in a low voice.

She was standing near the door, as far from him as possible. Edwin could not understand why. She had been more than happy to be close to him when she had struggled to help him up the stairs—ah, yes, now he remembered!

"Go?" he repeated before patting the bed beside him. "Why not join me?"

Vivienne stared, giving Edwin ample time to consider just how beautiful she was. "Wh-What on earth do you mean?"

Edwin grinned and patted the bed again. *Surely that would be enough to explain.*

"You are drunk."

"Just like Laura's mother," said Edwin promptly, as though he was being questioned. "I had not realized it was such a problem, but when I found out...her birth mother, I mean. Not Henrietta. Ha, Henrietta, drunk!"

It was a rather amusing image, though Vivienne did not laugh. Edwin couldn't think why.

"No, found her in London," Edwin nodded sagely. "Had the child off her within a week. A week! Just one week, and I had a daughter. A daughter—Laura, Vivienne. Vivienne?"

Soft hands were gently pushing him back, and he did not fight them. Why should he? There was softness all around him now, and Vivienne was here. Vivienne was wonderful.

"Vivienne..."

The next thing Edwin knew was pain and grogginess and regret.

"Vivienne!"

Edwin sat up in a rush, convinced Vivienne was right there beside him. After all, hadn't she only just been there, tucking him in?

"Ahhhh..." he groaned, raising a hand to his head. Why on earth did he have such a splitting headache?

And his mouth...it tasted as though he had been drinking lake water. Oh, it was disgusting. And he was...Edwin looked down. Fully clothed. What on earth had—

And then the memories of the previous evening rushed into his mind, and he was groaning for a completely different reason. Mortification, that was the only word for it. The things he had said—the nonsense Vivienne had allowed him to say!

"Dear God, Vivienne, you think after all we shared, all I promised, that I would not miss you? I missed you like the winter misses the sun. I felt your presence all over London, unable to escape it, yet never truly enjoying it because I was apart from you."

The vague memories were becoming sharper as they sifted into his mind, and Edwin closed his eyes. Perhaps that would help the headache, the dizziness, and the nausea, all at once.

While that certainly did decrease them, it could not remove the recollections of the absolute nonsense—or absolute truth—he had spouted.

"And then I did the most foolish thing in my life and married you. No, not you. Her. Henrietta."

Dear God, he had made such a fool of himself!

Hastily rising from his bed, Edwin did not bother to change but immediately stumbled toward the schoolroom with one thing on his mind.

To apologize to Vivienne. Miss Clarke. Perhaps it was best if, from now on, he only considered her Miss Clarke.

Edwin had been ready to knock on the door, but when he approached the schoolroom, he was surprised to see it slightly ajar. He could hear noises from inside, could see the scene before him.

Laura, seated her desk. There were blue ribbons in her hair, and she appeared to be smiling. She was speaking—was that French?

Edwin opened the door. Laura speaking French he had to see, but he was far more impressed by the fact that she was attending at all.

"Goodness, Edwin," said Laura in surprise. "You look terrible."

Edwin ignored her. "Viv-Miss Clarke, may I speak with you a

moment?"

She did not reply but instead placed her chalk onto the desk, silently left the schoolroom, and closed the door behind her.

They stood in the corridor, *both surely as embarrassed as each other*, Edwin thought wretchedly as he attempted to pull his hands through his tousled hair.

"I..." Edwin cleared his throat. "If I asked you to forget everything I said—"

"How can I?" said Vivienne quietly, not quite meeting his gaze.

His stomach did not stop squirming, though Edwin heartily wished it would. "I...I would really prefer to return to the way things were."

Vivienne's clear gaze finally met his own. "What, the angry bitterness? The complete inability for us to speak to each other without aiming to wound?"

Two halves of him warred within his battle-scarred heart as Edwin looked at her. All he wanted was her. He was starting to realize that. Everything she was, everything she had grown to become, it was all balm to his soul.

But he could not have her. He would not put himself in that place of vulnerability again, and he would not allow her to hurt him.

Conflicted though he was, there appeared to only be one solution.

"Yes," Edwin said, hating himself but knowing there was no other choice. "Yes, we have to return to that."

What little warmth had been in Vivienne's face disappeared. "Fine."

Without another word, she turned and entered the schoolroom. The snap of the door was a scalpel to Edwin's head, and he leaned against the wall as he raised a hand to his temple.

Dear God, what had he done?

CHAPTER NINE

January 21, 1816

DRESSING FOR DINNER. It was a habit Vivienne had never halted when she had been living on her own, above the Governess Bureau, in her small but serviceable apartment. It gave one the feeling of refining oneself, somehow. The custom, the routine, settled Vivienne's nervous heart each time she came to set her hair into something a little more stylish than her harsh bun.

When in London, it was a gift to herself. A reminder she was a lady and that even though she did not live in a large house or have a title or fabulous wealth, she was still a lady.

And ladies dressed for dinner.

She had paid little attention to it the last few weeks. Dining with Edwin and Laura, had been more ordeal than ideal. Edwin, with his dark silences and irritable remarks. Laura, with her dour expression and determination not to utter the word "father."

It had been left to Vivienne to attempt to make conversation throughout the painfully long meals, and she had grown quite tired of them.

Except...except for today. Today, Vivienne found herself

spending more time than normal before the looking glass she had been given. Today, she wanted to...

Vivienne swallowed. Look nice. *Nice? Nice for who? For what?*

"God, I've missed you, Vivienne."

If she had been advising another governess, one of her Bureau, Vivienne would have known precisely what to do, what to advise.

"Downplay any good looks you happen to possess," she could almost hear herself saying to a room full of hopefully Bureau governesses. "Just because one's hair naturally curls does not mean you are at liberty to permit curls to collect around your face. If your figure is particularly fine, hide it. A loose-fitting gown will do. You are not here to entertain. You are not here to please. You are here to serve."

Vivienne swallowed. She watched herself in the looking glass, her hair lit up by the small candle on the chest of drawers before the mirror. *Here to serve.* That was all she was here to do. That was all she should focus on. The task at hand.

"But why, Miss Clarke?" asked a governess from Vivienne's memory. A pretty girl, from what she could recollect. Proud. *Or was that just the filter of her memories?* Had she seen more rebellion than had been there?

"Because," Vivienne had replied to that governess, "the last thing you or this Bureau needs is accusations of...well. That you are attempting to tempt the master of the house."

Vivienne cleared her throat into the silence of her bedchamber. The candle flickered.

"I am not attempting to tempt the master of the house," she whispered to herself.

Saying it aloud did not appear to make it any less true.

Guilt prickled at the edges of her heart, but Vivienne ignored it. That was not what was happening here. She had her chance and stepped away from it most concertedly.

If she had wished to bed the master of the house, she could have succeeded.

"Why not join me?"

Vivienne's jaw tightened. No matter how tempting, she had managed to avoid the pitfall. Now all she was doing was attempting to make herself presentable to her master.

With a heavy sigh, Vivienne dropped onto her bed. What was she doing? What had she done, getting herself tangled into this mess?

The moment she had spotted that Edwin was not tired but drunk, she should have left him alone in that smoking room. She knew that now. That was the beauty of hindsight. What had felt obvious then felt ridiculous now.

The things he had said, the way he had looked at her…it was enough to make any woman wonder what, precisely, to wear to dinner.

Vivienne tried not to think about the things he had said, but it was impossible. His words were engraved on the inside of her skull, echoing in her ears.

"Dear God, Vivienne, you think after all we shared, all I promised, that I would not miss you? I missed you like the winter misses the sun. I felt your presence all over London, unable to escape it, yet never truly enjoying it because I was apart from you."

What did it all mean? Vivienne had never believed it possible to discern the truth or sense in a drunkard's ravings, but there had been such truth in the way he had spoken. Such vulnerability. Such pain.

She shivered at the remembrance of the pain in Edwin's eyes. He had suffered; there was no doubt about it. Had she not heard that when a person drank to excess, it was their secrets and their deepest fears that spilled out?

It was a gratifying thought, the idea that Edwin truly missed her, that he regretted his harsh refusal to bend to her request, his almost immediate marriage to another. Heady thoughts indeed, that he still loved her, still wanted her. At the very least, wanted to bed her.

Heat seared her cheeks, but Vivienne forced herself to think on. *Or was it just nonsense?* Were his words merely the ramblings of a person thinking of what could have been?

Worse, could she have misunderstood? When he had patted the bed beside him, giving her that look of desire she had thought she knew so well, had he merely been asking her to do precisely what she had done: to lay him down, tuck him in, and leave him in the darkness?

Vivienne bit her lip. There was no use wondering about it, she supposed. No amount of attempting to discern his truth would help her understand him, not when he was such an enigma, it seemed, to himself.

Rising to her feet, Vivienne looked at the three ribbons on the chest of drawers before her. Black, in case of mourning. Gray, for daywear. Blue, for best.

Her fingers meandered toward them, ignoring the black and going toward the blue.

She should not wear it. What if there was a ball to attend, for some reason, or a house party that Edwin threw, once their circle of friends and acquaintances returned from town? If she wore the blue now, a mere Sunday in the middle of winter, then what else could she wear?

The ribbon was soft under her fingertips. Vivienne picked it up, twisting it, trying to think clearly as emotions she knew she had to ignore rushed through her mind.

She was not usually one for adornments. She had never seen the point in them. Edwin had fallen in love with her all those years ago without pretty jewels and delicate ribbons. He had seen her for who she was and loved her.

Since Edwin, there had been little point in attempting to attract anyone's attention. She had lost her heart. It was not hers to give away again.

She wanted to attract attention now, and Vivienne was highly conscious it would lead only to bitter disappointment.

Edwin, she told her reflection firmly, *is not interested in you.* He sees you as naught but a servant, a servant whose life dream he wishes to crush. He was quite clear, wasn't he? His intention is to make the Governess Bureau defunct—and you want to impress such a man?

The ribbon twisted silkily between her fingers.

She did. She wanted to impress him. She wanted him to look at her and see the girl she had once been. She wanted him to touch her again, to hold her hand, to feel the rush of passion he inspired, and—

Vivienne cleared her throat, dropped the ribbon, and picked up the gray one.

A compromise then. *Besides*, she thought with a slow smile, *it was not for her, nor Edwin*. It was for Laura. Laura needed the example of a well-dressed, elegant lady, now her mother was, sadly, no longer with them. *It was for her benefit and her benefit alone*, Vivienne told herself sternly, that she was wearing this ribbon.

Or at least, attempting to wear it. It had been so long since Vivienne had bothered to do anything rather than a simple bun with her hair, her fingers seemed to have quite forgotten how to twist and turn her locks into something approaching a hairstyle.

The ribbon, too, was most disobliging. No matter what she attempted to do with it, twist it and tie it as she would, the thing just looked...

Terrible. Vivienne pulled it from her hair in irritation. As though she was trying far too hard. As though she was a pathetic old woman, trying to recreate her youth in a way that patently accentuated her age.

The ribbon had fallen in a tumble onto the chest of drawers.

"You are drunk."

She shivered. The Edwin she had known—albeit from a good many years ago—would never have touched strong liquor. *The very idea!*

But so much time had passed. Vivienne touched gently the lines at the corners of her mouth...lines which had crept up on her, appearing so slightly and so gradually she had not noticed them.

So much time had passed. Over a decade, closer to two.

What had he suffered? What agonies had he endured without her? Without her able to comfort him, understand him, stand by him just when he needed her?

But then her heart hardened. He could have had her, couldn't he? Vivienne had been open, wiling to be his wife, if only the Governess Bureau could succeed first.

And he had changed. The Edwin she had known, who had charmed her, wooed her, had been kind. Thoughtful. Caring. Considerate. Not the irritable, mood-swinging drunk, who had his appearance and wore his name.

Vivienne sighed, the candle flickering with her breath. Except when he was drawing. He had always been sketching in London, a sketchbook always in his pocket. Her hands, a curl of her hair, the way her eyes looked in the sunlight.

All these little parts of her had appeared in corners of the pages, until she had asked him to draw her portrait.

It had not taken him long. *Because I know you so well*, he had said with a smile.

Vivienne's heart clenched. *She should have told him the truth.* She should not have lied and said she had destroyed that drawing, the one piece of him she had been able to retain.

But how could she? Such an admission would have been near as admitting her feelings for him remained. Tantamount to a declaration of love. Absolutely outrageous. Impossible.

Vivienne took one more look at the tangle of ribbons on the chest of drawers and heaved a heavy sigh, which threatened to snuff the candle entirely.

She glanced at her reflection in the looking glass. There were a few additional lines around her forehead that had not been there before. *Of course, there were.* All this worry…

"That will just have to be enough," she said softly to her reflection. Edwin had been tempted by the young Vivienne, not the dour Miss Clarke she was now. And that was quite as it should be.

No matter how her heart fluttered when she looked at him.

It was as Vivienne stepped onto the last step in the hallway that her gaze caught the long row of paintings around her, and the words she had so thoughtlessly—or more accurately, ignorantly—spoken to Laura returned to her.

"Are you not interested in your ancestors? These people lived in these very rooms, walked these very halls, share your blood. They do not interest you?"

Vivienne winced. She had meant well, and in a thousand other country manor houses in England, it would have been the perfect thing it say. An excellent way to encourage a young child to trust her, feel affectionate toward her, know that she was on her side.

In the end, all that had happened was that she had offended a young girl.

Vivienne did not seem to have made a good impression at Byhalden Lodge on the child or the master, though the bargain she had struck with Laura was at least making lessons in the schoolroom less of a trial for both of them.

And it was not as though Edwin—when sober—had been supportive. Quite to the contrary, he had openly told her that he wanted her to fail! Her and her Governess Bureau.

Vivienne squared her shoulders in the silence of the hall. *His first mistake.* She was not particular about the world admiring her; at least, Vivienne did not think she was.

Some people liked talkative ladies, some, more silent. Some were musical, some artistic, and some had no discernable talent at all. Everyone had their preference, and Vivienne was not fool enough to believe she would be everyone's.

But her Governess Bureau was her life's work. Everything she was, the best of her.

To reject the Governess Bureau was to reject everything she was, everything she wanted to be. Her refuge, her sanctuary, her living, her home.

And that was precisely why she would not permit Edwin to win. He had wished her to set aside the Governess Bureau all those years ago, and he had not won that fight then. She was not going to let him do it now. She was more than enough to beat him. The Governess Bureau would rise again, and if that meant walking across Edwin to do so…

Vivienne swallowed. If that was what it took, then so be it. He had no love for her, barely any respect! Had he not proved it by his heartless attitude and his drunken nonsense?

"Why don't you join me?"

Just more nonsense, she told herself. She should ignore him. He certainly spent most of his time ignoring her.

It was unfortunate, perhaps, that it was these thoughts rushing through Vivienne's mind at the exact moment she opened the door to the dining room and found herself face to face with Edwin. He had clearly been about to leave the room. His intense proximity, the smell of him, the sudden surprise and lust and confusion on his face, was enough to render Vivienne entirely incoherent.

"I-I did not—hello Edwin, I mean my lord I—dining room…"

Vivienne felt the color rush across her cheeks. *What a fool she sounded!* How was it possible to speak such nonsense when she was, usually, so calm and collected?

"I was just going to—I did not mean to…hello," said Edwin, just as incoherently.

Vivienne wished he would step back, give her some distance so that she could collect herself, without once considering that she could do just such the same thing.

"Goodness, Miss Clarke, are you quite well?"

This came from Laura, who was seated—Vivienne gratefully took the opportunity to look past Edwin—at the dining table. Laura was staring at the two of them as though wondering why they were speaking a different language.

Vivienne chanced one final look at Edwin as she stepped around him as best she could, attempting to ignore her skirts brushing up against his breeches, and reached the dining table.

"Quite well," she managed in a breathless voice, as though she had run down the stairs three at a time. "Yes, yes, quite well, I thank you."

If only she had not just been thinking of Edwin sitting on his bed. The bed he had invited her into...

"You look quite done for," said Laura cheerfully.

"Be quiet," snapped Edwin from the doorway.

Vivienne carefully sat and made a big show of placing her napkin on her lap before looking up again. It was to see that Edwin had also sat, though he looked utterly wretched at having to do so.

If only she could stay calm for the entire dinner, Vivienne thought wildly. *If only the dinner was quick, over in less than thirty minutes.*

If it was anything like the previous dinners, it would take over an hour.

On the bright side, if there was one to be found, it was impressive to see Laura come a little more out of her shell. It was something she and Vivienne had discussed on multiple occasions over the last few days.

"He never wants to talk to me," Laura had complained bitterly just days ago. "He never wants to know what I think or discuss the book I'm reading. He never asks my opinion."

Vivienne had been forced to suppress a smile. How self-centered children were, even naively. The world went around them, and anything that wasn't to their satisfaction was an absolute disaster.

"Have you inquired as to his opinion on such matters?" she had asked lightly.

Laura had not replied at the time, but Vivienne had not pushed her. The best governess knew when to gently suggest something and then let it sit within one's pupil. At the right time, the child would decide for themselves whether they wished to continue with the idea.

"Edwin," said Laura as the first course was brought out, making Vivienne wince.

Well, that was perhaps her next challenge. How to encourage Laura to call her father by his...well, not his name. That was the point.

"Edwin, I wondered," Laura began. "Will you be going to town to join Society for a few weeks, as you often do?"

"Why?" snapped her father. "Looking to be rid of me?"

The girl looked at her plate and pressed her lips together, evidently upset by the harshness of his tone.

Vivienne glared at Edwin, who seemed utterly unaware of the pain he was causing. *Did he not see what a mistake he was making?* Could he not see how easy it would be to gain her affection, if only he made a smidgen of effort?

"No, that is not what I meant," said Laura quietly. "I...just wondered whether if you did, whether you could..."

Vivienne was impressed. It was not easy as a child, being spoken to so by an authority figure, let alone your only surviving parent. But Laura persisted. She gave the girl a gentle smile, which seemed to encourage her to continue.

"Wondered whether you could bring me back a few novels," said Laura timidly. "Or history books. Miss Clarke is teaching me about the Stuarts."

Vivienne beamed. It was a brave attempt, and one not without effort. *Well done, Laura*, she thought silently. She would have to make a mention of it tomorrow, back in the schoolroom.

Sadly, this effort went unrecognized by the person who should have been best pleased.

Edwin sniffed. "Just tell Harris the sort of thing you want. He can purchase whatever you want from York."

Vivienne's glare could have melted wax, melted iron. *What was wrong with the man?* He had not even looked at Laura. It was plain, right across that girl's face, that she was desperate for some attention, for some affection, from the man who meant most to her.

He wasn't even replying with any decency!

Vivienne took a mouthful of food—pork with its skin on, and a plethora of winter mushrooms and beetroot—and pondered the injustice of it all.

What was the difficulty that had arisen between Edwin and his daughter? The girl had been here almost ten years, more than enough time for affection to grow. Vivienne was sure that adopted children were just as beloved by their parents as those of birth. Sometimes more because they were more coveted.

It just did not make sense for Edwin to be so rude, to ignore her so thoroughly, to speak poorly to her when they did converse.

Time to inject this conversation with a little more heart.

"What a splendid idea, Miss Laura," Vivienne said brightly. "There are certainly more bookshops in London, each with a greater choice, I am sure than anywhere else in England. It is a good place to look for interesting books, especially if you have a rapport for the Stuarts."

Edwin did not even look up. He merely chomped on another mouthful, eyes downcast.

It was tempting to merely give up, to leave them to their own devices. Laura had evidently tried for years to gain the good favor of her father, and Vivienne was under no belief that she had a more favorable impression in his eyes.

But this was ridiculous. Two people, a parent and child, had to speak more than this!

Besides, wasn't this the very reason that she was here in the first place? To restore the Governess Bureau's reputation? Would it not be incredible to win round the one person in England who was determined not to help her?

Vivienne took a deep breath, smiled at Laura, and said airily, "Well, that's settled then. Miss Laura and I will go to York and choose a selection of books from the shops there."

That was enough to get his attention.

Edwin looked up. "What?"

"After all," said Laura with a hesitant smile, "it was the Duke of York who played such a pivotal role in the Restoration, wasn't it, Miss Clarke?"

Vivienne smiled warmly, but to her surprise, it was Edwin who spoke next.

"I...well, I am not entirely sure I agree. Although the Duke of York—and I assume we both speak of James—was influential, you do not believe Cromwell had a greater impact on the family?"

Vivienne held her breath. *This could be it.*

Laura placed down her fork. "Perhaps in terms of destruction, but not in terms of creating the dynasty."

It was a masterpiece. As the conversation continued on, various points of view brought forward by both father and daughter, Vivienne watched carefully. There were no lulls, no slowing of conversation. She was not required to nudge it along, and—

Was that a smile on Laura's face?

A rush of joy threatened to overwhelm her, and Vivienne could not help but beam.

This was what she had missed. The only thing, truly, she had missed about being a governess—seeing the difference one could make in a child's life. Watching them blossom and grow, challenge themselves, and overcome the challenges in their path.

Within a few minutes, Laura appeared to be an entirely different child. Open and alive and bright in a way Vivienne had never seen in her before.

Carefully finishing her pork with the smallest of movements so as not to disturb the conversation, Vivienne glanced at Edwin.

The change was there, too. In fact, it was quite remarkable how similar they looked: the same wide eyes, the same laughing expression as they attempted to disprove the other.

Edwin laughed. "But that is not what I meant at all!"

And in that instant, Vivienne was transported back, back to that moment she had first realized she had fallen in love with Edwin Bysshe.

He was still there, the same handsome features, yes, but now they were molded into the same joyful expression he had worn whenever he had looked at her. The same laughter.

She had been so convinced that gentleman was gone, but there he was—and as his gaze caught hers, smile still on his face, Vivienne's stomach lurched in much the same way it had back then.

She loved him. Vivienne knew it, and she could not deny it to herself, even if she were certain she would deny it to his face.

But this was a disaster. As Laura and Edwin's conversation continued, now meandering to the Tudors and whether Henry VIII was the last true medieval king, Vivienne felt her heart contract, her fingers tingle.

Because she could not be in love with Edwin. It would be the end of her—the end of the Governess Bureau.

"But mark my words, Miss Clarke, I will be doing everything in my power to demonstrate to the world that you and your Bureau are finished. Finished, over and done with. Forever."

Vivienne swallowed. This could not be happening, but it was about to get worse.

"—want to know is," said Laura, "how you two know each other? From before, I mean. I asked before, and you avoided the question. You do know each other, don't you?"

"No," said Vivienne in the same instant that Edwin said, "Yes."

What was he playing at?

The laughter on Edwin's face was more stilted now. "Well, what I mean is—sort of. We knew each other once in London, a long time ago."

Vivienne could not look at him. *Yes, a long time ago indeed.*

If only that had put Laura's interest to rest. "And did you know each other well?"

Vivienne risked another look at Edwin, who seemed to be enjoying this. "I thought so. Eat your peas."

But the girl was not to be fobbed off with such things. "I've eaten a great many peas, and how did you meet?"

There was nothing for it. Hateful though it was, Vivienne turned to Edwin with a brittle smile. *Wasn't it time he bore the brunt of his daughter's questions?* "Why don't you answer that question?"

Edwin held her gaze for a moment before turning to Laura. "We met at a ball, and—"

"A card party," interrupted Vivienne. *At the very least, the truth should be told.*

Now he was glaring. "Who is telling this story?"

"You," she said calmly. "Inaccurately."

Her heart was making that rather uncomfortable patter again. In another world, in another life, this could have been a flirtatious conversation. Yet here they were.

"The point is, we met," said Edwin, no longer looking at her. "And then we separated."

Laura looked between them, her smile slightly faltering. Vivienne wished to goodness that her cheeks would behave and cool, but she was certain they were flushed.

Much to her relief, Laura appeared to tire of the topic. "What is London like? Are there balls? How wide is the Thames, and can you swim in it?"

"One question at a time!" laughed her father, putting down his cutlery for the preferred consumption of conversation. "The Thames is so wide in places…"

Vivienne could not eat a single bite, but she had at least managed to direct the conversation away from herself and Edwin.

But for how much longer? How much longer could she suffer here in this house with him?

Chapter Ten

January 26, 1816

THE KNOCK ON the door so startled him, Edwin almost rose from his seat.

Which was foolish. He was the one who had issued the order, and he should have expected Harris to be quick about it. So lost in his thoughts as he had looked out the window from the drawing room, the trees of the park wavering in the wintery wind, he had almost forgotten he had made the request at all.

"My lord," said Harris quietly as he stepped across the room to his master. "As you requested, I have procured everything on the list you bestowed upon me three days ago."

Conscious that both Laura and Vivienne were in the drawing room reading, Edwin nodded curtly at the servant. "Right. I must say, I was not expecting them so quickly."

There was a look of hurt on the servant's face. "You doubt my abilities, my lord?"

"No, no, not at all," said Edwin hastily. *Blast, this was always the problem when he spoke without hours of thought.* He always managed to upset someone.

In the butler's hands was a large folder of papers, all different sizes, wrapped carefully with a blue ribbon.

Edwin's heart skipped a beat, most painfully. He had, in truth, not expected his request to be completed this week, let alone by today. If he had known the butler would be able to procure so much in such little time, he would have added to his instructions that they were to be placed in the study for his perusal later. Alone.

As it was, the servant had done what he believed was right and brought the documents to him immediately. It was just rather awkward to have Vivienne in the room at the same time.

Edwin glanced at her. Her head was bowed, her eyes only just visible, as she turned a page of her book. Laura was beside her, just as intrigued it appeared, by her own book.

Letting out a small sigh of relief, Edwin looked back at his butler, who was showing signs of real distress.

"I attempted to do everything you requested, even though a few of the items you asked for were quite difficult to—"

"And I am very impressed," said Edwin with a brief smile. "Thank you, Harris. You have done well. Just…just pop them on the side table, will you?"

It took every ounce of self-control not to pounce on the materials and wrench them from Harris's hands, but that would be to reveal just how desperate he was to read them. He had no wish for either Laura or Vivienne to request to see them. That would be awkward indeed.

The butler bowed, placed them on the side table, and bowed again. "And is there anything else I can—"

"No," said Edwin quickly, rising from his seat and meandering over to the windows as though what the butler had just brought him was of no concern whatsoever. "Actually, it might be worth considering if additional firewood should be ordered. I have a feeling it will be a cold few weeks, and the coal delivery is delayed. See to it, will you?"

"Of course, my lord. Anything else?"

Edwin shook his head, still standing by the window. His

fingers itched to untie that blue ribbon and start reading. "Unless Miss Laura requires you, Harris, you may go."

Laura looked up. "What?"

"I would consider that your leave to go," said Edwin with a small smile.

Harris bowed, then left with a gentle close of the door.

Edwin's eyes snapped over the pile of papers and then away from them.

The drawing room had felt like such a calm place to sit. He had not protested when Laura and Vivienne had entered, bringing their chatter and then reading quietly with them.

A log shifted in the grate. It had been cold these last few days. Having a fire in the grate during the day was not unheard of in midwinter, but he could not remember a grate without a fire since Christmas.

Laura turned a page of her book, the movement attracting his attention. She was curled up in a large armchair, her feet tucked under her, her skirt falling all the way to the carpet. She was utterly transfixed by the story.

Edwin permitted himself a moment to look at her. *His daughter.* He knew the way to raise a child—with distance and respect, as he had been raised. Yet Laura continually surprised him. Whenever he believed himself understanding her, he was proved incorrect. Most strange.

His gaze moved back to the papers beside him. The instinct to start reading them immediately was strong. But he was no fool. Even he was awake to the inappropriateness of having Laura here as he read such salacious gossip.

Strange. He so rarely thought about Laura, yet recently, she had occupied his thoughts more often. There must be a reason for it, but he could not put his finger on it. He would have to think on it later.

At this moment, however, fingers cold on the windowpane before him, Edwin could not resist the pile of papers on the side table right where he was sitting. He must read them.

"Laura," he said.

His daughter looked up instantly. "Yes?"

A strange sort of joy fluttered in Edwin's heart. *She had not called him Edwin.* "I believe there is a little dessert left over from yesterday. I believe Cook will let you have it if you go now and say I sent you."

A smile crept across Laura's face, and his stomach lurched. *She really did look like him when she smiled. Far more than her mother.*

"Can I really go?"

Edwin matched the broad smile on her face. "Of course. Go down and see what they have and tell them I sent you. Tell them...tell them you can whatever you want."

It was a strange feeling, looking at a child that most of the time shared none of your features or expressions or likeness. And then suddenly, Laura seemed to come out of a cloud and look precisely like him.

She grinned just as he had as a child when told he could eat treats downstairs. "Truly?"

It only pained Edwin slightly that Laura looked at Vivienne as she spoke. As though she was the ultimate authority here. As though without Miss Clarke's approbation, there was no possibility she would obey Edwin.

Vivienne. She was intruding everywhere. A rare occasion during which he and Laura had a moment of understanding, of closeness, and there was Vivienne, inserting herself into the family. It was beyond irritating.

"Miss Clarke?"

Vivienne looked up from her book. "What did your father say, Laura?"

No longer Miss Laura, Edwin noticed. That was interesting. The formality was expected but not required, yet it was interesting to see it had already departed.

Laura's smile widened. "He said that I could go."

Vivienne nodded. "Then, of course, you can go. Always listen to your father, Laura."

The governess looked at her book, and Edwin smiled painfully as Laura looked at him joyfully.

Well, really! Who was Vivienne to set herself up with such airs! Always listen to your father…was that not a given? Was not a father to be respected and obeyed by his child? Why did Laura suddenly decide to obey him now Miss Vivienne Clarke gave her approval?

But Edwin did not have time to consider this rather strange line of thought. Laura jumped up from her seat, placed down her book, and raced over to where he was standing by the window. Leaning up, she kissed him on the cheek, and without saying a word, left the room.

It was as though a whirlwind had rushed through the room. Edwin swallowed, raising a slightly shaking hand to the place on his cheek where Laura had kissed him.

Had she…had she ever done that before?

Rack his brains as he might, Edwin could not recall a single instance where she had. Laura had been affectionate toward him. His daughter had willingly approached him. Had kissed his cheek. She had not called him father, but it was a start.

Edwin's finger grazed the place where she had touched him, then realized to his dismay that Vivienne was no longer focusing on her book but instead was gazing at him.

He dropped his hand to his side immediately.

Christ, the last thing he needed was to get all emotional in front of anyone—let alone Vivienne. Memories of the nonsense he spouted to her weeks ago echoed in his mind, and Edwin quickly turned away to the window.

Being vulnerable, being open…it was something he'd ceased a while ago. Henrietta had never been interested in hearing his thoughts. Over time, he had learned to let them go.

The strongest emotions ever stirred in him, after all, had been created by Vivienne, and she had rejected him, chosen the Bureau over her.

He would not permit himself to read into this any more than was necessary, Edwin told himself sternly. Laura was young, a child. She was bound to be affectionate sometimes. It was no reason to get soft on her, no reason to even consider telling her...

No. That secret had to remain with him for now.

When the time was right, and Edwin was certain he would know when, he would tell her. Then everything would come to light, and they could perhaps grow stronger together.

But not now. He had more important things on his mind.

Edwin's gaze meandered from the chilling, uninviting, wintery scene outside and toward the cold, uninviting scene inside. Vivienne was still staring, but as he met her gaze, she looked back at her book, head held haughtily as though she had been doing nothing wrong.

Jaw tightening, Edwin managed to prevent himself from saying anything. The papers Harris brought through were still waiting on the side table, and the desire to read through them only grew with each passing moment. In complete silence, he strode across the room, picked up the folder which had been brought to him, and sat down.

Reports, newspaper clippings, gossip, scandal sheets...much of what Edwin sifted through were things he had already read about the Governess Bureau.

As his gaze flickered over them, phrases leapt out at him: scandalous mystery of Miss Clarke's disappearance, confusion over ownership, governesses or mistresses...

The same old stuff, Edwin though with a sigh of disappointment. He had hoped by sending to London for the latest gossip, he would hear something new or different.

But this was just more of the same. More hatred, more vitriol, more confusion about why the Governess Bureau office was suddenly closed up.

Miss Clarke had not been seen for weeks. Edwin had to smile wryly at that. He had seen far too much of her, and his dreams— *well*. One could not help what one dreamt about.

The very last bundle of papers in the folder were perhaps the most anticipated. Edwin picked them up and placed the rest of the papers on the side.

A report for Edwin, Viscount Bysshe, from his most respectful servants, Anderson, Peters, and Smethly.

Edwin snorted. *Lawyers.* They always found a way to make something sound ridiculous, and once again, Smethly had managed it. *On the bright side*, he thought as he opened up the sealed report, it was written in Smethly's own hand, which was a mark of respect he had not expected.

His instructions to his lawyers in London had been very clear, find everything they could—but with the utmost delicacy. The last thing he needed was to have Society buzzing that Viscount Bysshe was investigating the Governess Bureau. *Although perhaps, if that would close the place down...*

Edwin shook his head to himself. No, that was dishonest. He wanted to prove the Governess Bureau was defunct, but he was not a cruel man. He would not sink to such levels.

Swallowing as he started to read, Edwin found a twist of guilt settling in his heart.

The Governess Bureau appears to have been founded in 1801 by two young ladies: Miss Vivienne Clarke (current owner) and Miss Evangeline Jones (now Mrs. Shirley, have confirmed in the parish records of Ettingham).

After an inauspicious start—NB. Scandal involving Miss Jones and her marriage to her employer, one of the Bureau's first clients, a Mr. Shirley—the Governess Bureau struggled for many years to capture the respect and trust of the best of Society, which they claimed to serve.

It was only in 1807 when...

Edwin's eyes lazily skimmed the next few paragraphs. It had grown in success, yes, he knew that. He had heard about it, attempted to ignore it, been forced to listen to his acquaintances discuss it. Should they hire a Bureau governess? Why not? The

Duke of Axwick had. The Earl of Marnmouth had. To have a governess from the Bureau was, for a time, the mark of success and nobility, Edwin could well remember.

What he could not recall was how it all managed to go wrong.

The marriages...yes, that was a particularly tricky thing. No one wished to hire a servant, bring them into one's house, trust them with access to one's entire family, only for a respected memory of the nobility and aristocracy to do something so foolish as to marry them.

It was unheard of! At least, it should be unheard of. But a few marriages surely could not bring down something as strong as the Governess Bureau.

> *It was after the fourth such marriage that complaints started to be made not only against the Governess Bureau itself, but against Miss Clarke, the proprietress who purported to have such strict rules but...*

Edwin looked up. The fire was still burning, and his mind was similarly aflame.

Four marriages? Surely not. He had heard of two, and four was surely an exaggeration. He could not imagine Vivienne permitting such things.

But as he turned the page and continued to read, Edwin's mouth fell open. Five marriages—and those were the ones that Smethly could discover in the time allotted to him! Five in the last few years, at the very least.

Edwin eagerly read through the next three pages, packed with the details of who and when and how. Well, it was truly scandalous, and that was no exaggeration. It would have been eyebrow-raising indeed if Vivienne's—if the Bureau's governesses had been marrying other servants. Footmen or stewards or butlers.

But friends of their masters! Brothers of masters, in one case—masters themselves!

Edwin had to put the pages down for a moment to attempt to take it all in. *What were they thinking?* Theses women who came into homes to teach children—could they not focus on the children themselves? *How did they find themselves so easily distracted?*

Edwin was certain he would be able to answer that question if he had not been momentarily distracted by Vivienne turning a page of her book.

It was the way her fingers moved, so elegantly, with such purpose, yet with a lazy ease that was most becoming. The hand returned to the book, and Edwin found himself staring at the small amount of her which he could see. Only when she turned another page did Edwin jolt from his stupor and realize a few of the pages on his lap had spilled to the floor.

A momentary lapse of concentration, he told himself. Nothing to do with Vivienne. It could have been anyone in that chair. Anyone at all.

Turning back to the report from his lawyer, Edwin marveled that things could have gotten so bad without Vivienne doing anything about it. If there was a single person who had an iron will and could force others to bend to it, it was surely Vivienne.

The idea that she could have let this happen...it truly was scandalous. No wonder so many people in London were up in arms about it all. The Governess Bureau had essentially been shipping off eligible—or so they clearly considered themselves—young ladies into the house of the nobility of England.

Edwin's eyes moved down the page, caught by the mention of a name he recognized.

The Duke of Rochdale.

Dear God. He knew Rochdale, had met him a few times in York. He had even, now he came to think about it, met the Duchess of Rochdale.

A pleasant woman, all things considered. She had not spoken much. To think that the woman who had stood there so prettily, hands on her stomach, which had been swollen with another child to add to the Rochdale brood, had once been...

Edwin looked down. *Miss Meredith Hubert.* She had once been a governess! Not just any governess, but a Bureau governess!

A shiver rushed down his spine. *A governess with a duke!*

He snorted. He could not help but laugh. It was ironic, really. Vivienne had been given a choice those years ago: marry him or lead the Bureau. She could not have known that he would become a viscount—even he had not known. No one expected one's brothers to die so young and without children.

So instead of becoming a memory of the aristocracy, Vivienne had ended up creating a business to service them...while her governesses, without her permission and against all the rules she had herself created, had gone on to marry far more prestigious titles!

Edwin snorted again. *Dear Lord, it was almost comical.* The sort of thing one would expect to see on the stage! All that pouring her heart into the Bureau, and what had it given Vivienne? No warmth, no embraces, no wealth as far as he could see. After all, she was taking wages from him, wasn't she?

God, hindsight was a strange thing. If Edwin could go back in time and tell his younger self how it would all work out...

Now that was a strange thought. Would he advise his past self to do anything differently? He could have Vivienne, naturally, but at the cost of Laura?

"What are you laughing about?"

There was such merriment in his soul that Edwin did not think before replying. "You should have called it a Marriage Bureau, Vivienne, not a Governess Bureau!"

It had been a thoughtless quip—a very thoughtless quip. It was the sort of humor that would be appreciated in the club at London or after dinner with port and cigars with his friends.

It was not, as Edwin looked into the furious glare of Vivienne Clarke, not a remark to make to a lady. Particularly when it was at that lady's expense.

With horror and a large smattering of guilt, Edwin could see he had greatly misjudged the situation. What he had thought was an amusing remark which would be gently laughed at was clearly a dreadful mistake.

The book had been lowered into Vivienne's lap, although it was closed on her finger as though to demonstrate just how quickly she would be leaving his conversational company, and she was glaring right at him.

"What would you know about it?" Vivienne said stiffly, a prickly expression on her face and a sniff in her voice. *"You*, Edwin Bysshe? You wouldn't know anything about a hard day's work. You've never done one in your life. Who are you to judge?"

It would perhaps have been a wiser idea to say nothing. Edwin knew this yet found himself replying, "Hard day's work? Look at you, Vivienne—sitting in my drawing room, heated by my fire and reading my books! I would hardly call that a difficult job!"

"Well not *this*, precisely," shot back Vivienne, book entirely forgotten. "I meant when I was running the Bureau in London! Interviewing girls, keeping track of everyone, reading reports, cataloging expenses, paying wages, trying to keep all these organized—it was a grueling position!"

Edwin waved his hand. *What nonsense.* "Any accountant could do that."

"I would not disagree you with you there, but the point was, I did it!" snapped Vivienne. "Me, Edwin! A woman, no access to a university education or an apprenticeship or all those clubs you men seem to belong to which give one a step in the door. Me!"

Fire was starting to rush through Edwin's veins. He could well remember their debates in the old days, full of passion and ideas and discussion.

But this was different. There was a hint of pain here that had not been present before.

"Do not attempt to tell me, Edwin Bysshe, that I do not know my business! I know what to do, I know how difficult it is, I lived that life—I live it still!" Vivienne said furiously. "You would struggle to keep control of five siblings in a schoolroom!"

Once again, his instinctual response was not correct. "They are only children."

He was rendered immediately speechless by the sharpness of her look, but it was her mirthless laughter that really made his stomach turn over uncomfortably.

"Dear Lord, Edwin, you already have enough difficulty with one daughter—you think you could manage five?"

The words stung. All Edwin's fears, his shame that he was no father to Laura, rose to the surface. She did not even call him "Father." Never had. They had been advised to tell her she was adopted, and it was one of his greatest regrets.

Vivienne's cheeks colored. "I did not mean—I did not mean to reference…you and your wife, you were unable to…"

Her voice faded away in an agony of awkwardness, and Edwin did nothing to help her. *She had finally come to her conclusion then.* Laura was adopted, and that meant he could not have children. He could not stable a schoolroom of five if he tried.

Edwin watched as Vivienne swallowed. "Governesses…governesses are highly skilled, clever women. They are vital for a household, very valuable."

"Yet not at the Bureau," Edwin said, pain adding bite to his words. "At your precious Governess Bureau, they seem far more eager to get married than stay working for you!"

He watched her stiffen, saw pain had been given just as swiftly as it had been received, and hated himself. *How had they fallen into this malicious pattern?* Two people who had cared so much about each other once were now at odds with each other, unable to share any conversation without sniping at each other.

The medley of confusion was overpowering: he had no wish to harm her yet was driven by a foolish instinct to hurt before he himself was injured.

And was it not she who had so injured him in the past? Had

she not rejected him out of hand, laughed at him when he had proposed, ignored his offerings of love and affection for that ridiculous Bureau?

"It is not my fault that they got married."

"They were in your employ," pointed out Edwin, unable to stop himself.

Vivienne sniffed. "Be that as it may, I believe I did what I could to prevent such goings on. I had—I have three rules at the Bureau. You must have an impeccable record. You must bring a special skill to the table. You must never fall in love…"

It was impossible not to smile. "And how has that worked for you?"

She did not reply immediately. Edwin had expected her to quip a retort, to argue with him, attempt to prove him wrong.

What he did not expect was for Vivienne to place down the book, lean forward, and look directly at him. "Edwin," Vivienne said quietly, "you know I am doing everything I can to retain my reputation and that of the Governess Bureau. Will you truly attempt to oppose me? After…after all we have been to each other?"

Edwin swallowed. "And what will you do if you are unsuccessful?"

Vivienne did not reply. The look on her face was so similar to the one that had appeared when she had received his proposal of marriage, so strikingly similar, that Edwin was at once transported back to that moment.

He had hoped to find somewhere a little more private for the question he wanted to ask, but the important thing was the asking.

And her reply.

"But this Bureau won't be your life forever."

Vivienne had frowned as though the Bureau was the only interesting part of their conversation. "Why not?"

And Edwin had taken a deep breath, known this was the moment, and moved to bended knee. *This was it.* The moment he asked Vivienne to be his bride. The moment she made him so happy, he would hardly know how to describe it.

"You know I love you," Edwin had said, clasping his hands over Vivienne's as she stared in shock. "And I want to marry you, Vivienne. Marry me, become my wife—I have little to offer but myself and my pencil, but it would mean everything to me. You...you mean everything to me. Leave the Bureau, and when it is closed, become my wife."

It had been a perfect moment, an almost perfect speech, Edwin was sure—but Vivienne had dropped his hands.

"When the Bureau is closed? You cannot mean that," Vivienne had said uncertainly. "You cannot ask me to give it up."

And Edwin had stared, utterly unable to comprehend. "Well, you can't expect me to—the Bureau is just...you'll be my wife!"

The words had not quite been right, but he had not had a chance to add to them.

"The Bureau is my life, Edwin, everything I've built for the last two years. It's still in its infancy. I need time to get it fully— you really would not wish me to be a part of it, as your wife?"

And Edwin had risen to his feet, all softness in his expression gone. "You wouldn't marry me until this Bureau of yours was larger?"

And then she had laughed. The pain of that memory had stayed with him over the years, never fading.

"Why would I wish to give up the Bureau for you?" the memory of what Vivienne said, her laughter still ringing in his ears. "It is mine, Edwin, all mine, something I created, loved, grew, succeeded at, and on my own! My Governess Bureau will be famous, and you wish me to give that up? Absolutely not. Goodbye, Edwin."

She had walked away without looking back. Perhaps that was the thing that had hurt the most, Edwin wondered as he sat now, looking at a Vivienne that was fifteen years older but apparently no wiser. Without a second glance, she had walked away. *As though he did not matter.*

"Unsuccessful?" said the Vivienne before him. She tilted her head up. "It will be successful. You mark my words, Edwin Bysshe. I have a few more wise years behind me now. The Governess Bureau will be restored."

Without another word, she disappeared behind her book.

Anger flowed through Edwin's veins, so visceral he could do nothing but rise, step toward the fire, and throw the reports Smethly had written into the flames.

"That's what I think of your Bureau," he said shakily to the book raised before him and then storming out of the drawing room.

CHAPTER ELEVEN

February 2, 1816

"BUT IT'S COLD outside!"

If I had a shilling, Vivienne thought darkly, *for every time a child complained that it was cold outside*...She was out here, too, wasn't she? Did they not think she was cold as well?

"No colder than yesterday," she said aloud in a bracing tone.

Laura groaned. "Are all governesses like you, utter savages?"

Vivienne grinned. "No governess is like me."

Ramming a woolen hat onto her charge's head, Vivienne carefully inspected her. They were standing in the hall of Byhalden Lodge, preparing to enter the elements, and Laura had protested so thoroughly that Vivienne had dressed her for the cold weather.

She had perhaps overdone it. Laura had thick, leather winter boots on her feet, beneath which were thick woolen socks. Two pairs. Her heavy gown had an additional petticoat underneath, and there was both a shawl under her pelisse and a scarf over it. Thick, knobby gloves, which looked like a knitting project from a few years ago, were stuffed on her fingers, and the woolen hat— borrowed from a gardener who would undoubtedly be experiencing much colder ears today—almost covered Laura's entire face.

Vivienne could not help but smile. "Ready for your expedition?"

Laura glower was coming on nicely. "You're no governess, but a torturer come to punish me."

It was not entirely true. There was little Vivienne would actually force her charges to do against their will, and if Laura looked truly distressed about going outside into the cold, there was no possibility she would make her. But Laura appeared to be enjoying the experience of gentle complaints and dressing up like she was visiting a polar bear.

Vivienne turned to the door and saw through the windows that the crisp wintery sunlight was glittering off frost still lying thick on the lawn.

She shivered at the mere expectation of the low temperatures. Bracing herself was not going to make any difference. It was mighty cold at the moment, a real winter snap that appeared to be lasting longer than anyone predicted—or wished for.

Yet leaving the warmth of Byhalden Lodge had one primary benefit, one that she could not reveal to Laura. Avoiding her father.

Edwin had become intolerable. Just when she thought he had finally softened, was starting to understand her and her drive to restore the Bureau, he cut her down so utterly…

Vivienne paused, closed her eyes for the briefest of moments, then opened them again. She would not permit him to overwhelm her. If only it were as simple as closing one's heart.

"You'll enjoy it when you're out there," she said vaguely to Laura, as though that would convince her. "I am sure."

Anything was better than staying inside, Vivienne thought bitterly. Each day gave her unwanted opportunities to run into Edwin. It was like a slow torture, being locked inside his house, at any moment running the maze to discover him at the end, an unwelcome prize.

Why she had thought coming here to be a governess for a Bysshe, she did not know...

Vivienne recalled her ledger at the Governess Bureau, all names crossed out.

She knew precisely why she had been forced to come here. She had no other choice.

"We could just stay inside and—"

"Come on, Laura, the sooner we are out there, the sooner we will start to adapt," Vivienne said with a smile. "You'll enjoy it once you're out there."

It took only a few steps for her to reach the front door, and she opened it without giving herself time to hesitate.

Perhaps she should have done. Vivienne gave a sharp intake of breath at the sudden cold and immediately wished she hadn't.

Lord Almighty, had she ever known a temperature such as this!

"Ohhh, Miss Clarke, it's cold!" Laura whined behind her. "I don't want to—"

"Yes, thank you, Laura, I think you have made your opinion quite clear," said Vivienne brightly, as though there was nothing she wished to do more in the world than freeze. "Come on. We'll find a sunny nook to situate ourselves."

It was better once they started walking—or stomping, in Laura's case. Vivienne had not dared venture out to the gardens since her awkward encounter with Edwin in the parkland, and even in the midwinter, they were truly beautiful.

Orderly rows of trees, borders full of shrubs sleeping dormant in the cold earth. There were bulbs being planted by huffing and puffing gardeners in one bed and a tangle of roses being carefully tied back in another. Vivienne could see what was surely a kitchen garden in the distance if the red brick was anything to go by.

A very pretty place indeed. *Now, where was the sun?*

"Let's look down here," Vivienne announced, taking a left along a grass path that led to a gravel one. "I am sure we will find a suitable spot to sit."

Laura muttered behind her, low under her breath so that

Vivienne could not hear. It did not matter. The point was that the child was outside, in the fresh air, getting exercise.

The fact they were both freezing was quite another matter.

"This looks perfect," announced Vivienne after a few minutes and halted.

Before her was a bench, carefully carved from wood and facing southwest, full flush in the sun. With a large magnolia behind it and stocky shrubs on either side, it was out of the wind and, therefore, arguably the warmest place in the garden. *Which,* Vivienne only admitted to herself, *did not mean much.*

Laura shivered dramatically, and Vivienne tutted aloud. "Do not try to make me think that was a real shiver, Laura Bysshe, or I shall be having words with you."

Laura grinned wryly. "I suppose that was a little over the top—actually, my socks and stockings are keeping my feet marvelously warm. It's my nose that's cold."

Vivienne glanced at it. Laura's nose was a glowing rosy red, and she supposed hers was, too. *Ah well. It was not as though either of them was here to impress anyone.*

"Well, we'll be nicely out of the wind here," she said smartly, seating herself and indicating that Laura should do the same. "Goodness, it is good to get out into nature, isn't it?"

Vivienne found, to her surprise, that she was entirely serious in her statement. It was pleasant to be out here, though it was colder than she would have liked. London was warmer, certainly.

But warmer was not better. London was a sticky, smelly, overcrowded place that never had enough room for the people who wanted to inhabit it. Even in the summer, when the gentry and nobility retreated to their country estates, there were still far too many people.

Not here. The countryside offered air that was fresh, wonderful, with space between houses even in villages.

She felt more alive here, somehow. As though the wisdom of her years had finally taken her to a place she could thrive—excluding Edwin. But here, she could forget about him.

A robin dropped onto the gravel path before them, looked up at them with his head cocked, and chittered away.

"It's a robin!"

Vivienne nodded as the bird flew away, and Laura's face fell. "He'll be back. Gardener's friend, they call the robin. They like people. They like our ability to dig up the earth and turn it over, reveal so many delicious things to eat."

Now where did that knowledge come from? Vivienne was not consciously aware of having any insight into the birds and beasts of England.

"I hope he comes back," said Laura wistfully.

Vivienne glanced over. *Time to distract her.* Every child needed to be entertained and distracted at all times, and it was exhausting. How some of her governesses managed it, without a Governess Bureau to return to, Vivienne did not know.

"Here," she said, pulling a small sketching book from her pocket and handing it to the girl. "You've studied line, form, and shading. Now it's time to put those lessons into practice."

Laura looked fearful as she allowed the sketching pad to fall open on her lap, her pencil within it. "It's warming up, you know."

The February sun poured down, giving them every scrap of warmth that was possible—and with the plants providing a natural shelter, it was starting to become remarkably pleasant.

"Good," she said. "Now, where will you start on your sketching pad? The robin, perhaps, if he returns for you?"

Laura sighed. "Is there anything I could say that would make you take me inside?"

It was a most pleading look the girl gave, but Vivienne was entirely unmoved. "No."

Within ten minutes, the two were seated side by side in companionable silence, their pencils moving across their pages—sometimes swift, sometimes hesitant—but without the need for either of them to speak.

Vivienne had never missed being a governess, exactly. Perhaps if women had more access to professions, she would have chosen a different kind of business to found. There wasn't really any other choice, so she would never know. But it had been Evangeline who enjoyed being a governess, and Vivienne had seen the possibilities.

But now she was here and starting to wonder just what she had missed out on, not pursuing her own governessing career. The Governess Bureau would never have been created, of course, but…would she have been just as fulfilled, perhaps in a different way?

It was rather pleasant to issue orders and have them obeyed. It was like old times, like she was back in the Bureau. Laura was a willing child, and that made everything easier.

The same could not be said of her father. *The man was infuriating!*

A rush of heat seared across Vivienne's chest, warming her. It was an unpleasant, prickly heat. *Edwin Bysshe. What a gentleman for getting in his own way!*

Vivienne had thought, a few days ago, that he was starting to become amenable to her presence, perhaps in some way could return to the old way of thinking, of feeling, as she had…

But no. He was irascible in his views and irritable in his temper, and she would not permit him to take up any more time in her mind.

She dropped her eyes to the page of her sketchbook. Well, it was not as though she needed to put much work into the effort, after all. She was only here to keep Laura company and advise her on any tricky parts of the sketching image she chose.

It was perhaps for this reason that Vivienne permitted her mind to wander as her gloved hand, grasping her pencil, moved over the page.

Minutes soared by. After a bit—long enough for a page to be filled and for Vivienne to turn to a fresh one, a voice interrupted the serene solitude she'd created.

"What are you two doing out here in the cold?"

Every inch of her body stiffened. Instinctively closing her sketchbook to ensure nothing on the pages could be viewed, Vivienne looked up into Edwin's eyes, preparing herself for a fight.

Fingers tingling—though that may have been from the cold—Vivienne was ready to defend herself and her governessing choices to the hilt.

But she blinked. It appeared a fight was not necessary. There was a smile on Edwin's face, though a hesitant one, there was no mistaking that expression. There was a glitter in his eyes of barely concealed amusement, and he was wearing a greatcoat that dramatically showed off his broad shoulders and height.

Vivienne bit her lip, hoping he did not notice. *It was so darn irritating when the man you loved was both ridiculously handsome and a complete nincompoop!*

"Looks like you are practicing your sketching," Edwin said, sitting on the other side of Laura, who was looking downcast in expectation of critique. "Why don't you show me?"

Vivienne found she was holding her breath. It could all go one way or the other, and she did not know Laura well enough yet to know how it would go.

Would the child be willing to share something so new, so vulnerable—or would she react strongly against it and refuse to engage with him.

"Y-You want to see?" came the cautious reply.

Edwin nodded. "If you will let me."

It was well done, Vivienne thought, eyes staring furiously at her own sketchbook, so they would not consider her staring. If he had been too forceful, Laura would surely have refused.

As it was...

"I like the lines you have here, for the robin's beak," said Edwin, his attention wholly focused on his daughter's sketchbook. "How have you created such a likeness? You do not have a pet robin, as far as I know."

"One stopped here, right on the ground in front of us!" Laura said excitedly, brightness in her eyes and red in her cheeks. "And I looked at it carefully, and I thought that the beak wasn't entirely straight, you see, it has a slight curve…"

Vivienne smiled despite herself. When they were not thinking about it, when they could focus on something other than themselves, Edwin and his daughter were able to keep a conversation going rather well. Their chatter continued, unaided, and she continued to stare at her own sketchbook, closed as it was.

When Edwin was not thinking about it, she wondered, *he became a nicer person.* That was strange. Had she ever noticed that before?

When attempting to impress or show off or demonstrate that he was the one in charge, Edwin was intolerable. Cold, harsh, unpleasant to the extreme! But when relaxed—or drunk…

Vivienne swallowed. *Which was the true Edwin?*

It was such a shame. He could be a better man, a better father. It was all there within him, locked away but able to surface when he least expected it.

"—but then your little one will have no legs!" Edwin said with a smile, and Laura chuckled as though he had said something immensely clever, which as far as Vivienne could see, he had not.

But that was parenthood. A child wanted to love her parent, wanted to adore and be adored in return. Something that, for Laura, had been distinctly lacking.

It was pleasant, sitting here, listening to them chatter away. Though Laura was starting to leave childhood behind, there was still much of a child within her. She wished so much for her, Vivienne was starting to realize, even though she had only been here some weeks.

Laura deserved to be loved. Like any child, she deserved to be wanted by her parents.

"—when attempting this section, try tilting the pencil on its side—yes, like that—and you'll be able to create…"

Edwin was leaning toward his daughter and had placed his

arm not around her, but along the back of the bench. Vivienne was only conscious of that when she realized his fingers were mere inches from her shoulder.

Her stomach tugged most uncomfortably. Ever since that dinner, when she had realized that the love she had for Edwin had been dormant rather than removed without a trace, she had been forced to confront a terrible reality.

Edwin did not care for her. He did not even respect her, or he would not speak so poorly to her about her Governess Bureau.

The idea that he would love her was ridiculous. Though it pained her, Vivienne knew that Edwin did not care for her at all, and yet the emotions she had been certain had disappeared forever were returning with greater and greater force.

She loved the softness in him, deep within, the vulnerability, the artist, the caring father. Vivienne glanced through her eyelashes, determined not to but unable to help herself.

Edwin was leaning close to Laura, smiling and advising, teaching his daughter something that he truly loved himself. Vivienne's heartstrings twisted. He was a good man, underneath...underneath so much else.

Laura shivered violently, dropping her pencil onto her sketch pad, and Vivienne looked hastily away.

"Goodness!" Edwin said with a laugh. "May I be so bold as to suggest that you might be cold, Laura?"

She giggled. "Miss Clarke says the cold is good for me!"

A terrible thought hit Vivienne at that very moment. *Had she permitted Laura to be out in the cold for too long? What if she were to become unwell?*

"If you wish to go inside, you can," she said stiffly.

Vivienne half expected Laura to stay, to be close to her father and experience more of his artistic teachings—but the temperature overrode the warmth of their conversation.

"Thank you!" said Laura immediately, closing her sketch pad, thrusting it at her governess, and rushing off toward the house while shouting over her shoulder, "I'll see you later, Edwin!"

Vivienne smiled wryly. *So close, and yet so far.* But one could not expect to restore a relationship—or grow one—overnight. It would take time. She just had to hope that Edwin would be patient.

And speaking of Edwin…

The gentleman moved along the bench toward her. "And what are you working on?"

Before she could say anything, before she could put away the sketch pad in her hands, or demure that she was not working on anything, or stand up and escape him, or shoot him a cold, icy glare that would make him move away from her—Edwin took her sketch pad.

Time froze. Vivienne felt it freeze, the cold air rush into her lungs, surrounding her, freezing her so she could not move.

Edwin opened it up, while Vivienne wanted to shout that he must not, that it would be a disaster, that once he saw, they would not be able to—

There he was. Image after image of him, sketch after sketch. She had allowed her mind to wander, and what had it wandered to? *Him.* Different angles of his face, a close up of his eye, his hair, the collar around his throat, even his hands—it was unmistakably him.

Vivienne's heart stopped. That was it. She had died. She would never survive this depth of embarrassment. This was too much. She should never have come! She had thought she was stronger than this, and the truth was…she wasn't.

She felt the weakness in her bones. Embarrassment was weakening her, crushing her, making it impossible for her to move or speak or justify herself at all.

The silence continued too long. Though it took a stupendous effort, Vivienne managed to turn her head ever so slightly and look at Edwin.

His face was expressive, overpowered by an emotion that she had not seen on his face in a long time.

"Y-You…" Edwin attempted. He swallowed, attempted to

speak again, but only a gargle came out.

Heat flushed up Vivienne's chest.

"These...these look like summer clothes."

It was such a strange thing for Edwin to say. Vivienne was not sure she had heard correctly. *Summer clothes?*

But then she saw that he was pointing at one of the busts of him she had drawn. He was correct. He was wearing a summer collar, cravat, and jacket.

Vivienne nodded. Her voice, like the rest of her at the moment, was not to be trusted.

Was this what happened to others? There must be other people who have loved, lost, then been forced to confront the person they had once believed would make them the happiest they had ever been. How did they stand it? The awkwardness, the fear, the terror one may say the wrong—or right—thing?

"So...so you did this from memory?"

Vivienne swallowed. Edwin appeared to have his faculties about him, and he had not walked away, which he most certainly should have done. That meant he actually wished to converse about this. She would have to speak. She would have to make herself.

"Yes," she managed.

"But...but it was so long ago," said Edwin quietly. He had not looked up from the sketch pad, his fingers brushing over one of his face. "Years, yet you have recalled it exactly."

"I..." Vivienne knew she should not speak, but the time for holding back was passed. "I have so many memories of you, Edwin. You think I cannot recall what you look like in the summer? You think I cannot draw you?"

And that was the trouble, wasn't it? So many memories, so many encounters, moments of joy and laughter—only to be followed by pain and regret. There was so much unspoken between them, the opportunities for reconciliation they had not taken, the misunderstandings—the arguments.

It was all so long ago, but now it appeared it was too late to do anything about it.

Edwin cleared his throat. "Where did we go wrong?"

His voice was low, uncertain. What she wanted to do was ask far more important questions. Did he truly miss her? He had said he did—when he had drunk too much—but she could not be sure to trust that particular version of Edwin. Did he care about her? Did he find himself looking for her in every room he entered, as she did? Did he...was there a chance he could love her again?

"You should have called it a Marriage Bureau, Vivienne, not a Governess Bureau!"

Vivienne hardened her heart. She already knew the answers to those questions; and she just didn't like them. She had to protect herself, could not permit herself to fall into that trap again.

"What went wrong?" she said as lightly as she could, looking away from him and at the shrubs in the border opposite. "I cared too much about my business in your eyes."

Vivienne had attempted to remove any bitterness from her voice, but it was difficult—though her heart skipped a beat as Edwin responded.

"I wasn't willing to listen."

Did—did that mean he wished he had made a different decision?

"You did not understand how I felt about the Bureau," she said softly.

Edwin laughed bitterly. "Oh, I knew how you felt about it. You chose it over me!"

And there it was. What was that? Almost two full minutes of them being open and honest and kind to each other? Vivienne should have known it would not last.

"It did not have to be a decision between you and the Bureau," Vivienne said curtly, "but you made me choose."

How had they managed to descend once more into an argument? But it was the habit they had fallen into. She could see that now.

"This is precisely why I did not ask for your help," she said quietly. "You did not believe I could succeed in the first place."

"Well, isn't it failing?"

Vivienne opened her mouth to retort but closed it again. There was no point. As she looked at Edwin, she could see in his eyes that he had no desire to be won over or convinced. He had made up his mind; it was there in the tightness of his jaw.

Grabbing her sketch pad from his hands, Vivienne stuffed it in her pocket. "I do not understand why every conversation between us ends in one of us storming off."

She rose as she spoke, ready to almost run to the house. *To safety. To a place without Edwin.*

He was glaring. "Wasn't that our problem in the beginning? That we ran from our problems and therefore each other?"

Vivienne stared. *Was he asking her to stay—or was he just blaming their past selves for never managing to do anything different?*

She swallowed. The words she wanted to say were bubbling up in her and were surely the wrong decision, but she could not help it.

"I am not the one," she said, her eyes affixed on him, hoping he did not see the hurt in her face, "who immediately married someone else, Edwin. That was you. You gave up on us, on what we could have been. You ran away. *You.*"

This time, however, it was she who strode away, tears falling from her eyes despite Vivienne telling herself that she did not cry.

Chapter Twelve

February 5, 1816

It was starting to get rather annoying. He had never noticed his servants in this way before. He had grown up in Byhalden Lodge, and because of his two older brothers, had never expected to live here forever.

Thomas and Mallory, named for his father's penchant for medieval literature, had been two strapping lads when their rather scrawny youngest brother had been born. Edwin could well remember his father saying, not in a cruel way, that of all his sons that he expected to outlive, it was Edwin.

His father had died later that year, and the three Bysshe brothers had grown up relatively in harmony. There were always little scuffles between brothers, but Edwin could recall no great enmity between them. Thomas, the eldest, had no concern with his brothers staying at the lodge as long as they wished.

"Just because you're not the heir," he had always said with a smile, "doesn't mean you should be homeless."

It had been a rather unpleasant shock to hear of Thomas's death by a fever, a gangrenous wound weakening him within a matter of days. Mallory had inherited, and to much surprise, had succumbed just a year later to an agony in his side.

Edwin had never gained a clear idea from the doctor who came from York precisely what was wrong with his brother, but he had, to his great pride, been there with his brother when the end had come.

And that had left Edwin. Their mother, having died so many years earlier, Edwin slipped into the role of the Bysshe at the lodge, and the same servants who had watched him grow—or more likely, their children—had continued on with their tasks, keeping the house running as only a well-organized set of servants could.

But he did not actually *know* them. Edwin was not certain he could pick out a single name of a Bysshe servant, save for Mrs. Jenner and Harris, who arguably did not count.

It was just part of being a part of this family—of any family of a servant rank. One's house was full of servants. By numbers, he supposed it was more their house than his own.

And he had never noticed them. Well, Harris brought him things when ordered, and Mrs. Jenner made a fuss of ensuring he did not spot a single maid going around lighting fires, but that was all.

Until now. Until one of them in particular.

Edwin gritted his teeth as he tried to put all thought of Miss Vivienne Clarke from his mind, but it was impossible. Wherever he went, there was Vivienne. No matter how he attempted to avoid her, his efforts were futile.

She was truly everywhere. If he went to the garden to sketch, she was there. If he went to the drawing room to think, she was there. If he went to the library to retrieve a book, anything to rid his mind of the thoughts of her, who was he to find there?

Never on her own, of course. Edwin had to give her that; she was almost always with Laura. Lessons, it seemed, were for mornings only, the only time he was safe—unless the weather was pleasant, or Laura had a music lesson, or she was simply too tired for lessons.

At first, Edwin had believed that Laura was manipulating Vivienne into restricting the number of lessons she actually endured. He had been so impressed, it took a few days to realize that something quite different was occurring.

Laura was still Laura, the little scrap of a girl he had taken into his heart and home all those years ago. But she was different. Better behaved if Edwin had to put his finger on something specific, which was difficult. Calmer. Just…nicer to be around.

It felt terrible to think such a thing about one's child, but then Edwin had never been of the belief that one would always like one's children. Love, of course. But like? That was quite a different matter indeed.

The change was rather pleasant. Just when he was starting to run entirely out of patience with the girl, here Vivienne had come, and somehow the girl was…easier to talk to.

Indeed, last evening Laura had said something rather witty, which had made him roar with such laughter, he had spilt wine on his waistcoat. His valet would never let him hear the end of it, but that was beside the point. The point was, he'd had fun. With Laura.

The idea would have been unthinkable this time last year—even a few months ago.

He had been disappointed when the dinner had been over, and Laura had gone upstairs to bed. Had that ever happened before? He could not recall it. And so that was why he sat here, having breakfast alone—Laura had decided to break her fast with the servants, as she did occasionally—and he was…lonely.

Edwin cleared his throat. The noise echoed uncomfortably around the breakfast room.

He had waved away the footman almost as soon as he had entered the room. "Go away," he'd snapped, regretting his harsh tone immediately but unable to do anything about it.

The footman, whatever his name was, had bowed and disappeared before Edwin could think better of his rudeness and apologize.

And that had left him alone. As Edwin poured himself a cup of steaming tea, he looked at the empty chairs and wished, for the first time in his life, that Laura and Vivienne were here.

Where had that thought from? Edwin sipped the scalding liquid, hoping it would shock him into sense, but it did not. All he felt was a growing sense of being completely alone.

Was he starting to…become dependent on their company? Was he missing not just Laura, but Vivienne herself? Edwin shook himself. Surely not. He was just tired, that was all.

But as he slipped two eggs onto his plate with a side of bacon—Mrs. Jenner believed the cold weather would make him ill without a hot breakfast—Edwin could not help but allow his thoughts to meander around the memories of Laura.

She really was a bright young thing. *He had always thought she was*, he mused, *but had seen little evidence of it until now.*

He had always enjoyed the solitude of the breakfast room. For so long, Laura had not been permitted to eat here. Henrietta had taken breakfast in bed, and so that had given him one short hour in the day when he would not be irritated by either of them. But now he wanted her here. Her and Vivienne, though that thought was pushed firmly from his mind.

Edwin looked down at his plate. His food was gone. *What on earth had happened?*

Then he noticed the knife and fork in his hands, stained with egg yolk and bacon grease. He had become so lost in his thoughts, he had not even noticed he was eating. He could taste the food on his lips.

There was utter silence in the room.

Edwin placed his cutlery down on his plate, wincing slightly at the noise. It was odd how one could sense the silence at all times but not care about it, but once one noticed it, one could do nothing but notice it.

Silence. He was alone.

Now Laura was more amenable to polite—and interesting—conversation, Edwin found himself wondering whether he could include her more in his daily routine. His meals, perhaps. Certainly, he should spend a little more time with her. *But was it that she was more interesting, or that he was starting to understand her better?*

The thought was most upsetting, and Edwin pushed his plate away as though that could force the thoughts away.

He was not a bad father; at least, he had never considered himself a bad father. He had been the same sort of father for Laura as his father had been for him and his brothers. Stern, strong, aloof. Providing a wonderful home and a good name. *What else was there?*

A great deal, he was starting to realize with discomfort growing in his stomach. There was so much warmth he had not realized was missing. Had Laura? Was that, perhaps, why there had been such distance between them?

The thought did nothing to calm the growing pain in his lungs as they tightened, making each breath a challenge.

And he knew why. Because whatever he thought about his role as her father, he had to admit it was not a change in him which had brought Laura out of her shell, softening her to the world and making her a far more interesting conversationalist. *No. It was Vivienne.*

Vivienne had arrived, and within weeks, had understood his own child better than he did. *And now he was thinking about Vivienne.*

Edwin's heart skipped a beat, its traitorous symptom a sign of how his mind could not stay away, even if he wished it.

His attempts to restrict her presence within his mind had been utterly futile. The more he tried not to think of her, inexplicably, the more he thought of her.

In the past, he had not needed to make friends with two brothers who were such pleasant company. Their deaths as adults had rocked him, he could see now, greater than he had known. And now...

Edwin sighed heavily. The noise echoed around the room,

the chandelier tinkling.

Alone. That was what he was, without Laura and Vivienne. Their company was …pleasant. Even if he and Vivienne did not appear to be able to have a conversation longer than twenty minutes without it descending into chaos.

He would not permit himself to seek them out. His emotions were already too frayed, too close to the surface. The last thing he needed was to start thinking of her as he had before.

Rising from his seat, Edwin left the breakfast room and meandered up to his bedchamber with the vague idea of perhaps changing into his riding clothes.

A ride; yes, that was it. It would take him far from the lodge and Vivienne, where his heart may accidentally start sliding into bad habits, and away from Laura while she was in the schoolroom and utterly unattainable.

It was perhaps ill fortune—or an unconscious decision of his foolish mind—that Edwin's route to his bedchamber took him past the schoolroom. Though the door was closed this time, it did not prevent laughter from seeping through it.

Laughter!

Edwin halted by the door. This was foolish. He was not wanted there; it was not his place. Yet his feet did not start moving again. Instead, he stood there, listening to the laughter, aching to be with them.

He was so alone.

The thought had never occurred to him before, but Edwin felt it now in the very core of his being. He was alone. Laura had been alone, too, and they had not got on particularly well, but at the very least, they had been alone together.

Now she had been taken away from him. Vivienne had made Laura into her own creature, and he was the one standing here on the outside.

The urge to open the door and be with them almost overpowered him, roaring through his veins, making it almost impossible to think clearly. The laughter was dying away now, and the sound of their conversation started to be audible.

"But really, did Pythagoras say that?"

"Are you doubting my word, Miss Laura?"

More laughter. Edwin's jaw dropped. *They were laughing about—about math?* Now that certainly did not make any sense.

It had been many years, admittedly, since he had been at Harrow, but he could not recall math being anything other than an instrument of torture.

But they continued, still apparently having the best of times.

"And Archimedes—in the bathtub?" Laura sounded exhilarated. "He really said 'Eureka!'?"

"Well, the historian Vitruvius tells us that—my lord."

The last two words were cold, and Edwin could see the coldness in her eyes as she said them. Only then did he realize that he could see that precise temperature because he had opened the door and stepped into the schoolroom.

Laura and Vivienne stared, and Edwin found heat flushing his neck. *This was preposterous!* This was his home, and he could go where he liked. Even if his daughter and her governess appeared to think otherwise.

"Yes?" said Vivienne coldly.

It was a little like a nightmare; those where you find yourself where you shouldn't be, before people who were very stern, and you were told to explain yourself.

And you couldn't because you weren't entirely sure yourself how you had got there.

Edwin could see Laura staring with barely concealed confusion.

"What do you want, Edwin?" Laura said hesitantly.

This was foolish. Laura was his daughter. Vivienne was the one who should feel unwelcome here. So why was it he who so clearly felt the outsider?

"I-I..." *By Jove, he needed to get a hold of his tongue and force it to make some sense.* "I was just going to...to say..."

Vivienne blinked, somehow communicating in that small

gesture just how tired she was of this interruption.

Edwin swallowed. *He was near forty. This was not the time to become a boy!* "I wanted to say that I was looking forward to having dinner with you tonight. Both of you."

Why had he added those last words? Perhaps because he had glanced at Vivienne at that moment and was overwhelmed with a sense of desire. A desire he most certainly should not be displaying in his daughter's schoolroom!

"But it is not Sunday," said Vivienne quietly.

Edwin was well aware of that. He had been clear when Vivienne had first arrived—and with Mrs. Jenner and Harris—that the governess was only to dine with the family on special occasions. Sundays, Easter, and Christmas. And that was already far too much.

And now here he was, on a Monday, suggesting that she join him!

"That sounds wonderful," he heard Laura say.

Edwin blinked. The schoolroom came back into focus—that is, his entire mind was not filled with the image of Vivienne, but with the rest of the room too.

He smiled weakly at his daughter. "Yes. Good. Fine. I will see you then."

Edwin felt the biggest fool in the world as Vivienne and Laura watched him as he backed out of the room, closed the door behind him, and leaned against it.

What did he think he was doing? He had promised himself he would spend less time with Vivienne, not more! All he had to do was confirm that Laura was to dine with him. Wasn't that what he wanted?

What did he want?

"Miss Clarke," Laura's voice in the other room came gently under the door. "Do you...do you think Edwin is lonely?"

Edwin's heart lurched. That was precisely not the sort of thing he ever wanted his daughter to worry about—and the person he did not want her to ask that question of!

He waited, heart frantically beating against his ribcage now, for the answer. When it came, his shoulders drooped.

"Perhaps," said Vivienne crisply. "But that is none of my concern. Now, Pythagoras's theorem. As you can see with this triangle..."

It took Edwin the entirety of the day to convince himself of three things.

First, he was a complete and utter fool and should not be trusted to do or say anything.

Second, even with the specter of Vivienne looming, he was genuinely looking forward to seeing Laura at dinner, which was something he had not experienced before.

Third, Vivienne was absolutely not getting under his skin whatsoever. No matter what his mind thought or body felt.

It was after a great effort that the last of these could be forced into his mind, but it meant that when it came for dinner, Edwin could sit at the head of the table with remarkable equanimity and listen to Laura talk about her lesson on ancient Greeks and mathematics.

"—and I had not realized how much they had discovered at that time, but so much of what we know now comes from that time," Laura was saying, eyes bright and food ignored. "For instance, did you know..."

Edwin watched, transfixed, a smile on his face and his own food similarly forgotten.

It was difficult not to marvel at the change Vivienne had wrought in his daughter. When had it started? When the governess had first arrived at the house? Surely he had not been so ignorant for so long?

Laura was a changed child: bright and eager, a pleasure to be around.

"—and then I attempted it, and I was able to calculate the length immediately! Well, not quite immediately, Miss Clarke had to give me a small hint about..."

Edwin nodded, hoping Laura could not see how his mind was

wandering.

A changed child. What was wrong with him? He should not have been hoping for this; he should have loved the child he had. Was he in such a hurry to change Laura, to mold her into the type of daughter he wanted?

The pain of hypocrisy seared through Edwin's heart, though he tried to keep it hidden from the two women seated on either side of him.

He was a terrible father. Edwin had known that for some time, had known it as soon as Laura had arrived, but he had always thought it was because Laura was such a difficult child. Willful. Bad-tempered.

But was she in fact, merely responding to how he had treated her? It was not a pleasant thought, but Edwin forced himself to consider it.

As he thought of Laura, Edwin suddenly took in what she was saying.

"—Edwin learn this at school?" Laura asked—and Vivienne replied.

"I am sure your father learned all the same mathematics you are," she said quietly, her plate empty—the only one at the table, now Edwin came to look. "He is very learned, and that is why he wished for you to be as well educated. Isn't that right, my lord?"

Edwin wanted to reply with words—actual, real words. But he merely laughed awkwardly. *Dear God, what was wrong with him?* Had this woman really reduced him to this?

"Yes," he managed to say, clearing his throat and looking down at his food. Food he should eat. *Why was he so distracted?*

After another twenty minutes, he and Laura had managed to clear their plates, though his daughter was looking morose.

"I'll go upstairs now," she said quietly and slipped from her chair.

Edwin rose, the movement an unconscious thought. "Well, as you have such grown-up things to talk about, why not join us in the drawing room?"

Laura hesitated. He could see the temptation in her face, but as she yawned, Edwin realized he had made a catastrophic mistake.

"I'm sorry, Edwin, I am far too tired," Laura said, stifling a second yawn. "But Miss Clarke will go with you, so you have the company. Goodnight."

She had scampered off before Edwin or Vivienne could say another word—but it would be most indecorous of him not to extend the invitation now, and Vivienne knew it.

Damn.

Edwin glanced at Vivienne. He had not wished to be alone with her at all, let alone in the darkness and intimacy of the drawing room. So…should he offer her his hand?

Just before he reached out to lead her into the drawing room, Vivienne had risen and sailed past him without waiting, to Edwin's relief and sadness.

You just wanted to touch her, a dark little voice in his mind said. *You just wanted an excuse for contact, and now you've lost it. You're pathetic.*

Edwin attempted to push aside both the thought and the desire to touch Vivienne. Yes, he had touched her when drunk on that rather delicious bottle of port, and yes, it had made him feel more alive than he could remember. But that did not mean it was a good idea.

Vivienne looked uncomfortable in the drawing room, seated by the fire, and it took Edwin a moment to guess why, until the memory of the last time they had been alone together resurfaced in his mind.

"You should have called it a Marriage Bureau, Vivienne, not a Governess Bureau!"

Stomach in knots as he sat, Edwin wondered whether deep down, he was a bad person. Here she was, a woman who had hurt him, yes but was by no means a terrible person herself, now apparently fearful of his cruel words and cutting sarcasm.

Dear Lord, he was a blaggard.

"May...may I offer you a drink?" Edwin said, starting to walk toward the sideboard.

Vivienne sniffed. "No, thank you."

Edwin had reached out to pour himself one when the memory of that night forced its way back into his mind. *Perhaps not.*

"Look," he said instead, seating himself opposite her but ensuring that the armchair was a good three feet away, "I...I wanted to congratulate you. On Laura. I do not know how you are doing it, but you are doing an excellent job."

The astonishment on her face was further proof that Vivienne had expected harsh words, which made Edwin feel even more ashamed.

"How have you done it?"

"Why, by listening, of course," said Vivienne simply.

The way she spoke, as though it was obvious. Edwin blinked. *It could not be that simple, could it?*

"Tell me, Edwin," Vivienne said quietly. "Tell me about Laura."

To his surprise, Edwin found here, in the warmth by the fire, the darkness of the room, and with Vivienne, he was able to speak on a topic he'd told himself he would take to his grave.

"Henrietta and I...well, we had been married five years, and no child had come," he said with a heavy sigh. "I was not that bothered, to tell the truth. I have plenty of cousins who will continue the Bysshe name, and this lodge will be a home for many other Bysshes after my death. But Henrietta...she was upset. She wanted a child."

Edwin paused. That was the story everyone had been told, and the world had accepted that. *Why wouldn't it?*

Did Vivienne deserve the whole truth? He glanced at her and saw the interest in her eyes, the lilting smile on her lips.

Edwin swallowed. *No.* Until they had a civil conversation, until he could be sure she would not use the whole truth to benefit her Bureau, certain details he would keep to himself.

"We considered adoption, but it appeared to be so complicated," he continued, his voice gaining strength in his decision. "My lawyers looked into it but finding a child that would be suitable...it was complex. Henrietta was getting more—difficult, shall we say. I came to the realization that my wife would not be happy without a child."

"Some women are like that," came the gentle response from Vivienne.

It was on the tip of his tongue to ask Vivienne whether she was one of them, but Edwin managed to restrain himself. He had not yet earned that particular right.

"I wanted to ask," said Vivienne suddenly before he could continue on with his story. "I know I have no right, but...what was Henrietta like?"

Edwin did not have to consider his response. "Very beautiful and very empty."

Vivienne frowned.

"Do not misunderstand me," he said with a heavy sigh. "She was very pretty, had a fantastic dowry, and with two elder brothers, I needed money. Then Thomas died, and I became the heir. Henrietta liked the pageantry that came with a title, but she had no interest in me."

"You speak as though you did not love her."

Vivienne had spoken quietly, but the intensity of her gaze did not leave him. Edwin swallowed. They were meandering into dangerous ground now.

"She did not love me," said Edwin heavily, "and made no attempt to make me love her. We were companions, I suppose you would say. Perhaps I should have made more effort, perhaps she should have done—at any rate, her requests for a child were...unceasing."

How much more he could say, Edwin mused, *yet he should not*.

There was a strange look on Vivienne's face now—part pity, part disgust.

"People like me," Edwin said sharply, "do not usually make

love matches."

Unsaid words rang out between them. Vivienne looked at her hands.

"We found Laura in London and brought her here, and I thought for a time that all our problems would be solved," Edwin said. Now he had started the story, he may as well finish it. "But it turned out Henrietta was never going to be happy. She adored misery and saw no reason to actually mother the child."

Vivienne nodded slowly. "A child has to be loved. Desperately loved, desperately wanted."

Edwin nodded as though he knew what that looked like. Oh, his parents loved him, as you could love an asset to the family name. But there was little more affection than that.

"Love is..." Edwin swallowed. "Complicated. I have never known it not to be."

She looked up then, as he knew she would. If only he could know what she was thinking. If only she could know what he was thinking, what he was feeling.

But instead of consoling him, Vivienne rose to her feet. "I think...I think perhaps I should leave."

Edwin nodded. She was right. This had been a mistake, agreeing to Laura's suggestion. As she moved past him toward the door, Edwin was in the perfect position to reach out and touch her.

His fingers tangled with hers, and she halted. Edwin's breath caught in his throat, the intensity of that moment was so glorious. *Vivienne's fingers, touching his own.* A connection he had only dreamed of.

A hint of something to come if they could be bold. If they left behind all that animosity and found, instead, the heat of passion that had been so tantalizingly close during their courting.

A closeness which had never come to its full conclusion...

"What...what are you doing?" Vivienne whispered, looking down at him.

Edwin swallowed and spoke honestly. "I don't know."

The attraction between them could not be denied, but it could not be consummated either. They were stuck, half together, half apart.

Edwin rose to his feet, their fingers still entangled. She was close to him, too close. Mere inches away. Her breathing seemed to have quickened, and it only heightened the response in him.

He shifted slightly, leaning toward her, and Vivienne did not move away.

But she did speak. "We...we must not go down this page. We know where it goes."

Every inch of Edwin—some inches more than others—wanted to ignore her, to push aside her worries with a passionate kiss that would show her just how much she meant to him.

But she was right. She was always right.

Regretfully and with his heart crying out against the decision, Edwin dropped her fingers and took in a deep breath. "Fine. But don't leave me, will you?"

He glanced at the armchair behind her. Vivienne hesitated.

"You were the one," he said with a great effort, "who said our conversations shouldn't end with one of us storming off."

She had to smile at that one, and though it took another few heart-stopping moments, Vivienne turned and sat back down in the chair she had vacated.

"Do you honestly think we can have a civil conversation?" Vivienne asked, eyebrow raised.

Edwin lowered himself into the chair. "I would like to try."

CHAPTER THIRTEEN

February 11, 1816

VIVIENNE POINTED TO Liverpool. "And why is Liverpool an important place, Laura?"

She waited, face turned to the map she had carefully pinned to the wall.

"Laura?"

Still nothing. Vivienne sighed, turned around, and saw precisely what she had expected: Laura making faces when she thought she wasn't looking.

"Laura Bysshe!"

Laura stopped pushing her nose back, crossing her eyes, and waggling fingers by her ears, but her face did not return to that of a happy child.

She was sullen, eyes downcast, and Vivienne knew it was going to be a long morning.

"Laura Laura Bysshe," said Laura in a sing-song way. "You shouldn't call me that."

"But it is your name," said Vivienne with some bewilderment.

It had been such a long time since she had been a child. It was only in moments like these that Vivienne felt the misfortune of being so much older than the governesses she typically set out to assignments.

Many of them were in their early twenties and could still remember the frustrations and terrors and joys of youth. But for her...they were a lifetime ago. *Thirty years*. She could barely remember what it was like to be a child, how deeply everything seemed to be felt.

Everything was important. Every day was the end of the world. If it was exhausting for her, how exhausting was it for Laura?

"It's not my name," said Laura petulantly, all the good humor of the last few days gone. "Not my real name. I don't deserve to bear the Bysshe name, I am not truly of the line."

Vivienne realized her hand was still pointing at Liverpool on the map. She allowed her hand to return to her side and wondered precisely how she was going to navigate this one.

The origins of Laura were not a topic she relished. In her conversation with Edwin—one which had gone late into the night—they had not touched on Laura again. It had certainly been difficult, hearing about Henrietta, but Vivienne had persevered. She had wanted to know, wanted to understand how Laura had come to be a part of this family.

It was evidently a topic not spoken of. She had only attempted it once with Mrs. Jenner and was halted in her tracks with a very kind look and a shake of the head.

"We do not speak of *before Laura came*," the housekeeper had said pointedly. "She is the master's daughter. That's all I know."

Which was very admirable indeed, Vivienne thought darkly but was not of great use.

Some days were easier than others. She knew that. Sometimes Laura seemed entirely settled here, starting to talk to her father more easily—and others...

Vivienne could see she was entirely consumed with thoughts of her natural parents. Who they were, where they came from—

and most importantly, why they had given her up.

Vivienne swallowed. "Laura, focus. Geography is the subject for today, not history."

The quip was rather clever, or at least she thought so, but as it was at Laura's expense. She should not have been surprised to see a disappointed look on the girl's face.

"Is that all you can say? Geography. What's the point, I ask you, of all this?"

Vivienne blinked. "This?"

"This!" said Laura, waving her hands to indicate the entire room. "I am not a boy. I will not be the next Viscount Bysshe. So why bother educating me? I will never need to know all this, any of it. It's not like I'll be working for a living!"

A delicate flush tinged Vivienne's neck, though she attempted to conceal her reaction to the slight Laura had unwittingly paid her.

A corresponding flush was now starting to creep across Laura's face.

Poor child, Vivienne could not help but think. There was nothing like that middle stage between being a babe in arms and being an adult. Awkwardness was never far away.

"I-I didn't mean...well, you know what I meant," Laura said quietly. "There is no adventure in my future, no opportunity to do anything great. I will marry a dull gentleman, who will never want to have a meaningful conversation with me, or I will never get married at all."

It was difficult not to agree. Options for a lady did not exist; at least, Vivienne had not found them, and she had searched high and low before founding the Governess Bureau.

To be a woman, it appeared, was to be an object, to be a mother, and then to be quiet.

Nothing else was expected—by some men, nothing else was tolerated.

It was an intolerable situation, but there it was. *So it had always been, and so it would always be*, Vivienne thought. It was not as though there would one day be lady doctors, or lady lawyers—or lady politicians!

That was a fantasy world, a fairytale she would not do Laura the disservice of attempting to convince her of. Even a girl who was turning out to be as pretty as Laura and who would end up well educated could hope for very little.

"Well," said Vivienne decidedly, with no idea what was she was going to say next, "that's as may be. I don't want to lie to you, Laura, and pretend the world is other than it is. But I can tell you this. You are going to make your way in the world, married or not, and you will want to ensure your conversation makes sense. After all, you don't want to make a fool of yourself and talk about taking coals to Liverpool!"

Vivienne snorted, a rare lapse of good manners, but the joke was far too good to miss.

When had she stopped laughing? At the Governess Bureau, it was her place to be stern, severe, and foreboding, to give governesses a sense of their place in the world.

She had never noticed that the cost was her own joy.

Laura did not laugh. She was looking at Vivienne as though she was deeply concerned for her welfare. Her face dull, her expression downcast, Vivienne stopped laughing.

"Your jokes are always so terrible."

That was what Edwin had said to her, what felt like a lifetime ago. She had attempted to make a jest about the weather the first time they had walked out together. He had met her at Apsley gate of Hyde Park. He had assured her it would not rain. They had huddled together under an umbrella, laughing at the raindrops bucketing down, her hem getting wet, Vivienne's heart beating frantically as they huddled together.

He had been so close to her. So close.

Vivienne swallowed.

"Liverpool," she repeated, turning back to the map and pointing. "Come on now, Laura, we covered this most extensively last week. You do remember—coals are from Newcastle, not

Liverpool. But that latter place is known for..."

Vivienne allowed her voice to trail away, hoping her young charge would fall for the trick of wishing to complete her sentence.

It worked so easily on young children; that is, it had worked all those years ago. Vivienne was starting to wonder whether her memories of obedient children were merely fabrications of her mind, blotting out irritating, long mornings like this one.

Laura was looking out the window. The sun had not bothered to make an appearance yet. "Nothing matters, none of this. What is the point? Geography is so...so dull."

Vivienne privately agreed. Of all the subjects she herself had learned, Vivienne had found geography to be the most mind-numbingly boring—, but that was probably not something to say to Laura. Once said, that sort of thing could not be unsaid.

There were few subjects with so little applicability, especially those taught to the daughters of nobility. *Geography. What were they going to do with that?*

The world's men were not exactly going to permit ladies to start exploring or buying up land or...or running mines of anything!

If there was only a way to make it more interesting to her. But York, the nearest city, was a subject of history, not geography. It rained a lot, but that was England all over.

"It's all the same anyway," Laura was saying, gaze still at the window. "The more I learn about England...it's all the same. Nothing changes."

She had the soul of an old woman, Vivienne thought dryly, *but she just might be able to turn it to her own advantage. If she could just think of—*

"Fine, forget Liverpool," she said. "London."

Laura did not exactly snap back to attention as Vivienne had hoped, but she did at least look around from the window.

"The capital city," she said dully. "I have never been there."

Vivienne needed to think of something interesting about

London, and despite having lived there for the majority of her life, everything she knew about it flew out of her head.

It was most provoking. What sort of governess was she, despite all she had said to Edwin, if she could not rustle up an interesting fact about London!

"It...well, the Thames is a very important river," she said lamely.

She heard how pathetic her words were as soon as they were out of her mouth, but there was little she could say to improve it.

The Thames is a very important river. What utter bilge!

Laura sighed. "Bigger than the Ouse? It's so wide sometimes I don't know how people swim to the other side. I've never been swimming. I've never seen the sea."

And with that pronouncement, she turned back to the window.

Perhaps if Vivienne had been clever, she would have halted the lesson there. Laura was in no mood for learnin. It did not take a Bureau-trained governess to see that. There was almost nothing of import that could be shared with her, and Vivienne would have been much better off instructing her to practice her music or read a novel.

Anything except staying here in the schoolroom.

But that was the trouble, wasn't it, thought Vivienne wildly. If she could not get Laura to concentrate on a day where she struggled, what kind of governess was she? The Bureau was hardly going to be restored by giving up at the first hurdle.

And that was why, without really thinking, Vivienne said, "Goodness Laura, do at least attempt to pay attention! I would have thought you would be more interested in London, seeing as that was where you were adopted from!"

She had not thought it was a secret. Edwin had not told her to keep the information quiet, nor had he told her that the information was not to be shared.

But as Vivienne saw Laura's jaw fall, her body turn to the blackboard, and her eyes widen, it was suddenly very apparent that she had just told the girl something she did not know.

"Truly?" Laura's voice was no more than a whisper, as though speaking louder would shatter the moment. "Truly, I...I am from London?"

Vivienne swallowed. The evident fascination on Laura's face—something she had been trying to achieve for a good hour—was nothing compared to the panic rising in her body.

She'd just told Edwin's daughter something he'd evidently decided to keep from her.

Why? What harm could it be, letting the girl know where she was from? It did not make her any less his child, and London was a large place.

"Miss Clarke, I am from London!" Laura crowed, all hesitancy forgotten, eyes still wide and bright with excitement. "Tell me more—where in London? Do you know the area, the street? Perhaps the very house where I was born. I assume it is still standing?"

Vivienne hesitated. This was not what she had intended. If the word should get back to Edwin...would Laura speak to him? To a servant, who would surely report it to their master?

Had she just ruined any chance she had of not only restoring the Governess Bureau's good name but her own?

"Oh, I don't know," she said slowly, trying to play the whole thing off as something not particularly interesting. "London, that's all I know. Now, the Thames—"

"No wait—so does that mean," interrupted Laura with all the enthusiasm of a child, "that I am a Londoner? No, more importantly, does that mean my real mother, is still there? In London?"

Vivienne was entirely out of her depth, and she knew it. No amount of training that the Governess Bureau could offer would make it possible to navigate this conversation properly.

Talking to an adopted child about their parents was a fraught topic at the best of times. Some parents liked to keep it a secret entirely, some were open, and others, like Edwin, decided the easiest thing was to simply state that the child was adopted and leave it at that.

She looked at the eager child before her. *And that led to this. A child who simply wanted to know where she came from.*

Taking a deep breath usually helped Vivienne navigate even the most complex of conversations, but for some reason, this was not helpful.

Had her governesses ever had to deal with a situation like this? What did they do?

Vivienne wracked her brain to see whether she could recall any reports that mentioned such things. But it had been—what, eight years since they had last performed governess services for a family with adopted children, and that had been entirely different.

The two Montgomery sisters both had children, and when one died, the other had taken in her nieces and nephews. There were no questions about birth parents or where one originally came from.

"Miss Clarke?" urged Laura, a pleading smile on her face. "You know, don't you? What is her name? What job does my natural father do—or are they…are they dead?"

The child clearly thought she knew more than she did, and Vivienne grasped at the truth as a lifeline that could save her from this most distressing conversation.

"You will have to trust me, Laura, when I say I know nothing else save the location of London," Vivienne said firmly. "I speak the truth," she added, as Laura's face showed immediate disbelief. "I would not lie to you, there would be no point, and I am not a liar."

Laura's shoulders slumped. "You…you truly know nothing else except London?"

Vivienne could not regret bringing up the topic anymore. This had been foolishness; that would teach her to speak without thinking, a habit she thought she had beaten long ago.

"I should not be speaking of—forget what I said," she said finally. "We are speaking of London in general, so we will start with the Thames. This is a tidal river, and do you know why?"

Somehow, Vivienne was not entirely sure how, she managed to progress the lesson along almost normal lines after that. True, every sentence felt an effort, and she could see that Laura's interest was not truly there—there was only so much one wished to learn about a river, after all—but the point was, they managed it.

Laura's answers came mostly correct, and she became a little more compliant when it came for her to draw a map of England in her sketchbook.

By the time the clocks in Byhalden Lodge started to chime ten o'clock, Vivienne did not know who was more grateful that the day's lessons were almost over her or Laura.

"And that draws us close to the end of today's lessons," she said gratefully as Laura looked up from her sketchbook, having only drawn the southern shores of England. "One hour to go, Laura. How are you getting on with your drawing?"

"Getting there," she said quietly.

Vivienne nodded. There did not appear much else to say. Lowering herself onto the chair behind her desk, she watched the child concentrate, brow furrowed, on attempting Cornwall and Wales on her little map.

At least this would give Vivienne some time to think, and she certainly had plenty to think about. For a start, the absolute disaster she had only just managed to avert when speaking of Laura's origins in London.

She appeared to have diverted it, but at what cost? How many questions at dinner would Laura ask? Perhaps she should have told the girl not to mention to anyone else that she had revealed her London origins, but would that not have only heightened the girl's interest?

And worse of all, and Vivienne felt tension grow in her shoulders and neck at the mere thought of it, what would Edwin say if he found out what she had revealed?

Their conversation last night had been...pleasant. More than pleasant. More than anything they had managed since she had arrived here.

Vivienne cleared her throat and shifted uncomfortably in her seat. The sense of his fingers in hers, it was too much. Her whole body had responded to his touch in a way that was most alarming.

She had not realized such emotions were still present within her, that they could be so easily unlocked. It had been like going back in time. Years ago, when he had taken her hand like that, she had tingled all over in much the same way she had shivered yesterday.

And she had wanted...

More. Though she would never admit to as much aloud, she had wanted to kiss him. To feel his strength around her, his arms encircling her.

But she knew where that led. They had been at the foot of that path before, leading up to the mountain, with all the pleasures that the peak promised, and they had never ventured up it before, despite much provocation.

She was not about to make that ascent now, not without some sort of assurance.

Vivienne almost laughed to herself. *Assurance!* What sort of assurance could Edwin offer her that would induce her to consider such a thing?

In the intervening years between then and now, she hoped she had a little more wisdom than to simply repeat one's mistakes. She had not changed, and neither had Edwin. Not really.

Glancing up, she saw Laura's pencil drawing had reached the northwest shoreline. *Good.* She should have a rough draft finished by the end of today's lessons.

Vivienne looked at her desk. It was absolutely covered in letters—letters which bore a London postmark yet were unopened.

In all her frantic attempts to make the servants like her, to understand Laura, to not fight with Edwin—a true challenge—her desire to restore the name of her Governess Bureau had not diminished, exactly, but it had fallen by the wayside.

She had not even managed to open the post that was being sent on from London.

What if there was good news in there? Vivienne picked up a letter, the handwriting unrecognizable, and wondered. *Good news.* The fate of the Bureau restored. Everyone ready to welcome her back to London and the Bureau with open arms.

She had almost started to open it when she halted. Bad news was more likely and would surely only depress her. Good news would take her away from Laura…from Edwin.

Her stomach lurched. *She may still be in love with Edwin*, she told herself firmly, *but absolutely nothing was going to happen. It wasn't!*

Footsteps along the corridor outside the schoolroom were perfectly normal, but they made Vivienne stiffen. She knew those footsteps. Would know them anywhere.

Her heart leapt, her pulse quickened, joy poured through her heart—and then she chastised herself silently. Wishing to see Edwin? Was she some fresh new girl in Society, hoping that anyone would spot her?

Edwin burst into the schoolroom. "Get up, get up, lessons are canceled!"

"Hurray!" said Laura, closing her sketchbook with a grin as Vivienne's mouth fell open.

"Canceled?" she said blankly, trying to quiet her racing heart. "What do you mean?"

"I want to go for a carriage ride, and I'll be perfectly dull without Laura," Edwin said cheerfully, grinning at his daughter. "And you can come, too, Miss Clarke. If you want to."

He had not looked at her as he spoke, and Vivienne could not tell whether he actually wished her to join them or whether he was merely being polite.

"Oh, a carriage ride!" said Laura, clearly thrilled. "I will go and retrieve my bonnet—wait for me here, Edwin!"

She rushed out of the schoolroom, leaving Vivienne and Edwin alone.

Vivienne cleared her throat. "You do not have to invite me. If you do not wish to."

Why was there a smile on his face? "I know."

Before Vivienne knew it, they were, somehow, all three of them, getting into the carriage on the Byhalden Lodge drive.

"—interesting book, I thought you might like it," Edwin was saying to his daughter as she settled next to him in the open barouche. "I have a spare copy."

"That sounds wonderful, thank you!" said Laura, a wide smile on her face. "Is it like…"

Vivienne watched them. They spoke so easily when they were not thinking about it. She sat opposite Laura, her back to the driver and the horses, and was given the entertainment of watching father and daughter discuss novels as the carriage jolted to a start along the drive and toward the road.

"—sounds terrible!" Edwin was teasing his daughter. Despite Vivienne's misgivings, Laura was laughing. "You cannot honestly tell me that you have read such nonsense!"

"I challenge you to read it yourself before you criticize!" said Laura forcefully, though still with a smile on her face. "See, I knew it—you won't read it!"

The conversation continued on in much the same vein. Vivienne was not required to contribute, and she was not entirely sure she would be able to. The wind rushed through her hair, the gray, dull day now sparkling with the delight of the Bysshes' conversation.

It was almost like…being a family.

The thought speared into her mind like an ice pick, although that might have been the cold wind. Vivienne swallowed, glancing at father and daughter. They were the family, and it did not include her. She had to remember that.

When she got back, she must read those letters. If all went well, she would be gone by Easter.

Chapter Fourteen

February 13, 1816

And that was why, in the end, it was all the same to her. As long as she had Peter, everything in the world was as it should be.

E DWIN'S GAZE FOLLOWED the last line of the book until the very last word. It could not be the end. He had been enjoying the book so much, he hadn't noticed he beheld the final page.

He turned over the page to the back, as though that could contain any more story. It was blank.

His heart sank as Edwin looked up and found himself right where he had sat down hours ago, in an armchair in the library. The book had so absorbed him that he had barely noticed where he was or what the time was.

There was nothing like reading a good book. His gaze was vague, not focusing on any of the books before him but instead ruminating on the pages he had just read.

It had taken him just this sitting to read it. Edwin knew he should not have rushed and should have savored each chapter, each page, each paragraph. It was a slight volume, he could tell by the binding, and once he realized the story was excellent, he should have slowed down and allowed himself more time to enjoy it.

But that was the problem with a good book, as he well knew. The better it was, the more one raced through it, and it was over so much quicker, to his great frustration.

The truth was, he had not expected it to be any good. The title had not promised much, and the author was entirely unknown to him.

But Laura had insisted that he could not criticize it unless he read it, and though Edwin was not one to usually say this, she had been right. He could see, now that he had turned the last page, why she had recommended it to him. It truly was a masterpiece of literature.

"You won't read it," she had said just last evening at the dinner table. "People always say that they will do something, and then they never do."

True, he had put it off a few days. After Laura had first mentioned it during their carriage ride, Edwin had looked at the book, the cheap binding, the complete lack of gold leaf, and assumed it was a dud.

But there had been such disappointment in her eyes, and the way she had spoken, such sad acceptance that he would never do something she wished…

His daughter could not have tugged at his heart strings with any more force.

Now he had bothered to complete his side of the bargain and read the stupid thing, Edwin had quickly realized it was not stupid at all. Far from it. It was a small work of art, one that had to be treasured.

He would have to ensure that Harris procured a copy, for he was loath to give this one back to Laura. The depths of the prose...he would have to think a while on the themes, too. He may even, surely to her great surprise, have to read it again in the next few days. Just to make sure he was not overly impressed this time.

Edwin smiled ruefully. He was not a great reader, in general. In fact, he could not recall the last time he had read a book cover to cover like this, let alone in one sitting. Laura had much to teach him, if only he could prevent himself from being so stubborn as to learn.

Only when he placed the book on the table beside him did Edwin look up at the clock on the mantelpiece to discover, to his genuine surprise, that it was late.

It was difficult to tell in these winter months, of course. It grew dark so early, one could be sitting in candlelight at four o'clock in the afternoon, and it looked no different to ten o'clock at night.

It was, in fact, almost eleven o'clock. The candles he had brought through were low, the fire almost out. He had neglected both, utterly lost in the story. A truly excellent book. Nothing but that could have absorbed his attention, forgoing cigar, wine, anything else that normally would be required of an evening.

He would have to remember to tell Laura. A slow smile crept over his face as Edwin pondered the conversation they could have about this impressive book. Would she be delighted that he had read it—grateful? Surprised?

There was certainly enough in the book itself that they could discuss. For such a slim volume, it had some important themes in there. Love. Loss. Family. *Themes*, Edwin thought dryly, *he had more of enough of in real life.*

Groaning slightly as he rose from his seat, Edwin stretched his arms and felt his joints creak. He was getting old. He rarely thought of it until he stood after a long period of sitting, then his body reminded him in no uncertain terms that he had passed the halfway point of life.

The candelabra only had two lit candles remaining, but Edwin blew them out without a second thought. He knew Byhalden Lodge like the back of his hand. Every room, every corridor, was precisely as it had been when he was born. The day he could not navigate it in the dark was the day to put him out to pasture.

The library door opened without a sound. He must remember to commend Harris on the footman who had done such an excellent job in keeping hinges in the place smooth, Edwin thought as he stepped out into the hall. There were few places with such quiet—

Movement. Edwin halted, silent in the doorway of the library. There was a light appearing at the top of the stairs. A single candle if he judged rightly by the spread of the light.

What was someone doing coming downstairs at this time of night? Heart thumping painfully in his chest, Edwin held his breath as though they would hear it across the gloom.

Laura should be in bed; the servants were either finishing closing down the kitchen or abed themselves. Who else could be—

As the light grew brighter, the candle came into view, held by Vivienne Clarke.

Edwin swallowed, then hoped she had not heard that, then chastised himself as a fool for thinking that she could hear such a thing. *Vivienne.* Why had he not thought of her?

The single candlelight transfused over her a strange sort of ethereal beauty.

Edwin had always known Vivienne was beautiful. It was one of the first things he had noticed about her. *Well, by God, he was a man, wasn't he? He had eyes, didn't he?*

But the shy, smiling girl he had met years ago was nothing compared to the majestic creature who was slowly and elegantly descending the stairs.

This woman's long hair was not tied up into a restrictive bun but was instead loose, fanning down her shoulders and back like molten gold, glittering in the candlelight. Her figure was effortlessly emphasized by the candlelight as she appeared to be wearing naught but a nightgown—and a cotton one at that.

Edwin swallowed. Now he had noticed that, he could not look away. The delicate material fell from her shoulders to the carpeted floor, but the way it clung to her curves...

Dear God, it was criminal what it was doing to him. Parts of him were awakening that certainly should not be. Not if he wanted to sleep tonight without a cold bath.

Vivienne was still slowly walking down the stairs, and Edwin knew she would probably wish to know that she was being observed. He should say something. He should make his presence known, make it clear to Vivienne that she was not alone.

Yet he stayed silent. *Was that not the pleasure of a Peeping Tom?* Was it not the looking when one knew one should look away that was so tantalizing?

Edwin's fingers itched to reach out and touch her, but he was both too far away and far too sensible to do such a thing. No, he would stand here, alone in the darkness, gifted with a sight he believed he would never see.

Vivienne's beauty was rather like that of a garden. Even in the drabbest of days, you could see that it was a pleasant place to be—but when the sun came out, you asked yourself how you had ever managed to stay away from it.

Edwin swallowed. That was the trouble with a woman whose mind was just as stunning as her outer appearance. When one attempted to focus on the mind, the wit, to protect oneself from the absolute dynamite that lay on the outside, it was easy to be blinded.

He felt blinded. Reaching out his fingers, he was surprised to find the doorframe still there. For all he knew, the world had disappeared, and all that was left was himself, standing here, and Vivienne, walking down the stairs.

She had reached the bottom now. For a terrible moment, it looked as though she was going to move toward the library, which would have necessitated a rather awkward conversation—but no. She moved across the hall to the door of the corridor for the servants' hall.

And then she was gone, taking the light of her candle.

Edwin swallowed. His mouth was dry, his heart pounding, and he seemed to have forgotten to breathe during the encounter.

He took in a deep, rattling breath and really did lean against the doorframe now. That he should witness such beauty, that he should be within touching distance of her and yet restrain himself…he should be a saint.

But he wasn't. Edwin knew the right thing to do was to immediately go to bed. Up the stairs that Vivienne had so seductively traipsed down, into his own bedchamber—most definitely alone—and attempt to sleep while his body raged for her sweet touch.

That was what he should do. It was late. It was not as though Vivienne had invited him into her chamber or even been seeking him out. She had descended for something in the kitchens perhaps, not his opinion or counsel.

Or company.

Edwin's jaw tightened. She was not even fully dressed. No, a gentleman would do the right thing and go upstairs immediately. A true gentleman would not have looked.

But even before the decision was made, Edwin knew precisely what it would be. *Well, he was not made of stone!* A better man, perhaps, would resist, but he was not that man and had no wish to be.

Whatever desire for Vivienne, which had lain dormant, was now awoken, though if Edwin could be honest with himself, it had been stirring since the moment she had set foot in his home. *His home. The place that should have been her home.*

Without a second thought, Edwin crossed the hall, reaching out in the darkness for the door to the servants' corridor.

Light poured out from under the door of the pantry, however, and then it blossomed into the kitchen as Vivienne reappeared with a pitcher of milk in her other hand. Setting it down on the table and then the candle, she moved silently across the room. A small earthen beaker was selected, and Vivienne returned to the table to pour a little milk.

Edwin watched her, transfixed. It was such a small thing, coming downstairs for a drink of something, yet at the same time so intimate. No one else had seen her. No one in the world had ever seen Vivienne like this.

Yet if things had transpired in a slightly different way, that would not have been the case. He would have seen this a thousand times, would have known precisely the way Vivienne's long blonde hair fell down her back, how she pushed it behind one ear when it got in the way. Edwin watched her fingers move, a loving look that he was glad she could not see.

It would certainly not do for that sort of nonsense to continue.

But he could not look away. What if they had wed? What if Vivienne had accepted his offer of marriage, if she had been able to look past her obsession with the Governess Bureau, and had been led, instead, by love of him? How would this scene be different?

Edwin smiled wistfully. He would probably have come downstairs to retrieve the milk for her. He could not imagine Vivienne leaving the warmth and comfort of her bed if she could smile and make him do it.

It was because he was not truly paying attention but instead was wrapped up in ideas of what their marital bliss could look like that Edwin accidentally knocked the doorframe with his boot.

It was a small sound. Any other time, it would have been hidden by the clatter and noise of the servants' hall; but there was no one else here but each other.

The noise echoed around the place as though he had sneezed in a cathedral. Vivienne immediately looked up, fear in her eyes. It could not be more clear that she considered herself in danger.

"Who's there?" Vivienne said, looking out into the darkness, evidently not entirely sure from whence the noise originated. "Mrs. Jenner? Is that you?"

Edwin held his breath once more. If he could just stand here, perhaps she would think it only the shifting noise of the timbers. Old houses made noises all the time, after all.

Vivienne was still looking around warily. "Show yourself!"

Edwin slowly let out the breath within him. *Well, it was not as though he had any choice.* She was correct in assuming someone was there, but she probably thought it was a maid who had forgotten a small chore or a footman who had left a newspaper down here.

What would she do when she saw it was the master of the house?

Stepping out into the glow of her candle, Edwin was not entirely sure what sort of expression he should show. A smile? Would that seem too predatory? *Was he being predatory?*

There was no time to interrogate that thought just now. Vivienne's eyes fell upon him, and her shoulders lowered as relief rushed over her.

"Oh, it's only you," she said with a sigh.

Then the fact of where they were, at what time, and what she was wearing appeared to catch up with her. Two tiny dots of red appeared on her cheeks, her gaze lowered, and she smoothed down her nightgown—then immediately fluffed it up, realizing just how clear her figure was through the material.

Edwin's jaw tightened. *Very clear.*

The sudden vision of a woman he had craved for over a decade was enough to entirely topple his self-resolve, and it took all within him to prevent himself from stepping forward and crushing her to him.

That, however, did not prevent his manhood from stiffening at the very vision of her. *Blast.* He needed to keep control, needed to prove to himself, if not to her, that she was not in charge of him. *He* wasn't in charge of him, but...

Edwin cleared his throat, and Vivienne looked up as though expecting him to speak, but there was nothing in his mind other than the fact that anyone would forgive him, surely, for the very physical reaction his body was having. Sweat trickled down his temple into his sideburns, his heart pounded, and there was a rather indignant lurch in his loins that were making demands he simply could not fulfill.

Well, it was not as though he was a monk with a vow of celibacy! And Henrietta had been gone a long time.

Moving a mistress into the place, though a tempting thought, simply had not been an option. Not with Laura in the house. He would never do anything to hurt her, and he could not imagine seeing her mother replaced, and with a harlot, would do much for their connection.

But whatever Vivienne was doing to him, albeit unconsciously, had to stop.

It took all of Edwin's concentration, but he was not a man of eighteen. He had learned self-control, knew what it was to deny himself to give a woman pleasure, and he would need to use all that self-control now.

So it was just a small step he took toward her. "Do not look so embarrassed," he said quietly. "What have you got to hide?"

It was a foolish thing to say, even he could see that. She had everything to hide; she was no virginal youth, but she was a maiden, and she was standing here, Edwin was only too painfully conscious, before him in her nightgown.

A nightgown that could so easily be removed. *With his teeth.*

Vivienne stepped away and flushed as though she could hear his licentious thoughts. "Despite...despite everything we shared, Edwin, we did not share that."

More's the pity, Edwin thought darkly. He had few regrets in life, there was simply no point in dwelling on them, but that was one. A few stolen kisses, that was all he had managed to share with Vivienne, despite his body groaning for relief as they had danced together, walked together, sat entwined on a sofa discussing music, art, science, their future...

That regret was growing with every passing moment as Edwin allowed his gaze to leave her face and trail down her body.

Dear God. She had been a wonderful girl then, but she had matured into an even more lovely woman.

And he could appreciate the beautiful form of a woman, couldn't he? That was not too outrageous. As long as he did not touch. *Christ alive, he wanted to touch her.*

"We did not share that," he said quietly, "even though I wish we had."

It was an idiotic, vulnerable thing to say, and Edwin was not entirely sure why he had said it. If he could not be honest with Vivienne now, when he could?

Vivienne managed to meet his eyes. "You...you think about that?"

"Yes, of course," Edwin said, the words tripping off his tongue uncensored. And why not? When he had been courting Miss Vivienne Clarke, one of the things he had loved was how honest they could be with each other. "But even more so since you came here. Since you arrived at Byhalden Lodge, Vivienne, it has...damn. It has been something I have thought of too often."

He could not stop staring, knew he had to look away, but what possible sight in the world could give as much beauty as she?

Vivienne's voice was almost a whisper as she said, "So have I."

It took Edwin a moment to take in the three syllables, and even when he assured his brain that was what she said, it did not seem to register. *Did...did ladies think of such things?*

Vivienne laughed. "Do not be so surprised! There are...desires that even ladies have, even if one does not speak about them in public."

"No, it was just...I did not think you thought of me at all?"

"How can you say that?" Her voice was gentle, soft, but at the same time reproachful. It was a dagger to his heart. "After all we have shared, all we had been to each other...have been to each other. You think I can forget..."

Vivienne's voice appeared unable to continue, though Edwin

was desperate for her to share more. *What did she miss?* Was it the same things he yearned for, or perhaps little moments of romantic perfection that he had, over time, forgotten?

He caught her gaze and saw such desire that he almost staggered back, overpowered by the sense of passion.

Dear God. She had not been jesting with him nor lying to make him feel better. Vivienne desired him. She wanted him, just as he wanted her.

Edwin stepped toward her. "Do you remember the first time we kissed?"

A mischievous smile crept across her face, the candlelight flickering. "You should not have kissed me then, either."

"I know," said Edwin softly. "But I wanted to."

Fifteen years ago. How could fifteen years disappear so quickly, taking with them all the promise a year could bring? All the opportunities missed, all the days spent apart...Edwin could hardly bear to think about them.

The smile on Vivienne's face had not disappeared. "It was about to rain—"

"It was raining."

"It was about to rain," she repeated, almost chuckling, "and you said that you shouldn't keep me out any later."

The memory was sorrowful and beautiful. Its bittersweet taste was soaring through his heart, and it ached with the desperation to return to that moment. A moment of pure bliss, Edwin remembered. Even in the rain.

"I shouldn't have kept you out that late," he said hoarsely as the memories of that first kiss rushed over him, as though it had been yesterday.

A lazy smile had flickered over his face, but Vivienne now looked...upset?

"You...you cannot turn back the clock, Edwin," she said in a low voice. "No matter how much we might...it is not possible. We are not those people anymore."

Edwin's breath was tight in his chest. "I know that, but sometimes it is like—like we are discovering each other all over again. As though the hurt and the pain of the past could be wiped away."

He was mere inches from her now, a tantalizing distance that was playing havoc with his ability to think. Perhaps that was why he was saying such nonsense.

"Besides," he said, trying to catch his breath. "I don't need to go back in time. I have you here, now, right before me. Don't I?"

It was the merest nod, but Edwin saw it and took it as the permission he needed. Pulling Vivienne into his arms, where she belonged, filling the gap that had been left fifteen years ago, Edwin pressed his lips on hers and almost cried out with the joy of it.

He was home. She was it; she was everything. The glory of their connection, her warmth beside his, his heart beating against hers.

Edwin pulled her close, his hands deliciously sinking into her flesh, the nightgown proving no barrier to his touch, and he knew that this was it. He would never kiss any other woman again. He had no need to. He had no wish to.

The kiss ended, regretfully, far too early. Edwin stood there, Vivienne in his arms, and they looked at each other in silence.

Thinking was not particularly possible, but Edwin did his best. What happened next? Other than Vivienne never leaving him and accepting him once and for all…

"W-What does this mean?" Vivienne managed.

Edwin hesitated. This was a vulnerability he had not known. When he had first courted Vivienne, he had hardly hidden his intentions; the world could see and smile for all he cared.

No longer. Whatever he had thought when following her here, it had been a lustful consideration, not anything logical.

Vivienne's frown had reappeared. "Don't you think you should work that out before you kiss me again?"

"Again?"

The slight flush reappeared in her cheeks. "I can't help but feel this is going to hurt us."

"Kisses only," Edwin said. Whatever reassurance she needed, whatever he would say to prevent her from thinking he was taking advantage of her.

Which he wasn't. Was he?

Vivienne did not look impressed. "You're making me promises now?"

Edwin tried to think, but the warmth of Vivienne's breasts against his shirt was certainly not helping. He could promise her nothing; he knew that. She knew that, too, or she would not be looking at him with such an unamused expression.

This was dangerous, and they both could see that. Had they not earned the opportunity to be happy?

"No complicated promises," he said quietly, looking deep into her eyes. "I will expect no more of you, not tonight—but tonight, I do want this."

Edwin lowered his lips once more to hers, and was met with an answering moan and Vivienne's tongue meeting his. *Kissing for tonight.* If that was all he could be promised, well—he would take all he could get.

Chapter Fifteen

February 19, 1816

THERE WAS SOMETHING incredibly satisfying, Vivienne thought as she looked down at the carefully constructed sandwich on her plate, about eating food one did not pay for.

Admittedly, she would be receiving a higher wage if she were expected to feed herself with the proceeds, but still. In the kitchens at Byhalden Lodge, there was food aplenty and little concern for helping oneself—unless it was from whatever was stewing, baking, roasting, or frying, which was Cook's domain.

Woe betide any footman who decided to sneak a little for himself.

The initial rush of luncheon had already occurred that day. Vivienne, delayed by her tidying of the schoolroom, had descended to find most of the food platters empty, and those that were left being taken away by one of the scullery maids for the stock pot.

Mr. Harris saw her forlorn expression. "Don't you fret, gel, we'll find ye something."

The soft, Yorkshire roll of his voice did just as much to calm and console Vivienne as the food that was offered: a tray of bread and butter, slices of ham, a pot of mustard, two cold sausages, a tomato, and more drippings than Vivienne knew what to do with.

The butler's eyes had twinkled. "If it's too good for those upstairs, I say, then it's good enough for us down here. Go on, gel. Eat your sandwich."

Vivienne had met the Earl of Sandwich—at least, the son of the man who had invented the sandwich. She wondered as she chewed happily on the delicious succulent ham sandwich, how anyone had managed to live without it. He had been a pleasant man, as earls went, but far too interested in ensuring that everyone knew he was the Earl of Sandwich.

That was the trouble with aristocrats. The truly great ones never needed to prove that they were important. They just...were. Take Edwin, for example.

Vivienne's cheeks flushed as the thought trickled into her mind. She really must not think of the man—at least, not in public. Not if her cheeks were to immediately give her away.

"Besides, I don't need to go back in time. I have you here, now, right before me. Don't I?"

She had managed, in the main, to conduct herself as a rational, calm human being all morning. Laura had inquired about London a few times, which had been tiring, but Vivienne had guided her toward the important topic of Latin, and that had endured all morning.

Because she really should not be thinking of Edwin. Of how warm and safe she had felt in his arms. How right it was that they had kissed, right here, in this hall—

"Miss Clarke!"

Vivienne rose hurriedly, napkin falling to the ground, at the sudden sound of her name, her cheeks aflame.

"Now then, I did not mean to startle you," Mrs. Jenner said as she passed a few maids to reach the table, a distressed look on her face. "Oh, let me help you."

To Vivienne's shame, the housekeeper reached down herself

to retrieve the fallen napkin and offered it out to the governess.

"I did not mean to interrupt your luncheon," said Mrs. Jenner with a warm smile. "Please, sit yourself."

Vivienne slowly lowered onto the chair and wished to goodness that she would not look so startled to hear her own name spoken in the servants' hall. Was she not a servant, too, like the rest of them?

"I think you wanted the newspapers from the last few days," said Mrs. Jenner, as though nothing had happened—*which*, Vivienne reminded herself, *was the truth*. "Here, I collected them from the library and thought I would share them with you before little Bessy used them for laying under the carpets."

Vivienne nodded, cheeks still flushed, not trusting her voice. *Why was it impossible for her to converse about something as dull as the master's newspapers?*

She knew why. Because now he had kissed her, it was as though Edwin had branded her. As though she expected the world to look at her and *see*, just by the way his lips had touched hers, that they had passionately shared what should only have been shared between a husband and wife.

Vivienne swallowed. It had been a strange few days since that unexpected encounter. She had not attempted to entice him, had not expected him to spot her.

Yet he had, and since then, Vivienne had felt the strangeness of the situation in her very bones. Every step she took was one after Edwin had passionately kissed her. Every item of clothing she wore was one Edwin had not touched as he brought her into his embrace.

And it had been hot and glorious and wonderful and…

Never to be repeated, Vivienne told herself firmly. That was the mistake that would be easy to make, and she was determined not to make it.

What had it meant? She did not know, and she had seen in Edwin's eyes that he had not known either. *Probably just the last hurrah of a passion never spent*, she thought bitterly. The last remnants of the desire he had for her from all those years ago.

And now it was over. Edwin had shown no sign of wishing to repeat the encounter, other than informing her through the housekeeper that the governess was required to dine every evening with him and Laura.

Vivienne swallowed. When she had first arrived here, she had been determined to ensure that she would not be hurt. Now she was not so sure if that was possible.

"I had thought there would be more."

Vivienne blinked. "More?"

Mrs. Jenner stared with great concern. "Newspapers, Miss Clarke, newspapers. I said, I thought here would be more, but then his lordship has been in York the last few days."

Vivienne nodded silently. That would indeed make sense, and she had no desire to make a fool out of herself by attempting to speak anything else.

Besides, she had been highly conscious that Edwin had been out of the house. The lodge did not feel the same without him, somehow—which was nonsense. She was not its mistress to miss the presence of the master. *Even if she did.*

Mrs. Jenner rustled the newspapers and narrowed her gaze. "So, do you want them?"

"Them?"

"The newspapers, Miss Clarke!" For the first time, Mrs. Jenner sounded exasperated. "I don't know what's got into you today, but you are mightily distracted. Did you sleep poorly?"

"Sleep poor—yes, I slept very ill," said Vivienne, grasping gratefully at the excuse.

A softening expression covered the housekeeper's face. "Ah, I know what it is to struggle with sleep. You have my sympathy. Why, I said to Mr. Harris only the other day…"

Vivienne nodded at all the right places as the story washed over her. Perhaps she should start mentioning that excuse frequently. It was a fine one, very difficult to disprove, and would prevent her from being accused of not attending.

"—and so here you are," finished Mrs. Jenner, placing the newspapers on the table.

She smiled. "Thank you, Mrs. Jenner. I am most grateful."

There was a loud sniff from behind her. Vivienne turned to see Mr. Harris looking unimpressed.

"All those London newspapers," he said disparagingly. "I don't know why you need them, Miss Clarke, if I may be so bold. The place is miles away, a hundred miles! Far more interesting things happen near hereabouts."

Vivienne smiled. It had been her observation at her first governessing post, and all those subsequent, that it was most people's belief that the world centered around them—or at least if not them, their small community.

"I am sure, Mr. Harris," she said aloud. "But it is part of my role to keep up to date with political affairs, you see, so that I may educate Laura on the ongoing situation in France."

"France!" sniffed Mr. Harris if possibly even louder. "Well, thems as has the misfortune not to be born an Englishman cannot be helped, I suppose."

"Indeed," said Vivienne with a slight smile. "Well, if you will excuse me, Mr. Harris, Mrs. Jenner, I will start reading to ensure Miss Laura's education."

It was a polite enough goodbye that the two older servants left her quite happily, and Vivienne was able to open up the pages of the newspaper with one hand while happily eating the remainder of her sandwich with the other.

Her eyes darted over each page. She had not been entirely truthful when giving Mr. Harris the reason why she wished to read the newspapers, but then, it was a rather personal matter.

The Governess Bureau. Vivienne sighed as she turned the pages, the paper crinkled under her fingers. She had neglected her Bureau, the very reason she had come to Byhalden Lodge, and that had to change. If she was not careful, she would be here far longer than she needed, merely because she had not given the Bureau the attention it deserved.

The Governess Bureau's reputation had to be restored, and that could only be done once the gossip about her and her governesses had died down. Vivienne had promised herself she would keep a close eye on the slander in the newspapers, a task she had abandoned.

She had not been able to avoid paying the interest on the loans she had taken out, of course. Vivienne had known it was a risk, and at the time, it was a calculated risk. A risk that now felt reckless.

Avoiding the Governess Bureau had been a habit she had slipped into at the lodge. It was easier to avoid the potentially damaging truth.

But no longer. As she finished the last delicious mouthful of her ham sandwich, Vivienne looked carefully over the headlines, then scanned the paragraphs below.

It was only when she reached page twenty that Vivienne noticed she had not yet seen her name. Nothing had been said about the Bureau. There had not even been sarcastic flippant remarks about her when denigrating someone else.

Her heart fluttered, skipping a beat. *Maybe she had missed it.*

Turning to the front page, Vivienne took more care this time, scanning more slowly and attempting to make sure that she was not missing anything.

This time she had reached the editor's letters before noticing that she still had not seen a mention of the Governess Bureau. No snide remarks, no jests at her expense…nothing.

Vivienne stared at the print beneath her fingertips. She was not sure she believed her eyes. For months, she had been plagued with upsetting articles, letters, remarks, all at her expense. She had become the laughingstock of London and, therefore, in her mind, the world.

Unable to pick up a paper without seeing something shameful—and usually incorrect—mentioned about her, Vivienne had given up hope, for a time, that it would ever end.

But here was the proof. The second newspaper proved to be

just as empty of harsh remarks about the Governess Bureau. True, there were a few more advertisements seeking governesses than normal, but Vivienne had to assume that was because no one was able to procure outstanding governesses from her Bureau. It appeared the nobility of England was having to resort to shilling advertisements.

She swallowed. *So...was it over?* Had she managed to weather the storm, even if it had meant leaving London entirely and throwing herself into a governess position?

Most exciting of all, did this mean that she could return to London, opening up the Governess Bureau again, and slowly but surely welcome new governesses and new clients?

It was a heady thought. Vivienne's mind spun with the possibilities: the delights of being back in London, seeing the sights she was so accustomed to, living in her own apartment again over the Governess Bureau.

But as with any opportunity that could be grasped, there was a corresponding cost. To return to London meant, by definition, to leave Byhalden Lodge.

Vivienne looked around her. The servants' hall was almost entirely empty now, servants returned to their chores. There was a pleasant hum of busyness through the archway to the kitchen, and there were teasing shrieks of laughter coming from the two scullery maids.

She smiled. It appeared the gossip of Hannah's affection for one of the footmen was spreading like wildfire.

Perhaps that was what was making her hesitate. At the Governess Bureau, she was the stern and aloof Miss Clarke; no one was friendly precisely because she made it perfectly clear that no one was to be so.

It was far more important, she had always thought, to hold herself a distance from them. The governesses.

Only now did Vivienne wonder whether that had been part of the problem all along. None of them had felt able to come to her for help or advice, and she...she had been lonely. She could admit it now, in the warmth and security of the servants' hall.

Perhaps that was what she did not want to give up.

Liar, thought a mischievous voice in the back of her mind. *The companionship of servants, you think that will hold you back from proving your point? No, this is all about Edwin.*

The mere thought of his name made her stomach squirm. It was true; she could not deny it to herself. The success of the Bureau would mean an end to whatever was burgeoning between them. It would mean her removal, her abandonment of him.

No, not abandonment. Vivienne tried as she rustled the pages of the third newspaper, to push that thought from her mind. She was not abandoning him. If she stayed here, she would surely be abandoning the Governess Bureau.

A bitter chill seemed to sweep down her body, and Vivienne tried but failed to concentrate on the printed words before her.

It always seemed to come down to this, a pull between Edwin and the Governess Bureau. It had been that way when they had first been courting—and now here they were again.

"Are you finished with that tray, Miss Clarke?"

Vivienne looked up. Mrs. Jenner was standing politely beside her, evidently waiting for her to leave the servants' hall.

Pushing back the chair hastily, Vivienne stood up. It was not precisely a rule—nothing so formal as that—but it was expected that once a person had finished consuming their meal, they would leave the servants' hall. It would then become the domain of the butler and housekeeper for their ledgers. Their little place of operation.

If anyone understood that, it was Vivienne. Had she not her own office at the Governess Bureau? The people in charge needed a place to be in charge, she knew.

"Yes, I thank you," said Vivienne aloud, smiling and lifting up the tray. "I will take it through—and you may give the newspapers to Bessy. I am finished with them now. Thank you for saving them for me."

The housekeeper inclined her head. "My pleasure, Miss Clarke. Good afternoon."

It was a polite but firm dismissal. As Vivienne took her tray through to the scullery maid for cleaning, she saw how industriously the kitchen maids were being worked.

"Lumpy sauce, oh wonderful," said Cook with a stern look. "That is precisely what I wanted, thank you Abigail!"

Vivienne slipped out of the kitchen before Cook's temper could be really riled. Besides, everyone else was busy at their afternoon tasks, and she...she had nothing to do. It was a rather awkward situation, but there it was.

A child the age of Laura did not need babysitting. She had much to learn in the mornings, and perhaps as Lent began, Vivienne would start to increase the amount of time the child spent in the schoolroom—but Laura had many other calls on her time.

As Vivienne walked along the corridor toward the east side of the house, she passed the music room. Mozart soared under the door until a rather unpleasant discord.

"No, Miss Laura, more care on your finger work, please!" came the irritated voice of Monsieur Pierre. "Again, please."

Vivienne suppressed a smile. If there was one frequent and consistent complaint from her governesses' reports over the years, it was the conflict between governess and tutors. She had not understood it back in London, reading letter after letter of complaints. She did now.

What else had she missed by not taking up appointments herself? It was a strange thought, one Vivienne did not wish to dwell on. A great deal of things, she suspected.

The drawing room was, to her relief, empty. Vivienne had endeavored to avoid Edwin after their passionate kissing in the servants' hall, and his journey to York had made that easier—but he had returned now.

Seating herself in the soft armchair by the window, Vivienne tried to think logically.

So, the newspapers had not mentioned the Governess Bureau. More, they had not used her as a standing joke, referenced the Bureau to mock another, nor printed any hateful letters about her or her governesses.

Vivienne took a deep, slow breath. Of course, that did not mean that no letters had been received. Wouldn't they have printed them if they had them?

Perhaps not. Perhaps she was old news. Perhaps there were more interesting things to complain about at the moment, though she could not for the life of her think what.

So was that it? Was this the end of her trial and tribulations? Was it worth considering now what her plans were in terms of leaving Byhalden Lodge?

Even the thought depressed her. A heavy, sinking feeling fell into her stomach like she had swallowed an iron weight, and Vivienne did not like it. She had promised herself no entanglements when she came to the Bysshe household—not purely because it was in direct contradiction of the third rule, but because Edwin...

Edwin. Vivienne felt the iron weight shift and hated herself for being so easily won.

"*No complicated promises. I will expect no more of you, not tonight—but tonight, I do want this.*"

Vivienne hardened her heart. *He had been right.* There was nothing to be promised, nothing that could justify any further entanglements of that sort.

Though in the moment, she had felt as though everything was soaring toward a wonderful conclusion—precisely what, she could not guess—there was absolutely no knowing whether what she felt for him was merely stirred up remembrances of the past or something...

Something new.

What had he said to her? Try as she might, Vivienne could not perfectly recollect all that Edwin had said, his breathing heavy against her breasts, his fingers stroking her waist teasingly, sending her mind into a spiral of delight which could not be satisfied.

That was always the trouble with Edwin's kisses, she was remembering now. They were so delectable, so overwhelming, that anything around them faded into insignificance.

If only she did not love him. If only, Vivienne thought darkly, *she would tear these feelings from her heart and be done with them.* What good were they doing her?

None, and yet she was lumbered with them. Unable to lie to herself and unable to move forward, Vivienne could not help but think about that wonderful kiss again. She shivered. It was most unfair that Edwin should be so handsome. *If she could go back…*

The proposal in the park could have ended so differently, she supposed, yet how would that have helped? Would she have been here in this very armchair, looking out at the cold frosty day, just as lonely, just as trapped by circumstances?

Would the love have faded, disappearing after a few years, leaving them with nothing but contempt? Would she, in fact, regret not pursuing the Governess Bureau far more than she now regretted not pursuing Edwin?

"Am I disturbing you?"

Startled, Vivienne looked around to see Edwin. He was standing by the fire, warming his hands. *When had he entered the room? Why had she not noticed him?*

It was on the tip of her tongue to say that yes, he was disturbing her greatly. "No, not at all. Why not join me?"

Her hand rose unconsciously to indicate the sofa opposite her, and Vivienne looked down at it in astonishment. *Now what had possessed her to say such a thing?*

It appeared she could not stay away from him. Vivienne sighed internally and wondered whether this was the perfect example of why she should return to London. *What good could come of torturing herself here?*

She was certainly not to be trusted. As Edwin stepped across the room to join her, Vivienne wondered just where her self-restraint had gone.

The longer she stayed here, however, the more obvious it was becoming that she had lost something in remaining so distinct from others. The warmth of human kindness.

"I hear you have been reading my newspapers," Edwin said conversationally.

Vivienne swallowed. "I—Mrs. Jenner said it was permissible once you had finished with them."

He shrugged in response. "Oh, it doesn't matter. I should have thought to ensure two were ordered daily so that you could keep up to date with the goings-on in London. I will have Harris make a note."

It was a small act of kindness, one that Vivienne should not have been surprised by. Edwin had always been kind when she had known him in their youth. It was why his cold and harsh temper had taken her by such surprise when she had come here.

But that was thawing. Like the snow after a long winter, he was warming to her.

Vivienne glanced toward the window to prevent herself from merely staring at the gentleman opposite her. It was starting to snow.

"I don't read newspapers much anyway these days," said Edwin easily. "They just seem to say the same things that I was reading twenty years ago."

Vivienne smiled. "You don't think the world ever changes?"

She turned back to him, could not help herself. Any chance to look at him was one she would take. After all, she would not be at Byhalden Lodge forever.

Edwin shrugged. "Some important things don't change, but everything else does."

The way he looked at her as he spoke…Vivienne was not entirely sure whether to be pleased or concerned.

"Well," she said lightly, "I do not believe you have changed that much."

He laughed at that. "For better or for worse?"

For an instant, Vivienne was concerned she had offended him—but he did not look upset. There was a knowing grin on his face.

"Well, perhaps both," she admitted.

Edwin looked at her for a moment without speaking, then said, "You know, it's strange, talking of the past. You were so...so beautiful."

A flash of red-hot anger and shame rushed through Vivienne's body. *The blaggard!* How dare he speak to her like that? To be sure, she had noticed the faint signs of time upon her face and person, but there was no reason for—

"It just goes to show how little time matters," Edwin continued. "You are far more beautiful now than you ever were if that is possible."

Now it was Vivienne's turn to laugh. "You cannot be serious."

But Edwin was not laughing. "What, you think I don't see those curves? Didn't feel the softness of your skin, the warmth of your body? You think your eyes have lost their hue, their sparkle? You believe your smile to be less captivating?"

He could not be serious. He could certainly not be in his right mind. What did he think he was doing, speaking of her like that?

"That smile, ever knowing," said Edwin, his voice hoarse but his eyes never leaving her. "Those lips, tantalizing and inviting and yet so delicate. So precious..."

His voice faded away. Though Vivienne tried to look away, she found she could not.

Here they were, on a precipice. She could feel it, the opportunity to fall into something...something they should deny themselves. *Or should they?* Was this their second chance at happiness? If they allowed themselves, they could be happy.

Yes, happy for a time, but how long? Vivienne knew it would end somehow, and then would they not feel worse?

Edwin coughed. "I have embarrassed you."

"A little," Vivienne said honestly.

He chuckled. "Well, that is only fair. I never feel far from embarrassed with you. I always feel off kilter."

Her astonishment must have shown on her face.

"Do not misunderstand me. I like it," Edwin said quietly. "I like feeling off-kilter with you. As though at any point, I could kiss you again. That you would want me to kiss you."

Vivienne swallowed. This was no nighttime accidental meeting, when bodies were tired, and self-control was low. This was the middle of the afternoon when anyone could catch them. Anyone could hear them.

The fact that she wanted to kiss him, to be kissed by him, was neither here nor there. This was a slippery slope down into potential disaster.

Edwin had made her no promises. She had to hold onto that fact. Though, in a way, she did not want them, it could not be denied that he was not thinking about this logically; he did not appear to be thinking at all.

Vivienne swallowed. *In a few months, she would be leaving.*

"Of course, I will not be kissing you," Edwin said with a heavy sigh, and Vivienne found her heart twisting with disappointment. "Couldn't be discovered kissing my daughter's governess. That would be scandalous."

"It would indeed," Vivienne agreed softly.

"But would it be so bad?"

Vivienne stared, utterly overwhelmed. Hot and cold, warm and unkind, Edwin was confusing her greatly. Who was he? What did he want from her?

"This could have been our home, you know," said Edwin quietly, his eyes never leaving her, "with our daughter down the corridor, murdering Mozart."

Vivienne rose to her feet. *This was too much.* "You must excuse me, my lord."

"No, wait, Vivienne—"

"I do not know what is worse," said Vivienne, taking a few steps away from the outstretched hand that was so tempting.

"Your ice-cold temper, or this strange warmth! Storming off in a huff or staying here and starting to realize that I...that I—"

"Yes?" Edwin had risen, too, and Vivienne knew she had to leave.

She swallowed down what she could have said, that she did not understand if he was just doing this to hurt her, and strode away. "This is too much—you want too much from me!"

CHAPTER SIXTEEN

February 23, 1816

"You must know where it is," said Edwin, temper fraying at the edges but so far, unheard in his voice.

At least, that's what he hoped. He was doing his utmost to keep his frustration from his tone, but then Laura always had a special knack for hearing irritation where there was none. There was no hope that she would fail to hear it when it was actually there.

"I said," said Laura in the same clipped tones, "I have no idea where it is."

Edwin took a deep breath. This would not have happened if Laura had good habits about tidying things away. On the rare occasion that she actually did it, no wonder she found it difficult to remember where a single thing was.

Children. He had little experience of them save Laura, but surely they could not all be this untidy, this forgetful, this...this annoying!

Laura was still rummaging through the pianoforte stool. The lid lifted off and provided the perfect place to store sheet music, which was why he had expected the music to be there. Where it should be. Where Laura should have been keeping it the entire time.

"It's not here," she said unhelpfully with tired eyes. "I don't know where else to look."

Edwin took another deep breath. Why was this so infuriating? Why was he permitting himself to be so easily swayed by his emotions at the moment?

One answer came immediately to mind, of course, but he pushed it away. This had nothing to do with Vivienne. Nothing at all. His mind wasn't constantly affixed on the woman who was in his house and not in his bed. *Blast*.

"Well, you would know where it was if you kept this place tidy!" Edwin exploded, finally pushed beyond endurance as he rubbed at his eyes.

The clocks of the lodge started chiming the hour. Nine o'clock, far past Laura's bedtime. She should go upstairs, leave the music for another day, but she was determined.

I wonder where she gets that from, Edwin thought wryly.

"I said it should be here, and it isn't, which means it has been put somewhere else and not by me!" cried Laura defensively, rising to her feet, cheeks pinking with indignation.

"You are the one who should be keeping this place tidy," said Edwin, raising a finger to point at his daughter while wishing he had not. "When you asked for a music room—"

"It was your idea!"

"All young ladies learn the—"

"What in God's name is going on?"

Edwin blinked. That had not been Laura. The doorway to the hall was open, and standing in the frame was…

He tried not to show how easily he was distracted by the vision of perfection. Vivienne looked utterly astonished, her gaze moving between himself and Laura.

Only then did he realize he was still holding out a finger pointed at his daughter. Edwin dropped it, feeling the foolishness of his position. Surely there could not be many fathers shouting at their daughter about a little lost sheet music.

"Well?" said Vivienne as she stepped into the room with an eyebrow raised. "What is all this ruckus about?"

It was most unfair, thought Edwin darkly as he attempted to remain calm. There was something about the way a governess could look at you, even if you were in your late thirties and older than the governess in question.

There was a particular pitch or tone that made it impossible to speak back to her. One felt about five years old again, more likely to be sent back to the nursery than be able to have a civilized conversation.

And it was not as though he'd had many civilized conversations with Vivienne since...well. Since one that had been almost shamefully blatant about his regard for her, and she had left the room without as much as a suggestion that she cared for him, too.

Well, a small suggestion. But nothing compared to what he had admitted.

It had been most embarrassing, and Edwin had ensured to be in York the last two days. No dinners with Laura and Vivienne when he could not stop snarling at one and wanting to kiss the other.

Besides, it was not as though he could say much else to Vivienne. There were no promises Edwin could make, nothing that could restore the time they had lost.

Yes, he wanted to bed her. Edwin had accepted that finally; there was no point in attempting to lie to himself. But what else did he want? Vivienne in his life? Vivienne by his side, forever?

Edwin cleared his throat. "We...we were..."

His voice trailed away as Vivienne's sharp gaze moved to him. Why did she have to be so damn beautiful? Why did she leave him breathless right when he wanted to speak to her, tell her what she meant to him. *If he knew what she meant to him.*

Laura was speaking, attempting to explain the predicament they found themselves in, and Edwin allowed the words to flow over him. He was far more interested in looking at Vivienne.

She was wearing a rather fetching sky blue gown he had not seen before. Or perhaps he had never noticed it before. It set off her blonde hair beautifully, a fact he was certain she was well aware of. And even if he did speak, offer himself once more, ask her for a second time to be his wife...

Edwin shivered. *She would not marry him.* He knew Vivienne, perhaps better than she knew herself. She had her precious Bureau to return to, didn't she? That was the reason she was reading the newspapers, there could surely be no other reason.

"My lord?"

She was waiting until the furor died down, then she would return. She was a smart woman, his Vivienne. Find a country gentleman's home to hide in, and then return to London when it was possible to start rebuilding. The best he could hope for was a single night of passion. *Was that enough? Could he live with it?*

"My lord?"

Edwin could hardly believe he was asking himself that question. After being sidelined once before because of the Governess Bureau, was that not enough?

Was he really willing to live alongside it in Vivienne's affections?

"Edwin!"

Edwin started. Laura was staring, and now he was paying attention, he noticed Vivienne was staring at him, too.

Ah. He had become lost in his thoughts. How embarrassing.

At least he wasn't drooling.

"Yes, right," he said aloud, conscious he had probably been asked a question and with no clue what it was. "So the situation is as follows. Laura has lost—"

"Mislaid!" interrupted his daughter, taking a step toward him in fury. "Mislaid, Edwin, it is only momentarily not in the place where I had expected it to be!"

Edwin smiled. All of a sudden, the whole thing seemed rather small and insignificant. Almost joyful. He was having a domestic dispute with his daughter. When was the last time they had done such a thing? He could not remember.

No, Laura would have always gone to Mrs. Jenner, or in dire need, Harris.

But she had come to him. It was he who she had asked to help find the music, and though he had neither found the music nor restrained himself from shouting at her, they were doing it together. It was a small victory in his rather incoherent parenting, but it was one he was willing to celebrate.

"Mislaid," he said softly.

Laura opened her mouth—in all likelihood to argue, Edwin thought—then closed it.

He glanced at Vivienne, who was smiling, and this caused a ridiculously large grin to creep over his face.

"Laura has mislaid some of her pianoforte music," he continued aloud. "We are looking for it. Rather unsuccessfully, though, I say so myself."

Laura crossed her arms with a huff but said nothing.

"Hmm," said Vivienne. "A definite pickle. I think it may be a worthwhile endeavor, Laura, if we investigate the schoolroom and leave your father to look elsewhere, too. Come on."

It was a suggestion spoken with no expectation of disagreement, and Edwin was not surprised to see Laura meekly lower her head and follow Vivienne out of the room.

The only downside to this was that Vivienne was no longer here. Edwin felt the loss of her presence like a hole in his heart, twinned rather surprisingly with the absence of his daughter.

The two women in his life who truly meant something. Edwin cleared his throat in the silence of the room. He was starting to get a little sentimental there.

He should be looking, too. He could well imagine the fallout in tempers if Vivienne and Laura were to return to discover he had not moved an inch. The trouble was, Edwin could not for the life of him think where Laura might have put her sheet music that wasn't right here in the music room.

Edwin closed his eyes as though that would help him think better. Was there a chance perhaps that in the busyness of the day, Mrs. Jenner had not examined the papers closely and instead merely put them in his study? He had instructed, after all, that all papers left about the house should be placed on his desk. It was the only way he could find things that he himself left around the place.

Edwin opened his eyes with a wry smile. *Perhaps he and Laura were far more alike than he thought.*

It was a possibility, and so far, the one place that he could think the music could be. With that in mind, he left the drawing room and started towards his study.

The study and the music room were, by design, on entirely different sides of the house. It was while Edwin was walking along the corridor that he attempted to remind himself that he was starting to become sentimental, and it would certainly not do to become so.

Vivienne was not Laura's mother.

It was not something he had actively thought, but the way the two of them laughed together, read together, walked in the grounds and sketched…

Well, it was easy to see how the connection could be made.

At the end of the day, Edwin thought sadly, *Henrietta was not much of a mother to Laura in the first place.* She had wanted a doll, really, a little girl who would obey without question and permit herself to be dressed up. He should have bought his wife a pony.

As it was, Vivienne was a far better role model for Laura, but she was not a mother. She was not his wife.

Even if he may… Edwin stopped himself as he turned a corner onto the west corridor which had the study at one end. *No.* He would not even permit himself to think it. This was going nowhere, and he needed to remember that.

He never locked the study, for he saw no need, with servants coming in and out to clean and tidy it, and Mrs. Jenner and Harris often returning papers he had scattered about the place back onto his desk.

There were still the dull embers of a fire in the grate, making it possible to see across the room. His desk was utterly covered in papers.

"Blast," Edwin muttered as he approached it.

If he had not been so...well, distracted by a certain woman living in his household, perhaps he would have been able to keep the damn place tidy.

But as it was, the desk was stacked high with a mess of papers with no discernable order to them. Receipts, bills, wage slips that required his signature, tenant requests that needed reading, a note from his lawyer about a strange letter he had received about Laura, his banker's reminder that interest rates were soaring, or falling, or whatever they were doing...

Edwin heaved a heavy sigh. And, of course, the newspaper clippings, letters, and reports about the Governess Bureau.

He had almost forgotten he had commissioned those. It felt like such a long time ago that Smethly had written to him, and his emotions had changed about the whole thing.

That was the trouble. They changed on an almost daily basis.

Making a mental note to throw out all the papers regarding the Governess Bureau at the earliest opportunity, Edwin tried to sift through some of the paper detritus to look for the sheet music. It was almost impossible not to cause an accidental avalanche as a tranche of papers slipped from one side of the desk and onto the floor.

"Damn it," Edwin muttered, though with an element of good nature.

He would have to dedicate some time tomorrow into sifting through all this. Vivienne would have to wait—she certainly would, as she had no idea how drastically his affections had changed from the moment she had arrived here.

Edwin half hoped that below the top layer he would immediately find the sheet music. It was not just the principle of the thing—Laura needed to learn how to look after her possessions—

but a practical matter. Excellent sheet music was hard to find out in the provinces, as Vivienne would surely call it. York had a plentiful collection, but nothing of real note.

No, it was not there. Perhaps in one of the drawers? Mrs. Jenner did always try to be helpful, Edwin remembered.

Pulling out the three drawers that made up the left portion of his desk, Edwin stuck his hands in and had a good rummage.

The sheet music did not rise to the top. Something else, however, did. Something he had not recalled he still possessed. Something that, until this moment, he had not remembered he even had. Edwin pulled it out with shaking hands and sat very slowly in his desk chair.

It was a portrait of a young woman. She was staring rather fiercely at the artist, one eyebrow raised, the glint in her eyes was rather fearsome to behold.

Edwin gazed at it, transfixed. *Vivienne. When had he drawn this?* It was from life, he knew that. The lines were rapid, rough, hasty. She had evidently declined his request to draw her, and he had managed to get this profile complete before she had undoubtedly moved.

Over fifteen years ago. That was when he had put pencil to paper and drawn this. Silently, Edwin moved his hand and brushed over the face on the page.

Where had they been—his rooms in London? Surely not, that would have been risqué, even for them.

She was a young woman, and he a third brother, never expecting to have a title. His courting of her was natural, expected. No one had blinked an eye when the vivacious Miss Vivienne Clarke had been pursued by a Bysshe. He had no title. Not then.

Edwin smiled at the frown lines that were delicately traced on the drawing. She had been such a joyful woman, often glaring ironically but then laughing, unable to hold the expression.

Now it was the most familiar one on her face. She was always glaring…or frowning…or raising an eyebrow in disapproval.

Except when she was kissing him.

Edwin swallowed. It was a sobering thought. Vivienne had not led an easy life, he knew that—neither had he, if it came to that, but there was a different type of harshness to life when one was always provided with a roof over one's head, a shirt on one's back, and food on one's table. Vivienne had none of that. She had worked hard for years to have those things. And they had been taken away from her.

Edwin stroked the hair of the drawn Vivienne. *His Vivienne. To think, he'd had this drawing all along.*

"We couldn't find it in the end," came Vivienne's voice.

Edwin started and looked up. The door was open, and light was surely spilling out onto the corridor. She had probably guessed where he had come.

"But I sent Laura to bed," said Vivienne, appearing in the doorway with a tired smile. "She is far too exhausted to—what do you have here?"

Far too late, Edwin attempted to hide the drawing in his hands—but there was undoubtedly a small part of him that wanted her to see it. Wanted to see her reaction. Wanted to know what she thought, whether she felt anything, by seeing it.

Vivienne stared. She stepped into the study, hesitantly at first but then with purpose, and reached out a hand.

Edwin said nothing. Wordlessly, he passed her the drawing. It was only a piece of paper, not backed or mounted, but it was quite clear what it was.

Her gaze fell on it, her eyes wide, her mouth open. Yet she said not a word.

After almost a full minute, Edwin wanted to speak—but he had no words either. It was a fragment of a time that he had thought lost. Evidence of a love affair that had ended, at least in his case, in tears.

"I...I did not know you still had this."

Vivienne's words, when she spoke, were so soft, Edwin could barely make them out.

He didn't need to. Not really. He could see enough of what

she said on her face.

"I honestly did not know I had kept it," he said quietly, not able to take his eyes from her. "I thought...well. I just found it, this moment."

Her eyes had not risen from the drawing, giving Edwin far more time to look at her, which he did so greedily. Would he ever grow tired of her? The radiant beauty that put all others to shame, even now in the late of the evening.

Age had touched her gently. Even Edwin would not deny it, but the fine lines around her eyes and mouth merely enhanced the beauty. Like an elegant gold frame around a portrait.

"Do you...do you look at this often?"

Edwin shook his head rather too rapidly. "No, I swear, I-I only found it right now."

There was a too-knowing smile on Vivienne's face. "I never know whether you are teasing me or not."

If he had known it was there, Edwin thought privately, *he certainly would have looked it at more often. Regularly.*

To think, he had a drawing of her right there, which he could have looked at any time. No more relying on his memories, searching for the right remembrance of Vivienne laughing, of her talking, of her correcting him with that quizzical smile on her face...

There it was now. "You know, you are rather good at this. Drawing, I mean."

Edwin spoke without thought. "Well, I cannot have been that proficient. I mean, you did not keep yours."

He wanted to say more. Something more, something to explain the pain it had caused him to know she had so easily disposed not only of himself but his drawing representative.

The tension between them grew, his gaze not leaving hers but nothing spoken—yet it was not the tension of two people about to argue and fiercely debate something.

No, it was more passionate than that. Edwin wanted the tension to lengthen, to tighten, to bring them closer in a way that they had not permitted themselves in a good while. But how to do it? how to force Vivienne to confront feelings he hoped she was hiding?

"Indeed," she said quietly. "In a way…it would have been nice to have something of you."

"You should not have sent it all back," said Edwin, with no censure but a little sadness in his voice. "The miniature, the locket…"

Instead of disagreeing, she nodded.

"Yes, I know, and what a pretty parcel it made," she said sadly. "But it was painful, Edwin. Surely you must understand that. The thought of having anything of yours, anything with me that could remind me of you… I regretted it in the end. I was in half a mind to write to you, ask for them back, but I knew I could not. It would open old wounds. Wounds that needed to heal."

Edwin swallowed. This was dangerous territory they were meandering into, and he could see on Vivienne's face that she knew it. He should say something, something light, non-committal. About Laura's sheet music, perhaps.

"Do you think things could have turned out differently?"

That was certainly not the question that he had meant to ask. Edwin blinked, astonished at his own words, but they were said now. The only thing to do was to wait and see whether she would respond.

At first, Vivienne hesitated. Then, "I did not say no to you because I did not love you, Edwin. It was not because I could not have both. It was you—you made me choose. It was one or the other with you, and you forced that upon me."

Edwin could barely speak with astonishment. "You mean…you mean to say that if I had accepted the Governess Bureau as a permanent part of your life, all those years ago, you…you would have married me?"

It was a wild idea he could barely countenance. He had been so close—far closer than he had imagined. Vivienne and the Bureau; it would have been a strange life, indeed, but was not every life strange in its own way?

The smile on Vivienne's face was wistful. "You were the son of a viscount, Edwin. You think you could have had a wife who worked? I mean to say, you are a viscount now! A viscountess cannot run an enterprise."

"Says who?" Edwin had risen to his feet, stepping around the desk. He had to be close to her, now they were finally speaking the words they should have said over a decade ago. "Society's rules, society's regulations—have they ever made us happy?"

Vivienne placed the drawing on a table beside her, then turned to him. "They…they have not."

"And I want to be happy," Edwin pressed, hardly knowing where this conversation was going but knowing he wanted to go there with Vivienne. "Don't you, Vivienne? Don't you want to be happy?"

She answered not with words but with her lips. Leaning forward, Vivienne kissed him, nervously at first, but then with greater ardor as Edwin's fingers moved to her waist and pulled her closer to him.

Dear God, this was glorious. This time she gave herself willingly, initiating the kiss, and what a kiss it was. The sweetness and tenderness evolved into something darker, just as sweet but with a hint of spice that made Edwin groan in her mouth. Her tongue dazzled him, both teasing and giving pleasure until he could barely tell whether he was standing or sitting.

He knew what he wanted to do.

"Oh, Vivienne," Edwin moaned.

Pulling her around, he pushed her onto the desk and moved between her legs, Vivienne easily giving him entrance as her skirts tangled around him.

This was everything, this was glorious, his head spinning with the sensation of Vivienne pressed up against him—but then he stopped.

Edwin attempted to catch his breath, his hand hanging low. *Not like this.*

"W-Why have you stopped?" Vivienne said, her breath caught in her throat.

It gave him such joy to hear her ask that question, but Edwin had to ask a question of his own. He simply could not continue without it, and Vivienne's answer was one of the most important things anyone would ever say to him.

"Vivienne I...I want to love you. I want to make love to you. Will you let me? Will you let me finally show you the depths of my affection?"

CHAPTER SEVENTEEN

Vivienne could hardly believe it. The words rang in her ears, making even less sense as she heard them repeated.

"Vivienne I…I want to love you. I want to make love to you. Will you let me? Will you let me finally show you the depths of my affection?"

He could not be serious. Yet Edwin had never looked more serious in his entire life. She had never seen him looking so…so earnest. As though she could destroy him if she did not respond in the positive. *As though he was already destroyed by the lack of her.*

And she wanted to say yes. Finally, after all these years, wondering whether life would ever catch up with her as she raced through the world creating the Governess Bureau…

Now finally, there was a gentleman who wanted her. Who desired her, not as a governess, but as a woman. And it was Edwin. Of all people, it was the gentleman she had wanted the most in the world and been devastated to lose.

True, it was not the sort of declaration of love she had expected—if she had ever expected one at all.

"Will you let me finally show you the depths of my affection?"

No boundless praise, no declaration of permanent devotion, no proposal of marriage…

Yet that was not what she needed. Vivienne knew that now, in a way she had not before. What she needed was him. *Edwin.*

Without all the finery, without the title, without the grand speeches and declarations and whatever else viscounts were surrounded with.

Edwin. Open, vulnerable, honest. The traits she had fallen in love with in the very beginning. The man she had known, had loved. The man she had been sure would never look at her with anything but disdain after the way things had ended between them.

Fifteen years. It felt like a chasm between them, but, somehow, Edwin had crossed it.

Vivienne swallowed. Time was stretching out now, and she knew she needed to give an answer, but she could not think of one that made sense.

How could she say yes? The path Edwin wanted her to step down had no ending. A woman always needing a plan, a direction, found this map had no markings.

She had no idea what would happen if she accepted his offer—his delicious offer of previously forbidden joy. But surely, Vivienne reasoned with the last remaining morsels of her mind, whatever was at the end of this journey had to be better than what they had now.

Barely controlled desire and love and also confusion and hatred, at times, for what they had done to each other, for the way they had found themselves so easily parted.

Was it not unfair? And could not some of that unfairness be undone if she were just brave enough to accept it?

Thoughts whirled through Vivienne's mind, and she could see that Edwin was waiting patiently for her to think, not wishing to rush her—which was all to the good, because she was not sure she could be rushed.

They had loved each other in the past. He loved her now—*whatever Edwin thought of as love*, Vivienne found herself thinking. She knew she loved him, truly loved him, wanted to be a part of his life forever.

And she knew just as clearly that that would not be possible.

There was not a journey toward permanent devotion. She was no fool, no scatterbrained girl who could have her head so easily swayed. No, if any other gentleman had suggested such a thing…

"I…I would never wish to rush you into anything," came Edwin's gentle voice. "You know that, Vivienne. It's just…well. You know how I feel about you. How I have always felt about you. None of those feelings have changed, at least for me."

It was perhaps one of the most emotional speeches Edwin had made since she had arrived at Byhalden Lodge, after everything had changed for them.

Though still nestled in his arms, Vivienne had enough wits about her to take a closer look at Edwin and see him quiver. He wanted this; he wanted her.

But not so much that he would force her. It was evident that this would end if she decided not to accept his offer. The fact that it was a real potential option gave her courage.

"I care about you, Vivienne," Edwin said softly. "You know that, don't you?"

Vivienne was not entirely sure that she did know that. Even with Edwin saying those words right now to her, they did not sink in as she heard them. *Edwin cared for her. For her.*

It was an honor, Vivienne thought, *to be a part of his life in any small way*. That was what she had missed all those years ago, that was what she had not understood.

That losing Edwin was not just losing a lover but losing a part of herself. He was a complex paradox of kindness and fury, and she had missed him. More than anything. More than kisses, though they were sorely welcomed. But it was him. The Edwinness of Edwin that she had lacked.

It was an honor to be loved by him. Earning Edwin's love had been easy, but earning his trust? That had been far more difficult. Now she had it, was she strong enough, foolish enough to even consider giving it up?

It was, therefore, with a slow and slightly nervous smile that Vivienne said, "You know…you may regret this tomorrow."

A sentence she wished she did not need to say, but she had to. She could never live with herself if she did not give him fair warning that their affections tonight may look very different in the cold light of day tomorrow.

To face Edwin's ire in the morning...that was something she could not face.

Edwin kissed her lightly on the lips, his gently brushing her own. "I won't."

Vivienne captured his lips with hers, her hands entwining themselves in his hair as she pulled his head closer to hers. She did not want to give him up. She did not want to lose the chance to know what it was to be loved, truly loved, by Edwin Bysshe.

It may be an opportunity she never had again, but then that was the consequence of rejecting him in the first place. At least this time, she knew what to expect. Almost.

"Then," Vivienne said hurriedly, breaking the kiss, "then let's do it."

Edwin blinked as though he had not quite understood her words. "You...you agree? You wish to make love?"

It felt so foolish saying it aloud, but Vivienne could see that was what he needed. He needed to hear it from her own lips him.

"Make love to me, Edwin."

After a quick kiss that made Vivienne's breath entirely disappear, Edwin took her by the hand. "Come with me."

Vivienne nodded, grateful she was no longer expected to speak. What could she say? The whole world had changed around her, the sense of balance, which had never before failed her, rocking her feet as she attempted to take a step forward.

This was it. No going back. Though she was sure many people assumed she had had her fair share of dalliances as a younger woman, this was uncharted territory. For all her wise years, she was as experienced as a chit of sixteen. But not for much longer.

The sensation of being a rebellious harlot, finally doing something she had been forbidding herself for many years, overtook Vivienne as they stepped along the corridor, hand in hand.

Was this not the very thing that she had forbidden her governesses to do? Yet they had surely felt the same heightened excitement, the same rush of blood flowing, the same painful pattering of their hearts.

They had been filled with the anticipation that was now roaring through her veins.

No wonder so many of them had succumbed, finally, to the temptation.

Barely taking in where they were going, Vivienne was surprised to find herself standing, hand in hand with a viscount, outside the master bedchamber. *Edwin's room.*

"Here we are," said Edwin softly, leaning forward with his free hand to open one of the double doors. "Come on in."

Feeling as though every step was into enemy territory, half expecting herself to change her mind at any moment, Vivienne let go of Edwin's hand and stepped into the bedchamber.

It was difficult not to gasp aloud, but Vivienne just about managed it. She had never seen such a room. It was enormous, larger probably than her entire apartment above the Governess Bureau!

On the one occasion when she had stepped in here, Edwin had been drunk, and the whole place had been dark. She had been far more interested in getting him safely into bed and then herself out of there to pay any real attention to its size or décor.

The carpet seemed to roll luxuriously in all directions as far as the eye could see. Vivienne could make out a chaise lounge, a desk, several armchairs, and the largest bed she had ever seen. Lit by several candles in two candelabras on either side of the bed, the light glittered off the chandelier, glinted off the gold leaf on the painting frames, shone on the velvet of the bed hangings.

She shivered unconsciously. *A man's bed. Not any man's, but Edwin's.* Here she was, in Edwin's bedchamber. Not as a servant helping her master, but a woman invited by her lover.

For a moment, Vivienne hesitated. Thoughts of the Bureau intruded her mind, making it difficult to think clearly—and it was hardly easy before that.

Was she about to make the same mistake that so many of her governesses made? How did she expect to be able to restore the Governess Bureau if it was discovered that she had given herself so delightfully and so easily to Edwin's advances?

Was she willing to risk it all just to have a taste of the pleasure a man could give?

Vivienne swallowed as Edwin closed the door behind her. She knew what she wanted, and it was him; but it was also the Bureau. Why did the two demand so much from her, taking everything she was?

Risking it all. That was what she was doing. Vivienne knew the price for losing one's innocence, and that was Society's disapproval—forever.

You must never fall in love...

But she had already long crossed that line, had she not? Why, she had loved Edwin for years, nearly decades. *She loved him.* The thought solidified in her mind. *She loved him.* Vivienne loved Edwin, and there was little that would stop her now she was so close to discovering what it felt like to be so loved in return.

"Vivienne?"

She turned to see Edwin looking at her, concern mingled with desire on his face.

"Are you quite well?"

Vivienne nodded. Not trusting her voice, she tried to show him, rather than tell him, all the complicated thoughts rushing through her mind.

And he understood. Edwin took her hand in his. "Vivienne, you know that tonight doesn't have to be...this offer is open, and a refusal now does not mean you have lost your only chance. I respect you too much for that."

All fears disappearing, she saw in his face the truth of his words and knew that she could never love another, never feel this bold and true with another.

Edwin Bysshe had not merely her heart but now her soul.

Kissing him, gently at first, and then with more passion, Vivienne purposefully left behind her concerns and cares. What did it matter if the world would consider her despoiled after tonight? Who else would she consider giving herself to?

No one. This was all for Edwin, his strong arms around her, his teasing fingers on her buttocks, his lips trailing kisses down her neck...

"Edwin," Vivienne gasped.

"Vivienne," he replied, and she could hear the desire in his voice. "Let's get these clothes off you, I want to see you, see all of—what's the matter?"

Edwin had immediately released her, taking a step back from her and placing his hands behind his back as though he had been scalded.

Maybe he had. Vivienne certainly felt as though she had been, a desperate heat she had not understood but knew to be akin to shame rushing through her.

Vivienne swallowed. "I...I..."

"I don't want to force you to go too fast," said Edwin slowly.

His eyes had not left hers, seeking insight, and Vivienne wanted to give it to him...she just did not know how to explain it. Her hands twisted before her as she tried to encapsulate the sudden rush of panic that had overwhelmed her.

"I...well, I am not..." *Young*, Vivienne thought silently.

This was a mistake. The last time they had kissed like this, truly kissed like this, she had been near twenty. Though he had not managed to get his hands under her gown then, Edwin had known what to expect, and that was a young woman, fine and fresh, untouched, unaged.

It was not the body she possessed now. He undoubtedly expected...*well*, thought Vivienne wretchedly. *All that she was not.*

And she could not bear to disappoint him. To see displeasure on his face would be the end of her. She would never be able to face him again, nor herself. She would have to leave.

The wrinkles and rolls, the sunspots and age marks...they

were all evidence of a life led, and Vivienne had never been ashamed of them before. She was not precisely ashamed of them now. It was more...well. She had never expected anyone to have a chance of seeing them!

Edwin waited, but as it became clear she was not going to say anything, said quietly, "You know, we are in no rush. The night is still young, and we don't have to at all. If you don't want to. It was only an idea."

Vivienne licked her lips, swallowed, then tried to explain. "It is just...you will expect, but you won't find...and the years, they have been kinder to some than others, and I am not wont to complain, but you might be surprised by—and if you are, that is understandable, and I would not—"

"Slow down," said Edwin gently with a wry smile, "and I will have a far greater chance of understanding you. Are you trying to tell me that you are embarrassed?"

Vivienne pursed her lips. "Not—not embarrassed as such, more—oh, I am explaining this so poorly! You might think to see...you might expect me to look as I cannot, and—"

"Peace, Vivienne."

She halted. She was not entirely sure whether she could keep going in any case, the shame rushing through her and making it almost impossible to think.

Edwin stepped toward her and took her hands into his own. "Vivienne...Vivienne the gift of your love is more than enough. You think I do not know your concern? But every inch of your skin is majestic and worthy of love, no matter what it looks like. The honor you do me of even considering... Any gentleman not willing to see the beauty of the wise years on your skin simply isn't worthy of you."

She had not expected him to be able to explain it in any way that made her feel beautiful, yet he had. He understood. He truly did.

"I...thank you," was all she could manage.

And then there was fire in his eyes as Edwin gripped her

hands tightly. "No. No, don't ever apologize for being appreciated as you ought, Vivienne. God knows you've probably gone through life being underappreciated, and I will not have that here. I am honored to be—you make me feel so..."

Vivienne kissed him. The well of love for him—not gratitude, but adoration—was such that she could no longer prevent herself from kissing him. She wanted to taste him, to know him. To tease him with her tongue and feel him quiver in her arms.

And he was not reticent. Edwin returned her passion with that of his own, his fingers moving to slowly unhook her gown all the way down her back, brushing up and down her figure to tease what was coming next, and then before she knew it, Vivienne's gown was pooling down on the carpet below her.

If it had been summer, Edwin may have been greeted with the view of her naked body—but as it was midwinter...

"Dear God," Edwin laughed. "Three petticoats or four? I had not realized I would keep needing to unwrap you like a parcel!"

Vivienne laughed. *How did he do it? Put her at ease so utterly?* "Here, let me."

The little boldness she had found was used entirely on removing the rest of her clothes. As Vivienne stood before him, naked, she suddenly realized the import of what was happening and attempted to hide certain parts of herself with her hands.

"God, I'm falling behind," said Edwin distractedly, attempting to take his boots and breeches off without looking away from her.

He managed to strip himself remarkably quickly, and Vivienne could not help but stare at the manhood standing to attention. *Dear Lord.* She had seen statues in the art galleries, of course, when ladies were permitted to attend, but nothing had given her any indication of...

Well. Its size.

"Vivienne Clarke," said Edwin, pulling her into his arms as she gasped at the intensity of his skin on hers. "I want to kiss you all over."

"What! No, you wouldn't dare," said Vivienne with a gasp,

hardly certain whether it was a jest, a tease, or a threat.

A mischievous look appeared on Edwin's face. "Never dare me, Vivienne."

In a swift movement, he had pushed her onto the bed. After the initial terror at falling, Vivienne found herself lying on soft sheets and looking up at a man who quite clearly adored every inch of what he was looking at.

"Dear God, you are beautiful," he said before joining her on the bed.

He did not, however, move into her arms as he had expected. No.

Vivienne shivered as he kissed her foot, just above her ankle. "Edwin, what are—"

"Did I, or did I not say I was going to kiss you all over?" came the low reply as Edwin kissed up her leg to her thighs. "I think I did."

Vivienne quivered with the intensity. Parts of her body she had never considered to be particularly desirable were now tingling with the pressure of his kisses, and she was growing warm between her legs.

"So beautiful," murmured Edwin as he kissed her hip, then her belly. "Dear God…"

Vivienne arched her back as Edwin took one of her nipples in his mouth, the other nipple caressed lightly at first and then firmly with his hand.

"Such beauty deserves to be seen," he said quietly as he kissed her neck, finally looking down with a smile. "And I am the most fortunate of men to be so chosen."

Vivienne captured his lips with her own for a heady kiss, filled with anticipation for more, and as he pulled away, she said what she was thinking without any censorship. "You still haven't kissed everywhere."

Edwin's eyes widened only for a moment. "Christ, Vivienne, I had no idea you had it in you."

Neither did she, but she knew what she wanted. She wanted

all of this, everything, and she knew Edwin would give it to her.

"Edwin!"

It would have been impossible not to cry out as his lips touched her secret place. Her warmth welcomed him in, and Vivienne's eyes closed with unrestrained pleasure as his tongue entered her, slowly at first, nibbling, licking, and then increasing in intensity and pace as he suckled her until Vivienne cried out his name for a second time, the pleasure overwhelming her until she fell over a crest of ecstasy she had not known was possible.

Her whole body shaking at the unexpected glory, Vivienne managed to pant, "I...I did not know that was even possible!"

"Oh, there is so much I want to show you," said Edwin, eyes bright as he settled into her arms. "The question is, what do you want?"

Vivienne stared through the haze of pleasure she had already experienced. *More?*

"Come on," he said quietly in a gentle yet encouraging voice. "You asked for what you wanted before. Tell me what you want. I want to pleasure you, Vivienne, I want to please you. I'll do anything you ask. Just command me."

It was beyond all her wildest dreams. She could see the truth in his eyes, see he wanted nothing more than to be told what she wanted more than anything.

Never before had she such an opportunity, and all the dark and delicious thoughts she had hidden started to surface, her body quivering not just with the pleasure it had already received but the pleasure it would soon receive.

"I...I want you to touch me," Vivienne managed.

Edwin smiled with a teasing grin. "Where, how?"

Vivienne swallowed, and knew that if she did not speak now, she would always regret the chance. "Pull...pull me into your arms and touch my breasts. Like you did before."

In an instant, he obeyed, and Vivienne arched her back once more as his tongue teased first one nipple, then the other, his hands pulling her close, his manhood pressed up against her like a promise, waiting in the wings.

And heat was building in her, but not to the peak it was before, and Vivienne was desperate for more. "Now...now *there*."

"There?"

"You know what I mean," said Vivienne breathlessly, hardly aware of where she was but all too conscious of whom she was with. "Please, Edwin."

He groaned as he kissed her, his hand moving to between her legs and capturing her gasp as he slipped a finger inside her.

He knew the rhythm she wanted now and was able to bring her to a swifter climax than before, Vivienne holding on for dear life as her body performed wonders she had not known was possible.

"More, more," Vivienne gasped as the peak crested, not willing to wait this time. "Enter me. I want you, Edwin. I want you."

Only now did Edwin hesitate. "Are...are you sure?"

Vivienne's gaze met his. "More sure about this than anything. Please, Edwin."

It took him but a moment to find a French letter and place it upon himself before he was inside her, and Vivienne lost all reason, all sense.

Being so connected to another person, having him inside her, feeling every movement; it was an intimacy that she could not have imagined, and all ability to ask for what she wanted disappeared.

She wanted him, she had him, and now the path was unclear. All her wise years could guide her no further.

"Just...just love me, Edwin," she begged, unable to stand the delicate pressure. "Take control, Edwin, and show me what you want."

It was not a subtle lovemaking. *Perhaps it would be the next time they shared this*, Vivienne thought vaguely as she clung onto Edwin's shoulders as he raised himself almost out of her and then entered her again and again, and the pressure grew as the friction stoked the flames within her, and she knew that this was perfect, the perfect lovemaking for both of them, and she could see and feel the pleasure building in him and any moment—

"Vivienne!"

"Edwin!"

He collapsed into her arms, spent, as Vivienne felt the shivers of afterglow soar around her body. Finally, they were where they should be. Together.

CHAPTER EIGHTEEN

February 24, 1816

EDWIN HAD NEVER really understood the phrase "skip in one's step." It was the sort of thing that children did, growing out of it as soon as one realized just how embarrassing it would be to trip over one's feet and fall flat in front of someone.

He understood it now. Every step he took seemed to bounce with energy that was not entirely his, flowing through him, a mere vessel of joy.

He had done it.

The weak wintery sunshine seemed to be as glorious as midsummer as he walked down the corridor, beaming at everyone he passed.

Finally. After all these years, after a courtship over a decade ago, after thinking everything was lost, after believing she was lost to him, after longing and misunderstanding and joy and confusion…

Edwin grinned. *He had made love to Vivienne. Several times.*

"Good morning!" he cried as he threw open the breakfast room door.

There was no one there. He had not expected anyone;

Vivienne broke her fast with the servants, and Laura had taken to having her breakfast in her room like a married mother.

Still, he had not the heart to enforce her presence here. If having a few hours in the morning to herself made her feel better, more adult, more trusted, then who was he to argue?

The sight of an empty room did not fill him with dread as it had done for the last few weeks.

A shiver ran down Edwin's spine. Best he not think about their bed if he was to have any control over himself for the next few hours. It was difficult enough leaving Vivienne lying there, her hair spread across the pillow like a golden halo, her gentle breathing moving her body ever so slightly as he watched her.

But he had forced himself to leave. After such dramatic scenes yesterday, a breakthrough in understanding he'd never predicted, it was best he give her time this morning. If she were anything like him, she would want to take time to think about what had happened.

Edwin sat at the table and started pouring himself a cup of tea. All he could do was think about Vivienne. *Vivienne.* The way she had smiled at him. The astonishment on her face when she had seen the drawing he had created of her and kept after all these years. The way she asked for what she wanted, so inexperienced and yet so desirous.

Edwin took a sip of scalding tea and flinched. *Too hot.*

After so much waiting, so much desire, so many years of telling himself he would never see her again, let alone hold her, or touch her, or kiss her…he had made love to Vivienne. More than once.

It had been better than he could ever have imagined. On the rare occasions when he had permitted himself to think about what possessing Vivienne would be like—something he had avoided once married to Henrietta—the actual details had been rather fuzzy. Try as he might, Edwin had been unable to imagine past bringing Vivienne into his arms and kissing her.

That was all they had permitted themselves to do in London.

Perhaps that was why his mind could give him nothing more; his imagination simply couldn't conjure the beauty of the woman.

Vivienne. Vivienne Clarke, a woman who had waited. A woman of wise years indeed.

Steam swirled up from his teacup, and Edwin found himself watching it twist in the air.

He was going to have to be careful. This was not some floozy or harlot he had picked off the streets of London, nor a courtesan he had met in a particular bordello that he could see one evening and forget the next.

No. This was Vivienne, and what's more, she was residing in his house. *She was supposed to be here to teach Laura, for goodness' sake!*

He was going to find it difficult to keep his hands off her, Edwin thought with a wry smile. She was far too tempting, far too delicious now he knew the taste of her, the feel of her under his skin. *Will they repeat the evening?*

Edwin pushed the thought away. He could not expect that, could not ask that. Vivienne herself needed to bring that up. If he was going to ensure she was comfortable here, he must ensure that power remained in her hands.

A clock chimed—then the rest of the clocks at Byhalden Lodge joined in. *He must speak to Harris about that first one*, Edwin thought hazily to himself as he continued to eat. It really was outrageous that one of them could be so out of time.

Thinking about time swiftly led Edwin to think about the future, but that was another dark and misty idea ahead of him. *The future.* He had been careful last night to make no promises, and Vivienne had been just as astute.

Last night had not been about the future. It had been about the past, restoring something, completing something which should have been resolved a long time ago.

But now that was behind them, the future lay before them. Edwin picked up his teacup and took a sip. The liquid was not quite so scalding this time.

The future could be simple as far as Edwin was concerned. It was quite obvious that the Governess Bureau was finished. Vivienne was no longer a young woman, with the vitality and energy—or time—of a younger woman.

She could not seriously think to remake the Governess Bureau; it had been a wish, a desire, but she would surely not withhold herself from pleasure and fulfillment merely because of a wish that would never come.

A slow smile crept over his face. The Bureau was finished, whether Vivienne had yet admitted it aloud to herself or not. She was a clever woman, wise far beyond her years. She would not cling to such a useless hope.

Only a fool would attempt to revive it, and Vivienne was no fool.

She could be his mistress…

A mistress in the lodge—the convenience! Edwin had considered it before, naturally, but had never wished to bring anyone into the house who may unsettle Laura.

Here was the perfect solution, so entirely desirable for all three of them that Edwin wondered he had not considered it before. Laura already liked Vivienne; they liked each other. Vivienne would be assured not only of her profession and a wage but of his affection.

It was so obvious, Edwin wondered why he'd not suggested that when she first arrived.

"But mark my words, Miss Clarke, I will be doing everything in my power to demonstrate to the world that you and your Bureau are finished. Finished, over and done with. Forever."

His smile became rueful. *Ah, yes. That was why.*

It was incredible to think that after so long, after such misery on both sides, they would finally be able to be happy. And that was all he wanted. For Vivienne to be happy. For him to be the one to make her happy. To see her smile, truly smile, not that curt smirk that appeared sometimes when Vivienne was conscious she needed to smile, yet felt no joy within her. Edwin knew her; he could not be fooled.

After suffering for so long in a loveless, warmthless marriage with Henrietta, he was finally going to be happy. He could consider actually looking forward to each day, knowing that it would contain joy rather than misery, interest rather than boredom—and the nights...

Edwin's loins tightened. *Well, the nights would take care of themselves.* If last night was anything to go by, they would be absolutely marvelous.

And he was still hungry. *Well, that's what happens*, Edwin told himself cheerfully, *when one stays up half the night pleasuring one's mistress.* One does build up quite the appetite.

As Edwin piled up three pieces of toast onto his plate and started slathering butter onto the first one, a noise interrupted him, making his butter knife pause.

A sound. No, sounds. Footsteps. Someone was walking in the hall—it must be Laura.

"Come on in!" Edwin called out, not bothering to rise from the breakfast table. Why should he? He was the master here. He was the one who gave the orders, made the decisions, and paid the bills. "Come on in, I say, and join me!"

The footsteps halted. Then they slowly yet steadily increased in volume as the walker approached the breakfast room door.

When it opened hesitantly, it was not Laura but Vivienne who appeared there, her hair still slightly fluffy from their night of pleasure. There was no Laura beside her.

Edwin looked at her side, expecting his daughter to appear. "Where is Laura?"

Vivienne's cheeks turned scarlet as she closed the door behind her and then leaned against it. "Good...good morning, my lord."

It was fortunate indeed that Edwin had not at that moment been chewing a mouthful of toast, for his jaw dropped wide open.

Good morning, my lord? When had Vivienne ever been so civil to him as to call him my lord when they were alone? It was unheard of. Try as he might, Edwin wracked his brain but could not pinpoint a single occasion.

Yet as Edwin looked up at the woman standing by the door, he suddenly realized what strange emotion was playing on her features. *She was shy.*

His first instinct was to be flattered, but he pushed it away immediately. He was not the sort of man to revel in another's discomfort. Seeing Vivienne so at odds with the world was a rather disorientating sight.

No, if he was any sort of gentleman, he would do what gentlemen for ages past had done—put everyone around them at ease.

"Good morning," Edwin said with a broad smile. "Come on in, have something to eat. The bacon is still warm, so are the eggs, and the potatoes—the tea perhaps too much so."

He had intended to be warm, inviting. He had poured his affection into every syllable and ensured his smile did not disappear as he spoke.

Yet Vivienne hesitated. She said nothing, eyes roving across the table as though looking for something.

Eventually, however, it appeared she had no option but to reply with, "Th-Thank you. I will join you."

It was not exactly a resounding affirmative, but Edwin tried to ignore this. It was a strange situation for the both of them, to be sure, but this was his house. He had the upper hand, always did, and so he needed to be understanding for Vivienne. Even if the way she walked toward him, hips swaying, was enough to turn him mad within minutes.

"Excellent," he said aloud, rather than reveal what his thoughts had been dwelling on mere moments ago. "And where is Laura, still upstairs?"

Vivienne nodded. She sat beside him, eyes downcast. She did not look at him as she spoke. "Yes, Laura is not feeling well—a head cold, I think, nothing more serious than that."

Edwin's ears pricked up. "A head cold? Should the doctor be called for? No expense is to be spared when it comes to my daughter's health."

It did not appear to him to be such a strange statement, but a corner of Vivienne's mouth turned up at his remark. "No, I do not believe there is any danger, just a little discomfort for the poor child. I have recommended that she spend most of the day in…in bed."

The word "bed" was enough to make her flush, something Edwin studiously ignored.

He was not going to bring up the subject until she did. He was determined to have more self-control than he usually managed, and it was down to Vivienne to raise the topic of their evening. If she wished to.

"I see," Edwin said smartly, starting to slather butter onto his second piece of toast, for want of somewhere to look that wasn't the angelic beauty of Vivienne Clarke. "Well, Laura always gets terrible head colds each winter, poor child, she really suffers. I suppose we shall just have to leave her be. She'll be fine after a few days. I'll make sure Mrs. Jenner takes up plenty of tea and cake."

He had expected Vivienne to say something after this pronouncement—praise his care as a father, maybe, or even more delightfully, make a suggestion about what the two of them could do while her charge was in bed, with no need of her.

Edwin's spine shivered.

But she said nothing of the sort. In fact, Vivienne was entirely silent. She did not move to put any food on her plate but instead poured a cup of tea with steady hands, then looked into the teacup, waiting for it to cool sufficiently to drink.

Edwin's stomach twisted, but he took a bite of his toast despite it. Well, he had hoped the whole encounter this morning would not be awkward, but sometimes these things just happened.

And he had to admit, this was far more strange for Vivienne, wasn't it? After all, she had lost her innocence last night, whereas he…*well. It had been many a year since he had considered himself innocent.*

But he could not permit this to become increasingly more and more strange. No, he would have to say something. Even if he was not entirely sure yet what it would be.

"Honey, for your tea?" Edwin said, picking up the pot. "It's local."

It's local. What was wrong with him? Edwin raged at himself for the insipidity of his words. It was one step up from talking about the weather, which was hardly impressive.

He was a gentleman, a well-born, well-bred gentleman with years of experience in Society. And he was talking about the source of his table's honey?

Vivienne laughed. It was a gentle laugh, not mocking, just merriment, but it put an ease between them that nothing else had.

"You don't find this awkward at all, do you?" she said with a smile that was finally natural. "After everything we…you don't think this is strange?"

"A little," Edwin admitted. "It is just as new to me as this is to you. I have never done…*this*…before."

And there was truth in those words, he realized as Vivienne happily spooned honey into her tea. True, he had made love before, but he had never bedded another woman in this house. His one indiscretion early on in his marriage to Henrietta had been conducted far away in London.

"Neither have I," said Vivienne quietly.

Edwin swallowed down the multitude of questions that rose up from this pronouncement. Her innocence had been assumed by him, and it had seemed too impolite before now to ask.

Perhaps it would still be impolite, but Edwin was desperate to know precisely what she meant by that statement. She had never had breakfast with a man after bedding him? She had never bedded a man as she had done last night?

Or had she truly been an innocent and had never bedded a man at all?

Edwin cleared his throat as though that would dislodge the thoughts from his mind. It was a caveman's line of thinking, and he would not shame her nor himself with it. Whether or not Vivienne had bedded a thousand men, none of them surely had made her cry out like he had done. What they had was special.

"Well, it's only as awkward as we make it," he said aloud in a bracing tone.

"Yes," said Vivienne dryly. "That was what I was afraid of."

They laughed together, the room echoing with their merriment.

Edwin glanced at her as Vivienne took a sip of tea. She was not only beautiful; he could see that now. Witty, clever, sharp—the best sort of person he had ever known.

Her beauty, though fantastic, was just one part of her. One part of perfection.

Her left hand was resting gently on the table between them, and before Edwin really knew what he was doing, he was holding it.

"After so many years apart," he said in a low voice, his gaze meeting her slightly startled one, "cannot we just be happy that we are together?"

Vivienne nodded. "Yes, of course, but…but I have to think of the future."

There was his Vivienne, Edwin thought warmly. Always planning, always attempting to make sure everything would be settled. She was just built that way, and he adored her for it.

Naturally, she would wish to ensure that she was provided for. She was a practical woman for all her beauty. *She had learned to be*, Edwin thought with a little prickle of sadness, *because she had never had the support of another*. Vivienne had gone through life alone, always ensuring she had everything prepared because one day, she would need to fall back on a plan like that.

Poor Vivienne. It broke his heart to think that their separation had meant misery and pain for the both of them.

"Of course, you wish to think about the future. That is only natural," said Edwin, finally breaking their gaze and lowering his focus to his final piece of toast. He started buttering it as he continued. "I will ensure there is a pension laid out for you on the occasion of my death, which we will have to hope will be many years hence."

When he looked up, Vivienne was sipping her tea, her cheeks scarlet. *Well, there was no predicting who would be more embarrassed about a conversation of money*, Edwin thought. He had expected it would be him, after her work at the Governess Bureau, but there it was.

Ah, yes, of course. The Governess Bureau...

"After all," he said cheerfully, "it is not as though this Governess Bureau of yours is going to be taking up any more of your money or time, is it? So that's all settled then."

Placing his butter knife down, Edwin took a large bite of his toast. Melted butter seeped into his mouth, and he sighed happily.

The only thing that would make this morning better would be the appearance of Laura, healthy and happy—although admittedly, it would certainly make his conversation with Vivienne more stilted.

As he thought of Vivienne, Edwin glanced at her—to see to his surprise that she was staring with some confusion.

"Why will the Governess Bureau take up no time?" she asked quietly. "If anything, it will take up more time. Getting it going again, securing new clients, bringing back my governesses, or training up new ones...it will almost be as though I am starting the whole endeavor again, from scratch."

Although her words individually made perfect sense, they did not make sense together. Why would Vivienne wish to start the Bureau again? Had he not proved, conclusively, that she could be happy here with him?

Why would she wish to choose strife and difficulty—not to mention financial uncertainty—along with facing all those critics, all those gossiping slanderous fools in London?

"Wait—wait a moment," Edwin said slowly. "You cannot

seriously be thinking about attempting to resurrect that old thing again, are you?"

The moment the words were out of his mouth, Edwin saw he had said the wrong thing.

Vivienne stiffened. "You mean my life's work? Yes, I had rather thought of returning to that. You would have me abandon it completely, admit defeat?"

"Well, yes," said Edwin. The instant look of anger on Vivienne's face made him add hastily, "I mean, it is more that...well, we have found each other again, after all this time. So many years apart, not knowing that we still felt this way, not knowing we could be together again—and you wish to separate us? I...well, I had assumed that you would stay here."

If he had expected a warm reception to his words, he was very much mistaken.

Vivienne raised an eyebrow. "What, as your mistress?"

"You say that as though it's a bad thing!"

She took a long, deep breath, and Edwin felt the hope he had built up in only the last hour of waking come crashing down around him. *It was all over, wasn't it?* He was going to lose her again—lose her to the same foolish Governess Bureau.

But this time, he would not lose her without a fight. Desperation made him think fast.

"I have no wish to make the same mistake as last time," Edwin said quietly.

Vivienne's eyebrow did not descend, but her expression softened somewhat. "Well then...try harder. Because that is exactly where we are heading."

Edwin opened his mouth, could think of nothing to say, and closed it again. *What could he say?* There appeared to be no option of compromise within Vivienne's heart; it was the Governess Bureau or nothing. And the idea of having nothing...

"I admit myself genuinely astonished that you will not even consider giving it up," Edwin found himself saying, probably foolishly. "Do I not have enough to offer you?"

"A man is not the only thing," said Vivienne quietly. "Nor is wealth or status. I knew you would not understand."

Edwin swallowed down his retort that he could make quite the same accusation to her and tried to think. He had to get this right, but they appeared to be barreling too fast toward a natural conclusion.

He had to slow this down. Somehow.

"So...so was last night something never to be repeated again?" he asked quietly.

It was painful to think he would never touch her again, never kiss her again—but this was more than just the physical pleasuring of Vivienne Clarke.

No, it was the very real pleasure he gained by her presence. Any mistress could provide comfort, but Vivienne was everything, everything he wanted.

He had to be a part of her life, or he would...the idea of her leaving...

"I have not decided that—last night was so...I am not thinking that far ahead."

Edwin could not help but chuckle. "That's not like you."

"I know," Vivienne said with a wry smile. "But you do something to me that prevents me from thinking clearly!"

And it was then that Edwin realized the problem. *He was asking too much of her.* Vivienne had been overwhelmed enough as it was last night, and she was still thinking about what they had shared, what they meant to each other.

While his mind raced ahead to pensions on the occasion of his death—a tad macabre, now he came to think about it—Vivienne was still trying to understand what had just occurred.

This time, Edwin did not just take Vivienne's hand in his own, but he kissed it. "I am sorry. I have no wish to rush you. We will—we will work it out in our own time."

It was just a hint of sadness that crept into her face as Vivienne did not reply.

"We will," affirmed Edwin. "Now, let me pour you some more tea."

CHAPTER NINETEEN

VIVIENNE HAD NOT expected to find it. She had not even remembered it was there. It was only due to an accident, dropping the notebook she had brought with her, tallying up the interest due to her debtors, that a few loose leaves slipped out.

A note from the Duchess of Rochdale which Vivienne had never replied to. It was too shameful seeing a governess of her own Bureau reach such a height.

A bill of sale for the Governess Bureau building. Vivienne smiled as she sat on the end of her bed. She had wondered where that had got to.

And a letter, folded several times and unfolded just as many, slightly dog-eared at one end, and with the stain of a red wine glass on one corner.

Vivienne's heart shivered. That letter. She had thought it lost years ago. It had been a great deal of time since she had read it, but perhaps there was no greater time.

Now her mind whirled with thoughts and dreams and hopes of Edwin's lovemaking, and the way he smiled at her over a cup of tea...

As Edwin proposed—not marriage. That would be too much. Vivienne's heart twisted. Even if it was what she wanted. Even if she could not admit that to herself. Even if his hints toward an arrangement—*arrangement*, she knew what that meant—were delicately made.

You must never fall in love…

Vivienne swallowed. There was a reason she had created that rule, and the reason was now in her hands.

Perhaps she needed to face reality.

Placing her notebook and the other ephemera which had slipped from it beside her on the bed, Vivienne slowly opened up the letter which had brought her such consternation all those years ago.

The letter which had set her life onto one direction that she would never have imagined. And it had all started with this betrayal.

Vivienne's eyes caught the name at the end of the letter before she started reading it again.

Miss Evangeline Jones.

Her stomach tightened, and her jaw clenched. Once her closest friend in the world. Vivienne tried not to think about her too much, tried not to wonder what Evangeline was doing. She had purposefully not kept in touch. The letters which had arrived with the Shirley seal had gone unopened and therefore unanswered, into the fire.

Each time, Vivienne had regretted it. Eventually, the letters stopped coming.

But she had kept this one. This first letter which had revealed the depths of depravity…

No, she could not think that way. Had Vivienne not proven herself how easy it was to slip into such things? Had she not found herself bedded by her master?

Vivienne swallowed. But that was different, she told herself. She had known Edwin for nigh on sixteen years. Evangeline had known her master but a matter of months. The situation was entirely different.

The letter lay on her lap. The handwriting was as familiar to her as her own.

Knowing she would in some way regret reading it and reliving that time of pain, Vivienne could not help herself. The letter was a long one, but in a way, she knew parts by heart.

My dearest Vivienne,

I must hope this letter finds you well, and healthy, and happy, as it leaves me. I also hope it has reached you before any hint of rumors have done so, for it is important to me that I explain—or at least try to explain—everything from my heart to yours.

Oh, where to begin?

My pen has dried of ink twice since I started this letter, yet I have explained nothing to you. Forgive me, Vivienne, for it is hard to know where to begin.

In a way, it begins with you.

The Governess Bureau was always your idea. I own, it is a good one. I can see much success for you in the future. A future bright and full of possibilities.

Creating a place where the nobility of England and Ireland can procure high-class governesses is something no one—certainly no man—has ever conceived of before. I know we are merely a year into our enterprise, but I am certain it will last many years.

And that is where it all began. What I am trying to tell you, I mean. You know full well that I never saw myself as a governess; never hoped to be one, yet saw the necessity of one of us going out into the world and drumming up a secure reputation for the Bureau.

You are so good at bookkeeping, managing people, and sorting everything out. Of course, it was I who was the governess.

I know my letters of late have been a little lackluster. I admit, teaching is not my skill, and in many ways, I think it is relief that I no longer—but I have not explained.

I told you in my last letter, in fact, I think all my letters, that I have found it hard here at Ettingham Park. The Shirley boys are, in the main, good children. Too energetic at times, but what small children are not?

But it was the master. It was...oh Vivienne. I love him.

Sir Mark is all that I would want in a gentleman. So kind, Vivienne—no, I can see your head shaking already, though I am not there!

I promise you, I had no intention of falling in love. It fell...well, it fell like snow. One cannot stop winter coming, and one cannot beg the snow to stop falling.

That is what love has done to me, and though I hesitate to state it, I know you have experienced somewhat of that nature.

My intentions were honorable. I had no idea that Sir Mark would return my affections—that he would wish me to.

I cannot write it. I can barely say it. The whole thing feels unreal.

Vivienne, I do not do this to hurt you. But I cannot live without him. A life without him would be no life at all. He has asked me to be his wife, and I have accepted.

I know this will be a shock to you. I know I have given little warning that my affections were in any way engaged, and I know you will not understand my desire to give up the Governess Bureau to become a wife, and perhaps one day, a mother.

But I know you would not stop me. I know you will wish me well on this next stage of my life's journey.

When you meet him—and I do hope that will be before the wedding, though Sir Mark wishes to hasten its approach—I am certain you will see all his amiable qualities and thoroughly comprehend why I have found it impossible to live without him.

The more time I spend with him, and the older I become, the more I realize that love if found, must be grasped. No matter if it arrives in strange garb.

I certainly never thought to be stepmother to two small boys!

I babble on the page—forgive my meandering thoughts and know that I will still recommend the Governess Bureau to all. I am sure a small marriage like this could not possibly damage our—your reputation.

Write back to me soon with all your love and affection, so that I can be sure that you are not offended by your devoted friend,

Evangeline Jones

Vivienne swallowed hard, emotions threatening to well up against her will.

It was painful to read such a letter, even years after she first received it. So much betrayal, so much pain in those lines. Evangeline had been thoughtless indeed to believe that the scandal of a governess marrying her master would not affect the Bureau.

But it had rallied. The third rule, *you must never fall in love*, had been put in place, and that had protected her for a while.

She had never met Sir Mark. Vivienne had received the wedding invitation, all gold embossed, and sent a short, curt refusal. That was when the letters had started. After about two years, they had halted.

Hot, burning tears were threatening to fall, but Vivienne dashed them away. She would not cry.

How could she mourn a friendship that had been over for a decade? It was her fault, after all. Evangeline had done nothing wrong.

She could see that now.

Now Edwin and she were starting to move toward some sort of understanding, not that she knew what it was, she could see how easily Evangeline had slipped into affection. When one met a man who changed the world for you, you wanted to stay in that world.

No matter the consequences.

Vivienne's gaze caught a few more lines from the letter.

I promise you, I had no intention of falling in love. It fell…well, it fell like snow. One cannot stop winter coming, and one cannot beg the snow to stop falling.

A wry smile appeared on her face. Well, that was one way to

put it. She certainly had felt that loss of control recently. With each step that she and Edwin took toward each other, the pain melted away, and the love grew.

Was that what Evangeline had experienced? Vivienne sighed. She had never known. She had never asked.

It was too late now to retrieve the friendship of a woman who had, if Vivienne was honest with herself, truly helped to establish the Governess Bureau all those years ago.

But it was not too late, perhaps, for her.

"I have no wish to rush you, we will—we will work it out in our own time."

Vivienne bit her lip. He was a good man. A great man, at times. Everyone had their faults, and she was hardly perfect.

Perhaps perfect was not necessary. Perhaps it was the journey toward each other, even after terrible odds, that made it perfect.

Vivienne carefully folded up Evangeline's letter and sighed heavily. Perhaps, after all this time, she could find her own version of happiness.

Chapter Twenty

March 1, 1816

Edwin looked down at the long list and saw to his surprise that the majority appeared to be ticked off. No, that was not quite right. All of it was.

He blinked to ensure he was not misreading his own handwriting—something which had been known to occur. He was hardly going to win any prizes for his penmanship, but it had always, at least, been legible.

But as far as he could see, the long list that had been a dreaded burden of the beginning of the month had disappeared in less than an hour.

"And that is all, my lord," said Harris, looking up from his own corresponding list.

Even hearing from his butler's own mouth that they were finished with the day's tasks did not convince Edwin. He looked at the paper on his desk, certain they'd forgotten something.

"Surely not," he said distractedly. "Have we discussed the Easter celebrations?"

"We have, my lord."

"And the flowers that are to be sent to the village church?"

said Edwin, looking for it on his list. *Where was it?* "It was always a Bysshe tradition that Easter day would be decorated with the blooms of the estate. It has been organized?"

The butler bowed his head. "As ever, my lord, I have fixed things with the reverend, and he sends his thanks and compliments."

Edwin nodded. *Yes, yes, the rhythm of the estate continued as it always did—as it always had.* When one of his cousins, or more likely their children, inherited the place from him, the same flowers would be sent to the same little village church, as it should be.

As it always had been.

But that meant, if Edwin was reading his list correctly, they were finished. *Goodness.*

He could hardly believe it.

The first of each month, he was usually trapped in his study, going through things first with his steward, then Mrs. Jenner, then finally with Harris to ensure Byhalden Lodge and its surrounding environs continued on much in the same way as they always did.

This time of year, darkness would fall hours before he and the butler finished; but somehow, they had come to the end of the list with no fanfare and no disasters.

"Are you quite sure?" Edwin found himself asking. *Not that he wanted to be proved wrong, but...* "We have covered everything? The invoices, bills, wages—"

"Rent agreements and the letters from your lawyers, yes, my lord," interrupted Harris with a well-meaning smile. "I know we have completed the tasks a little earlier than before, but be assured, we have left nothing out nor missed a thing."

Edwin nodded. *It sounded too good to be true.* Perhaps it was. Perhaps he was merely more efficient than normal. Perhaps a change in his life had brought benefits in other areas...

A smile crept across his face. *Vivienne.* He would happily ascribe any good fortune to her presence in his life, as long as he could maintain it.

They had made love again last night. Soft, gentle, and slower than before. A new exploration of each other, of what they liked, of what they could not bear to stop before ecstasy was found.

The memory soared within him, making Edwin certain that it was Vivienne's presence that made everything else...better. He could describe it no other way.

More importantly, the phrase "Governess Bureau" had not been uttered between them.

Vivienne did not always have to speak for Edwin to understand her. True, in the past, he had managed to get a few things monumentally wrong...but that was then. This was now.

If she truly intended to return to London, would she not have said so? Would she not be talking endlessly of the Governess Bureau, how vital it was for her to restore it? Yet she had said nothing. The Bureau had become silent between them, precisely how Edwin liked it.

The clearing of the butler's throat brought Edwin back to himself. "Sorry, did you say something, Harris?"

The man nodded respectfully. "I am afraid I did, my lord. If I may be so bold as to note that you have been remarkably happy this last week..."

The comment wiped Edwin's smile from his face. *Ah.*

That was something he had not considered. They had been very careful around Laura, who, at any rate, had spent most of the last week in bed, suffering as she said from a head cold. It had been easy to keep their burgeoning affection from his daughter, but his staff...

Edwin swallowed. He should have thought about this earlier. He made a point of only hiring intelligent servants, for a servant with good brains was far less difficult to manage. They practically managed themselves, which was all very well until they started to notice things.

Vivienne's reputation was in his keeping, and Edwin would be damned if it would be destroyed before they had agreed what sort of arrangement they would make together.

It was difficult at the best of times to keep gossip from other people. It was something Edwin had endured when he and Henrietta had adopted Laura, and he had no wish to endure it now. Besides, picking an orphan off the streets of London to adopt was interesting but hardly salacious. A viscount bedding his daughter's governess, on the other hand…

Edwin found his throat had gone quite dry. *Blow the Bureau; it was his own reputation that he had to maintain! And Laura's.* His stomach lurched painfully. If any harm was done to Laura due to his own recklessness…

"What do you mean by that?" Edwin asked sharply.

His butler looked astonished at the harshness of his tone, and took a step back.

Blast. Edwin regretted the way he had responded—too harsh, too quick, too severe. If he had merely thanked the man for his observation, the whole thing would be over by now.

"I-I just thought," said Harris, holding himself straight and stiff, "that you were happier, my lord. I don't mind telling you that after her ladyship…we thought you would be mourning forever."

Edwin's heart softened. That was the benefit of hiring generation after generation of servants from the same family. They almost became a sort of family to you.

He had mourned when Henrietta had died. He was no monster; theirs had not been a love match, and they had both been disappointed that love had not blossomed. He had mourned her with all the dignity she had deserved.

"But that seems to be coming to an end," his butler was saying, still hesitant. "As though the end is in sight, if you don't mind me saying, my lord."

Edwin forced a smile on his face. It was not difficult; he was touched by the man's awkward phrasing, even if the whole topic was rather uncomfortable.

Harris had been with him for his entire time, since he inherited the title—had been the butler for his brothers before him, and for a few years, their father before that. He had earned the right to make slightly more personal remarks.

"You know," said Edwin slowly, "I do know what you mean. I do feel as though I am coming out of the end of a tunnel, rather. Thank you, Harris, that will be all."

It was a polite dismissal but a firm one. Edwin had no desire to open that topic of conversation, for then it could descend into questions, and all of a sudden, Vivienne's name was being pulled into the mirk.

And he would not have that. No, Vivienne and he would discuss it all, slowly, as and when she felt comfortable.

"Thank you, my lord," bowed the butler, closing the door behind him.

Edwin was left alone in the study, the sun still shining, and with a few hours of his afternoon entirely free. It was such a novel development on the first of the month that he had no real idea what to do with himself.

Life, in short, was starting to return.

Edwin found he was smiling. Just as the world was starting to awaken, so was he. He had not really realized he was dead—well, not dead precisely. In hibernation, perhaps.

After their break in the park all those years ago, it had been Vivienne's absence from his life that meant it was not worth living. Not worth enjoying. Laura was the one ray of light, and she had continued to be difficult.

He still had no success in encouraging her to call him "Father." Edwin's jaw tightened. *He supposed he had to earn it, but still.* No other child had to be persuaded to call her father by that loving endearment, not his name.

A figure moved outside, catching his attention. From this distance, it was difficult to see precisely who it was, but as the figure turned, Edwin could see it was a gentleman carrying a leather briefcase.

Ah, Monsieur Pierre, the music tutor. Yes, he had forgotten

to cancel the music lesson, so now the poor man would have to travel all the way to Harrogate. Edwin made a mental note to pay the man double for his trouble.

The music lesson certainly could not go ahead today. He had almost visited Laura that morning, having not seen her for a few days, but Mrs. Jenner had persuaded him not to.

"She must be mighty sick, the poor child," the housekeeper had said as the breakfast things were being cleared away. "She told me days ago that she wished for only one person to come near her to reduce the risk of infection, and she asked little Bessy to do it. Kind, thoughtful child."

With all this time and Laura in bed, this was a perfect time to see Vivienne. Edwin's heart warmed at the thought of her. *Every minute spent in her presence was precious, as though it could be pulled away at any moment.*

The thought was painful, and he pushed it away.

In any other circumstances, the master of a household seeking out the company of a servant—a governess, no less—would be absolutely scandalous. But not here. Not Vivienne.

Edwin's smile was bright and bold as he wondered just what he could suggest. A carriage ride, perhaps? An excuse for the two of them to get out of the house, away from others, into the slow country lanes where they could talk openly. Perhaps, if he drove them himself, they could even find a new way of loving under the blankets…

It was a delicious prospect, one Edwin relished. No one would be surprised to see the master of the house and one of his most respected servants out on a carriage ride, particularly with Laura bedridden with a cold. What were they supposed to do, wait around for the child to be well again before they did anything?

Edwin could hardly believe it, but everything had suddenly fallen into place. Vivienne was here, she and Laura got on like a house on fire—almost too well—and what he had wanted all those years ago was finally coming to fruition.

When Edwin reached the schoolroom, it was to discover, as he had expected, that Vivienne was seated there alone. There were papers all over her desk, mainly workbooks from what Edwin could see, and she was going through them with a pencil, her forehead lined.

The lines disappeared as soon as she looked up and saw him in the doorway. "Edwin!"

"Vivienne," he said warmly, stepping toward her with hands outstretched.

He wanted to touch her, be surrounded by her, know himself to be with her.

Vivienne rose from her chair and quickly stepped around the desk, moving into his arms so willingly, so naturally, that Edwin wondered that they had only been blessed with this understanding for a few days rather than a few years.

Her kiss was soft and warm and sweet and precisely what Edwin wanted.

"We should be careful," said Vivienne, pulling away from his kiss but not his arms.

"Why?" teased Edwin, glorying in their connection. Teasing her was like hearing a melody from one's childhood, once beloved and still adored. "You think a servant may decide to take up Latin or feel a sudden need to learn the kings and queens of England?"

"No, not that!" Vivienne laughed as she looked down. "No, it's just that I know Laura's music tutor is here. I do not wish Laura to see us this way."

Finding her governess in her father's arms? Edwin shivered at the thought. No, that would be a most inauspicious start to explain to Laura precisely what was going on here.

"Well, I suppose that is true," Edwin said, reluctantly releasing Vivienne, so she could lean against her desk. "Though I saw the music tutor leave not ten minutes ago, so goodness knows where Laura is at the moment."

Vivienne laughed. "Well, I suppose she is in bed, bless her.

She really is a most docile child when she is unwell, I have experienced far worse."

Edwin laughed in turn. "Which is odd, for I have never known her to be so obliging. You know, Mrs. Jenner told me that to reduce the number of people exposed to her, Laura told her only Bessy would attend to her. Was that not thoughtful?"

It was rare that Edwin ever had a chance to boast about his daughter, and he thought it was rather prettily made—but for some reason, the joy in Vivienne's face was fading.

"Bessy?" she repeated.

Edwin nodded. "Yes, I think that's what she said—or Betsy, maybe. I will be honest, many of the lower servants' names fly by me, and I simply cannot retain them."

It was not well of him to admit such a thing, to be sure, but there was no reason for Vivienne to look so unhappy.

"Bessy," she said again. "You are quite sure it was Bessy?"

Edwin shrugged. "What difference does it make?"

Only then did he start to notice signs of real distress in Vivienne's face. Her eyes roved around the room as though attempting to calculate something complicated, and she gripped the side of the desk with her fingertips.

"In God's name, what is it?" said Edwin quickly. "Vivienne!"

Perhaps it was the mention of her name that revived her or the tone of panic that was starting to seep into his voice. *What was going on?*

"I...I happened to speak to Bessy just this morning at breakfast," said Vivienne, still refusing to look at him. "It was a coincidence of seating only, I had no purpose in speaking with her. She said...she said..."

Fear gripped Edwin's heart. It must be terrible, or else Vivienne would be speaking openly. *What could a mere maidservant possibly have said to upset Vivienne so?*

"She said Hannah told her...that Laura had asked Hannah to wait on her. Hannah, and Hannah alone," said Vivienne, in almost a whisper, her eyes wide and tears starting to form.

Edwin swallowed. *No, this was not possible.* "So...so Bessy has not been attending to my daughter?"

"I think..." Vivienne could hardly get out the words. "Bessy thought Hannah was caring for her, and you believe Bessy was. Which means—"

"Who was the last person to see Laura?" Edwin asked, turning away from Vivienne and striding to the door, heart beating so quickly he thought it would wrench itself out of his chest. "I have not seen her these past four days, but someone must have. Who?"

His shout did not receive an answer as he pounded down the corridor toward Laura's bedchamber, his mind rattling with thoughts he could not put in order.

It had been days since he had seen her. When had Vivienne seen her? If Mrs. Jenner, Bessy, and Hannah had not been tending her—

"Edwin, wait!"

Edwin did not wait. Blood boiling, he reached out a hand and pushed the door open.

Laura's bedchamber appeared before him. It was tidy, which was unusual in itself, and enough to make the hair on the back of his neck prick up.

There were her books, her playthings, which Laura insisted she had outgrown but just as vehemently insisted she could not part from. There was her bed, all pillows and blankets for these cold winter nights.

It was made. And it was empty.

Vivienne appeared behind him, panting with the effort. "She...she could be anywhere, Edwin, there is no need to—"

"To panic?" said Edwin, turning on her with sheer terror in his voice now. "You think I should not be concerned that my daughter is missing, has somehow constructed a way that no one has seen her for near on a week, you think I should stay calm?"

"She could be anywhere in the house, in the stables. She could have tried to get to York for a book," said Vivienne wildly, as though she sensed how nonsensical her words were. "She could be—"

"Gone," said Edwin quietly, turning back to the empty bed, which seemed to scream out into the silence. "She's gone."

His daughter was gone. Laura. Laura was gone, missing, and where to, he could not think. The terrible truth that his daughter had perhaps been gone for hours, days even, and no one in the household had realized...

Something terrible prickled at the back of his mind. A letter, one he had ignored. A letter from Smethly...someone had been making written inquiries to them about the origin of Laura. Edwin had dismissed it out of hand, but had Laura...

"You know how Laura hates the cold. She wouldn't have just..." Vivienne's voice trailed off, and then it became firmer again. "We need to search. Organize a search of house and grounds. We could be seeing things here! She may have—have slipped down to the library. It may all be a misunderstanding between Bessy and me!"

It was an eternity, the time it took Edwin to hurtle downstairs to the library. It was empty.

"Or the drawing room," said Vivienne, and even Edwin, in his befuddled state, could hear the fear in her voice now. Even she did not believe it. "The drawing room is very pleasant."

When they crashed into the drawing room, almost falling over their own feet in their haste to open the door, it was to find a rather surprised Harris in there.

"My lord, Miss Clarke, what is all this to do?" the butler said as he straightened up from inspecting the polished grate.

Edwin's stomach lurched. "Laura is missing."

"Laura may not be missing," said Vivienne slowly in that governess voice Edwin both loved and loathed. "We have just...misplaced her."

Edwin was astonished to see the man's face whiten.

"Miss...Miss Laura is missing?" said Harris in horror. "Why? Where did she go?"

Hearing the words said aloud by another was somehow far

worse.

Edwin fell heavily onto an armchair with his butler's words going round and round his mind, sounding far worse each time they echoed back to him.

"Miss...Miss Laura is missing? Why? Where did she go?"

Excellent questions, ones Edwin could not even begin to answer. Vaguely in the distance, he heard Vivienne and Harris talking, but he could neither make out the words nor summon enough energy to care.

His daughter was gone, who knew how long. *Oh, she was a smart one, his Laura,* Edwin thought numbly as he twisted his fingers together. *Far too smart for him. But where would she go?*

"—search of the grounds," the butler's voice said as it pierced his thoughts. "You stay here, Miss Clarke, with the master. I will send a footman with any news."

Hurried footsteps—and then a soft hand touched his shoulder. "Edwin?"

Edwin looked up, tears blurring his eyes. "She's gone. My daughter."

"We will find her," came the reassuring words, but they could not impose on his heart.

Gone. Laura. Edwin could not put the two thoughts together, but there they were. His daughter was gone. The child he loved beyond anything. *Had he ever told her that?*

"There was so much I was going to tell her," he said quietly, staring up into the eyes of the one person right now he could trust and rely on. "So much she wasn't yet ready to know but...but perhaps I should never have kept it from her in the first place. Perhaps...did she deserve to know?"

Vivienne could not answer him, and Edwin knew that, but the question had to be asked.

Vivienne, on the other hand, was thinking on more practical matters. "We have to tell the village, put word out to York to the justices and magistrates to let them know a child is missing. We must all be on the lookout."

"I...York?" stammered Edwin. His heart was racing, head spinning, and nothing seemed to make any sense anymore. "Why would she go to York? Why would she go anywhere? There isn't anyone in the village or York she really knows. All the neighbors, all our acquaintances, are in London—she knows that!"

There was a desperate tone to his voice, and Edwin could feel himself collapsing into the terror that she had been taken. *But by whom, and where?* No, this journey, wherever it was, had been taken on her own steam. But where would she try to go?

Out of the corner of his eye, Edwin saw Vivienne's face change. It was slowly, and if he had not been hyper-aware of everything he was thinking and feeling, perhaps he would not have noticed it.

A slow, terrible understanding was appearing on Vivienne face.

"What is it?" Edwin demanded.

"I..." Vivienne's voice sounded strangely hoarse. "I mentioned to Laura that her natural mother had been in London."

Silence fell between them as rage, pure unadulterated rage, poured through Edwin's soul.

"You said what?" Edwin's voice was low, controlled, but controlled as a fire was just before a glazier dipped molten glass within it. Burning at such high temperatures, one could not understand how it did not tear down the factory with its heat.

This was why he should never have got his hopes up. This was why they had not worked before, why he and Vivienne had taken such different walks in life. Just when he thought they could have an understanding, Vivienne proved just how dangerous she could be.

"You—you have ruined everything!" Edwin shouted, standing up as though ready to fight, staring at Vivienne, who had collapsed onto the sofa. "What have you done, Vivienne?"

"I-I'm sorry, I—"

"Sorry doesn't bring my daughter back!" he spat, unable to contain himself. "Sorry doesn't find her! Christ alive, the nights are still long, frost is on the ground each morning, we have no clue how long she has been gone, and you are *sorry*!"

Lashing out wasn't helping to find Laura, but Edwin found to his surprise, that it made the pain in his chest lessen, so he allowed the words and venom to pour out from his fearful heart.

"I made a mistake. I am sorry!" Vivienne said, tears in her eyes.

"Sorry doesn't keep her safe. Sorry does not mean she is alive."

It was the first time either of them had spoken the awful truth: that Laura may already be...

"Do not worry," said Vivienne grimly. She, too, stood up, her head held high. "I have a plan."

Chapter Twenty-One

March 2, 1816

IN ALL OF Vivienne's previous nightmares, she had been able to wake up. No matter what had faced her, no matter how fast her heart was racing, regardless of whether she thought she could escape or not—she would awake, the nightmare would fade, and she would sit with a candle until morning. It had been her habit all her life, and she wasn't about to change it now.

But this wasn't the same. This nightmare did not end, no matter how much Vivienne wished to wake to find the whole thing had just been the wild imaginings of her sleeping mind.

Because it couldn't be real, Laura couldn't be missing.

She couldn't be out there in the world, alone. Vivienne could not comprehend it, but it must be true. The hours the entire household, including gardeners and stableboys, had spent looking for her had proven it.

After turning the place upside down, even the attics, which had prompted Mrs. Jenner to cough and say they really must start cleaning up there after all this was over, there was nothing to do but accept that she was gone.

Laura had gone.

The carriage jolted, and Vivienne opened her eyes. It was pitch black outside, but it could be two o'clock in the morning or coming up to seven, and the sky would look no different.

In the darkness of the carriage, however, she could still make out Edwin's face. He sat opposite her, his eyes open, sleep evidently eluding him just as it was her.

The carriage jolted again, and Vivienne reached out a hand to stop herself sliding.

They had not been able to find Laura. The idea she could have attempted to reach London had never seemed real to Vivienne, even after she had admitted her unconscious part in the whole debacle, so when the news came that Laura was nowhere to be found, she had most uncharacteristically burst into tears.

Edwin had not comforted her.

But Vivienne had not permitted sorrow to overcome her for long. There was a steel inside her, she knew, that made her perfect in a crisis, and within minutes, she had dried her eyes, wiped the tears from her face, and resolutely created a plan.

That plan had brought them here, and she could only hope that it had worked.

A painful twist of her stomach reminded her of her guilt, the feeling rising up her throat telling her she may just throw up if they reached their destination to no avail.

No. Vivienne could not lose hope, not when Edwin already had.

She chanced a glance. Edwin's face was pale, his eyes ringed with tiredness. Had he slept at all since Laura's absence was first noted? Vivienne could not recall it.

And that was because, that cruel, sharp little voice in the back of her head reminded her, *this was all your fault.* Your betrayal. Your thoughtless words that made it possible, that spurred on Laura to abandon her father, all she has ever known, to find some dream of a mother who gave her up years ago.

Vivienne's head hurt. *It was all her fault.* Try as she might to quiet that vicious voice, it was right. If she had not been so foolish as to give Laura that piece of information, the whole thing would have been different.

That was what gave her the most pain. That she was the instrument of Laura's misery—for she was surely miserable at this moment, wherever she was—and Edwin's agony.

To think she was the cause of such disaster…

Vivienne closed her eyes. She would not think of it. She could not possibly berate herself any more than she already had done. She should not have said anything about London to Laura. That had caused hurt to two people she…she truly cared for.

And, underlying all of that self-loathing and panic was the painful knowledge that it was downright infuriating to realize she had created her own worst nightmare. A child missing. How many times had this occurred to a governess of the Bureau?

How would she have advised a governess in her position?

Vivienne opened her eyes as the sad truth seeped into her mind. She would probably have fired her. Any governess who lost a child, really lost one, was not fit to work at the Bureau.

It was a sobering thought. All this time trying to bring the Governess Bureau back into Society's good graces, and perhaps she was the biggest liability of all. Perhaps she herself was someone not to be trusted.

Vivienne pulled her pelisse around her tighter. It was cold in the carriage, though she could no longer see her own breath.

Where was Laura? Each time Vivienne attempted to picture where she could be, she was forced to stop herself. It was too painful. Laura in a ditch somewhere. Laura in a barn, struggling to keep warm; or worse, Laura taken by a man of no morals…

Vivienne blinked. Movement in the darkness. Edwin had slowly lowered his head into his hands and, by the small snuffling noises she could hear, he was crying.

Edwin was crying. The thought was almost enough to bring tears to Vivienne's eyes once more. She had never seen Edwin cry before, and now she had hurt him terribly.

She reached out a hand, so close it almost touched his hair, but then Vivienne drew it back. She was not wanted. She knew that now. Edwin would never consider her to be someone he could trust after this monumental failure. She was as good as destroyed.

After all her training, all the training she gave others, after championing the Bureau, saying with such confidence again and again that she would be able to face anything...

Now she faced the worst situation imaginable.

And it was not just a child. A child missing was bad; but this was Laura. This was a girl she had laughed with, taught, embraced after successes, and comforted after failures. It was a child she had hoped, in time, to reconcile with her father.

Vivienne had hoped, in her heart of hearts, to hear Laura calle Edwin "Father."

It was her fault. She was the one who Edwin had trusted with precious information; that Laura had come from London. She was the one who had told Laura without any purpose or caveats. And that was the reason she was gone.

"All you had to do was be a governess!" Edwin burst out, raising his tear-stained face.

Vivienne bit her lip. Was it strange, in this moment, to look back longingly on the days when all they had to argue about was whether or not he had spoken carelessly to her or whether she had not given Laura the right type of Latin lesson?

Now it was all ruined. All the progress they had made, the small understanding she thought they had come to... It was over. It could never be made whole again.

They had tried, perhaps unknowingly, to capture something of the romance they had experienced when they were young, and for a time, Vivienne believed they had achieved it.

But she was wrong. *It was all over.*

"I don't know how I will ever be able to forgive you," Edwin said dully.

Vivienne nodded. "I do not think I will ever be able to forgive myself."

Their eyes met in the gloom of the carriage, and for a moment, Vivienne wondered whether he understood what she was trying to say. How sorry she was, how hard she would work to make this up to him.

How she would never rest until she had found Laura and how she knew it was entirely down to her that they were in this nightmarish situation.

Perhaps, a small part of her wondered, if he could see, could feel how awful he felt, then he could forgive her.

But then he looked away. Edwin turned, as though no longer able to look at her, and peered through the window. Dawn was starting to arrive. Cold, slow dawn.

Another day, and still Laura had not been found.

"I…" Edwin spoke softly, his voice hoarse, as though tiredness and exhaustion had rid him of all strength. "I should never have trusted you."

Vivienne swallowed. It was harsh indeed to hear such words from the lips of the man she loved, but then… "Perhaps not."

That certainly got his attention. Edwin turned to her, surprise on his face. "You are not going to defend yourself? That is not the Vivienne Clarke I know."

Vivienne nodded, keeping herself as upright as possible. "I will always admit fault when it is merited. I thought I had done something small and inconsequential, but I…I was wrong. I am sorry for it."

The surprise on Edwin's face lingered, but after a few heart-stopping moments, he turned away.

"I can never look at you in the same way," he said quietly. "After all we had built, I thought…but no. You have broken that trust, Miss Clarke. It is not possible to go back and change the past. I should have known that. I should never have invited you into my home."

Sorrow clutched at Vivienne's throat, and she thought once again that she would cry, but with great effort, she managed to keep her tears at bay. There would be plenty of time to mourn the loss of whatever this might have been another time, when she could be alone.

"I can never look at you in the same way."

Vivienne knew she would never be able to look at herself in the same way either. Due to her incompetence and thoughtlessness, a child was missing. Alone on the road, unprotected.

God only knew what had happened to her.

Silence fell between them, which was almost welcome to Vivienne's weary soul. She was not sure she could take much more conversation with Edwin if it was to tear her heart again and again, with no purpose save to increase her guilt.

Nothing could rectify her mistake, nothing.

Except maybe, this. Vivienne had not expected the carriage journey to last this long, but then, she was no expert in northern geography. She had no idea just how far Rochdale was from York. Harris had said it could take a few hours if the roads were good, but they had been bad—so bad that the driver had taken an entirely different road.

But they would be there soon, Vivienne comforted herself, with absolutely no knowledge whether that was true. And God willing, they would find what they sought.

It could have been another five minutes, or perhaps fifty, when Edwin spoke again, Vivienne was not sure.

"I don't understand how you know she's there."

Vivienne swallowed. "I don't. Not really. But I believe in the Bureau."

There was a snort from the other side of the carriage. "Your precious Bureau. The faith and trust you put into that thing is laughable."

In any other situation, perhaps Vivienne would have laughed with him or challenged him in debate. It certainly did seem ridiculous—that she expected her contacts in the Governess Bureau over the last fifteen years to offer up a solution to the challenge of a missing child.

But that was only a symptom of a deeper problem, Vivienne knew. It was the challenge of bringing together these two parts of her life, the Governess Bureau and loving Edwin, Viscount Bysshe... that was the real problem, wasn't it?

No matter how hard she tried, reconciling the two together had been a task she had been attempting for years now, and what did she have to show for her efforts?

A devastated father and a missing child. Hardly the grand romantic gesture she meant.

And besides, the success of one was at direct opposition to the success of the other. Vivienne knew that if the Governess Bureau had once again been restored—something she should certainly forget now, for it was not going to happen—then she would be taken back to London, away from Edwin.

And if she had agreed to something as wild and delicious as being Edwin's mistress... Well then, how could a harlot to a viscount run a respectable business?

In short, it was impossible. Vivienne knew there was too much pain there, too much history, too much betrayal now on both sides for any reconciliation to be attempted.

They had only just been starting to put everything together, to start to understand whether there was a way back to each other, and now that was all ruined. Laura's disappearance, even if they found her—*when they found her*, Vivienne determinedly told herself—was a stain on their relationship that nothing could ever wipe clean.

It was no wonder he would not look at her.

"Of course," Edwin said bitterly, still looking out of the window, "even when you try to clean up your messes, Miss Clarke, the dratted Governess Bureau is still wrapped up in it somehow. Even when you bring disaster on my house, you want to use it as a way to justify your disastrous actions."

He was speaking from a place of pain, Vivienne knew, but that knowledge did nothing to lessen the pain he caused. Controlling her temper was key here, which would have been so much easier if she'd had enough sleep to think straight.

"I do not know what you mean," she said as coldly and as

aloofly as possible. "I am merely using the resources that are available to me."

There was a hearty sniff from Edwin.

"There are Bureau trained governesses up and down England," continued Vivienne stiffly. "Every manor, every mansion, every town, every city holds one. It took but an hour to write out a short note indicating the emergency to each of them—"

"Spreading gossip about the scandal of my family!"

"—to Bureau trained governesses who know how to hold their tongues," said Vivienne fiercely, trying to keep heat from her words. "I trust my governesses, my lord, even if you do not."

It pained her to speak to him in such a formal manner, but as he had returned to "Miss Clarke," it was only appropriate that she did the same. No matter how much it tore at her soul.

"And by the return post, we heard tell of an unaccompanied girl with plenty of money just yesterday at an inn, about Laura's age, wearing a pelisse identical in description to the one that is missing," said Vivienne slowly. In a way, this recitation of what they knew and why they were journeying at breakneck speed to Rochdale was rather soothing. "According to Miss Hubert, the girl refused all help but demanded that she be given the best room in the inn and a stock of all the novels in the building."

Was that a smile on Edwin's face? It flashed before her so quickly, Vivienne was not entirely sure she caught it.

He sighed heavily. "That does sound like her."

The instinct to reach out and comfort him was high, but Vivienne managed to keep to her side of the carriage. That was a line that could not be crossed now, no matter how much she wished it. Edwin would never again receive her tender embraces, and she would never again know what it was to be kissed by him.

Vivienne swallowed. The wide expanse between them filled the carriage. She was not sure whether she could overcome it. She was not sure whether she deserved to.

When—if Edwin ever chose to marry again, and of course, it was not known whether he would ever choose to, he deserved a woman who did not put Laura in danger.

Something she had done within months of arriving in his household.

A sudden change in the carriage made Vivienne look out of the window. It was slowing down. They had arrived.

"We're here," said Edwin, his voice cracked and his eyes searching hastily out of the window for what Vivienne knew was a glimpse of his daughter. "Stop the carriage!"

The great speed at which they had rumbled along the road meant it took almost a full minute for the carriage to stop. Every second seemed to drag on most painfully.

They had stopped outside a large coaching inn. Several horses were being led across the yard, and sleepy-looking drivers were starting to hitch up their steeds to the carriages. There was little noise that could be heard, even when Edwin threw open the carriage door and stumbled out onto the cobblestones.

"Laura?"

Edwin raced out of the carriage without waiting for Vivienne nor offering to assist her, but that was the least of her concerns. She half stepped, half fell out of the carriage herself, her bones crying out after the stiffness of the journey, and rushed forward toward the archway over the entrance to the inn.

Under its cover stood a woman with dark chestnut hair and sharp eyes; a woman Vivienne knew. It was Miss Meredith Hubert—or the Duchess of Rochdale, as she supposed she would have to call her now.

And beside her, wrapped in a heavy woolen cloak, was a bundle with blonde hair.

"Ah, Miss Clarke," called out the Duchess of Rochdale.

Edwin started, then started running toward her. *Of course*, Vivienne thought as she reached them. He had never met the Duchess of Rochdale *nor knew she had once been one of her governesses.*

"I believe this is what you are looking for, Miss Clarke?" said the Duchess of Rochdale with a smile.

The blonde bundle looked up at Vivienne and Edwin, exhausted eyes matching those of her father's. There was a small, muffled sob.

Laura was not permitted to speak. Edwin pulled her into such a tight embrace that Vivienne was astonished he had not knocked the wind out of the child.

"I-I thought I'd lost you," was all the muffled words Vivienne could make out from the distraught father.

Vivienne looked at the duchess. "I cannot thank you enough, I—"

"What did you think you were doing, running away?" asked Edwin, pulling back from his daughter to look at her.

Laura's face was glazed with tears. "I didn't run away. I was running towards! To my parents!"

"But Laura," Vivienne could not help but say before Edwin could open his mouth, "your father is here."

There was genuine distraught and exhaustion on Laura's face as she wailed, "I mean my birth parents!"

There was silence for a moment, other than the gentle nickering of horses. Then—

"I think I will take my leave of you," said the Duchess of Rochdale delicately. "Always a pleasure and an honor to see you, Miss Clarke. My lord."

The stately woman stepped away, but Vivienne paid her no attention. All her focus was affixed on the man and child before her.

Edwin grabbed Laura's shoulder and started walking. "Come with me, Laura."

It was such a strange reaction that Vivienne blinked, then realized he was taking the child to the carriage. There was a very real possibility he may choose to leave her behind if she did not keep up, and so Vivienne followed them.

No one spoke as they helped Laura into the carriage, Edwin sitting beside her and Vivienne opposite them both. Edwin said nothing as he tapped the roof of the carriage, and the driver turned it around and started off for home.

Vivienne looked closely at the girl before her. She looked sulky, absolutely exhausted, and smelt to high heaven, but she was there and whole and safe. It was a miracle.

"Laura," said Edwin quietly as the carriage rattled on, albeit at a slower pace than on their way to the inn, "why would you want to go to London to find your mother?"

Laura gave what Vivienne believed was a shrug, through it was difficult to tell under the heavy woolen cloak. "Henrietta is gone. I wanted a mother, someone who I could talk to."

Edwin took a deep breath, and Vivienne saw the pain on his face, knew what he was going to say before he said it. "Laura, your…your birth mother is gone, too. That was one of the reasons that we—that I wanted to adopt you."

Vivienne said nothing. From her recollection, when Edwin had told her only briefly about Laura's introduction to Byhalden Lodge, it had been Henrietta who had wanted to adopt a child, not himself.

Laura had resorted to one of her favorite expressions: a good, solid, scowl. "Fine. My father, then. I was looking for my father."

"I am your father," said Edwin in a rather strangled voice.

"Fine!" Laura snapped, tiredness evidently shortening her temper. "My birth father."

And then Vivienne saw it. She could not have believed how she had not seen it before.

"Yes," said Edwin quietly, his eyes not leaving his child's face. "Your birth father. Me."

Astonishment flowed through Vivienne's mind as she stared at the man she had believed she had known. Edwin—Edwin was Laura's father? Her birth father?

Laura's face was an absolute picture, showing all the confusion that Vivienne felt.

Edwin sighed heavily and put his arm around his daughter. "I should have told you before, but there was never a good time, and as time went on…your mother was my mistress. You are my daughter, Laura, though whether from blood or love, I don't think it really matters. If you were adopted with no connection to me whatsoever, I would love you no less. What matters is that…is that I love you, Laura."

Vivienne was full of questions but knew better than to interrupt.

"I had no idea you existed at first," Edwin was saying quietly, "until I received your mother's letter. She was sick, she was…she knew she was…"

Laura's eyes were full of tears again, but she said nothing.

"I left for London immediately, but she died the night after I arrived," said Edwin softly. "And there you were. My daughter."

There was such warmth, such depth of emotions in his voice. Vivienne had never seen him like this. This was the answer, then. This was the girl who finally unlocked Edwin's heart—not his lover, but his daughter.

"Father," whispered Laura.

Edwin burst into tears and hugged his child as she embraced him with the same affection.

Vivienne wished heartily she was both not in the carriage at all so as not to intrude on this moment, and a part of it.

But it would not be long after they arrived back at Byhalden Lodge that she could fulfill one of those instincts. It had all become too much.

He'd had a mistress, then. Securing for himself a wife was not sufficient, so he had two women at his beck and call while she had been alone and miserable in her small room in London.

Edwin had immediately wed, and then by the sound of it, found solace in the arms of another. Who was to say that he would not do so again, even if they somehow were able to reconcile to each other?

No, it was over. Vivienne allowed her eyes to close and pretended to fall asleep in the carriage as Laura and Edwin excitedly spoke. She had enough to think about. She needed to plan her return to London.

CHAPTER TWENTY-TWO

March 3, 1816

E DWIN COULD NOT only feel the patter of his heart but hear it, so loud was his pulse. The house was dark. He could not see her, knew Laura was somewhere within but could not find her.

"Laura?" His voice sounded low, quiet, no matter how much he raised his voice.

What strange situation was this?

A strange noise, somewhere far from him. Edwin turned around hastily. He was standing in the hall but did not know which direction to take. To the kitchens? The servants' hall? The library? The music room?

Perhaps she was in the smoking room, though why Laura would be there—

The noise again. Was it the muffled cry of a child in pain? Edwin could feel the terror overwhelming his senses, but he tried to push through them, determined to find her. He had to find her. *His daughter.*

"Laura, where are you?" Edwin stepped forward—any movement was better than nothing.

But as he opened up the door to the dining room, the library came into view. Edwin's mouth gaped. *This did not make any sense;*

this was the dining room. Except it wasn't. Instead of a table and chairs in the center of the room, the walls were lined with books.

Edwin stepped back to the hall, growing unease prickling the hair at the base of his neck.

"Confused," he muttered to himself. "Just confused."

He stepped forward for a second time, this time to the morning room—only to find himself in the kitchens. The place was eerie, pots cluttered and bubbled on the stove, yet no servants could be found.

Nowhere led where he expected. No one was here. And he could still not find Laura.

The confusion rose like a constricting belt around his chest, making it increasingly difficult to think, but think, he must. Edwin knew he had to find Laura, that was the only thought on his mind, and yet he could not find her—she did not seem to be anywhere.

"Laura," Edwin tried to shout but found he said nothing. As he raised his hands to his mouth, he found to his horror that his mouth was clamped shut, and nothing he could do could help him scream—

Edwin sat bolt upright in his bed, hands clammy, face coated in sweat, his heart racing so quickly it threatened to break a rib.

It was only after Edwin had hurriedly rushed out of bed, almost fallen to the floor because one of his legs was asleep, tried to pull his boots on then his breeches over his boots, and actually fell to the floor, that Edwin remembered.

Laura. They had found her.

Only after minutes of slowing down his breathing and attempting to remember did Edwin slowly sit up, pull both breeches and boots off, then get back into bed.

Every bone ached. That was what happened, he supposed, when one hurtled off in a carriage halfway across the county and then hurtled back at much the same speed to get Laura into bed and a doctor to her.

"Sorry doesn't bring my daughter back! Sorry doesn't find her!

Christ alive, the nights are still long, frost is on the ground each morning, we have no clue how long she has been gone, and you are sorry!"

Edwin pulled a pillow behind him and sat up in bed, trying to calm down. His lungs still ached with the tension from his dream—more a nightmare. Dear God, to think that his mind had not yet caught up with the truth: that Laura was safe, at home, and likely to be forbidden from ever leaving the place again.

It was still a slight blur, how it had all come together. Vivienne—*Miss Clarke, he would have to forever think of her as Miss Clarke*—put out the word; that's what she had said.

Well, he could only pray that the news of the matter never reached the gossip sheets. He was not sure he could bear the scandal if it did.

But they'd found her. *Laura.* Wrapped up like a sorry little beggar, cared for by some woman Miss Clarke had called both a duchess and a governess of the Bureau, which figured.

And he had told her. Now Laura knew.

They had arrived back at the lodge late, Edwin now recalled, too late for further conversation. Laura had been bundled up to bed by Mrs. Jenner, with many warnings of cod liver oil and such like, and Edwin had collapsed into a chair in the morning room, the closest to the front door. It had been Harris who had managed to encourage him to go upstairs to bed.

Edwin sighed. It felt almost as much of a dream as his nightmare had, though of course, with a much happier ending.

Laura was home. She knew the truth of her parentage, and she had called him Father.

In some ways, Edwin thought ruefully, *it was a pleasant end to the whole debacle.*

Reaching for his pocket watch, which Edwin had lain on the chest of drawers beside his bed, he saw it was past nine in the morning.

Despite his poor night's sleep and the stress which had been his constant companion the last few days, Edwin smiled to himself. *Laura was his daughter.*

She always had been. Blood mattered little to him when someone as wonderful as Laura entered his life. He would have loved her whether or not she came from his blood line, Edwin knew that.

But she didn't. He had taken her into his home, given her his name, but perhaps not the warmth and affection that she had expected. That Laura had needed.

Everyone needed to know where they came from, Edwin reflected. Even if one did not like the answer. There were plenty of people—lords, mainly—who did not get along with their father, never had done. But they knew who he was.

Perhaps that had been his mistake, amongst many. It had not mattered to him either way, but it had mattered to Laura, clearly.

Edwin sighed heavily, finally starting to feel the effects of the nightmare wearing off. There were many other mistakes, of course, some more important than others. There would need to be a great unpicking of his approach to Laura, a revisit of how he spoke to her.

They would work on it together.

His heart flickered with a paternal love he had always known but never really sought to display. Fathers did not display affection. Come to think of it, many noble mothers did not.

Well, that stopped here, Edwin thought to himself. If the cost of not showing his true feelings were the potential loss of his daughter, it was far too high a price to pay. The terror which had entered his very soul at the thought she could perhaps never be recovered...

Edwin shivered. It was as though a cold breeze had entered the room, though no such thing had occurred. It had, instead, entered his soul.

He had almost lost her, and it had been due to Vivienne's idiocy and incompetence that it had happened. A dark scowl overcame his face. But it had been Vivienne's cleverness, her connections, her...her dratted Governess Bureau, which made it possible to find Laura.

Edwin folded his arms across his chest. *There she was again, Vivienne, making everything complicated for him.*

The numerous times in his past he had needed her, wanted her, and she had not been there. Edwin could think of five immediately when his world had been dull, boring, lonely, or grief-filled, and he had wanted Vivienne by his side, where she could not be.

But this time, when he had truly faced an emergency of epic proportions, Vivienne had snapped into action more competently than any man.

She had been there right when she had needed him.

A slow smile spread across Edwin's face. He had needed her, and in a strange way, she had rescued him. Rescued Laura. *Rescued them both.*

But then the smile disappeared as the very real and painful truth dawned on him. Laura would not have needed rescuing if Vivienne had not told her the last known location of her mother. She would never have run away at all, would not have gone to the lengths she did to concoct a head cold to keep her out of sight for days if she had not been given a location.

Edwin sighed heavily and considered just rolling over and going back to sleep. Nightmares were frightening, true, but he could at least wake up from them. This sort of waking confusion was one he could only escape in dreams.

It was all so...so complicated. Edwin was not one to listen to gossip, preferring real facts rather than bold supposition that had no merit in truth.

This meant he was often unaware of scandals in London or elsewhere until someone mentioned it to him in passing, and he had no idea what the reference could possibly mean. But he had to assume that most people did not live their lives with increasing complexity, as he appeared to be doing.

At his time of life, moving into middle or later age, there were usually complications. Illegitimate children, debts, arguments with family and friends. Edwin had always considered himself to be fortunate only to have the one.

But Vivienne was an entirely new type of complication. Not mistress, not lover, yet hardly an acquaintance. Something so much more and yet not enough.

"Sorry doesn't bring my daughter back! Sorry doesn't find her! Christ alive, the nights are still long, frost is on the ground each morning, we have no clue how long she has been gone, and you are sorry!"

Edwin cringed at the memory of his harsh words. He had not acted particularly well then, but he did not expect anyone would react any better.

Besides, Vivienne had made a mistake. Was he to pretend that no one ever made mistakes? That his own life was entirely perfect?

"How did you find me?" Laura had asked in the carriage last night, looking between the two adults.

And Edwin had tried not to catch Vivienne's gaze but had been unable to look away. Her eyes had been red-rimmed. She had been crying, and he had not noticed.

"With difficulty," was all Vivienne had said.

Edwin had nodded at the time, accepted that if Vivienne—Miss Clarke—wished to tell Laura how she'd been tracked down, safe and sound, she would tell her.

So he had kept his counsel.

He rather regretted that now. Edwin could see the benefit of telling Laura the truth—that Vivienne had so many loyal friends around the country that it had taken but half a day for someone to share the news that she had been spotted. Now he came to think about it, it was rather impressive.

Emotions tore at each other within his heart so tempestuously that Edwin hardly knew what to think or what to feel. What was it that he had thought, when he and Vivienne had finally succumbed to their passion for each other?

That he had come home.

Now she was surely expecting him to dismiss her. Edwin would be fully within his rights to be, he knew, but that did not mean he wished to. A sudden ice sunk into his heart. *Vivienne—leave Byhalden Lodge?*

There were still plenty of conversations to be had, and he was not entirely sure he had forgiven her in his heart. But the idea of Vivienne leaving his employ before those conversations could be had were anathema to him.

The idea he might not be with her—that he could not happen upon Vivienne in the garden, enjoy her company at dinner, relish her sweetness in his bed…

Edwin sat up straight. *He had to find her.* He needed to…well, not precisely apologize for what he had said when Laura had been missing, for he had meant every word.

But he wanted to speak with her. Reconcile, find some way that they could share their lives. Forgive her. Forgive each other.

They were too old, too wise in years to be arguing over such things. He had never told her, not properly, how he felt about her. If he had learned one thing from Laura's escapade, and he had learned many, it was that words thought were not the same as words spoken.

It did not take Edwin long to get dressed. His coat was somewhere downstairs, but a shirt and waistcoat would do very well for the conversation he planned to have with her.

It was not as though Vivienne hadn't seen him in less, anyway.

Edwin's heart was racing. *If he was not careful*, he thought wryly, *he would need to see his physician, the exertion all these adventures were placing on his heart.*

He had to be with her. It was as though he was being pulled inexorably toward her, as though he would not be complete until Vivienne was before him.

Somehow, he needed to make this right. There would be difficult times ahead of them, to be sure, and navigating the Governess Bureau would be one of them. But if they were facing the challenge together, side by side, as they had done to find

Laura—that was what mattered.

So lost in his thoughts had Edwin become that it was not until he was standing on the landing, pulling his second boot on, that he realized he had no idea where Vivienne was.

Another glance at his pocket watch told him that it was near ten o'clock. No point in going to the servants' hall, for they would have breakfasted long ago.

Unless Vivienne had also risen late, as he had? They'd arrived late last night, after all.

Edwin did not bother going the long way round. Taking the servants' staircase and surprising a footman who was carrying up a great deal of bedlinens, Edwin rushed down to the servants' hall to find a few bemused servants hastily ceasing their chores to bow or curtsey.

"Yes, yes," said Edwin distractedly, looking for Vivienne's face. "Where is—"

"Ah, my lord, can I say again how relieved we are to have Miss Laura back in the fold again," said Mrs. Jenner, rushing toward him with a slightly harried expression on her face. "When Mr. Harris told us she was missing, why, I half thought—"

"Vivienne," said Edwin.

The housekeeper stopped to stare. "I beg your pardon?"

Ah. Edwin tried again. "I am looking for Miss Clarke."

That at least made more sense, but it did not prevent a few eyebrows being raised by maids, and a footman muttered something to another, receiving a wallop on the shoulder.

"Goodness, I do not know," said Mrs. Jenner slowly. "She didn't come down to breakfast, I can tell you that. Perhaps she is asleep? I can ask Hannah if she will go up and—"

"No need," Edwin said hastily, turning immediately to race upstairs again. *Bedchamber, why hadn't he thought of that!*

He passed the schoolroom on his way, and Edwin poked his head in there for good measure but saw precisely what he had expected. Neither Laura nor Vivienne were there.

When he reached Vivienne's bedchamber, he entered without knocking. *Well, there would be so much gossip downstairs in the servants' hall already*, Edwin reasoned, heart soaring in anticipation of seeing Vivienne. *Why not add a little more?*

"Vivienne, I know this is wild and radical, and I should not be here," Edwin said in haste as he stepped inside. "But I need to explain myself and apologize—not for everything, but for some of…"

His voice trailed away. The room was empty. Vivienne was not there.

It took a moment for Edwin to realize why this was so surprising. After all, Vivienne could be anywhere in the house, in the grounds…but it wasn't just that she was not in her bedchamber, which jarred.

It was more than that. All of Vivienne's belongings were gone, too.

Edwin leaned against the wall and slowly slid down it to sit on the floor.

No. It wasn't possible. He had only just managed to get Laura back; he could not now lose Vivienne. But was it any wonder?

"Sorry doesn't bring my daughter back."

Edwin dropped his head into his hands. He had meant every word, and though he could not take back the sentiment, it had come from a place of pain. Why was this so confusing?

Taking a deep breath, he willed himself to do something, but he was all out of ideas. There was nothing else he could do. *Nothing.*

"She…she really is gone then?"

Edwin looked up. Laura was standing in the doorway.

Before the last few days, Edwin would have immediately risen to his feet and attempted to pretend that he was entirely in control. Instead, he sighed and nodded.

Hesitantly, Laura moved from the doorway and came to sit beside him. "I did not really think she would go."

Edwin looked at his daughter. "You knew she was going?"

Laura shrugged. Despite the exhaustion of the last few days, she seemed far more comfortable around him now.

He sighed. He should have been more open years ago. All

this time they had lost—something of a theme in his life.

"She said something about finding her place," said Laura quietly. "When she came up last night to tuck me in."

Pain gripped Edwin's heart. Not only had she given a hint to Laura, but Vivienne had once again proven that she knew what to do as a parent far more than he. *Why had he not come upstairs to tuck in his daughter?*

"But her place is here." Only then did he realize he had spoken aloud.

"That's what I said," said Laura quietly, "but she said she had to go. She said I would understand when I am older, but I'm older now, and I still don't understand."

Edwin blinked, unseeing, at the bed before him.

Why did this feel like a betrayal he had never known before? Because he could not blame her for going. Vivienne had felt his wrath, seen his bitter anger at her mistake, and gone. And she had made the mistake in the first place which had caused his bitterness…

Oh, it was such a mess.

"Well," he said heavily. "I suppose it is just father and daughter left."

Laura smiled. "I suppose so, but I still wish she was here. She…she made me comfortable. In myself. Do you know what I mean?"

Edwin's smile faltered. "Yes. Yes, I do."

They sat in silence for a few moments until Laura piped up again. "I don't know why no one ever wanted to marry Miss Clarke. She's so wonderful, but she's never been married, I asked her."

There did not seem to be any point in attempting to hide it from her now.

"I proposed marriage to her once," Edwin said quietly.

Laura's face was a picture of astonishment. "So is she my—"

"No," he said hastily, foreseeing the problem on the horizon. "No, she is not your mother. Sometimes I wish she could have been a mother to you, though, if we could have found a way to…

I hope that does not upset you."

Laura blinked up at him. She was still so young, Edwin realized with a heavy weight in his chest. She could surely not understand the complexities and vagaries of the adult heart.

With luck, she would never have to know the ill-fortune he had suffered in that regard.

Without saying anything, Laura rose and left the room.

Edwin sighed but made no move to leave. Well, he was not entirely sure how he had managed to upset his daughter, but he supposed that was what being a father was all about.

How long he sat there, Edwin was unsure. His thoughts swirled painfully around him, preventing him from focusing on any one thing for more than a moment, but as there was nowhere for him to go and no one to see, he remained where he was.

Until a stern voice spoke in the doorway. "Come on, you need to pack."

Edwin looked up. Laura was frowning. "What on earth do you mean?"

"I've organized it all with Harris and Mrs. Jenner," said Laura firmly. "I told them that we are going to London, and the carriage is almost ready. Pack. We're going after her!"

There was such brightness in her eyes that, for a moment, Edwin almost believed it.

Then his hopes died. "Laura, you can't understand how... I cannot lose Vivienne again. I have already done so twice, and a third time would..."

A warm, soft hand took his own. Edwin looked up into the eyes of his daughter.

"I promise I am not using this as an excuse to go to London," Laura said seriously, though there was a hint of mirth in her voice. "For a man of many years, you are not very wise. If you think you can be happy without her, we won't go."

Edwin looked at her. *Twelve years old and almost wiser than he.*

He stood up, Laura's hand still in his own. "Well then. We had better get packing."

Chapter Twenty-Three

March 9, 1816

Vivienne sighed and rubbed her temples. *God save her from stupid men!*

It had been a constant frustration in her life that she had never been able to overcome; why the men around her were so often the ones being utterly useless, while there were perfectly intelligent women around the place who could do the job just as well, if not better.

Never had this thought been so apt than as she faced this completely idiotic man.

Corpulently fat and red with the effort of walking up a single flight of stairs, the man stood a little too close to her with an unpleasant leer.

Vivienne curled up her nose to prevent his stench from overpowering her. She had had it absolutely up to here with him, though there seemed little she could do to avoid him.

The conversation had to be finished, and at least, by now, they had completed any of the walking up and down stairs that would be required. This negotiation had to be completed. Her life and livelihood depended on it.

Vivienne's gaze focused once more on Mr. Russel, who stood before her. An agent, he had told her, purchasing on behalf of another. It made little difference to her. Whoever purchased the building that had once housed the Governess Bureau would, undoubtedly, put it to some use that was entirely none of her business.

As she stood in her office—*her old office*—Vivienne attempted not to notice everything around her that demonstrated just how much of a failure she had been.

Most of her furniture, almost all, was packed in crates in an orderly queue along one wall. Her desk was still unpacked, though Vivienne thought that was primarily because it was difficult to see how a solid mahogany desk could be lowered down the staircase without someone damaging it. Or it damaging someone.

Now she came to think of it, it was hard to imagine how the thing had been brought up here in the first place.

There were a few paintings still on the walls, and Vivienne's own personal luggage was still upstairs, but the packing was almost complete. Where she would go was as yet uncertain. It would all depend on this negotiation—which was probably why she should pay greater attention to it.

Vivienne took in a deep breath and regretted it immediately. It was rather unpleasant to breathe in deeply around Mr. Russel.

"—know what I mean, Mrs. Clarke," the irritating man was saying.

"Miss," said Vivienne stiffly.

Mr. Russel shrugged. "Whatever. As I said in my note, the place simply isn't worth what you are asking for. I mean, you bought it for less than that!"

"Fifteen years ago," Vivienne said curtly, holding herself up to her full height. "I think you will find, Mr. Russel, that property prices in these parts have risen quite substantially."

She knew for a fact. She had inquired, discreetly of course, as to the price of two buildings for sale just two streets over, and their prices were astronomical. If they could ask such vast sums for those run-down, damp, squalid places, she was well within her rights to demand what she wanted for the Governess Bureau.

"Not that substantial," said Mr. Russel in that patronizing voice Vivienne had noticed men used when they were sure they could convince a woman of something quite contrary to what they wanted. "You will have to trust me on this, Mrs. Clarke. I know what I am about."

Vivienne stared distastefully. He looked more as though he knew how to avoid a good bath. *Trying to tell her the place wasn't worth a thing—how dare he!*

Summoning up her greatest stare, Vivienne said fiercely, "Mr. Russel, I am not a woman to be trifled with. I know this building is worth several hundred pounds more than your customer is willing to—"

"Damp," interrupted the man flatly. "Damp, everywhere!"

Vivienne was almost beside herself. "There is no damp in this building!"

"Riddled with it," said Mr. Russel with a heavy sniff. "Difficult to spot unless one knows what one is doing, of course, but I seen it. The signs."

He said it with such aplomb, Vivienne felt her certainty start to melt away. She had been confident in her pricing, and several hundred pounds were needed for her next venture. She could not start again with less.

Confidence starting to trickle away, Vivienne knew she had to maintain her certainty. She could not permit Mr. Russel to think he had got to her. Even if he was starting to.

"Look, Mr. Russel, I know what this place is worth, and furthermore, I know what I need," said Vivienne sharply. "I will be establishing a school in the countryside, and if I am unable to raise the funds—"

"That, my good woman, is none of my concern," said Mr. Russel smoothly.

Vivienne narrowed her eyes. *She was certainly not his good woman.*

"All I am here to do is ensure that my client does not get fleeced by buying this building over the odds," he continued, his gaze roving around the room. "It'll need a good deal of work to it to bring the place back up to scratch, I can assure you."

Vivienne could see the greed on his face. There was no client, she was almost sure of that. No, Mr. Russel was going to buy the place—he thought—for a knockdown price, give it a lick of paint, then sell it on to some unsuspecting person who would hear about all the hard work he had to put into getting the place watertight.

She could already see the pounds, shillings, and pence pouring into his pockets.

"That is what you are concerned about?" Vivienne asked. "*Me*, fleecing *you*?"

Now she had heard everything. If she had thought the agony of leaving Edwin and Byhalden Lodge could not be topped by anything, she had at least seen that the foolishness of others had no bounds. No bounds at all.

But that was not what she should be thinking about. Vivienne forced Edwin from her mind and focused on the task at hand. The closure of the Governess Bureau.

Vivienne smiled slowly and saw, to no surprise at all, that Mr. Russel smiled back. *Men. They were so predictable.* It was almost enough for her to give up on them altogether.

Why had she warned her governesses to stay away from men? Because they could not be trusted. *The only consistency in men*, Vivienne thought darkly, *was their inconstancy.*

It was safer to stay away, guard one's heart, and hope to never come across them again.

"Will you not sit down while we discuss this, Mr. Russel?" Vivienne said genteelly before realizing there was no place for him to sit. The only chair left was behind her own desk.

Mr. Russel did not appear to care, however. He started walking around her office—*the room*, Vivienne reminded herself, looking up at the ceiling.

"As far as I can make it out," he said slowly, not looking at her, "your business has failed. You've poured everything into it, and it's failed. Now you have to get rid of your assets, liquidate. Start again. All over again, at your age."

Vivienne bristled. *What had her age got to with a damned thing?*

But she swallowed down her words. There was no point attempting to engage with this cretin. The Governess Bureau had not failed. The world had failed her, perhaps.

"I need to sell the building," she said aloud, trying to prevent her emotions from seeping into her words. Moving over to her desk, Vivienne sat behind it in some attempt to regain the power she had felt when the Bureau had been alive and prosperous, and she had been its queen. Strangely, it did not restore those feelings within her.

She had been so certain, hadn't she? So determined when speaking to Edwin that the Governess Bureau would rise again; that she would be able to resurrect it, make it whole again. Make the world see how wrong it had been to discount her.

And she had been wrong. She had failed.

Now she would start again, at any age, when she had rather hoped to be taking a step back from hard work, rather than toward it. But Vivienne knew she would have plenty of time to be miserable later. Right now, she needed to ensure she had a future in which to be miserable.

"You have debts, right?"

Vivienne blinked. Mr. Russel was standing by the window, looking at her with what he evidently thought was pity.

She crossed her fingers underneath the desk. "No."

Mr. Russel sighed and shook his head. "I can see your fingers."

Vivienne flushed. *Damn.* "Whether I have debts or not has no bearing on the value of the building, Mr. Russel, and that is what we are here to discuss. Now, if I might return to the asking price which I think is more than—"

"It has everything to do with your debts!" Now Mr. Russel appeared to be angry, quite unsettlingly so. "Your debts, madam, which I believe are probably numerous and most grievous to you, are likely costing you a pretty penny. Am I right?"

Vivienne did not dignify his rudeness with a response, even if it was true.

Her wages from Edwin had been enough to cover her initial costs of the interest but not enough to reduce the debts themselves. It had been her own fault. Every business required investment, she knew, but this…this was more than she had bargained for.

Mr. Russel leered. "As I thought. And the size of your debts, madam, tell me just how eager you are to have this place off your hands—how little you are willing to accept."

Vivienne again stayed silent. She was going to say something coarse and rude in a moment if he did not hold his tongue. *Woe betide any man who got her truly in a rage.*

Now the man had stepped closer, his leering eyes were no longer fixed on the building but on her. Most uncomfortably so.

If only she had not been seated, Vivienne would have been able to take a step back; but as it was, she was powerless to prevent Mr. Russel from growing closer and closer to her, his wide eyes lustily gazing.

"After all," he said in a low voice, "there isn't exactly a line of people going down the street, hoping to buy this place. Some things are a little past their sell-by date."

"How dare—" Vivienne halted before she said something that she would regret. She was alone here with this man, and there was no knowing what he might do if he was truly slighted. He was hardly a man to be trusted; he had made that plain.

Still, she needed to sell the Governess Bureau. *If that meant accepting a few insults…*

A painful smile crept across her face. "There may not be a queue of people looking to buy this place, Mr. Russel, but there should be. There is a great desire for property in London and simply not enough people selling. Besides, I have not informed several other agents that this place is available. When I do, I am sure the competition will be great."

For a moment, she had been certain that she had won the day. Vivienne could see Mr. Russel's eyes narrow as he tried to take in her most recent words.

They were not strictly true, of course. Vivienne had no idea who else she could attempt to sell the Governess Bureau to if these stilted negotiations with Mr. Russel came to a halt, but there was no need for him to know that.

The man sighed heavily. "A hundred pounds. That is my best offer."

Vivienne looked at him closely and saw to her horror that he spoke the truth. He was not going to offer her any higher and if she were not careful, her rudeness may in fact, drive him away before he shook on the deal, let alone before he signed any paperwork.

"One hundred guineas," Vivienne said slowly.

It was a small difference, only about five pounds, but it would be more to tide her over. Her heart thundered in her chest, desperately hoping that he would go for it.

But Mr. Russel sensed the weakness within her and smiled. "One hundred pounds."

Vivienne tried to prevent her shoulders from sagging, but she knew precisely what she was going to do. She was going to accept the offer. She had no other options, no choice but to make the best out of this terrible situation.

She would leave London, leave all of this pain and misery behind, and try to build a new life for herself. It would never be the life she wanted, *but then*, Vivienne thought darkly, *she had lost the life she wanted a long time ago*.

It was time to start putting her hopes where they belonged: in the past. She hadn't learned that so far, but it was time to start being a little wiser with her decisions.

Vivienne took a deep breath. "One hundred pounds?"

"Two hundred pounds!"

Vivienne blinked. That did not make any sense—but then, Mr. Russel's mouth had not moved. It had not sounded like him, either. It had sounded like a gentleman she knew well, but that was surely just wishful thinking. There was absolutely no possibility it could be—

Edwin stepped into the office.

Vivienne rose to her feet so hastily that her chair fell down behind her. "Edwin."

There was a smile on his face, a smile she had not expected considering the last words they had shared together: pain and bitterness and accusations.

"Vivienne," he said quietly.

To her shame, Vivienne found her cheeks flushed to hear him speak her name. *He was here.* Why, she had no idea. It could surely not be a good reason…

"Laura," Vivienne said quickly, fear rushing into her heart. "Laura, she's not—"

"Oh, she's quite well, waiting in the carriage for me below," said Edwin hastily. "Fear not. She is safe."

Vivienne had expected her heart to stop its painful flutter once she heard those words, but for some reason, it merely increased in speed. *What was he doing here?*

"Excuse me!"

Vivienne looked at Mr. Russel. *Dear Lord, she had almost forgotten he was here.*

His cheeks were flush red, and he glared at both her and Edwin before saying, "I am in the final stages of negotiating with this woman."

"And I really don't care, my good man," said Edwin breezily, not taking his eyes from Vivienne. "She is mine."

This was so irregular; Vivienne almost laughed aloud with the strangeness of it all. *What was happening?* There was no possibility of her dreaming, was there?

It was clear, however, that Mr. Russel was just as confused as she was. "Dear God, man, you think I would spend days negotiating with Mrs. Clarke about this place to allow you to pick it up piecemeal in my wake? No sir!"

Edwin sighed, and Vivienne wondered if it was worth her attempting to explain. But before she could even concoct which words to speak, Edwin had pulled out a sheaf of banknotes from his pocket.

"Here," he said, throwing what appeared from Vivienne's view to be almost a dozen ten-pound notes. "Take them and go."

Mr. Russel stared—but unlike Vivienne, he did not stay silent. "What on earth is this?"

Edwin smiled coldly. "To go away. Be off with you."

And so, scolded as though a schoolboy, Vivienne watched with some delight as Mr. Russel disappeared out of the office, his footsteps heavy on the stairs. She stood in silence as she heard the door slam and knew that the horrible man had gone.

Which left her alone with a man of quite a different nature.

Vivienne managed to look into Edwin's face, but it was quite an effort. *Here he was, then.* She had thought he would choose to stay away, but no. He was here, no doubt to crow over his victory. To celebrate her failure.

It was just...that was not the Edwin she knew. The man she loved would see her failure as a cause for sadness, not celebration. Yet, for what other reason could he be here?

Vivienne drew herself up. She would not be walked over, not ever.

"You may leave by the same door," she said as icily as she could manage, conscious she could not sit down without lifting up the chair. "Isn't everything else enough for me to deal with? Do you wish to shame me even more by buying my property?"

Edwin took a step toward her, and Vivienne knocked her heels against the chair as she attempted to back away. There was such a strange look on his face, she was quite overcome.

"Vivienne, you have misunderstood—let me explain," said Edwin in a low voice.

Vivienne was not entirely sure whether she would survive an explanation from him; Edwin's mere presence was causing her whole body to shiver. All those years without him, and now he was here, in her Bureau. It was too much, too much to bear.

"I want to buy it as...well. A gift to you."

Vivienne blinked. *She could not have heard him correctly.* "I beg your pardon?"

Edwin threw up his hands. "If I cared about you less, I could explain this better! I was wrong, Vivienne, that's the most basic way I can explain it, and I will say it again and again until you believe me!"

Yet still, she stared. Vivienne could not think what to say, unsure what to believe, unsure whether her own senses were lying to her.

Because he could not be saying that. He could not be speaking these words, the words she had been desperate to hear so long ago, during a time when she had been young enough to still have hopes, still have dreams.

But there was nothing but sincerity on Edwin's face as he looked passionately at her, now only the other side of her desk.

"Please, never leave me again," Edwin whispered. "Don't just disappear. I can't bear it. I can't bear life without you."

"What? No, I-I don't understand...this is nonsense!" said Vivienne finally, her voice breathless, her mind turned in circles. "We go back and forth, Edwin, back and forth, and nothing changes!"

"Not anymore," said Edwin sharply. "No, I've learned from my mistakes, finally. Believe me, over the years, I have learned what I can live with and without, and I have come to the firm conclusion that I cannot live without you. Vivienne..."

There was such longing in his voice that Vivienne's mouth fell open. *Was this not what she had wanted? Were these not the words she wished he had said?*

But they were older now and supposedly wiser.

Vivienne steeled herself to say what she knew could only

bring them both misery for now but would make sense later. "Edwin, we...we have had two chances, and we have both managed to ruin them!"

"So we've learned," said Edwin with a wry smile.

Vivienne had to laugh at that. "I am no longer the picture of a blushing young bride!"

"And neither am I," Edwin said. "Or at least, bridegroom. You know what I mean. You are wiser in years than I—you were wiser than I fifteen years ago, so I suppose that is no surprise. I am serious, Vivienne, in complete earnest. Marry me. Make me the happy fool I want to be."

It was on the tip of her tongue just to say yes. *Yes to happiness, yes to joy, yes to a home and a family and a husband, which had slipped through her fingers so long ago.*

But she couldn't bear to grow so close again and fail. It would ruin her; she would never survive it. And he had to know that.

"Edwin. Edwin, I..."

"Yes?" His eagerness was written across his face.

Vivienne took a deep breath and found her voice cracked as she said, "I can't have my heart broken again."

Somehow Edwin had come around the desk and pulled Vivienne into his arms. His comforting strength, his familiar scent, the way he held her: it was enough to break down the walls, and Vivienne clung to him as she had never done before.

"I know," said Edwin softly. "I am sorry."

Vivienne breathed in, her head against his chest, her eyes closed. She was fast losing all possibility of resisting him. *Did she want to?* Or did she wish to accept him, take this opportunity of happiness which had somehow presented itself?

"How can I trust you?"

"You know I'll make mistakes. I can't promise I will not," said Edwin heavily, and Vivienne snuffled a laugh. "But I can promise that whatever I get wrong, which I will, I will do all I can to make it right."

Vivienne opened her eyes and looked up into the gaze of the

man she loved. Only when Edwin grinned in return and started lowering his lips to hers did Vivienne pull away.

"Vivienne—"

"I need to show you something," she said quietly, speaking over him.

Edwin chuckled. "Dear Lord, woman, I have traveled far today—I am not sure whether I have the energy to—"

Vivienne tapped him on the arm. "Not that!"

Her heart thundered painfully as she stepped over to one of the few paintings still on the wall of her bare office. Her fingers tingling, and sure she was doing the right thing, she took a deep breath and turned over the painting.

There, pasted on the back, was a drawing. It was of a young woman who looked in many ways remarkably similar to her. Perhaps a little younger, perhaps a little more naïve. On the bottom right of the paper was a signature.

E. Bysshe.

Edwin gasped. "You—you kept it."

"I did," said Vivienne with a shy smile as he stepped toward it, staring as though it was a holy relic. "I did, indeed."

"But—but you told me that you got rid of it!" said Edwin, turning to her bewildered.

Vivienne nodded. "I did, didn't I?"

For a moment, Edwin just continued staring, utterly confused—then he laughed. "You know, I am not going to be able to keep up with you, am I?"

Vivienne shook her head as she stepped into Edwin's waiting arms. "No, but that is exactly where I like you to be."

His kiss was sweet and warm and welcoming and promised of more to come. Much more.

Epilogue

March 21, 1816

It was difficult to believe in a way. Almost as though Christmas had come around again far too quickly. As though all his dreams had come true, more than he had ever expected. More than he deserved.

Edwin beamed as he looked around the room and sighed, his entire body relaxed. It was something he had not experienced in many years.

"—and the scenery! I truly believed I was right there in Normandy, France," Laura was saying excitedly to a wide-eyed Vivienne, the two of them nestled under a blanket on the sofa opposite him. "The way she paints a picture with words, I felt like I could reach out and touch the bark of the trees!"

Edwin smiled indulgently. *Books.* He was reading much more now, a conscious choice to bring him closer to his child. If that was what it took, it was more than worth the time.

And the books weren't half bad, though he would admit that to no one but his ladies.

"I thought the hero far less believable," said Vivienne with a gentle wink at Edwin, which Laura thankfully missed. "No man is that perfect."

"Oh, but wasn't it romantic? The way they fought to get back to each other, against all odds!" said Laura blissfully, clutching the offending volume to her chest. "And at the end...will you do my hair like it is described, all up with a gold clasp?"

"Of course," came the initial reply, but Edwin was keen to put a stop to that.

"Hold fire, woman," he said good-naturedly to the lady who, just a few days ago, had become his wife. "You must be careful, now."

Vivienne smiled as Laura looked at him in confusion. "Careful?"

Edwin smiled. "She'll be making you up to be a woman, Laura, and I am not yet ready for my little girl to grow so wise."

His daughter beamed but made sure to stick out her tongue, too, which made Edwin chuckle.

"Oh, there's no harm in a small gold clasp, at the very least," said Vivienne indulgently, looking at Laura with the same devotion Edwin looked at his child. "But your father is right, Laura. There is more than enough time to deal with being a woman and all the difficulties and adventures that come with that. Far more exciting to enjoy where you are right now. Besides, did you hear about the sequel to this one?"

Laura's eyes opened wide. "There's another book?"

Edwin watched the two of them converse easily, pausing only in his observations to put another log on the fire.

Their chatter meandered from books to gowns to hair clasps to music, to the dancing Laura might learn from a new tutor, to just why girls had to learn to dance at all, and back to books. Vivienne was more than a match for her stepdaughter, and Edwin knew in time, maybe, he would be able to catch up with them.

The important thing was he had his family back together again—the family he wanted. Though the time apart was painful, and he would not necessarily have given up Henrietta entirely, this was where he wanted to be. With the people he loved.

Besides, without Henrietta, there would not have been the indiscretion which had led to Laura, and that surely would not be a life worth living.

He was a fortunate man, Edwin knew that. Now all he had to do was start demonstrating that he understood just how precious the jewels in his keeping were.

Edwin's gaze fell to Vivienne. There was laughter in her eyes he had not seen in years. All the joy wrenched from her by their misunderstanding over a decade ago had finally been replaced now they had come to a true understanding.

And what a stepmother she was already proving to be. Careful with Laura, never assuming too much, never pretending to be her mother, yet at the same time gentle, while pushing Laura to try new things and be braver at which she already loved.

Vivienne was not going to be a mother who was walked over, that was for certain.

Edwin shivered, despite the warmth of the fire by his side. It was times like this that he could hardly believe what he was seeing.

He was not an old man; at least, he did not consider himself old. But he was no longer young. When he had been young, this had been precisely what he had wanted. Vivienne and a family.

Now he had both.

Edwin sighed as he picked up his glass of port and smiled as the evening continued in perfect happiness.

"So, are you going to be giving me a sibling?"

Edwin snorted into his port. Vivienne's mouth fell open, and from what he could see, Laura grinned at each of them in turn.

"No," said Vivienne firmly.

"Why?" asked Laura pointedly.

Vivienne's gaze met Edwin's, and he shrugged helplessly. *Well, he had always assumed that Henrietta would explain to Laura that…that part of life.*

He certainly hadn't planned to.

"What would be the point?" asked Vivienne sweetly. "We

have the perfect daughter already."

Laura rolled her eyes but giggled so Edwin was not too concerned. The hour was growing late, and she tried to hide a yawn behind her hand.

Vivienne was not so easily convinced. "Bedtime, young lady."

Laura immediately turned to her father with a pleading look, but Edwin was not to be so quickly won over.

"Come on now," he said with a smile. "You heard what your governess—what your mother—what Vivienne said."

Well, he had ruined it. All the gentle comfort of the evening seemed unstuck, and Edwin hated himself for making such a foolish error.

Why had he not thought to ask Vivienne before this what she would like to be referred to by Laura? At least he had warned her, right before he had proposed in the Governess Bureau, that he would make copious mistakes.

But Laura just laughed. "Dear me, I will let you work that out. You are a fool, Father."

She spoke so good-naturedly as she rose and kissed him on the cheek that Edwin did not really know what to say. It was only after Laura had shut the door behind her on her way to bed that Vivienne collapsed into giggles.

"Well, what was I supposed to say!" said Edwin defensively.

Vivienne laughed and shook her head. "Just pick one, Edwin! Vivienne is probably easiest. Poor child. Such a fool for a father, she is quite right."

Edwin rose and moved to the sofa to sit beside Vivienne.

"I have to admit," he said, kissing her on the head lightly, "I still see you as a governess in a way—not Laura's governess specifically, but a governess generally."

Vivienne smiled. She did not appear offended. "I have spent so much of my life being one, I suppose it's no surprise that I still feel like a governess."

Edwin nodded. *There was an obvious logic to it.* "But what about in public—what shall Laura call you then?"

Vivienne raised an eyebrow. "My name is not sufficient to be spoken in public?"

"You know what I mean," Edwin said hastily. "Now tell me again how I managed to snag such a beautiful, intelligent, and witty woman?"

"I have no idea," said Vivienne dryly.

Edwin sighed as he pulled his wife into his arms. *She was right, of course.* After all his stupidity, being certain that ruining the Governess Bureau would make him happy—he had been blinded by his love for her, and he was grateful that in the end, they had managed to find their way to each other.

And really, they owed it all to the Governess Bureau...

"Evangeline finally replied to my letter."

Edwin looked up. "She did?"

Vivienne looked shyly pleased. "I was concerned, I admit, that she may not wish to hear from me. It has been so long, but she warmly accepted my invitation. She, Sir Mark, and their brood will all be here for Easter."

Edwin beamed. It did his soul good to see his wife—his wife!—happy. That smile that had disappeared for so long had finally returned.

"Good," he said heartily. "I am intrigued to meet this friend of yours."

Vivienne nodded. "Much has changed in the intervening years...but not too much."

"I suppose she knows about us," Edwin said. "I imagine there hasn't been much else on your mind since the wedding!"

"You know," said Vivienne hesitantly, snuggling into her husband. "I have been thinking."

Edwin smiled. "Should I be worried?"

"Maybe. I was thinking...about the Governess Bureau. About how maybe, in the future, when Laura is a little older...how I might open it again."

It was evident that he had much work to do, Edwin thought ruefully, *seeing Vivienne speak of her Governess Bureau to him with hesitancy and concern.* He had much work to do there to gain back her trust, and where else to start, but here and now?

"I am pleased to say that I have already thought about it," said Edwin, tightening his hold around her. "But...well. I would hate for you to get hurt again if, by mere circumstances, it did not work."

Vivienne sighed. Edwin felt the movement against his chest and tried not to get lost in the softness of her skin and his growing desire for her. *This was important. This was a conversation that truly mattered.*

"I suppose I will have to accept that some things have their time," said Vivienne slowly. "The Governess Bureau was wonderful. It was glorious. The friends I made, the joy I found...it was truly special. But everything has its season, and there is no reason to believe that I will never find joy again."

Edwin nodded. "Perhaps, you know, there is something more with the Bureau you could do, other than resurrect it to find new governesses for noblemen."

Vivienne looked up. "Meaning?"

"Well, I don't know," said Edwin, not expecting to have to provide an example. "You could...you could always publish some materials to show the marriages that occurred were true love, couldn't you? Write some books to tell the tales as they ought to be told. Show them what true love is. Love that couldn't be fought. Love that didn't compromise."

"Perhaps we could," Vivienne said with a smile. "Ours would certainly be a good example of that. But who would want to read them?"

Edwin thought for a moment, and then an answer came to him as though it had been there all along, waiting for him. "People who need to know how wonderful you are, of course. People who need to know that the Governess Bureau was glorious and respectable. And people who need to be reminded what love is."

About Emily E K Murdoch

If you love falling in love, then you've come to the right place.

I am a historian and writer and have a varied career to date: from examining medieval manuscripts to designing museum exhibitions, to working as a researcher for the BBC to working for the National Trust.

My books range from England 1050 to Texas 1848, and I can't wait for you to fall in love with my heroes and heroines!

Follow me on twitter and instagram @emilyekmurdoch, find me on facebook at facebook.com/theemilyekmurdoch, and read my blog at www.emilyekmurdoch.com.

CPSIA information can be obtained
at www.ICGtesting.com
Printed in the USA
LVHW040931290322
714698LV00014B/572